STAR TREK®

NEW FRONTIER

PROMETHEANS

STAR TREK®

NEW FRONTIER

PROMETHEANS

Martyr
Fire on High

PETER DAVID

Printing History: Pocket Books paperback March 1998

Printing History: Pocket Books paperback April 1998

Published by arrangement with:
Pocket Books
A division of
Simon & Schuster Inc.
1230 Avenue of the Americas
New York, New York 10020

ISBN 1-56865-742-0

Visit our website at *http://www.sfbc.com*
Visit Pocket Books's website at *http://www.simonsays.com/startrek/*

PRINTED IN THE UNITED STATES OF AMERICA.

CONTENTS

MARTYR 1

FIRE ON HIGH 213

MARTYR

FIVE HUNDRED YEARS EARLIER . . .

Ontear could tell which way the wind was blowing.

Even so, it seemed that everything and nothing was clear to him as he looked at the Zondar horizon. The smoke that hovered over the cityscape far in the distance was drifting off to the north. It was not his favorite direction, for the stench from the charnel pit was wafting in as well.

How many of his people had died, he wondered, during the bloody civil war that had enveloped the planet? One million? Two? He'd lost count. For that matter, he'd even lost interest, which was both ironic and unfortunate, considering that the war had been fought in his name.

Ontear felt old . . . older than he had felt in quite some time. He had been sitting at the entrance to his cave, but now he rose to his feet, stretching his cramped legs. He was bald . . . indeed, completely devoid of body hair, as were all his people. His skin was leathery and shiny, with a sheen that made it look as if the Zondarians were perpetually wet or glistening. His eyes were set wide apart, and when he blinked, it was with eyelids that were clear and made a soft clicking sound. His nostrils flared visibly as the charnel stench moved toward him and then past. He wondered how many bodies burning there were people he knew. People he had blessed, or at whose birth he had officiated, or weddings he had performed. For that matter, how many of them had come to him for guidance, had sought out the wisdom of the prophet Ontear? Ontear, the prophet who had seen a great and glorious destiny for Zondar. Ontear, who knew all that was to come. Ontear, who could not help but feel that he was single-handedly responsible for the chaos that had erupted all around him.

He had long felt that he was in direct communion with the gods. But today, of all days, he believed that the gods were going to communicate with him directly, and with a vengeance. Today, Ontear felt, was going to be his judgment day.

He heard scambling below him, heard grunts and arguments and words of indecision. He was being approached by acolytes. They were not exactly being subtle about their advent, and whatever it was that was on their minds, clearly it was accompanied by a certain degree of volume. This was not of tremendous consequence to Ontear, because truthfully there was very little any acolytes could say that would come as a surprise to him. This was an inevitable state of affairs, after all, when one is a prophet.

There were three of them, approaching Ontear with bedraggled and exhausted mien. It was not the easiest of climbs, for Ontear's cave was set upon the upper ridges of a small mountain. There were paths that led to the plateau where Ontear was seated at that moment, but they were not forgiving for the clumsy of foot. There was a thick layer of pebbles along several lengthy patches, and those wishing to come and visit Ontear oftentimes felt the ground slipping beneath them and they would skid several yards back down the steep path before regaining their footing and slogging forward once more.

Based on the difficulty of approach, no one was quite sure just how Ontear managed to survive there. There was no food to speak of, although water might be available through a mountain stream (not that anyone could really be sure). Perhaps Ontear had hidden resources. Perhaps he had unknown allies. Perhaps, as some speculated, he was actually dead, and merely a very animated and lively corpse.

The trio continued to approach, and Ontear recognized the closest of them as Suti-Lon-sondon, one of his oldest and most dedicated students. He remembered the first time that Suti had come to him, scared and confused, daunted by the task that had been put to him: to approach the prophet and learn at his feet. That had seemed an eternity ago.

It had not been difficult to convince Suti of his veracity as a prophet. Indeed, it was no more difficult than it had been to prove it to anyone else. Unlike other prophets, false prophets, who had contented themselves with speaking in broad and unspecific predictions (the more precious of them choosing to quote their vagueness in rhyme, as if that added some aura of respectability), Ontear had been amazingly specific in his prognostications. He had predicted the great earthquake of Kartoof. He had predicted the rise in power of Quinzar the Wicked and Krusea the Black, and the defeat of Krusea's son, Otton the Unready.

Oh, there were the skeptics who believed that Ontear's predictions were so specific that they became self-fulfilling prophecies. For instance, his prediction that a conqueror named Muton would be born in the eastern territories and dominate half the region had resulted in no fewer than two thousand eastern territory newborns in the last year being given the name "Muton." The confusion this created in schools alone was nothing short of calamitous.

But the debates over Ontear meant nothing to Suti, for he believed in the man and his powers. There was a serenity about Ontear, a confidence that seemed to lift him above all that surrounded him.

Suti was surprised to see Ontear seated in front of his cave. Ontear rarely left the confines of his rocky home. He had a particular spot that he simply sat upon, apparently day and night, for Suti never saw him move from it. Yet here was Ontear, outside, apparently taking a tremendous interest in the skies which were darkening overhead. Suti gestured for the others who had accompanied him to hang back, desiring to address Ontear on his own first. Slowly he drew near to the prophet, and Ontear acknowledged his approach with a slight nod of his head. Suti began to speak, but Ontear put out a raised hand and Suti promptly lapsed into a respectful silence.

"Can you smell it, Suti?" asked Ontear after a short time. "There is a storm coming. A storm of great significance. I have foreseen it."

This, to Suti, did not exactly seem to be the stuff of prophecy. One did not have to be a seer to tell that a storm was on its way. One merely had to look at the growing blackness. Of far greater concern to Suti, however, was the smoke on the horizon. The smoke that was a lingering and mute testimony to the war that had enveloped Zondar. A war that had begun in the western regions but had spread to consume the whole of the planet.

"I do not dispute that, Ontear," Suti said, "but we have other matters to consider at the moment." Suti's skin had the same characteristic sheen that Ontear's possessed, but his eyes were darker and the contrasting youthfulness in his face was quite evident.

"Other matters?" asked Ontear.

Suti drew close and knelt nearby Ontear. "The war, Ontear. The great war."

"Wars are never great, Suti," Ontear said softly, thoughtfully.

"There can be great acts of heroism. There can be great causes. But the wars themselves are always terrible, terrible things."

"The Unglza, Ontear. The Unglza refuse to surrender."

"Do they?"

Suti was beginning to feel frustrated. It was as if he was having an impossible time just managing to capture and hold Ontear's attention. "They refuse to surrender," he repeated, trying to give added significance to the statement through weight in his voice.

"Yes, so you have said."

"But you said they would!"

"Yes, so I did."

Suti could hear mutterings from his companions nearby, and he did not like the sound of it. He began to pace furiously, the incoming wind whipping the hem of his acolyte gown. "Ontear . . . this . . . this war is because of you!"

"Is it?" Ontear still seemed to be only partly paying attention to what was being said.

"For years, Ontear . . . for years, the Unglza and the Eenza have desired the extermination of each other. They are two peoples who have racial and border disputes going back centuries! Every time there has been a move toward peace, the talks have broken down and new bouts of attempted genocide on the parts of both peoples broke out once more! But it's never been a full-blown civil war before! Never spilled over into . . . into an unyielding bloodbath! That's what it is, Ontear! A bloodbath!"

"That can be a good thing, Suti. A cleansing thing."

Suti made no attempt to keep the astonishment from his face. "A *good* thing? Ontear, as of six months ago, there had actually been greater advancement in the peace talks between the Unglza and the Eenza than ever before! And then you suddenly came forward with your . . . your . . ." He waved his hands about as if unable to find the words.

"Prediction?" Ontear prompted gently.

"Yes! Your prediction that there would be a great war! Your prediction that the Unglza would surrender, bow in defeat! Your prediction that the Eenza would finally dominate their hated rivals, once and for all! These were statements from your own lips, Ontear! I was there when you made them! We heard them. We *all* heard them."

"I remember, Suti," Ontear said patiently. "I was there. I may be old . . . I may even be approaching the end of my days . . . but my mental faculties remain as sharp as ever."

"But don't you see? When you made your predictions, the talks broke down!"

"I knew they would."

"But to what end?"

"End?" Ontear actually seemed puzzled by the question. "The end is the end, Suti. I am not responsible for—"

And to the shock of Ontear—in fact, to the shock of Suti himself—Suti grabbed Ontear by the front of his robes, and turned and pointed urgently at the haze of smoke hanging on the horizon. "You are responsible for *that!*" he bellowed. "You are responsible for the Eenza breaking off talks, emboldened by your predictions that the Unglza would be crushed! Don't try to deny that you had a hand in that!"

"I deny nothing," Ontear said with apparently infinite calm. "But the actions taken by the Eenza are ultimately governed by their own free will. My predictions are merely that. They are not absolutes, nor are they designed to absolve the participants of their own culpability."

"People are dying, Ontear!"

"People have died for eons before I came along, Suti, and will continue to do so long after I am gone."

There was a crack of thunder from overhead, as if the gods hidden by the rolling clouds agreed with him. Suti did not release his hold on Ontear. "Why haven't they surrendered? The Unglza—why haven't they?"

"They will."

"They haven't! Your predictions have only strengthened their resolve! They have sworn to fight to the last man, woman, and child!"

"Have they indeed?"

"Yes!"

Ontear shrugged. "They are to be commended, then."

Suti was stunned. He felt his fingers go numb, and Ontear gently disengaged Suti's hands from their grip on his robes. "Commended?" asked Suti incredulously.

"Yes. They fly in the face of prophecy. They fight a hopeless battle. It is only the hopeless battles, Suti, that are the truly interesting ones."

"The Eenza are asking me when the Unglza are going to surrender, Ontear! I don't know what to tell them! And I have asked you, and your response has simply been, 'Soon.' In the meantime, hundreds of thousands have died! Perhaps millions! When is 'soon' supposed to be, Ontear?"

And there began to be something in Ontear's eyes . . . something that Suti had never seen before. A sort of burning intensity that caused a chill to spread down Suti's back. "That depends upon your point of reference, Suti. To you, 'soon' means sometime within your immediate lifetime. Days, weeks, months at most. For one like myself, 'soon' relates to the galactic whole. What may seem an infinity of time to you is barely a fraction of a heartbeat in the body of the great cosmos. I speak within the frame of reference of our world's vast history, Suti. I speak on behalf of Zondar, and within the time frame of Zondar, the Unglza will surrender soon."

"You're . . ." At first Suti was having trouble framing words, so paralyzed was he by the enormity of what Ontear was saying. The other acolytes, who were outside of hearing range but could see the stunned reaction on Ontear's part, looked at each other with growing apprehension. "You're saying . . . that the Unglza may not surrender in my lifetime? Within the lifetime of *my entire generation?* That their surrender could be *centuries away?!"*

"Of course."

Suti's entire body began to tremble. "You're . . . you're insane!"

Ontear drew himself up, looking annoyed for the first time, and his glistening brow darkened in anger. "Do not take that tone of voice with me."

"Tone of voice? *Tone of voice?* Our people are dying on your behalf! The Eenza fight under the banner of Ontear, in the belief that their triumph is imminent! And you're telling me that you have absolutely no idea when the Unglza will surrender!"

"The Unglza and Eenza need no excuse to battle each other. Theirs is a hatred that transcends generations."

The wind was getting louder, and it was getting harder and harder for Suti to hear. "Ontear, you have to tell them!" he cried out. "You have to tell them that you were wrong! You have to—"

"Wrong?"

"You have to—"

"Wrong?" and this time his voice was audible above the increasing howling of the winds. And with a fury that seemed to mirror the anger of the storm clouds overhead, Ontear shoved Suti with a strength that was far greater than Suti would ever had suspected possible in the old prophet. Suti stumbled backward, losing his balance and hitting the ground with a bone-jarring thud, his elbows absorbing

most of the impact and sending a jolt of pain through him. He gaped in utter astonishment at Ontear. High above, the entire sky had become black, and currents of air were beginning to surge. Ontear was buffeted by the gusts, but didn't appear interested in acknowledging it. ***"Wrong?"*** he shouted over the noise of the wind.

Suti glanced in the direction of his companions, but they were already in full retreat, running before the pounding of the air. It was as if the very elements had risen up against them to defend the wounded honor of Ontear. Never before had Suti felt quite so vulnerable, so exposed. He knew that, at this point, survival was the primary consideration. Not vanity, not wounded pride . . . not even the lives of those already gone, because Suti had come to the realization that if he or Ontear died at this moment, that wouldn't do a damned thing toward bringing back any of those who had already been killed.

"You weren't wrong! I was . . . I was mistaken!" cried out Suti. "We need to seek shelter, Ontear! To get to the cave! To—"

"The cave will not serve as protection! I have foreseen that! I have foreseen all! Do you have any idea what it is like, Suti? Any idea what it is like to *know?* To be *aware?*" He pulled at his face as if he were seeking some way to tear the very skin from his bones. "It never stops, Suti! The knowledge never stops, no matter how much I desire it to! I am accursed, Suti! How can you have sought out my wisdom? I know everything and nothing! Everything and nothing!" His voice went to a higher and higher pitch, bubbling just short of total hysteria. "You want predictions? You want to know what to expect from the future? Look to the stars, Suti! All of you, look to the stars, for from there will come the Messiah! The bird of flame will signal his coming! He will bear a scar, and he will be a great leader! He will come from air and return to air! And he will be slain by the appointed one! Read the writings, Suti! Read of the appointed one and keep that knowledge secret, within the acolytes, for the appointed one must not know the destiny that awaits until the time of slaying! For in that slaying, the Messiah's death will unite our planet! And if he does not die in the appointed way, then the final war will destroy all! All! *All!*"

"What writings?! What do you mean?" Suti called out desperately.

There was a crack of thunder from overhead, a blast so massive that all Suti could think of at that moment was his childhood. He would tremble upon hearing the sounds of storms, and his parents would spin him fanciful yarns of how the gods would be having sport with one another, and that there was nothing to fear. He would take comfort in that, nestle in his mother's arms, no longer afraid.

He longed for those times now, for if there were indeed gods, they were furious about something.

Wind hammered Suti, stinging his eyes even though he tried desperately to shield them. He slammed shut his clear eyelids, and they afforded him some protection even as thousands, millions of infinitely small pebbles ripped up from the pathway, creating dust and dirt. Thunder doubled and redoubled, and lightning blasted from on high. The storm was everywhere, ripping down from the skies, and he felt as if the storm were within him. As if he had become a focal point for it somehow.

Through his eyelids, he saw Ontear.

And he saw something else. Something that filled him with undiluted terror.

Dropping down from on high, like a great black tongue, a blasting cyclone of air was descending and licking up everything with which it came into contact. The base of it was half a mile wide, and the howl of the air was so earsplitting that Suti was screaming at the top of his lungs and still couldn't hear himself. And it was bearing down directly toward them.

Completely panicked, Suti scrambled backward, trying to get out of the way of the oncoming cone of black air. He managed to gain his feet, ran some yards, and then lost his footing once more. He slid on a trail of pebbles, ripping the skin off his forearms, and suddenly he was yanked to a halt. For one horrified moment he thought that the wind had him, but then he felt the sharpness of the ground and twisted his head around to look. His foot was trapped, wedged into a crevice in the mountain path. He yanked in terror, but it seemed as if all the effort he put into it simply caused his foot to become more solidly imprisoned.

The entire sky was illuminated once more, and Suti howled in fear and sent a prayer to whatever gods there might be, hoping and praying that they were listening and were intending to do *something*. The mass of black air bore down on him, he felt the rippling of his clothes, and knew that he was beyond hope, beyond prayer.

And Ontear, with his arms outstretched, appeared to be laughing. Suti couldn't hear him, but his head was tossed back, his shoulders shaking with barely restrained amusement, and it was as if he were welcoming this mass of destruction that had erupted from the heavens like an inverted volcano. And the cyclone, which was driving straight toward Suti, suddenly veered off. Whether it was simply a shift in the air currents or—the more fanciful interpretation suggested—that Ontear was somehow actually summoning it, Suti would not presume to say. Perhaps it was even that this incredible destructive force had just noticed Ontear, and was abruptly realizing the reason for its presence.

Whatever the reason, amidst a blasting of rock, pebbles, and debris, the black air angled right at Ontear. It pulled at his robes as if inspecting him, trying to determine whether he was worthy of its attention. Ontear, for his part, was no longer laughing, nor was he showing any element of fear. Instead, he was serene, at peace with whatever his fate was going to be.

He did not have to wait long to determine what that fate was.

Suti saw air appearing between the bottoms of Ontear's simple footwear and the rocky surface upon which he was standing. The outlandish sight made no sense to him at first, but then he realized what was happening. As incredible as it seemed, Ontear was being lifted into the air.

Ontear kept his body perfectly still and stiff as he began to rise higher and higher. He was so unafraid, so completely at peace. In some ways, it seemed as if he were going home.

Then the wind turned on him. As gently supporting as it had been, suddenly it became savage. Ontear was about ten feet off the ground when he was abruptly snapped from one side of the funnel to the other. For the first time, Suti saw confusion, even fear, in his eyes. As if he had been expecting this, and had prepared himself for it . . . but now, faced with the reality of it, panic was setting in. It was, however, too late for any such last minute considerations or doubt. Ontear was whipped away from Suti's sight, caught up in the whirl of the destructive force, and now he was thrashing wildly, clearly trying to get away from the unstoppable force of nature that had yanked him away.

The dark air hesitated for a moment, as if choosing its course, and Suti's mind was far too paralyzed to pray or hope or conceive of anything except possibly, just possibly, surviving to the next moment. Then the funnel angled completely away from him, plowing toward Ontear's cave. Suti would have thought it impossible, but the mass of air ripped through the cave, blasting through solid rock. Shards and rubble flew everywhere, and Suti pulled himself into a fetal position, arms crisscrossed over his head to afford himself what protection he could. He felt his belly beginning to heave and he couldn't control himself as he vomited up the entire contents of his stomach. Worst of all, he wasn't even aware that he had done it.

Finally, however, he began to hear himself scream. It took a moment for him to realize that he was hearing his own voice, that the air mass was moving away. He continued to scream as if celebrating, with incredulity, his survival. He lifted his head and saw the funnel moving farther and farther away, apparently picking up speed. He could not make out any sign of Ontear, or what might have been left of him. For all he knew, the wind was of such intensity that it had simply ripped him apart.

Then the funnel suddenly began to retract into the sky. Its bottom dissipated, and then, with a final few crackles of thunder, the black column of air vanished as if it had never been there at all.

Suti's breath was ragged in his chest, and he was unable to tear his horrified gaze away from the last place that he had seen the deadly air funnel. He felt as if, were he to look away, the destructive force might return with more power and intensity than before. But after long moments his breathing slowed down and he managed to compose himself to some degree. With the immediate terror of the moment gone, he was able to work with quiet calm on his foot and was surprised to discover that it took only a few seconds' effort to extricate it from its entrapment. He stumbled to standing, wincing as he tried to put weight upon the injured foot. He took a few careful steps to try and shake it out and relieve himself of the pain.

Gradually he made his way over to where Ontear had been standing. He wasn't exactly sure what he was supposed to feel upon standing at the last spot that he had seen his mentor, but the fact—the embarrassing, humiliating fact—was that he was simply glad that it had been Ontear who had been carried off rather than himself.

Then he looked over to the ruined remains of the cave, and remembered that his original instinct had been to seek refuge there. It had been Ontear who had stopped him. Fortunately, as it happened, for if he had tried to secure himself there, he would have been carried off by the winds. Ontear had saved his life. He had known. Somehow he had known.

He walked up to the cave, pushing aside the remaining rubble with the toe of his shoe. So many times had he come there to discover Ontear sitting in the exact same place: quiet, serene, confident. Suti had sought to emulate it, sought to find the inner vision and peace that Ontear felt, even though there were critics who claimed that the serenity was nothing more than the self-confidence born of utter madness.

And then, when Suti stepped upon the spot that Ontear had occupied for so long . . . this time, he *did* feel something. At first he thought it was his imagination, but quickly realized that such was not the case. There was . . . there was something there. The ground felt different: harder, smoother, *warmer.* Was it a simple heating device? Something that Ontear used to help him subsist through the cold of the winter days?

No. No, Suti got a different sense of it altogether. He took a large step backward, and the moment he was away from the immediate area that had once been Ontear's within the cave, the feeling ceased. That was when Suti realized that it was more than simply the sensation of warmth. It was something that somehow had burrowed deep within Suti's soul, something that he felt permeating his very being. It was a sense of . . . of peace. Of knowledge and understanding. There were no particular facts floating through his head, but instead a simple and serene confidence that anything there was to know, he would eventually come to understand. It was addictive, like a drug. Without hesitation Suti stepped back upon the area and he felt it once more, this time stronger than ever. The ground was cluttered beneath his feet, but he kicked away the debris as quickly as he could and then dropped to his knees to inspect the ground. It was the same color as the rest of the area around him, but it was flat and smooth, and under his hands he could feel something that reminded him of a slow, steady pulse.

Then his fingers discovered an indentation, a tracing. He brushed aside the last of the dirt and dust to find a symbol etched in the ground. It was small, no larger than the palm of his hand, and it did not make sense to him at first. It appeared to be carved in the shape of a torch or flame. Why there was a small carving of a flame in the ground, Suti could not even begin to guess, yet something prompted him to extend one long finger and drag it across the intricate line carving.

He found, with interest, that it was one continuous line, and he traced it until his fingertip had reached the point from which it had begun. The moment it made that contact, it was as if a circuit had been completed. There was a soft rumbling from just beneath him, gears shifting, as if some sort of machinery had been set into motion. This time, however, he felt no immediate fear. No sense of panic as he had before. This time, for no reason that he could readily discern, it all felt . . . *right* somehow.

There was a loud, solid *click* and the flame symbol actually twisted in place, moving about ninety degrees and then slowly sliding upward, revealing a cylinder about the width of Suti's hand and a foot tall. It was made of gleaming silver metal and sparkled in the daylight, the suns rays filtering down in the wake of the storm that had passed only moments ago. With reverence, Suti reached over and removed the cylinder, hefting it experimentally. He turned it over and over, looking for some sort of seam, some hint as to what it might be and what it might contain, if, indeed, it contained anything at all. Experimentally he twisted the top in the opposite direction from the bottom, and suddenly the top unscrewed in his hands. He blinked in surprise as he felt the unexpected give of the device in his hand, but then did not hesitate to unscrew it as quickly as he could. It made a harsh rasping sound, as if feeling the need to put up some sort of token resistance before yielding its secrets, whatever those might be.

He finished unscrewing the lid and then upended the cylinder. Thin sheaves of papers slid out and onto the ground, where they lay for a moment before unrolling by themselves, without Suti touching them at all. He was hesitant to pick them up at first, but finally he did, and scanned them quickly in an effort to discern exactly what it was they contained. There was line after line of writing upon them, and immediately he recognized the penmanship as that of Ontear himself. His eyes grew wide with excitement as he recognized them for what they were: predictions. Page after page of thoughts and concepts by the foremost seer in the history of Zondar. And they were all in his hands.

He knew what he had to do, of course. He had to make these predictions public. He had to bring them to his people, let them know precisely what their future held. Ontear had been closed-minded, self-directed, and selfish, and the result had been an appalling civil war. Suti would not make that mistake.

He replaced the cylinder on the spot from which he had lifted it, and he saw it slide neatly back into place. The gentle vibrations, the feeling of power that he seemed to sense from beneath his feet were gone. It was as if the machinery beneath him, whatever it was, had gone silent. Perhaps he was imagining it, or perhaps it had somehow been keyed directly to Ontear himself. Was it possible that his foresight came not from within, but from without? That somehow this equipment had been responsible? If that was the case, then from where had the equipment come? Who had given it to Ontear, . . . and would they be back?

That, Suti realized, was clearly part of his destiny. He would wait. He would wait right there, for however long it took, to see if the potential providers of the answers would reveal themselves to him. In the meantime, however, he would use the information left behind by Ontear to continue the work and reunite the world. Information that he became more and more excited about as he read the material over.

Tentative voices called his name and he turned to see the other two acolytes who had accompanied him. They were a short distance away, walking carefully toward him, stepping delicately over the shifts in the path. "Are you all right, Suti?" they asked.

This was it. This was the moment to share the knowledge. To let them know all that was to befall the world, to produce the writings of Ontear. Why, with this concrete view of their world's destiny before them, they could mold it and shape it, they could . . .

They could . . .

They could share the power.

Knowledge. Knowledge was power. That truism rang in Suti's head as he read the writings in greater detail. Yes, that was the way of things, wasn't it? Knowledge was power, and there was tremendous power to be had here. Suti's mind raced: There were so many possibilities, so many things he could accomplish with this information . . . except that it would require that he kept it all to himself. Yes, that was the only reasonable possibility. After all, the world was already in disarray, civil war sweeping the different factions. If the information, the predictions, the last words and visions of Ontear were made public, different groups would endeavor to twist them to their own respective convenience. Everyone had their own intentions, after all, their own incentives. Everyone had an agenda, sometimes hidden and other times right out in the open.

There was information, knowledge here that many Zondarians simply couldn't handle. That was another problem. Either they would be driven mad by the knowledge of what was to come, or else would labor to try and invalidate it as had happened with some of Ontear's predictions. There were those who, once the future was revealed to them, felt compelled to do everything they could to change it out of some sort of sheer need for perversity and contrariness. As if once they were told, "This is how it will be," felt the juvenile need to protest, "We'll just see about that!" and labor mightily to change it all. And if that were the case, then one of two things would happen. Either Ontear's predictions would become invalidated, and the legends of Zondar's foremost seer would be challenged, diminished, and Ontear, who deserved reverence, would be lessened in the eyes of posterity. Or his predictions would remain true in the face of overwhelming odds, and what would be accomplished then? Fear, destruction, railing against the frustrating inevitability of fate. Nothing much else.

No, no indeed, what Zondar needed was one man. One good man, with a solid ethical foundation, who could use these predictions to lead the Zondarians into a new golden age. An age where the Unglza and the Eenza would be able to cooperate with one another and grow into two compassionate, cooperative groups. They were all Zondarians, after all, and it was simply madness that they were at war with one another.

And Suti was that man, of that he was quite sure. Ontear had been given power, but it had corrupted him. It had dragged him down even as he thought he was elevating himself, and he had completely lost touch with what was good for the people. That was something that Suti would never do. Not ever. And if fulfilling the destiny that awaited him meant keeping a few secrets, for the overall greater good, well, he was willing to make that sacrifice.

His back was still to the other acolytes as, without drawing any attention to it, he slid the rolled up papers into the inner folds of his robe. Then he turned to face the acolytes. He felt taller, more confident, as if the writings which he had secreted upon his person gave him an inner knowledge and strength.

''Hello, my friends,'' he said softly. There was an odd calmness to his voice.

The acolytes looked at each other nervously, and then back to Suti. ''Are you . . . all right? Where is Ontear?''

''Ontear . . .'' He paused for dramatic effect. ''Ontear is with those who have come before . . . and will come after. I am here now. The power is mine now, but I will share it with you. Bring the others. Summon them to me.''

''Ontear is . . . gone?''

He felt a brief wave of impatience. ''Yes, he is gone. But I am here, and that will suffice. Now bring the others to me that I may address them.''

''Suti, they're waiting for us back at the temple. We can all go to—''

"I said to bring them here!"

The acolytes were startled, jumping back in response to the anger and intensity of Suti's voice.

"They will come here," Suti continued with the same degree of intensity. "We will rebuild the cave, rebuild Ontear's place."

"Rebuild a cave? How—"

"We will find a way! We will do so, and we will create a shrine to Ontear, and that is just the beginning of my plans! And you will not question me again!"

They did not question again, but instead bolted down the side of the mountain to obey his orders.

Suti was annoyed, but it was quickly passing. They were going to have to learn, that was all. He was going to have to teach them.

And if they refused to learn, if they irked him or did not sufficiently cooperate, well . . .

Well, he might have to let the war continue a bit longer. Just to show them what they had passed up by proving difficult to deal with. He would hate to have to follow that course, but he had to start thinking beyond immediate gratification. When the whole of the future was at one's fingertips, one had to keep watch on the big picture.

NINETEEN YEARS
EARLIER . . .

"Get someone else,'' said M'k'n'zy.

''There *is* no one else,'' Sh'nab said. ''You are the one. It is the appointed time, M'k'n'zy, and your responsibility. I can't believe that you would want to shirk it.''

M'k'n'zy strode back and forth apprehensively within the confines of his fairly modest hut. His long black hair was tied back, although a few stray strands dangled around the twenty-year-old's face. The scar that ran the length of his right cheek had flushed bright red, as it tended to do when there was something truly frustrating facing him.

Sh'nab couldn't quite understand what M'k'n'zy's problem was. One of the tribal elders of Calhoun, Sh'nab had seen M'k'n'zy face down entire troops of Danteri oppressors. He had seen him command troops of men, send them into battle, fight for his life. He had witnessed M'k'n'zy dealing with every sort of challenge and problem under the Xenexian sun, and therefore could not wrap himself around M'k'n'zy's current problem. After all . . .

''She's just a woman, M'k'n'zy!'' Sh'nab said, for what seemed to him to be the umpteenth time. ''This should not be difficult for you. You are acting as if . . . as if . . .'' He shook his head in frustration. ''I don't know how you're acting. I am frankly not certain what to make of it.''

''Why can't D'ndai do it!'' M'k'n'zy said, annoyed with the sound of his own voice. He sounded whining, petulant, and even—gods help him—scared.

''Because,'' Sh'nab said patiently, ''D'ndai isn't here. You know that. He's on Danter at the moment, paving the way for the peace negotiations with the Federation overseeing the process. You know this."

It was true, of course. He had been there, after all, when the Federation had first shown up on Xenex in the person of Jean-Luc Picard, the man who had suggested to M'k'n'zy that he himself consider a career in Starfleet. Considering M'k'n'zy's frame of mind at that moment, perhaps the thing to do was to find out when the next shuttle was going to be available and to head straight out as soon as possible. But M'k'n'zy had not made up his mind yet as to whether Starfleet was the direction that he wanted to go with his life. Never before, though, had he regretted hesitating over a decision as much as he regretted it now.

"We can wait until he comes back, then," M'k'n'zy suggested.

Sh'nab shook his head. "The times are very proscribed for these matters, M'k'n'zy. Catrine's husband has been gone a year. She has not remarried; she has had no wish to, and that is her right by tribal law. But she maintains her husband's name, and her husband's fortunes, and she does not wish the family line to end with her. That is also her right."

"But I'm the warlord! I'm not the chief! D'ndai is the chief!"

"You are his brother. These responsibilities run along family lines. You know that—"

"Yes, yes, I know, I know!" M'k'n'zy's purple eyes flickered with frustration. "Sh'nab, will you please stop telling me things I already know and reminding me that I know them? It's most irritating to me!" He paced back and forth. "Can she wait until—"

"We're going in circles, M'k'n'zy! Besides, she—" Sh'nab paused.

"She what?"

Sh'nab muttered something that M'k'n'zy didn't quite hear, and when asked to repeat it, said, "I said she asked for you specifically. If she wanted to be flexible, she could likely wait until D'ndai's return, but it would put her beyond her current fertile cycle and she'd have to wait three months. She said she did not wish to wait, and she made it quite clear that she found you more . . . desirable . . . than D'ndai. I would ask that you do not pass that information on to your older brother. He might be hurt."

"Fine, fine," M'k'n'zy said with an annoyed wave. "Not a word."

"M'k'n'zy," Sh'nab said, not unkindly, "I admit that I am so accustomed to seeing you handle virtually any situation, that I'm not used to seeing you act like . . . well, like a nervous young man. You are, after all, only twenty summers old, even though you have served to liberate your people from an oppression that has gone on for centuries. Catrine is older than you, granted, but she is a comely woman nonetheless. It's not as if the task that awaits you is unpleasant. And it is not as if you have not . . ."

And then his voice trailed off as he saw M'k'n'zy's back stiffen slightly. "M'k'n'zy," he asked, with growing suspicion in his voice, "You *have* been with other women, have you not?"

M'k'n'zy laughed contemptuously. "Of course I have. I have had . . . dalliances, if you will. Experience."

"How much experience?"

"More than enough."

"M'k'n'zy," Sh'nab said, beginning to fully comprehend the situation, "I'm not speaking now of simple pleasure-giving. Of groping beneath sheets, or stolen moments in the darkness of a tent. Have you ever actually . . ." He found the resolve of his question beginning to fail under the intense glare and scrutiny of the look that M'k'n'zy was now giving him. He cleared his throat loudly and said, "Have you ever fully . . . well . . . consummated . . . ?"

There was silence in the hut for a time, and then M'k'n'zy said slowly, "Define 'fully.' "

"Oh gods, you're a virgin," Sh'nab moaned, sinking into a large, ornately carved chair.

"Only partly," M'k'n'zy replied defensively.

"Partly! One cannot partly be a virgin, M'k'n'zy! I don't believe this!" said Sh'nab. "A twenty-year-old warlord virgin?"

"Say it a bit more loudly. I don't think they heard you on Danter," M'k'n'zy told him with undisguised annoyance.

"M'k'n'zy, I don't understand! Every time you'd walk through the village square, women's heads would turn! Do you think a village elder doesn't notice such things? I was knocked aside once by three young girls who were trying to get your attention! How can you still have no carnal knowledge of women? The average Xenexian male is sexually active by the time he has seen thirteen summers."

"It was my choice, Sh'nab."

"I . . . I see."

Sh'nab was silent for so long that M'k'n'zy turned to look at him with concern on his face. "Do you?"

"Of course I do. It saddens me, I admit. But . . . perhaps it's understandable. Perhaps that is why you are so able to lead troops of men into battle. You are more . . . *comfortable* . . . with them.''

It took a moment for what Sh'nab was saying to sink in, and when he realized, M'k'n'zy wasn't sure whether to react with outrage or laughter. His voice caught somewhere in between in a sort of strangled choke. *''I do not prefer to have sex with men, Sh'nab!''*

''Oh,'' Sh'nab said mildly. ''I thought that was what you were trying to say.''

''If I had been trying to say that, I would have said that! Kindly do not 'help' me with a pronouncement of that magnitude, if it is all the same to you! All right?''

''Well, then I do not understand, M'k'n'zy. If you don't . . . I mean . . . if . . .''

Sh'nab was still seated in the ornately carved chair as M'k'n'zy sank onto the floor opposite him. M'k'n'zy had known Sh'nab for many years, felt a closeness to the elder who had on a number of occasions schooled him in some of the gentler arts of Xenexian life and culture. M'k'n'zy was not comfortable discussing such matters with anyone, really, but if he was going to speak of it, then at least Sh'nab was someone he considered an appropriate sounding board.

''Sh'nab, I did not expect to survive the uprising. Do you understand? I did not think that I would manage to live through the rebellion. I thought the Danteri would catch and kill me, or that I would die in battle. I faced death a thousand times, and to some degree I still cannot believe that I survived it all when so many others who were just as brave, just as resourceful, and just as skilled in battle as I wound up losing their lives. I saw the way women looked at me, Sh'nab. If it wasn't lost on you, it certainly wasn't lost on me. I'd see the lovelight in their eyes, and I . . . I did not desire any woman to form an attachment to me, for fear of not being there for her. I did not want any loved ones because I did not wish to leave a loved one behind. It might have hampered me in what I needed to do, and it would have been unfair to her. So now we are faced with a possible peace, and I find the prospect of . . . of intimacy . . . to be somewhat daunting. For that matter, I am suspicious of women.''

''Suspicious of them?''

''Well,'' M'k'n'zy shrugged, ''it is unfair, I suppose, to single them out. I am suspicious of everyone. But now I have a reputation as our greatest fighter, our greatest warrior. What if a woman is attracted to my title and reputation, rather than to me, for myself? For that matter, what if she expects me to be as . . . as skilled in the art of lovemaking as I am in the art of war? What if''—and he lowered his head—''what if I cannot perform to her satisfaction? What if I cannot perform at all? Can you imagine that? Can you imagine the things that would be said as word spread? People calling out to me, 'So, M'k'n'zy, having problems getting your sword out of its sheath, eh?' The humiliation of the thought, the . . .'' He shuddered, his voice trailing off in contemplation of such embarrassment.

''M'k'n'zy,'' Sh'nab said softly, ''you are a strategist. That has always been your greatest strength. As such, it has been necessary for you to give a great deal of thought to whatever situation you might be faced with. In my opinion, you are treating the prospect of sex with the same gravity that you would plan a military engagement. You are trying to foresee all possibilities, plan for every possible contingency. Intimacy is not a war, M'k'n'zy.''

''I know of some couples who might disagree with you, Sh'nab.''

Sh'nab allowed a smile. ''All right, I'll grant you that,'' said the elder. ''But you are overthinking things here. Simply allow matters to develop naturally.''

''That is not my nature, Sh'nab. I am one who feels the need to steer matters to a conclusion that I find satisfactory.''

''Relationships do not work that way, M'k'n'zy. In war, you give instructions to your men and they follow orders. Women do not take to that. Except the most passive of women, and I doubt that you would be satisfied with someone like that.''

M'k'n'zy made no immediate reply, and Sh'nab continued gently, ''Go to Catrine, M'k'n'zy. She is a good woman. If you do not wish to attend to her wishes, then tell her so. The likelihood is that she will understand. Give her some sort of explanation, though. She is entitled to that much, at least.''

''I suppose so,'' M'k'n'zy sighed. ''All right, Sh'nab, all right. I'll go to her and explain the situation. I'm sure I can get her to understand that it would be better for her to wait for D'ndai's return. He has far more experience in these matters. I should know. He certainly boasts of it enough.''

It had rained the previous night, and the great square was more like a large pool of mud. M'k'n'zy stepped through it carefully, his feet sticking in place every so often, and he'd have to fight to pull his boots free. He made his way across it, and angled off down the side road toward Catrine's home. The sun was already setting, its rays stretching across the horizon, and M'k'n'zy scanned the skies urgently in the hopes that, at the last moment, D'ndai's ship might suddenly show up overhead. But there seemed to be no sign of it.

Just his luck.

M'k'n'zy knocked gently on the door of Catrine's home, so gently that it seemed as if nothing short of a miracle would enable anyone to hear him. He waited exactly five seconds, got no immediate response, and promptly came to the conclusion that she wasn't home. He turned away, prepared to bolt, when the door creaked open and Catrine stood in the doorway.

She was at least ten summers older than he, with copious blond hair that framed a round and amused face. In contrast to the smile, though, there was sadness in her eyes. Sadness or, at the very least, loneliness. She wore a simple white shift, and there was gentle lighting from within that backlit her, tracing the curves of her muscular body.

"Greetings, M'k'n'zy," she said. He was surprised to notice that her voice had a somewhat enchanting lilt to it. "You have come to honor my request and give me a child?"

"I have come to discuss it," he replied.

"Discussing it is not how it's generally done," was her comment, and then she gestured for him to enter. He did so, looking around at the long tapering candles which decorated the inner hallway. "I appreciate your taking the time to come to me."

"I wasn't otherwise occupied," said M'k'n'zy.

He suddenly realized that she had taken his hand in hers. His palm felt clammy to him, but if she noticed it she said nothing. "Do you have a woman, M'k'n'zy?" she asked.

"You mean at present?"

"Yes."

"No. No, there is no one. I have not had the time. I have been . . . rather busy. Where are we going?"

"My bedroom." She stopped, turned, and smiled at him. "Unless you wish to take me right here on the floor."

"No!" he said quickly, his voice sounding higher and sharper than he would have liked. He composed himself and repeated, "No," in a slightly deeper voice that sounded like forced casualness.

"All right, then."

She brought him into the bedroom, and there were more candles surrounding the bed; so many, in fact, that he felt as if he were about to be tossed onto a slab and offered up as a sacrifice. The bed looked softer than a slab, though. Nonetheless M'k'n'zy looked tense, rigid, nervous. In short, he looked like a man who was about to do many things, other than have sex. The scent of her filled his nostrils, and he felt slightly dizzy. Her eyes picked up the flickering candlelight and seemed to be flickering with a heat all their own.

"Well?" she said.

He shifted his feet uneasily. "Uhm . . . well, uh . . . well, what?"

"What would you like to do? Do you wish to undress me, or shall I do that for you? Do you wish me to—"

"I don't know. Whatever you desire is fine. I am doing this for you, Catrine. It is . . ." He tried to find the words and adopted a scolding tone. "It is an obligation. That is all. Just an obligation. I'll do as you wish, since this is your desire, not mine."

If he could have pulled the words out of the air before they had reached her, he would have. But naturally, that was not an option. He saw the hurt on her face though, her large eyes going round with pain. She did not cry, but she sank slowly onto the bed, her back rigid. "I am sorry," she whispered.

"You have nothing to apologize for."

"No, I . . . I do. For you are young and beautiful, and I am . . ." Her fingers trailed along her throat. "I am . . . old. Old and unattractive."

"What?"

"Obviously that is the case. I—"

He wanted to console her, wanted to speak words of love or sympathy to her, but he didn't have the tools to do so. So all he sounded was brusque as he replied, "Don't be ridiculous. You are . . . you're beautiful. You are. You're beautiful."

"I'm not. I am old."

"You are . . ." He tried to find a way to phrase it that would pierce through her veil of self-pity and, in so doing, his voice automatically adopted a more sympathetic tone. "Every summer that you have lived has graced you with sunlight that you continue to carry with you. You shine with an inner light."

"Oh, please," she said with what sounded like cautious dismissal, as if she wanted to believe his words, but was reluctant to accept them for what they were. "Please, you will say whatever comes to mind so that I will not be sad. I'm flattered by your efforts, but do not patronize me."

"I would not patronize you," said M'k'n'zy firmly. He took her by the shoulders and turned her. "I knew your husband, Catrine. He was a good man. A good fighter. I respected him. If nothing else, I would not insult his memory by treating you in such a manner."

"So," her voice was very quiet and he had to strain to hear. "You . . . do find me attractive?"

"Yes. Very much so."

"And do you"—she looked up at him with hesitation that almost seemed girlish—"do you want me?"

"I—" He suddenly felt as if the temperature in the room had risen. "It is simply that . . . well . . ."

"M'k'n'zy, you act as if you've never been with a woman before. . . ." Her voice trailed off as she saw his reaction.

With an annoyed grunt, he turned away. "What is it, emblazoned on my face? Has the news been circulated throughout the town? How is—"

And then he heard something that he had not expected: laughter. Gentle, floating laughter, as he turned to see that her body was shaking with mirth. Somehow it was not exactly conducive to salving his wounded ego. "I'm sure it's very funny to you," M'k'n'zy said sourly.

"No! No, I . . . I think it's sweet!" she said.

"Sweet!"

"Yes. You were so busy fighting for the freedom of our world that you never had time for romantic entanglements. Besides, after a day of hacking and slaying, it must be difficult to be in the mood for soft words and softer women."

He was completely astounded to hear her say that. "Yes!" he affirmed, sitting next to her on the bed. "Yes, that's it exactly! How did you know?"

"It's obvious. Obvious to me, at least. Don't worry, M'k'n'zy," she said confidently, patting his hand. "Your secret is safe with me."

"That is . . . that is so kind of you," he said, squeezing her hand in return. "I cannot begin to tell you." Relief flooded through him and he flopped back on the bed. "I thought that you would—no, actually, I had no idea what you would say or do. I wasn't even planning to tell you. I was just . . . I . . . I don't know what . . . I just wanted . . ."

She lay down next to him, propping her head up with one hand. "What did you want?"

"I don't know," he said softly.

"You can leave if you wish. I'll wait for D'ndai to fulfill the requirements of law. I just . . ." She stared down at him.

"You just what?"

"Nothing, M'k'n'zy. It really doesn't matter."

He looked up into her face. She was quite lovely, really. And there was a mixture of sadness and resolution that reminded him, in many ways, of himself. "Catrine," he said slowly, "I do not . . . anticipate remaining on this world. I am seriously considering leaving Xenex. I am thinking of going far, far away. You've had such great loss, such great sadness. You deserve so much more than I can give, I think. You deserve more than simply what the law dictates. You deserve a man to be with you, to wake up next to you, to care for you. If you wait, I'm sure that man will come to you. If we did what you ask now, then—"

"Then I would have your baby. A baby who, I can only hope, will grow up to be as strong, as brave, as determined, and good as his or her father."

"But you should have a mate to—"

"You do not understand, M'k'n'zy. I'm not looking for such a man. My dear, lost husband . . . he was a good man. He was my soul mate. Perhaps someday in the far, far future I may be ready for another, but I do not envision such a time. But I am ready for a child now. A child to love, to raise in the teachings of Xenex."

"Catrine, I—"

She leaned over and her lips brushed tentatively against his. When he did not resist, she kissed him more thoroughly. The kiss was like a fine wine, sweet and bringing warmth to him. His hands, seemingly of their own accord, were running along her body, tracing the curves of her hips. Slowly she undid the front of his shirt and looked at his chest. She saw scars, bruises all over his torso, and she traced the line of one of the scars across his left breast.

"Sword slipped past my guard. Grazed me," he said, and he was surprised how choked his voice sounded.

"So many scars. So much fighting," she sighed as she gazed into his face. "How much death have these eyes seen?"

"Too much," he admitted. "Far too much."

"Tell me, M'k'n'zy of Calhoun, would it not be nice for a man who has seen so much death, slain so many people . . . would it not be proper and just and honorable if, the very first time you made love, it was for the purpose of putting a life back into the world?"

She kissed him on the throat and he sighed, his body trembling. "Yes," he admitted. "Yes, it . . . it would."

He somewhat lost track of what happened after that. He knew that her simple white shift had fallen to the floor, and his own clothes soon joined them there. She was gentle with him, and loving, and any fears he had over being unable to perform were quickly left far, far behind, along with the concerns of the real world.

She moved atop him, her face smiling down at him, and he was lost in the beauty and glory that was Catrine. Even though the goal was a straightforward one, she managed to prolong the moment, the heat building within him but not finding release until she was ready to let it go. And when she finally did, and he exploded into her . . .

He was silent. There was no outcry, no shout of joy. Nothing but complete and utter silence. Even in a moment of total ecstasy, M'k'n'zy could not completely let go. Catrine was struck by it as he sagged beneath her, spent and quiet, so very quiet. She touched the side of his face. ''Did you . . . enjoy it, M'k'n'zy?''

He smiled ruefully. His breath was coming in slow, ragged gasps as he said, ''You have to . . . remember who you're talking to.''

''I don't understand.''

And she was astounded to see a single tear roll down his cheek as he said, ''I enjoyed it more than anything else . . . that doesn't involve killing an enemy. Do you understand now?''

Slowly she nodded and wiped away the tear. She brought the wet finger to her mouth and tasted it. Then she slid off him and lay next to him, her arm draped across his chest, her head on his shoulder. ''Can we stay like this for a time?''

He nodded almost imperceptibly and she drew against him. Even though it was early evening, and the sun had only just drawn below the horizon, Catrine nonetheless fell into a deep and peaceful sleep.

When she awoke six hours later, he was gone. The side of the bed he'd been lying on was cool to the touch. Catrine turned over to face away from ''his'' side of the bed, as she would continue to do for the rest of her days, and ever so softly cried herself back to sleep.

NOW . . .

1

In the starkness of her room, Selar twisted and turned on her bed, the single sheet becoming completely ensnarled around her naked body. Sweat was pouring from her, even though the climate control for her quarters did a more than adequate job of duplicating the arid, dry-heat environment of her native Vulcan. Several times during the night she woke up, crying out the name of Voltak, her late husband, and then she would lapse back into her fitful sleep.

An assortment of images tumbled through her mind. She would relive the night of their mating, the horrible circumstance in which a heart attack took Voltak from her while they were in the throes of *Pon Farr.* She would see his face, floating away into the void. And then she would see another face, a curiously angled face with a smile that bordered on a smirk, and two-tone blond hair cut low to the scalp. It was the face of Burgoyne 172, the Hermat chief engineer who had taken a fancy to Selar and made several impassioned overtures before Selar had made it clear that she simply wasn't inclined to sate the demands of *Pon Farr* with the odd Hermat. But Selar had changed her mind, only to spot Burgoyne arm-in-arm with astronavigator Mark McHenry, heading off to what was clearly an assignation. This left Selar high and dry . . . and mightily frustrated.

Burgoyne was smiling at her, hish fangs peeping out from under hish lips. And then Burgoyne reached out with hish long, tapered fingers, and Selar saw herself, her arms reaching out toward Burgoyne. Burgoyne reached for her.

And there was a high-pitched beep.

The sound repeated itself, and it was enough to jostle Selar to wakefulness. Sitting up quickly, she misjudged her position and rolled off the bed, crashing to the floor with a rather loud thud. She lay there, entangled in the bedsheet, musing over the rather odd situation that had brought her to this particular sequence of events. Then, in the darkness, her brain fully cleared and she responded via voice prompt. ''Computer, Selar here,'' she said, her voice so casual that it never would have betrayed the fact that she was lying on the floor, naked and tangled up in a sheet.

''Doctor,'' came the concerned voice of Doctor Maxwell. ''Are you all right?''

''I am in perfect health, Doctor. Why are you inquiring?''

''Because you're over an hour late for your shift, and, well . . . that's unlike you.''

That explained why Maxwell had paged her via her comm badge rather than patch directly to her quarters. He'd assumed that she was already out and about, since Selar never slept late. Selar checked the chronometer on the wall. Had she been human, she would have moaned to herself, or jumped up in a panic. ''I . . . appreciate the summons, Doctor. I shall be along shortly.''

''Take your time, Doctor,'' Maxwell's reassuring voice came. ''Things are somewhat quiet here, for a change of pace.''

''Indeed. You are saying, then, that I am not needed.''

There was something in her tone of voice that clearly was puzzling to Maxwell, but he endeavored not to let it show. He was only partly successful. ''We can always use your guidance, Doctor. You are the CMO, after all.''

''The thought is appreciated, Doctor, as is the half-hearted argument regarding my indispensability.'' She paused, and then her thoughts began to drift, because she was feeling the building of the warmth once more. It seemed to have its origins in her loins and in her heart, and the two radiated outward, the circles of sensation intersecting within her. Something within her snapped her attention back to the fact that she had an open comm link and a puzzled doctor at the other end. ''I will be some time more, Doctor, if, as you say, all is calm. I have a meeting I must attend to.''

''Not a problem, Doctor. Sickbay out.''

Once again she had nothing but the silence of the room. For some reason, she fancied that she could hear distant wind chimes, and sense a warm desert breeze sweeping over her. Something had to be done about the *Pon Farr.* She had a plan; her research had been very beneficial in that matter. Now it was just a matter of summoning up her courage and doing what needed to be done. She had hoped she would be able to wait . . . wait indefinitely if need be. But that didn't seem to be an option. Nor was returning to Vulcan much of a solution either. For one thing, finding a Vulcan male in the right state of *Pon Farr* was possible but difficult in the time she had left. She could hardly just announce her need on the Vulcan planetary internet, and discreet inquiries took time. Besides, a choice of mate on availability alone would hardly be logical. Selar still retained enough of her logic to know that. She would at least choose a highly qualified father for her child.

No, she knew what she was going to do—what she had to do.

She dressed as quickly as she could, annoyed that her fingers were trembling slightly, thereby making it difficult for her to put her uniform on with efficiency. She glanced once in the mirror and turned away as quickly as she could from what she saw. She stumbled towards the door of her quarters . . .

. . . and it didn't open.

She stepped back, looked at the door as if to wonder whether anything on the vessel was going to go right for her this day, and tapped her comm badge. "Selar to Ops. We seem to have a maintenance problem with the door to my quarters."

"We're aware of that, Doctor," came Lefler's voice. "It's not just you. Engineering has some systems glitches they're trying to lock down. Doors all over the ship are opening by themselves or not opening when they're supposed to."

"Including turbo lifts?" asked Selar.

"No, thank God. Just doors. Burgoyne estimates another hour or so before they've got it cleared up . . ."

Selar tensed inwardly at the mention of Burgoyne's name. At that moment, the door to her quarters slid open, even though she was standing two feet away. "The door is open; apparently I have been liberated."

"We'll keep working on it. Ops out."

Selar headed out, relieved to be out of her quarters and away from the face she'd seen in the mirror. A face that she barely recognized as hers. One that seemed to have more ties to Vulcans of the past, with that burning and smoldering savagery, than anything that she vaguely related to her modern-day perception of her race.

A face burned in her mind, one that had not appeared in any of her dreams. And she was going to go to that person and have her situation attended to.

Or else she was going to die.

2

"The Great Bird of the Galaxy."

Admiral Edward Jellico's face, incredulity written in large letters all over it, glared disbelievingly out from the comm screen at Mackenzie Calhoun and Elizabeth Paula Shelby, who were seated in the conference lounge in apparently relaxed fashion. Jellico's tone of voice came as absolutely no surprise to Shelby; she'd had a sneaking suspicion what he was going to say before he said it. She could see the nice view Jellico had outside his window at Starfleet headquarters: the Golden Gate Bridge, the occasional shuttle floating past. It seemed pleasant enough, and yet she wondered how he managed to tolerate it. If Shelby didn't have stars to look out at, she was certain she would go completely mad.

"The Great Bird of the Galaxy?" he said again.

"Yes, Admiral, that's correct," Calhoun said.

"You're telling me," Jellico leaned forward as if somehow that would bring him closer to the captain of the *Excalibur,* "that the entire planet of Thallon was smashed apart by a giant flaming bird, clawing its way out to freedom, and that it then flew away to who-knows-where?"

"I find it hard to believe myself, but yes, Admiral, that's essentially what I'm saying."

"Captain Calhoun, what do you take me for? Calhoun . . . Shelby," Jellico began again with an air of forced patience, "I know you don't think much of me—"

"That's not true, sir," Shelby assured him.

''Absolutely not,'' agreed Calhoun. *In point of fact,* Calhoun thought, *we actually don't think of you at all.*

Calhoun reached down subtly to rub his right shin where Shelby had just kicked him under the table. He fired an annoyed look at her, and blocked his mouth from Jellico's view with one hand as he murmured, ''Striking a superior officer?''

Shelby reached up to scratch the back of her neck, shielding her face from Jellico's view long enough to mutter back, ''If you want to *stay* a superior officer, don't say whatever it is you're thinking.'' Without waiting for him to respond, she turned to Jellico and said, ''Admiral, how you are viewed or not viewed by the command personnel of the *Excalibur* has nothing to do with the matter at hand. The ship's log, the science log, even our visual records, all confirm what it was that we saw.''

''Visual records can be arranged, Commander. To imply that seeing is necessarily believing is a charmingly antiquated notion that hasn't had a shred of truth to it in about four centuries now.''

''Granted, Admiral, but the fact remains: Somehow this creature burrowed into the heart of the planet Thallon, and provided the energy-rich resources which enabled the Thallonians to become the dominant world that they grew into. It was the creature's imminent . . . *hatching,* if you will . . . that caused the drain of power, the destruction of the world, and the fall of the Thallonian Empire.''

''Commander,'' Jellico said patiently, ''empires fall because of any number of things. Economic collapse. Political infighting. Inbreeding causing a downward spiral in the quality of its rulers. Empires do not fall because giant flaming birds smash the home world to bits!''

''Well . . .'' Shelby paused, looked to Calhoun, who shrugged. She turned back to Jellico. ''Not as a rule . . .''

''Commander—''

''Admiral, be reasonable. Do you really think someone would go to all this effort just for the purpose of perpetrating some sort of massive hoax on you? With all due respect—''

''There's that phrase again,'' sighed Jellico. ''The one that always precedes something said with a total lack of respect.''

''With all due respect,'' Shelby said more forcefully, ''doesn't that sound like an odd view of the galaxy? I mean, really now. Ship's log, science log . . . all to pull a joke on us?''

''Or perhaps to cover up some sort of—''

''Of what?'' Calhoun now cut in, and the veneer of affable amusement, and even faint condescension, was gone. "May I ask, Admiral, what you are implying?"

"May I ask, Captain, what you are inferring?" countered Jellico.

"I am inferring," replied Calhoun, "that you think there may have been some sort of sloppiness on my part, and that the report we've given you was constructed—in all its outrageousness—to fool us. And that we fell for it. And if that is the case, Admiral," and his voice lowered in a tone that bordered on deadly, "then I am going to have to ask you to apologize."

"Apologize to you, Captain?" asked Jellico with clear skepticism.

"No, Admiral. To be perfectly blunt—"

"As if that were a change of pace."

"I couldn't give a damn what you think of me," continued Calhoun as if Jellico hadn't spoken. "But Elizabeth Shelby is one of the most capable humans I've ever known."

"Captain, this isn't necessary," Shelby tried to say.

But he ignored her and continued. "The notion that she would fail to see through *any* hoax is, frankly, insulting. And if you do not retract that statement, then I shall file a formal complaint with Starfleet Command."

"What 'statement,' Captain?" replied Jellico. "You're asking me to retract an inference that you yourself made. I am simply saying that I find this report of your activities in Sector 221-G, formerly known as Thallonian space, to be somewhat . . . dubious."

"If that is the case, Admiral," Calhoun replied, "if you truly think that running into a figure of mythology or history such as the Great Bird of the Galaxy is too preposterous, then I take it you will not want to hear about it should we happen to encounter . . . oh, I don't know . . . Apollo?"

"Or Zephram Cochrane?" Shelby added. "Or—what was his name—the knife murderer . . . ?"

"Jack the Ripper?" offered Calhoun.

"Yes!" She snapped her fingers as the memory came back. "Jack the Ripper. Thank you. You know, I have to tell you, Admiral, in comparison to those incidents, a giant flaming bird seems a fairly modest claim."

Jellico rubbed the bridge of his nose, suddenly looking rather tired. "Very amusing, Captain, Commander. You refer to Kirk, of course."

"Well, he *was* required reading at the Academy, sir," said Shelby.

"He was required reading because of his tactics and strategy," clarified Jellico. "His more 'outrageous' exploits were hardly required."

"True, sir, but in Kirk's case, sometimes the footnotes were far more interesting reading than the main events."

"That may be the case, Commander, but here's the truth of it: My great-grandfather was in Starfleet Command during Kirk's time. And the fact was, Kirk had some very staunch supporters. That served him well, because he also had any number of people whom he had angered with his constant glory-hounding and utter disregard for regulations. And it was widely believed in Starfleet that, every so often, he would file utterly preposterous reports, just to tweak those individuals whom he knew didn't like his style and his way of doing things. Such as the incident with the giant killer amoeba. And that totally ridiculous alleged occasion in which his first officer's brain was stolen. I mean, come *on,* people. Clearly, these things could not possibly have happened. Every time you heard uncontrolled laughter ringing up and down the hallways at Starfleet Command, you could tell that Kirk had filed another one of his whoppers."

"Did anyone entertain the notion that they might all be true, sir?" asked Calhoun.

"Yes, they did, and every single one of Kirk's crew swore to their dying day that every insane thing Kirk encountered was the absolute truth. To some people, that was sufficient proof of Kirk's veracity. To others, it simply showed the incredible depth of loyalty from his people." For just a moment, Jellico's expression seemed to soften, to become reflective. "Either way, I suppose, that made Kirk a man to be envied."

Calhoun and Shelby glanced at each other in undisguised surprise. Jellico actually sounded almost envious of the legend of Kirk.

Jellico seemed to refocus on Calhoun, and his brow furrowed. "This isn't about Kirk, and it isn't about me. From now on, I expect to receive reports that are not fanciful extrapolations of reality. Is that understood?"

"Fully, Admiral," Calhoun said quietly, but his purple eyes were blazing with undisguised annoyance.

"You have a good deal of latitude, Captain, out there in Thallonian space. You're the only starship out there. You're operating without a net, so don't expect me to be there to catch you when you fall."

"Understood."

Jellico looked from one of them to the other, as if expecting them, even daring them, to say something that might be considered challenging. But they simply sat there, tight-lipped, and Jellico grunted before saying, ''Jellico out.'' His image blinked off the screen.

''That was certainly a little piece of heaven,'' Shelby sighed, slumping back in her chair. She noticed the way Calhoun was looking at her. ''What's the problem?''

''You kicked me,'' Calhoun said.

''Oh, that.''

''Yes, that. That's a hell of a thing to be on the receiving end from the queen of Starfleet regulations. I'd be most interested to see the one where it says that it is acceptable to kick one's commanding officer.''

''It's more of an unwritten rule. You were about to say something that would get you in deep, Mac, and in so doing were dragging me along with you. Don't think of it as an assault. Think of it as self-defense.''

''I can't say I appreciated it.''

''I didn't do it to gain your appreciation. I did it to get your attention.''

''Well, next time might I suggest something a little less painful?''

''I would have tried a striptease. That's always worked in the past,'' she said with no hint of a smile. ''But somehow I think the Admiral might have noticed.''

''Perhaps. Certainly might have gotten you that promotion you've always wanted.''

She blew air impatiently from between her lips as she rose from the table. ''Don't bring that up.''

''Bring what up?''

''Did you see the promotion list recently? I was scanning it over and did a double take when I saw 'Captain Shelby' commanding the *Sutherland.* For half a second I thought I'd been promoted and someone forgot to tell me, and then I realized it was someone else. It should have been me, Mac. But instead, I'm still . . .''

''Stuck with me?''

She sighed. ''You know, Mac . . . the whole world doesn't have to be about you. That's one of the things you always did that drove me crazy. It's my problem, okay? Not yours.''

''It doesn't have to be yours either, if you'd only be happy with what you've got.''

''With what I've got?'' She leaned her back against the wall, her hands draped behind her, and she looked bleakly at Calhoun. ''This Captain Not-Me Shelby is in the thick of things. There's a major push going on with about three quarters of the fleet, and he's smack in the middle. And us, we're . . ."

"Exploring," Calhoun noted. "Last I checked, that's what Starfleet is supposed to be all about. *Grozit,* Eppy, you know that as well as anyone. Better than most, in fact."

She glanced at him. " *'Grozit'?* Reverting to Xenexian profanity?"

"Xenexian profanity. Sorry. I'll try to watch myself."

"Not on my account, although your command of terran profanity is fairly comprehensive."

"I have an ear for languages."

She half-sat on the edge of the table. "The problem is, Mac, that first and foremost, I'm a tactician. That's my strength, what I was trained for. Analyzing an enemy's weakness, seeing where they can be outthought or defeated. That sort of thing is where I really come alive, Mac. But here, I feel like . . ."

"Like you're wasting your time?"

She studied him and, to her surprise, she saw something in his eyes that she had thought he really wasn't capable of: Hurt. He seemed hurt over the very notion that she would want to be elsewhere or that she could think that her time as first officer of the *Excalibur* was not a worthy test of her skill.

"No," she said softly. "No . . . I don't think that at all. Face it, Mac, you'd be lost without me."

"I don't know if I'd be lost," he replied. "But I'd be far less eager to be found."

She was genuinely touched. It was times like this that reminded her exactly how and why she had become involved with Mackenzie Calhoun in the first place. How they had wound up lovers, engaged to be married, until the relationship had broken down under the weight of their conflicting personalities. "That is so sweet," she said.

He shrugged. "I have my moments."

She found that she was looking at him in a way that she hadn't in quite a long time. When she'd signed aboard the *Excalibur,* it had been for the purpose of more or less riding herd on Calhoun. Of making sure that he toed the line when it came to Starfleet policy. And she had been quite, quite sure that their history together and their past romance would not factor in to their day-to-day interaction.

But now . . .

"Do you really feel that way, Mac?"

He laughed gently, walked over to her, and put his hands on her shoulders. "You want me to be honest, Eppy? When you first came aboard and applied for the job as my first officer, I was relieved to see you. Then, after I agreed to take you on, I decided that I must have been completely crazy to do so. And when we began fighting over protocol and the official Starfleet view of procedures—''

''That's when you were *really* sorry that I was here?'' she said teasingly, although she had a feeling, deep down, that she'd actually put her finger on it.

But he shook his head. ''No. That's the point at which I became convinced that taking you on was the absolute right thing to do. You make me think, Eppy.'' He rapped the side of his head with his knuckles. ''It's not always easy to crack through this heavy-duty shielding into my head. I don't always agree with what you say, Eppy. But even when we're disagreeing, I'm still thinking about everything you say. You make me think, and that's not always easy to do.''

''So you always listen to me, then.''

''Always,'' he smiled.

The door to the conference lounge slid open, and standing there was Doctor Selar. She looked utterly composed, her arms folded across her chest. ''Captain, may I speak to you in private for a moment?''

''I'll just excuse myself then.'' Shelby left, smiling to herself. For reasons Calhoun wasn't certain of.

''This is . . . a delicate matter to discuss, Captain,'' Selar said slowly.''

''I appreciate that,'' Calhoun said. ''And I think you'll find that there is no matter so delicate that I can't be trusted with it.''

''Very well, Captain.'' She paused a moment, as if steeling herself. And then she said, ''It is my desire to have sex with you.''

''My . . . apologies, Doctor,'' Calhoun said slowly. ''Did you just say you—''

''Desire to have sex with you, yes,'' she nodded. ''There is an explanation, which can be summarized in two words.''

''Good taste?'' he suggested.

''Pon Farr.''

''Ah. Well, that would have been my second guess.''

''That is a sort of . . . of Vulcan mating ritual, isn't it?'' Calhoun asked slowly. ''I mean, I've heard rumors about it, but Vulcans tend to stay fairly closed-lipped about such things.''

''It is considered . . . inappropriate . . . to discuss the matter with outworlders,'' Selar told her. ''However, I feel I have no choice in the matter. Besides, it may be that my role as a clinician makes it . . . easier''—she forced the word out—''to discuss matters pertaining to a medical situation. It is not a ritual precisely. It is a . . . a drive. An urge that cannot be denied, no matter how much we may desire to do so.'' She put a finger to her temple, as if to steady herself, and then said more calmly, ''We must mate.''

''To conceive a child?'' asked Calhoun.

''Yes. You see, it could easily be argued that there is no logical reason to have a child. Ever. They are burdensome, they are limiting, they habitually expel bodily fluids out of a variety of orifices at high velocity, and they are extremely time consuming. So, for a race whose every action is defined by logic, that race would—by definition—face extinction.''

''But to allow the demise of your race just to avoid child-rearing is also illogical,'' pointed out Calhoun.

''In which case, perpetuation of the species becomes a chore. An obligation. To live with such an onerous situation is also not logical. Therefore our very nature, our bodies, have developed in such a way that logic simply does not enter into the conception of children.''

''Believe me, it's frequently no different on Earth,'' Calhoun said ruefully. He paused a moment, pulling himself back to the major topic at hand. ''But certainly you can't expect the captain—''

''I can and do,'' Selar replied evenly. She looked straight into Calhoun's eyes. ''You are the most appropriate individual to handle this matter, Captain. At the moment, my options are extremely limited. The *Pon Farr* drive is in remission for the time being, so this need not be attended to immediately. But it will resurge again and again: each time with greater impetus and a greater need to be satisfied. I am requesting that, upon the next resurgence, when the drive is upon me, you satisfy my genetically driven lust. Will you honor my request, M'k'n'zy of Calhoun?''

''I shall *consider* it, Doctor,'' Calhoun told her. ''I'm leaning towards 'yes,' but can I have a little time to think about it?''

Despite her Vulcan training, Selar let out a sigh and sagged slightly in visible relief. ''I am . . . pleased . . . to hear that. And yes, of course, take all the time you need. Just . . . not too much.''

''A request has been made of M'k'n'zy of Calhoun, the man I was,'' Calhoun said reasonably. ''I can't turn that aside. Doctor, if I do agree to it, kindly let me know when and where you will find my . . . services . . . required. Several hours notice would be appreciated if that's at all possible.''

"I will make every effort to accommodate you, Captain. And I would, in turn, appreciate if we could keep this matter between us."

"Sounds like a plan."

She nodded and, as if the matter were completely settled, she turned to leave to find that at some point in her conversation with the captain, the doors to his office had quietly opened by themselves.

At least half a dozen crewmen were walking past at the time. To say nothing of the fact that her voice apparently carried halfway down the corridor.

Selar visibly winced.

3

Word was beginning to spread.

It was sort of the reverse of a black hole: Instead of everything being sucked away into blackness and disappearing, the information was blasting outward in all directions. And it wasn't as if the stories needed to be built upon; the truth itself was so insane that exaggeration was not required.

Nonetheless, matters did tend to build upon themselves, passing on from one world, one system to the next and becoming bigger and more impressive with each one. The Nelkarites, for example, heard of the two giant flaming birds that had smashed apart Thallon and then fought against the *Excalibur.* The refugees who had settled on Nelkar listened to the stories with unfettered astonishment. By the time word reached the Lemax system, however, and the warring races which inhabited it, the *Excalibur* had apparently morphed into an even greater flaming bird and faced off against the two fiery beasts which had sprung from the smoldering remains of Thallon.

The Boragi, upon hearing the news that two great flaming birds and one large flaming sheep had fought a pitched battled against an armada of morphing ships from the Federation and led by the *Excalibur,* wisely chose—as they oftentimes did—not to believe any information that came their way, and to take no aggressive action unless it could somehow serve them.

On Naldacor, the residents received word of the Thallonian developments, and burrowed deeper into the subsurface hiding places in their world, concerned that somehow the great flaming cat of which they heard so much might somehow come to seek them out.

Comar, on the outer rim, spread word to Xenex, where the triumph of the former M'k'n'zy of Calhoun over the flock of great flaming birds prompted the creation of a planetary holiday.

The news eventually filtered to Starfleet headquarters, where Edward Jellico's head sank into his arms as he became convinced that the entirety of Sector 221-G had organized a massive hoax specifically designed to drive him completely insane.

And everywhere that word was received, there was much cause for speculation and wonderment as to what it all might mean. The name of Mackenzie Calhoun was repeated throughout the former Thallonian Empire with varying degrees of respect, awe, admiration, and even fear. This was, after all, the captain of the brave vessel which had withstood the attack of the giant flaming *whatever.* The valiant warrior who had settled a life-and-death dispute, driven by honor, when a world was literally falling apart around him. Clearly, a new force and power had come to the Thallonian Empire. He captained a mighty starship, with such servants as a being which seemed like a walking mountain, and Vulcans, and a feisty Earth woman (who, truth be known, would probably have blown her brains out if she'd known the word ''feisty'' was being attached to her). And even the fallen Thallonian noble, Si Cwan, was said to travel with him. The situation seemed ripe with possibilities. . . .

On the surface of it, Tulaan IV did not seem a particularly outstanding or impressive world. There were sections of it that were rather pleasant, with lush vegetation, warm climate, an abundance of water. The weather was fairly moderate, and overall it was attractive.

There was hardly anyone there. Instead there were machines, robots who harvested the food that grew there and shipped it elsewhere. There were a couple of individuals who maintained the robots, but that was the totality of the air-breathing inhabitants.

There was other terrain, however, that was cold and inhospitable. The nights were long, and the wind—nicknamed ''monster breath'' for the constant and remarkable chill that it always carried—blew steadily. Very little grew there except for a few stubborn patches of vegetation that appeared invulnerable to the hostility of the environment. The temperature never went much above freezing. All in all, considering the alternatives that Tulaan IV offered, this particular area, known as Medita, should have been fairly deserted. Instead, it was where the vast majority of Tulaan's populace resided.

They were not great believers in luxuries or comfort. They felt that it was anathema for their chosen way of life. Theirs, instead, was a life of sacrifice, of thoughtful contemplation, of reading over their holy books. And—most sacred of all—complete domination of any worlds which did not fall into accord with their dogma.

They had a variety of names among many races, usually spoken in fear or hushed whispers. The name that they preferred for themselves was simply . . .

The Redeemers.

They lived in simple homes, and their main gathering place was the Great Hall, the single most impressive structure on Tulaan. That is to say, it was impressive by Tulaan standards. Several stories tall, with spires reaching toward the sky as if trying to caress it, and atop the Hall was a statue carved from a gleaming metal that seemed to absorb even the most meager of illumination as provided by the several Tulaan moons. It was a statue of someone that no living Redeemer had ever seen, but his portraits hung everywhere, and elaborate statues were among the few indulgences that the Redeemers allowed themselves. Probably because they did not consider them "indulgences" so much as objects of worship and respect.

They were representations of the great god, Xant. He Who Had Gone On. He Who Would Return. And the Overlord awaited His return, as had all the Overlords before him, and all those who would likely come after him.

Prime One entered the Overlord's sanctuary and found him much as he always found him: seated in his Great Chair, his fingers steepled, apparently lost in thought. The Overlord's deepest thoughts were generally something that none of the Redeemers, no matter how high up in the Hierarchy, wanted to dwell on for very long.

The Overlord was the tallest of the Redeemers, and half again as wide. His skin was hardened and black, almost obsidian, and his eyes were deeply set and a soft, glowing red. Other races generally tried not to look directly into the face of a Redeemer; it was like experiencing a little foreshadowing of death. His clothing was as black as his skin, with a tunic that hung down to knees and black leggings tucked into his high boots. He wore a large black cape which draped around him, giving him, when he was in a contemplative, forward-leaning mood, a distinct resemblance to a crouching bird of prey.

Prime One said nothing, merely standing there and waiting for the Overlord to acknowledge his presence. This was not necessarily an immediate or swift event; once he had remained exactly where he was for the better part of a day as the Overlord said nothing. Prime

One had never been entirely sure whether the Overlord knew he was there and merely elected to let him stand around as some sort of test, or if the Overlord was truly so lost in thought or meditation that he didn't register Prime One's presence. In the end, it didn't really matter: Prime One had waited until the Overlord chose to acknowledge him.

On this occasion, Prime One was fortunate. He waited a mere hour before the Overlord's attention finally focused on him. "Yes?" said the Overlord.

"There is important news, Overlord." Prime One was so excited about it that he actually took a step forward. Any sort of approach to the Overlord was a breach of protocol and potentially punishable, but Prime One had always served the Overlord well and so he was inclined to let it pass for the moment. "I thought you should know as soon as possible."

Prime One remained the Overlord's main point of information. It was a large and annoyingly busy galaxy, and if the Overlord endeavored to keep up with all of the events and happenstances within it, he would never have time for the contemplation that was his first and greatest duty. Indeed, when it came down to it, there was little occurring in Thallonian space that required his firsthand knowledge. He had his meditation, he had the solid hold of the Redeemers upon their own section of space, and that was all that required his immediate attention. Prime One would come to him with news of another Redeemer conversion, or of some particular concern that the Thallonians might have in their ongoing dealings.

A wary truce had existed between the Thallonians and the Redeemers for some time. It was an understanding that went back many, many years, and one which no Overlord had been particularly inclined to disrupt since, truly, there seemed no point in doing so. Why disrupt matters when they were going so smoothly? The Redeemers attempted no conversions of those worlds that were of particular importance to the Thallonians, and the Thallonians in turn made no attempt to press their interests on those worlds which had undergone conversion. Nonetheless, the Overlord had a suspicion that the situation would not last. The Redeemers could afford to be patient, for in the end, Xant would eventually return, and then it didn't matter where the relations with the Thallonians stood. Xant would arrive with His great flaming sword and sweep all away beneath it. In the face of that inevitability . . . what, truly, did the Thallonians matter to the Redeemers?

When the Overlord spoke, it was with a voice that was a deep and forbidding rumble that seemed to originate from somewhere beneath his boots. ''What would you have me know, Prime One?''

''The Thallonians . . . are gone, Overlord.''

The Overlord's glowing eyes fixed on Prime One with clear curiosity. ''Gone, you say?''

''Yes. We had heard rumors, news from other sources, but we waited until we could verify it firsthand before we informed you, Overlord.''

''Gone where? Have they abandoned their world?''

''Their world is likewise gone, Overlord.''

This fully captured the Overlord's attention. ''The world itself? How is that possible? Was it''—for the briefest of moments, there actually seemed to be a moment of concern upon his face—''was it the Black Mass?''

''No.'' Prime One shook his head quickly to dispel any concerns on that score. ''No, not from without, but from within was the planet lost.''

Prime One then, very quickly and in as broad strokes as possible, outlined what had happened. As opposed to the exaggerations that were racing through the other populated worlds, the Redeemers' information was fairly accurate. Prime One spoke of the great bird, of the *Excalibur* and Captain Calhoun, of the destruction of the Thallonian homeworld, and of the survival of Si Cwan of the royal house. All of this was absorbed by the Overlord, his face inscrutable except for occasional flickers of greater interest visible in his glowing eyes. When Prime One finished, the Overlord seemed to mull over the significance of it all.

''We live in cold,'' he said after a time.

Prime One nodded. This much was, of course, evident simply by looking around outside. ''And we have lived in cold since the departure of Xant. We are darkness, Xant is light.''

''We are darkness, Xant is light,'' repeated Prime One.

''We are cold, Xant is heat,'' the Overlord continued, and Prime One—as he had so often in his life as a Redeemer—repeated the prayer. There were ninety-seven of them, each of them describing what Xant was as opposed to what the Redeemers were. It was their most sacred belief that all that they were had to be the opposite of all that Xant was. Only then could Xant truly turn their lives around upon his return. He was their beginning and end, their means to salvation.

There were other religions which endeavored to follow the specific teachings of their gods or messiahs, but to the Redeemers, that seemed preposterous. How could any mortal being hope to have an insight into the workings of as holy a mind as Xant's? When Xant had departed, there seemed only one reasonable course of action all those centuries ago. Rather than try to comprehend and obey His teachings in an imperfect manner, it was decided to operate in as far removed a manner from all that Xant was as they possibly could. Only in this way would Xant then be able to return and show them the right, true, and proper way to live.

And they knew that there would be signs signaling Xant's return. They had no idea what those signs might be, but they would come, of that the Redeemers had no doubt.

"The creature is flame to our cold," the Overlord said thoughtfully. "It is light to our darkness. It is great, and we are small."

"Could it be, Overlord?" Prime One seemed almost afraid to frame the question. "Could it . . . could it possibly be?"

"All things are possible, Prime One. The question is: Are they likely?"

He stroked his chin thoughtfully as Prime One waited for him to voice an opinion. But when none seemed forthcoming, Prime One forgot himself. He blurted out, "Well?" and was immediately mortified, looking for all the world as if he wanted to snatch the word back from the air. Trying to urge the Overlord to speak on a matter! It was presumptuous beyond imagining. The punishment for it would be—

Prime One lost control of his legs as they began to tremble. The Overlord stared at him for such a long time that Prime One felt as if he could actually sense death having entered the room, hovering over him and waiting for the slightest push in its direction.

And then the Overlord . . . smiled.

Oh, it was not much. It was rather small as smiles go, and rather unimpressive. It wasn't as if the Overlord had a good deal of practice at it, so it was understandable. Prime One couldn't quite believe what he was seeing. At first he thought he was imagining it, but it didn't waver and slowly, ever so slowly, the trembling stopped.

"It's a sign," the Overlord said.

Prime One began to ask, *Are you sure?*, but wisely managed to hold his tongue before uttering the words.

"If you wonder why there will be no discipline at this time for your transgression," continued the Overlord, "it is because I would be loath to soil this day with punishment or bloodshed.'' The Overlord rose from his chair, standing half a head over Prime One, and he clapped a hand on Prime One's shoulder. ''Yes, Prime One. A sign, most definitely. We cannot allow our frozen surroundings to chill our imaginations and perceptions as well. Nor should we permit our lengthy wait for some sort of sign to delude us into thinking that there never will *be* a sign. But this cannot be ignored or explained away, Prime One. If these stories are true—and I assume you would not waste my time with them were that not the case—then it presents a clear and concise signal to us, telling us that Xant is preparing to make His return.''

Prime One began to tremble once more, but this time it was with excitement rather than fear. ''To think, Overlord . . . after all this time, all this waiting . . . Xant is to return, and we are the fortunates who are alive to see it.''

''Indeed, Prime One. Come,'' and he clapped Prime One on the back in a manner that bordered on the jovial. ''Come, let us inform the brethren. Let us begin the preparations. Our prayers must not cease, that is to be understood, of course.'' Prime One nodded in brisk understanding. ''Nor must we be lax in continuing to spread the word.'' The Overlord held up a cautionary finger. ''It is, after all, rather tempting to simply sit back and say, 'Ah, well, with Xant on His way back to us, our job is finished. We need not spread His word, for He is come to take up the task Himself. No, Prime One,'' and Prime One just as quickly shook his head, changing cranial direction so sharply that it caused a slight cramp in his neck muscles. ''No, we cannot slacken.''

''Not slacken, no, Overlord.''

''We cannot let up.''

''Never let up, Overlord.''

''And after Xant has returned,'' the Overlord continued, ''after the new Golden Age of the Redeemers has been put before us, after we have taken our true and rightful place in the hierarchy of the universe . . .''

''Yes, Overlord, yes!'' Prime One was exploding with enthusiasm that was bordering on the orgasmic.

''Then, and only then . . .'' The build up was staggering.

''Then what, Overlord?!'' Prime One asked in exultation.

''Then . . . you will be disciplined for your transgressions.''

It brought Prime One screeching to a halt, both physically as he'd been matching the Overlord's strides, and emotionally as he felt himself brought to the brink of theological ecstasy only to be shoved off into an abyss. "My . . . my transgressions?" It took him a minute to recalibrate himself. "You mean for . . . before? When I . . . ?"

The Overlord nodded. "Of course," he replied matter-of-factly.

"But . . . but you said—"

"I said, 'at this time.' That does not indicate forgiveness, Prime One. Merely leniency. But it will not be for some time yet, so be of cheer! Celebrate!" He nodded approvingly and then, in one of his rare forays from his sanctum (which, in and of itself, was enough to alert the others immediately to the significance of the moment) he strode out with his hands draped behind his back.

And Prime One was left behind, to sink down onto the floor and murmur, "Hurrah," which was about all the enthusiasm for celebration he could muster at that particular moment in time.

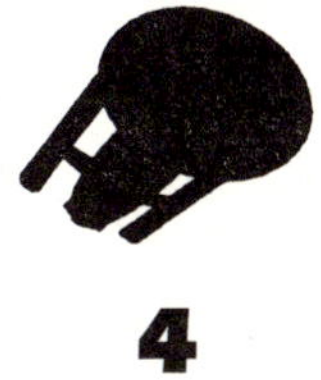

4

"Si Cwan?"

It was the fourth time that Robin Lefler had said Si Cwan's name without getting any sort of response. She was beginning to get just a little concerned. She sat on the other side of his desk in his quarters and saw him staring off vacantly, as if he'd forgotten that she was there. The quarters remained relatively simple in terms of decoration at this point. By Si Cwan's standards, it was even less than simple. It was rudimentary. Then again, one had to understand that Si Cwan's bed from his time as a Thallonian royal would likely have taken up the entire quarters just by itself. But he'd forced himself to make do, and was actually rather pleased with himself when it came to his ability to adapt. Still, he was much more pleased with himself than anyone else was with him.

She moved her hand flutteringly in front of his face and then said with more force, "Si Cwan!"

It snapped the Thallonian back to attention as he blinked at her with surprise. "I am sorry . . . what did you say, Robin?" He leaned forward, his fingers interlaced, trying to refocus his attention.

Robin stroked her chin thoughtfully, trying to find a way to phrase it without seeming combative, argumentative, or difficult. "Si Cwan," she said slowly, "I'm supposed to be serving you as your official liaison, correct?"

"Yes, Robin," he replied, looking mildly surprised that she felt a need to state the obvious.

"You've already gone through two other liaisons, in rather short order. There's an old Earth saying about 'three strikes, you're out.' Do you know what that refers to?"

He paused a moment, his red brow furrowing, and then took a stab at it. "Repeated labor disputes can result in the loss of your business?"

She began to laugh it off, but then reconsidered. "Okay, we can go with that," she decided. "And I wouldn't want you to be out of business when it comes to having a liaison. Someone to represent your interests to the captain, and at the same time to serve as an events coordinator for you."

"I should hope not," Si Cwan said reasonably. "We have been barraged with contacts from dozens of worlds, each with their own interests and agendas. There is a goodly deal of administrative work to be done, and I am an ambassador, not an administrator."

She held up a scolding finger. "Technically, you're not an ambassador either. You're forgetting you represent no government. But the captain has made it clear that he has no objection to your using that title, as long as you provide our vessel with guidance and aid in the exploration of Thallonian space."

"Yes, yes, yes." He was making no attempt to hide his mounting irritation.

"The first two people he assigned to this post got tired of your high-handedness in no time flat and made it clear they did not wish to remain in direct contact with you. The captain was prepared, at that point, to simply close up the position. But I volunteered, Si Cwan," and she leaned forward, tapping herself on the chest. "Me. I actually volunteered. Work an hour a day as your liaison, make myself available to you as emergencies require, and still maintain my bridge duties at Ops. I can do all that because I'm organized, which is the sort of person you need."

"I'm most appreciative, Robin. Can we get on with matters now?"

"Not quite," she said patiently. "What I'm trying to say is that my time is limited. I don't have oodles and oodles to play with in the course of any given day. Which is a roundabout way of saying that I sure don't have time to sit here and watch you nod off and stare into space."

"I was staring into space?" he asked, sounding confused. He started to turn in his chair to glance out the viewing port behind his back.

"No, I meant . . ." and she waved her hands in the direction of the area in front of his desk. He nodded in understanding. "All I'm saying is that something's distracting you, and it's not the most efficient way to manage the time.'' Then her voice softened. ''It's . . . It's Kallinda, isn't it?''

Slowly he nodded, and this time he genuinely did stare off into space, into the great void that glittered at him so frustratingly. ''I truly do not know which is worse,'' he murmured. ''To think that she is definitely dead and lost to me, or that she is alive somewhere out there, undergoing who-knows-what form of difficulty.''

''Zoran could have been lying,'' Lefler pointed out.

He nodded. ''That is true,'' he admitted. ''Zoran Si Verdin is my oldest, most vicious and unforgiving foe. He would say or do anything to hurt me. It is entirely possible that he created the spectre of my sister's survival in order to gnaw at me. To haunt my days and evenings. And do you know what, Robin?''

''It worked?''

He nodded sullenly. But then he seemed to shake it off with physical effort as he said, ''Dwelling on it will serve no purpose, save that which Zoran may have desired to attempt. And it is wasting your time. I have feelers out in a variety of directions, to try and bring me news of Kallinda. Those who are still loyal to me, who are still friends of the old regime, are operating to further my concerns. In the meantime, there is no need to delay you any more than necessary simply because of my inability to focus on important matters.''

She put a hand out to lay it on his forearm. She wanted to say something that would comfort him, wanted to establish some sort of ''human'' connection to the Thallonian. Her hand hovered over his forearm for the merest fraction of an instant, and she allowed it to settle as lightly as possible on the arm. She was surprised by the extreme coolness of his skin. If she were given to flights of fancy, she would have imagined that it was a reflection of the distance he forced himself to keep from the world around him. The distance that was part of the baggage he carried with him, what with being royalty (albeit fallen royalty), an ambassador, and a brother seeking the only member of his family who might still be alive.

He stared at her coolly, appraisingly, and she waited to hear what he would say next. The acknowledgment of her effort, the realization that it was possible to allow others to be close to him. To be his friend, to be . . . whatever.

''I do not like to be touched,'' he said, not unkindly.

''Ah,'' was all Robin could think of to say as she quickly withdrew her hand. Suddenly it seemed almost like an alien appendage, just hanging there on the end of her arm. Not quite sure what to do with it, she reached around with amazingly forced casualness and scratched the back of her neck. "That's . . . okay. That's fine, I can understand that."

"I've made you uncomfortable."

"No, not at all. Not at all." She cleared her throat loudly. "It was simply a . . . a human ritual. Don't think about it another minute. So, there's one more planet we've heard from, petitioning for the *Excalibur* to visit."

"That makes, by my count, twenty-nine." Si Cwan let out a soft whistle. "They are very, very curious about us, Robin. They want to know what the *Excalibur* is up to. They want to meet our captain. And of course . . ." He permitted a small half smile, not bothering to finish the sentence.

"They want to see you," Lefler was kind enough to complete it for him. "Well, naturally. That goes without saying."

"Yes, but thank you for saying it. I will present the captain with a detailed information list on the candidates, with order of suggested priority. He can, of course, deviate from that priority. But to do so would be quite foolish."

"That likewise went without saying."

"So which is the twenty-ninth world?"

She checked her readout. "Zondar."

A jolt of interest seemed to spark in Si Cwan. He had been seated, but now he came from quickly around his desk and leaned over Robin's shoulder to study her data padd. She became, for some reason, rather aware of the nearness of him, and endeavored to keep her mind firmly on her work. "Yes, Zondar. I have to admit, of everyone we've heard from thus far, they certainly seemed to be the most excited about the prospect of meeting with the captain."

"I am amazed," admitted Si Cwan.

"Why? Why should it be so surprising that they would want to see the captain?"

"It's not that. I am amazed that they would want to see anyone." Slowly he circled the interior of his quarters, stopping so often to check, totally unconsciously, for any hint of dirt or dust. "The Zondarians are an extremely acrimonious race. They always have been. They've been in the throes of civil war for well over eight hundred years. They would fight until they were exhausted, then work out some sort of temporary peace, which would hold just long enough for all involved to catch their breaths, and then they'd"—and he made vague stabbing motions—"have at each other again. They're not unique in that they seem rather determined to obliterate themselves from the memory of Thallonian space, but they were certainly the most insistent little bastards that my people ever oversaw."

"Oversaw how?" asked Lefler. She was reluctant to ask for details, for she was always concerned about some aspects of Si Cwan's past that she'd truly prefer not to hear about. But she didn't have much choice in the matter. She had to know as much as possible, and she simply had to acknowledge that, as part of a ruling family, Si Cwan may very well have been party to various acts that outsiders would consider to be barbaric or heartless, but in which Si Cwan had no voice and no choice. "Did you enslave them, or—?"

"Enslave them?" Si Cwan gaped at her in clear surprise. "Lieutenant, honestly. What do you take me for? Slavery!" He *harrumphed* at the very absurdity of the notion. "No, of course not."

"Well, that's a relief to hear."

"No, we threatened to destroy them."

"You—" She blinked in surprise. "You what?"

"It seemed a reasonable threat," Si Cwan said affably. "After all, they were well on their way to doing it themselves. When my ancestors were spreading the influence of the empire and arrived at Zondar, they saw a world at war with itself. One group called the, oh"—and he snapped his fingers for a moment to jog his memory—"The Unglza. Yes, that's it. The Unglza and the Eenza. They have assorted disputes, none of which they seemed interested in settling and, most discouragingly, many that they couldn't even seem to remember the origins of. Now is that the epitome of pointlessness? I ask you.

"In any event, we invited the Unglza and the Eenza to join the Thallonian Empire. They refused. So we took the next step we usually took in such cases, which was to inform them that they officially were members of the Thallonian Empire, subject to our rule, whether they liked it or not. Then we surrounded their world with about a half dozen of our heavy cruisers and informed them that, unless the fighting ceased immediately, we would wipe the planet clean of them. Our logic was that this solution, while violent, would satisfy everyone. Since they were out to destroy each other, this would save them the trouble. And we would be satisfied because we would still have conquered Zondar. Granted, no one would be *alive.* But their decomposing bodies would serve to fertilize the land, and if the Thallonian Empire had to wait an additional century or so in order to take possession, well, we had all the time in the galaxy. But they—as we made clear to them—did not."

He didn't continue immediately, and Robin prompted, "What happened?"

"They didn't believe us."

"What did you do?"

"Well, my great-great-great-great-grandfather gave them one more chance, and then obliterated the eastern seaboard of one of their main continents. Fired down from orbit, of course. Five hundred thousand Zondarians—perhaps more—wiped out, just like that, their shattered bodies sliding into the Great Sea. It's said there were so many bodies in the water, one could have walked from the remains of the eastern territories to the neighboring continent of Kartoof without fear of sinking. An early and rather impressive display of Thallonian might. The Zondarians quickly saw the wisdom in acceding to our gentle guidance, and put themselves under Thallonian rule."

She shifted uncomfortably in her chair. "And do you think what he did was right? Your great-great—your ancestor. Was he right?"

"It does not matter especially what I think. He did what he felt was right at the time. To leave them to their indulgence of slaughtering one another would likewise not have been a particularly positive endeavor, now would it?"

"It's called non-interference. It's the most sacred law of the Federation."

Si Cwan guffawed. "A federation has luxuries that an empire does not." But then he stopped laughing and shrugged. "Then again, my empire has fallen and your Federation yet stands. So who am I to judge, eh? Who am I?" He leaned on the edge of the desk. "The point is, even after that, we've always had to keep a very careful eye on the Zondarians. They would sneak skirmishes as part of their ongoing holy war with each other. They would try to deceive us at every turn. It was like trying to oversee petulant children. But they paid their taxes to us, albeit with complaining, and we had to discipline them only occasionally, so we managed. Not once, though, not ever, did they ever come to us or approach us about anything. They are very, very insular. So for them to be making overtures to the *Excalibur* is a most unusual gesture. The timing could not be better, either, for with the final fall of my family's influence and control over this sector of space, full-blown civil war could easily break out on Zondar at any time, if it hasn't already. The *Excalibur* is in a position to save a lot of lives, if the Zondarians are interested, for whatever reason, in meeting with Calhoun and getting his help or input.''

''Well, it's a good thing you feel that way,'' said Lefler as she glanced farther down the padd. ''Because according to their message, they're already in the process of putting together volunteers for a 'pilgrimage' to seek us out. They may be knocking on our back door just about any time.''

''If that is the case, then I suggest with all due sincerity that you be certain and let them in. I'll have that formal report together quite quickly. I don't wish to take up any more of your valuable time, Robin.''

''Oh, not at all,'' she said quickly, rising from her seat while making a few last minute notations on her padd. ''Not at all. It was . . . it was very educational.''

''For both of us,'' said Si Cwan. ''Robin, tell me, why did you *really* take on the assignment of being my liaison?''

She stared at him with a forcefully neutral expression. Stared at the corded muscles on his dusky red forearms, the broadness of his chest, the piercing eyes, the towering presence and charisma that just seemed to radiate from him.

''Aggressively seeking out new duties,'' she told him, ''is a good way to show one's CO that one is a determined, take-charge officer who should be considered for further promotion through the ranks of Starfleet. That's all. Why else?''

He nodded, slowly and thoughtfully. ''I had supposed it was something along those lines. Well, thank you for your time, Lieutenant.''

''Not a problem at all,'' and she exited rather more quickly than she'd intended to.

She headed down the corridor and greeted Commander Shelby. The first officer was heading in the other direction with what appeared to be a great deal on her mind, considering that she didn't even acknowledge Lefler's salutation. Robin Lefler shrugged and continued on her way back to the bridge.

Shelby, meantime, wasn't entirely certain where she was going until her feet, apparently of their own accord, guided her into sickbay. It was only then, as she stood there while various medics walked past her, glancing in her direction before going about their business, that she realized her body had already made the decision on behalf of her mind.

She glanced across the sickbay and saw Dr. Selar in her office, briskly going through assorted reports. She folded her arms since she didn't know what to do with them, and then let them dangle at her sides as she took a deep breath and then strode with authority across sickbay. For some reason that she couldn't quite put her finger on, she felt as if one leg was suddenly a bit shorter than the other. Since no one else seemed to be taking notice, she had to assume that it was her imagination.

She stood in the doorway of Selar's office, and at first Selar seemed to take no notice of her. Finally, however, without glancing up, Selar said, "Yes, Commander?"

"How'd you know it was me?" she asked.

"My hearing is sharper than the human norm, Commander, and you tend to tap your foot if you are impatient."

"I do?" Shelby was intrigued as she sat in a chair opposite Selar.

"Yes. Quite rapidly, I might add. Softly enough so that it does not disturb anyone, but it is detectable to me." She turned away from work and focused her attention on Shelby. "How may I be of service?"

"Selar—do you mind if I call you Selar?"

"If you are asking my preference, I prefer 'Doctor.' "

"Oh. Say, what do you call the person who graduates last in their medical class?"

Selar stared at her for a long moment. "Fascinating," she said at last. "I can easily believe that you and the captain have a history with one another. He reacted in exactly the same manner when I made the same request of him, with precisely the same joke. He was also under the impression that the answer—'Doctor'—was somehow funny. I had once thought that humans were difficult to understand, but I have become willing to widen the parameters to non-Vulcans as a whole."

"It's just that, well, I wanted to discuss something personal, and addressing you with a title seems to keep a distance between us."

"I find that preferable." When she saw Shelby's look, she added, "It is not intended as a personal slight, Commander. I assure you. I prefer distance when it comes to dealing with others. It is one of the qualities that makes me a good doctor: the ability to keep a professional distance between myself and my patients. A doctor must never become emotionally involved with her charges."

"Granted. But a doctor should at least show some empathy, don't you think?"

"Germs do not care about empathy, Commander. Nor do phaser wounds, multiple lacerations, cancer cells, stopped hearts, collapsed lungs, or any of the many calamities that can befall the human body." Selar sat perfectly motionless in her chair. She might have been carved from marble, and Shelby was having a difficult time picturing this woman in the throes of any mating urge. Selar raised one inquisitive eyebrow and asked, "Did you come here to discuss my medical techniques?"

"No," Shelby said evenly. "I came to discuss your request of the captain."

"Yes, that would be the logical reason for your visit. Since discussion of my personal life is doubtlessly moving apace throughout the entire vessel thanks to a faulty door, there is no reason that you and I should not converse about it as well."

"Look, Sel—Doctor . . . I could come to you as a first officer. I'd like to come to you as a friend."

"Friend?" She tilted her head slightly. "I was unaware that you consider us friends."

"I would like to. You must have friends. On Vulcan, at the very least."

"There are . . . others," said Selar after a moment's thought. "Other Vulcans with whom I associate. We have discussions of philosophy, and we devise puzzles of logic in order to hone our skills and direct our thought in proper channels. I do not know, however, that the human word 'friend' would apply. There is a Vulcan term—*Ku'net Kal'fiore*—which roughly translates as, 'One For Whom You Have Use.' "

Shelby tried not to make a face, and was only partly successful. "No offense intended, Doctor, but that doesn't sound very pleasant."

"I said the translation was rough," Selar said defensively. "On Vulcan, that is actually a term of endearment."

"All right, fine. How I want to talk with you is somewhere between a first officer and a friend. Can we agree on that?"

Selar let out a small sigh. "With all respect, Commander, if it will get you out of my office sooner so that I may return to my work, I will agree to virtually anything at this point."

"All right, fine. Here's the thing: You've put the captain in a very awkward position."

"Not yet," replied Selar matter-of-factly. "I do not envision utilizing anything beyond your equivalent of the standard missionary—"

"That's not what I meant," she waved her hands to get Selar to stop. "You asked the captain of this vessel to have sex with you! To sire your child!"

"Yes, I believe the news is just coming through on the Interplanetary Network. Do not worry; if we miss the broadcast, I am quite certain it will be repeated."

Shelby's lips thinned. "I was unaware that Vulcans could be so sarcastic."

"We have many exemplary traits."

"Mm-hmm." Shelby paused, and then pushed forward. "It was . . . inappropriate of you to approach the captain in the fashion that you did."

"Inappropriate for whom?"

"For protocol. A captain should not fraternize with his subordinates."

"That, Commander, is illogical. Since the captain is by definition the most highly ranked individual on a ship, that point of view would require that a captain remain celibate throughout his tour of duty. That does not seem reasonable."

"Perhaps. Nonetheless—"

"Besides, I am not asking for fraternization. Merely to have sex. I doubt there will even be a good deal of conversation."

"Doctor . . ." She tried to find a different way to approach it. "The captain of a ship . . . he's not like everyone else. In a way, he does have to keep himself apart. Because everyone, sooner or later, will come to him for a decision . . . a decision that may very well have consequences for everyone else on the ship. When a captain makes those decisions, he has to be able to make them, free and unencumbered by other, irrelevant concerns. If intimacies of any sort factor into the equation, it can skew the decision into a direction that may be the wrong one."

"I do not quite comprehend, Commander," said Selar. "Are you implying that, in this instance, the captain could develop some sort of attachment to me that would cloud his ability to make appropriate decisions?"

"Doctor," she said and leaned forward, resting her hands on Selar's desk, "trust me on this: I know Mackenzie Calhoun. He's not the type of man who simply has casual sex. If he is intimate with a woman, he immediately considers that they then have an ongoing relationship. He's not a love-'em-and-leave-'em kind of guy. It's not part of who he is, or the way he was raised."

"The way he was raised? Commander, it is precisely because of the way he was raised that I approached the captain in this matter."

Shelby opened her mouth a moment, then closed it. "I'm sorry?"

"Commander, I did not choose the captain simply because of his rank, his rugged good looks, or his 'animal magnetism.' As befits my heritage, I approached this in a logical manner. I researched all the males on this vessel for compatibility and cultural background that would lend itself to attending to my needs. The captain's background on Xenex was the most thorough match."

"I'm not following," said Shelby, her confusion evident on her face. "His background? You mean from Xenex?" In all their time together as a couple, Calhoun had never gone into excessive detail about his life on Xenex. From what she knew of it, it was so filled with memories of war, heartache, and loss, that even to broach the subject was painful to him. So they had not discussed it overmuch. "What about his life on Xenex can possibly apply to your situation. Xenexians don't have *Pon Farr.*"

"Granted, Commander. However, they do have their own traditions and customs. One of them is that if a woman of the tribe has become widowed, and she wishes to conceive, thereby fulfilling what is perceived as the woman's role in the tribal order—and please"—she put up a hand to forestall exactly what she anticipated Shelby saying—"do not spend time telling me that women are capable of fulfilling many more functions besides childbirth. Since you and I have both chosen careers in Starfleet, we can take that to be a given in both our personal philosophies. The point is, if she wishes to conceive, then it is the responsibility of the tribal leader to perform the necessary services. Mackenzie Calhoun was indeed a tribal leader. Therefore I am merely asking him, in a manner of speaking, to fulfill those same obligations."

"But he's not on Xenex!" pointed out Shelby.

"True. And I am not on Vulcan. Our specific geographical location, Commander, is irrelevant. We continue to carry our cultures and backgrounds within us, no matter where we are. Mackenzie Calhoun is, to all intents and purposes, the leader of our little tribe here on the *Excalibur.* I, a widowed female, have asked him to fulfill an obligation that a Xenexian tribal leader routinely fulfills. This is not a question of Starfleet regulations or Federation policy, Commander. It is a question of cultural backgrounds, for both of us. Traditions. As we both know, the honoring of individual cultures and their ways is sacrosanct, even in Starfleet."

Shelby was still working on getting a grip on what Selar had just informed her of. "So . . . so you're saying that Xenexian tribal leaders sometimes act as . . . breeding machines?"

"In a manner of speaking."

"For widows?"

"Not always just widows. If it is a desire of the family and the young woman in question, tribal leaders will have intercourse with young women who have just reached maturity. The purpose there is not conception, but more of a . . . a blessing."

Shelby's voice was barely above a whisper, for which Selar was rather appreciative. "A blessing? The tribal leaders have . . . have sex with adolescent women—"

"It is considered a great honor, and is always consensual."

"*Consensual?* What girl knows anything about anything when her hormones have just started kicking in, and there's . . . there's"—and she waved a hand in a direction as if she were pointing to an invisible person in the room—"there's M'k'n'zy of Calhoun, big, broad, and studly. Playboy of western Xenex!"

"Such traditions are not completely unknown in Earth culture, Commander, although they are not practiced as much anymore. For instance, the—"

"I don't care, Doctor," said Shelby sharply, and then instantly regretted speaking so harshly to Selar. Even though her face maintained that same inscrutability, it was clear that Selar had an air of polite confusion about her. However, she said nothing as Shelby very, very quickly pulled herself together. Then she slapped her thighs briskly and said, "Well, this certainly has been educational, Doctor."

"Yes, I have learned a great deal, too, Commander," said Selar. And as Shelby walked out of her office, Selar murmured, "I have learned that, when I see you coming toward my office, I should leave immediately."

5

Burgoyne 172, chief engineer of the *Starship Excalibur,* seemed utterly engrossed in a message from home that was scrolling across the computer screen, and the other members of the engineering department were tiptoeing around so as not to disrupt Burgoyne's attention. Finally, however, Ensign Ronni Beth had completed an assignment that Burgoyne had assigned her, and felt that delaying the report back to Burgoyne would probably not be a wise thing. So she stepped up behind the Hermat and said tentatively, "Shir?"

Burgoyne turned and looked up at her with those incredibly dark eyes. "That's 'sir.' Sir, or 'chief' since I'm chief of engineering. That would also be acceptable."

"Pardon?" said Beth in surprise. "I thought Hermats preferred 'shir,' feeling that 'sir' was too attached to one particular gender—"

"We did," said Burgoyne, tapping the computer screen. "But some new decisions have come down from the Hermat Language Council."

"The what?"

"The Hermat Language Council," repeated Burgoyne. "It's an organization that meets annually, composed of various scholars and linguists. They review our language: How we use it ourselves, how others use it, our interactions with other races. They adjust the usage, create new words that the language seems to require, or give approval to words that have worked their way into our own language."

"That sounds bizarre," said Beth. "A whole group just to govern your language?"

"If it is so 'bizarre,' why does the French government of Earth have the same thing?"

Beth was caught momentarily off guard, but then she shrugged. "Well, they're French," she said, as if that was all the explanation required.

"Oh," said Burgoyne. "Well, in any event, Starfleet representatives were complaining that we had created our own separate designation. That the fleet had no problem with separate descriptors such as s/he to reflect our bi-gender status, but contended that 'sir' was a form of Starfleet direct address and therefore exempt from Hermat requirements. The winning argument, I must admit, pointed out that it was the equivalent of changing the rank to 'commandher' so that females would have equal time with the word 'man' already included in the title. The Council went back and forth on that one, but finally decided that if we're going to be part of Starfleet, we should accede to their desires in this matter."

Beth leaned forward. "What other decisions have come down?"

"Well, the big one is that they've done away with 'hish,' " said Burgoyne. "It was decided we didn't need both 'hish' and 'hir.' 'Hish' was if you wanted to say, 'S/he bowed hish head.' 'Hir' was for saying, 'S/he didn't know what to do with hir.' But for a long time now, a lot of younger Hermats have been complaining that 'hish' is just too damn difficult to say, and that 'hir' can fulfill both functions. Apparently the Council agreed."

" 'Flutzed?' " Beth's gaze had wandered farther down the screen.

"Yes, 'flutzed.' Slang term, now made official. It means"—hir long, tapered fingers waved in the air for a moment as s/he tried to come up with an appropriate equivalent—"it means, 'messed up.' Not performing as expected due to some sort of error. If you want, we can discuss all the niceties of Hermat language later on. I'll be generating a memo for all personnel discussing all the pertinent changes. Computer off." The screen went obediently blank. "For now, I expect that you have a report for me?"

"Yes, sh—sir. I've been monitoring the readouts of the phase generators as they interface with the coils, and, well, it's still there, Chief."

"The energy wave readout?"

"Yes. I made a recording of it over several one-hour periods. Computer, access file Beth Wave One."

The screen promptly flared back to life. "Accessing," said the computer briskly, and a moment later the distinctive wave pattern appeared on the screen, undulating steadily.

"But it's not affecting engine performance," Burgoyne said thoughtfully, drumming hir fingers on the countertop.

"No, sir. I believe it was the source of some of the systems botch-ups we had earlier, although we have those under control now. In fact, if anything, it's improving energy processing."

"Look at that," Burgoyne said in wonderment. The energy readout seemed to turn steadily in a sort of undulating spiral. "It's almost beautiful to watch."

"It is definitely that, Chief."

"And my own research into this wave," continued Burgoyne, "indicates that we can trace its origin point almost to the minute after we passed through that Great Flaming Bird. Ensign," s/he turned back to Beth and indicated the screen, "do you have any explanation whatsoever as to the current curious status of our energy wave read-outs?"

Beth gave it a long moment's thought, and then she said with conviction, "I'd say it's definitely flutzed."

Burgoyne laughed softly, displaying hir sharp canine teeth. "Yes. Yes, I'd have to agree. I want you to find what's causing it, Beth. I want you to make it your top priority. I have my eye on you, Beth. I think you have potential, and it's fulfilling these types of assignments that gets you ahead."

" 'These types of assignments.' You mean assignments wherein the chief engineer has absolutely no clue as to what's causing it, and s/he's looking for some lucky sucker to foist the problem on."

"Well done, Beth," said Burgoyne approvingly. "You see, assignment of blame is an even greater skill than assignment of duty."

"Words to live by, sir."

"You'll likely need people working with you. Submit a list of those who you'll want on your team so I can clear them from other duties. Although I suggest you may want to leave Christiano's name off here."

"Christiano," Beth said slowly, feeling her cheeks coloring. "Is there a . . . uhm . . . problem with Ensign Christiano, sir?"

"Not from what I hear," replied Burgoyne teasingly. "My understanding is that you and he have become quite the couple."

"How did you—?"

"Word gets around a starship quickly, Ensign. We're a rather enclosed little community."

Not one to allow teasing to go entirely in one direction, Beth riposted with, ''Well, my understanding is that you and Lieutenant McHenry are quite the couple yourself.''

''Mark?'' Again, Burgoyne laughed, although it was in a slightly different tone. One that seemed to carry a bit of pleasure in it. ''Mark is . . . Mark is charming. A very original thinker. Neither of us sees the relationship *going* anywhere, really. We're more friends with fringe benefits, you could say.''

''Enjoying each other's company until something better comes along.''

''That's it precisely. So,'' and hir dark eyes twinkled, ''any other gossip you've heard about lately?''

It was very odd for Beth, talking to Burgoyne. She never knew quite what to make of hir. There were times when s/he was surly, brusque, bordering on the dictatorial. But there were other times when Burgoyne seemed in the mood to chat and gossip like . . . well, like one of the girls.

''Well, I assume you've heard about the captain,'' said Beth. ''I mean, that's the big one floating around the ship.''

''The *captain.*'' Burgoyne seemed intrigued, leaning forward in hir chair as if afraid that a word might slip through the already minimal distance between them. ''No, this I hadn't heard. Smart money is that he and the commander are—''

But Beth quickly shook her head. ''No, not the commander. The captain and the doctor.''

The smile remained frozen on Burgoyne's face as s/he said slowly, ''Which doctor would that be?''

''*The* doctor. Selar.''

''Captain Calhoun and Doctor Selar.'' Burgoyne was having trouble maintaining the smile now. ''The . . . the two of them are . . . together now?''

''That's what I hear. Apparently the doctor is having some sort of *Pon Farr* problem. Since she's been talking with the captain, people are speculating that she's looking to him to solve it. That's where my money is, at any rate, although there are some who are speculating that actually it's the doctor and Commander Shelby who—''

''This is none of our business,'' Burgoyne said sharply, all efforts to maintain hir smile now gone. ''You have work to do, Ensign, and so do I. I think we've spent enough time at this foolishness, don't you?''

And Burgoyne turned hir back to her, leaving a puzzled Beth stammering out, "Yes, sir," and walking quickly away.

Shelby entered the bridge and saw Calhoun looking over a report that Lefler had just handed him. He was studying it thoughtfully, and she thought she heard him say something about Si Cwan. She nodded, and then he nodded and said, slightly more loudly, "Sounds like a plan. Mister McHenry."

"Yes, sir," McHenry said briskly from the conn.

"Set us a course at two-two-three mark"—he glanced once more at Lefler's notes—"mark four."

"Aye, sir. Bringing her about."

"Warp factor four, Mister McHenry. Kick it."

"She's kicked, sir."

Shelby went to her chair next to Calhoun's, but she did not sit. Instead she half-crouched, with one bent knee in the cushion of the chair, and turned to face Calhoun. "Mind telling me where we're going, sir?"

"It is Ambassador Si Cwan's recommendation that we meet with envoys from a people called the Zondarians," Calhoun replied. "Apparently they already have people en route. We're going to be rendezvousing with them within thirty-six hours."

"I see." Shelby turned to Lefler. "The purpose of the meeting?"

"We're not sure, Commander," admitted Lefler, "but we are hoping that it is for the purpose of spearheading a peace initiative that will bring an end to a civil war stretching back nearly a millennium." She then proceeded to outline, in quick, broad strokes the details behind the rendezvous.

"Sounds impressive," said Shelby.

"Commander, are you planning to stay with us for a while?" Calhoun commented, noting her rather odd stance. "Feel free to sit down."

"Actually, I'd like to talk to you a few minutes, Captain, if you have the time. In your ready room, perhaps?"

He shrugged. "Of course. Lieutenant Soleta," he called to the science officer, who from her station was busy taking notes from long-range scanners on a collapsing star many parsecs away. She looked up, her eyebrows furrowed. "You have the conn," he said, as he moved toward the ready room at Shelby's side.

Soleta walked around to the command chair and slid into it. From behind her, Security Chief Zak Kebron, the mountainous member of the Brikar, rumbled, "You look entirely too comfortable there."

"I could get to like it," she said, rubbing her hands appreciatively on the armrest.

"I thought I knew you, Mac. I thought I, of all people—"

She was briskly pacing his ready room and he watched her go back and forth as if he were observing a tennis game. "Does anyone really know anyone?" he started to reply.

But she stabbed a finger at him and said angrily, "Don't you dare. I won't see you be flip about this. Not this."

"And I won't see you overreact!"

"Overreact! Mac!" She stopped in her tracks and calmed herself. "Mac, when we first became a couple, I know we agreed that our previous sexual histories weren't really relevant, and we weren't going to inquire."

"Yes, I know."

"But, jeez, Mac!" she said as she leaned against the table to steady herself, shaking her head in astonishment. "You might have mentioned this at least! You were Xenex's official sexual surrogate?!"

"Eppy, why do you care?" he said.

"You're doing it again. Calling me by that annoying nickname in hopes that I'll get distracted. It's not going to work, Mac. Call me 'Eppy' as much as your little heart desires."

"All right, then. Eppy, again . . . why do you care? Our romantic relationship was long ago. Why should you care?"

"Because it colors what went before, that's why! Because it's—oh, I don't know!" she said in frustration, thudding one fist on the table. "I don't know why I care. You're right, I'm being stupid."

"You're being who you are, and saying what you feel. That's never stupid."

She slid into the chair next to him, propping her chin up on her fist. "It's just that"—and her voice was so soft that he had to strain to hear her—"you were . . . you were very special to me back then, Mac. Our relationship was very special. And finding that your life before me included that facet of it, I . . . well . . . it just makes me feel—"

"A little less special?"

"Kind of, I guess. And I'm sorry, I don't care what you say, I am being stupid, because it was a long time ago, and I shouldn't be letting it upset me. I've been through a lot since then, and I shouldn't really.'' She paused, as if her mind was switching tracks, and then she blurted out, ''How many?''

''Pardon?''

''How many women were there? During your 'tenure.' ''

''You mean how many women did I service?''

She winced. ''That's a bit more blunt than I would have liked. I'd have preferred you put it somewhat more delicately.''

''How many women did I fill with the glorious seed of M'k'n'zy?''

''Okay. Let's go back to blunt. How many?''

''Are you sure you want to know?''

''Yes.'' With a forced demeanor of casualness, she crossed her legs and steepled her fingers. ''I admit, I may regret it, but . . .''

''Very well.'' He proceeded to murmur to himself, counting off on his fingers, muttering a string of names. Shelby felt her heart sinking. He looked at his hands, and then back to her. ''I'm out of fingers. I may have to use the computer to calculate it.''

''Aw, come on, Mac! Just ballpark it, okay?''

''Okay, okay. Ballpark, rough number, off the top of my head, and don't hold me to this now, but it was somewhere around . . .''

She braced herself.

''One.''

She didn't even realize that she'd closed her eyes in a grimace until the moment sustained itself, frozen in time, and she became aware that she couldn't see anything. She opened her eyes and stared at him, to see that he was laughing silently to himself. ''*One!*''

''Yes.''

''Just one? Just one woman!''

''Just the one. Her name was Catrine, and if you must know, she was also the first woman that I ever . . . serviced . . . in *any* capacity. Appropriate, I guess. Someone who fought for his planet's freedom from his early teens, naturally my first sexual experience would be in the line of duty.''

''But why only the one?''

''You sound disappointed.''

''Oh, I'm not!'' she said very quickly. ''I mean, I guess only in the sense that if I were going to be getting myself so upset about something, it'd have been nice if there were something for me really to get upset about. But one? How can I . . . ? Uhm . . . why just one?''

''I found at that point that I actually had a preference for swordplay.''

''Aw, c'mon!''

"Because I wasn't the tribal leader, Eppy! You keep overlooking that. I was the warlord; my brother was the actual leader. How many women he was involved with, I could not begin to tell you, and I seriously doubt that you care."

"Not in the least."

"Good, because if you did, I'd start wondering about you. One time I had to step in while he was off-world and perform that function. I was a nervous wreck, but it all turned out okay."

"And . . . did you have a child? I mean, that's the other thing that kind of threw me, I guess. The thought of dozens of little Mackenzie Calhouns running around."

"Yes. A son."

"What's he like?"

"I wouldn't know. I've never met him."

She was visibly startled. "Never?"

He shook his head. "I had left for the Academy before she gave birth. The one time that I returned, some years later, I learned that she'd moved out of Calhoun. No one knew where. I figured if she'd wanted me to be able to find her, she'd have made it easy for me to do so, so I decided to respect her privacy."

"I'm sorry, Mac. That must be very painful for you. You must miss him."

"Miss him? Eppy, you can't miss someone you never even knew. Don't worry about it. I'm fine. I haven't thought about him in years, actually. Years and years." He paused. "How many?"

She looked at him in confusion. "You're asking me how many years you haven't thought about him?"

"No, I'm asking you how many men you were with before me." He folded his arms expectantly. "It's a fair question, Eppy, considering the grilling you've put me through. How many?"

"One." And she hesitated, and then added, "Half."

"One *half?*" He laughed skeptically. "Bottom half, I assume?"

"It was at a party," she said in annoyance, "and I was, to put it bluntly, tired of being a virgin, and there was this guy who'd been after me for a while, so I let him because I figured 'What the hell,' but he'd only partially, uhm . . ." She hesitated. "Now *I'm* trying to be delicate. He had only partially—"

"Breached your warp core?"

"Yes, thank you. And then suddenly he . . ."

"Fired photon torpedoes?"

"I was going to say 'reached critical mass,' but if you want to mix your metaphors, you're the captain."

"I think you've made the point, Eppy." He smiled. "You know, Eppy, back then, I have to admit that your lack of comfort discussing sex bothered the hell out of me. But now, in a woman your age, I find it somewhat charming."

"Why, thank you. So, have you made a decision regarding Doctor Selar yet?"

"No. But whatever I do decide, understand that I will endeavor to keep the common good of all concerned as my first and foremost consideration. And now, if you'll excuse me . . ." He rose from his chair and exited the ready room.

She stood to follow him, then stopped.

"A woman my age?" she said slowly. "What the hell is *that* supposed to mean?"

6

The approaching ship was bristling with armament and ready for war.

It was a sleek, low-slung vessel, small but maneuverable, with foils that clearly indicated it was designed to function equally well in the depths of space or within a planet's atmosphere. McHenry had been tracking it for some time, and when it began to make its approach, he nodded as if confirming his own concerns. "Yeah, it's definite, Captain," he said. "They're definitely set to intercept us."

"How are they running?" he asked.

Kebron checked his sensor array. "Running weapons hot. They are not, however, targeting us."

From the science station, Soleta went over the weapons analysis. "They're packing phase blasters and torpedoes with nuclear warheads. Their weapons could hurt us, sir."

"Any thoughts, Commander?" he addressed Shelby.

She leaned forward, like a bloodhound on the scent. "They may be suspicious of us. Desirous to ascertain our identity."

"Have you managed to raise them yet, Mister Kebron?"

"Not yet."

The turbolift doors slid open and Si Cwan strode out onto the bridge. "Came as fast as I could, Captain."

Calhoun gestured towards the opposing vessel. "Recognize them, Cwan?"

Without hesitation, Si Cwan said briskly, "Zondarian. Definitely."

"They're not responding to our hails. Any thoughts?"

Si Cwan studied the vessel for a moment. "Turn around."

"You mean the ship?" said Calhoun.

"Well, you could turn around in your chair, but that would hardly alter the situation."

A deep voice rumbled from nearby, "Watch it, Cwan."

"I think I can handle this, Kebron. Thank you," Calhoun said. "Why should we turn around, Ambassador?"

Si Cwan hesitated a moment, as if ready to answer, but then he drew himself up even straighter, towering over Calhoun. "Looming" was perhaps one of Si Cwan's greatest talents. "If one of your officers gave you advice in a pressure situation, you'd take it on faith first and ask questions later."

"Correct," Calhoun said, arms folded. "What's your point?"

"Captain, five hundred thousand kilometers and closing. Still running weapons hot."

"Thank you, Mister McHenry." Calhoun paused, assessing Si Cwan's demeanor, and then he said, "Bring us about, reverse heading."

"Deflectors up, sir?"

"Yes."

Almost as quickly as Calhoun gave an affirmative, Si Cwan said, "No."

Calhoun's violet eyes narrowed. "*Yes,*" he said with emphasis.

Quickly the *Excalibur* turned about, and began to head back the way she came.

"Sir, pursuer is picking up speed! Three hundred thousand kilometers, closing fast, coming in at heading one-two-nine mark nine," McHenry informed him.

"Still no targeting from their weapons array. But they are on intercept course."

"Evasive maneuvers, Mister McHenry!" ordered Calhoun.

"Evasive manuevers. Aye, sir!" replied McHenry, and sent the *Excalibur* howling directly toward the expected point of collision.

There was a unified shout of alarm from virtually everyone on the bridge, Calhoun's voice above all as he shouted, "*McHenry, what are you doing!?*" The alien vessel loomed huge on the screen, looking as if it were about to park itself right on the bridge.

"Evasive maneuver, sir," McHenry said calmly. "Three . . . two . . . one . . ."

The starship passed the point of intersection seconds before the oncoming vessel, and then hurtled away, missing the other ship by barely one hundred meters. Shelby fancied that she could actually hear the roar of the other ship's engines.

". . . Zero," finished McHenry. "Evasive maneuver successful, Captain. Orders?"

"Bring us around behind them. Lock phasers on target, Mister Kebron."

"Gladly, sir."

"Send them a warning that if they do not stand down, we're going to blow them halfway to hell."

"You are going to needless trouble, Captain," Si Cwan said. "They were endeavoring to show 'dominance.' They do not like to have discourse with any race that they feel inferior to. So they make a great show of bluster, like that Earth animal . . . a gorilla . . . pounding on its chest. If you had simply stayed on course, they would have veered off on their own. No evasive maneuvers, as charmingly unorthodox as they were, were necessary."

"If that's the case, Ambassador, I appreciate their desire to deal from perceived strength. But if it's all the same to you, I'd prefer to operate from genuine strength."

"We're getting an incoming hail, Captain."

"About bloody time. Put them on visual, Mister Kebron."

The screen wavered for only a moment, and then two Zondarians appeared on the screen. They were staring, almost in wonderment. "It is you? Mackenzie Calhoun?"

He was struck by the odd sheen of their skin. They looked fairly similar to one another, except that one was taller than the other. "Yes. That's right. Identify yourselves, and explain your attempted attack upon my vessel."

"We would never have injured you, Mackenzie Calhoun," said the shorter one. "We are the Zondarian pilgrimage, come to meet with you."

"You have a very odd way of trying to make a positive first impression," Calhoun informed them. "If you *wanted* to meet with us, why did you take a combative attitude?"

"We would have communicated sooner," said the shorter one, and he glanced in annoyance at the taller one next to him, "but my Eenza associate insisted that he have the honor of having the first communication with you, since it was one of the Eenza who foretold your coming. But it was my belief that I had equal right to the first communication, considering all the hardships my people, the Unglza, have suffered at Eenza hands."

"As if the Unglza hands are clean," snorted the taller one.

"I told you Mackenzie Calhoun would not be familiar with your convoluted methods of greeting newcomers by way of challenge,'' the shorter one said testily. ''Attack, dive. Which idiot member of your clan dreamt up such—''

''Gentlemen,'' Calhoun said firmly, ''there are certainly more constructive ways to spend time than arguing over who said what. I'm willing to chalk this unfortunate incident off to miscommunication and''—he glanced at Si Cwan—''rather odd greeting rituals. The point is, we're talking now. You desired to speak with us. Here we are.''

''Yes. Yes, of course. I am Killick,'' said the shorter one, ''and my associate is—''

''I can introduce myself. I am Ramed,'' said the taller. Calhoun noticed that there was another difference between the two of them. Ramed's eyes were darker, more serious. He had the air of being perpetually disturbed about something. His gaze flickered to Calhoun's right, and he nodded slightly in acknowledgment. ''Lord Si Cwan.''

''Ramed. We meet again under unusual circumstances,'' Si Cwan replied.

''Odd how things develop, isn't it?''

''Odd indeed. To see an Unglza and an Eenza side-by-side.''

''We have been brought together by common cause,'' Killick spoke up. ''We humbly petition that you meet with us as soon as possible. We wish to share the joy of this moment with you, so that you all may understand.''

''Do they have matter transport capability?'' Calhoun said softly to Si Cwan.

Si Cwan shook his head. ''Not to your degree of sophistication. They can transport from one construction transmat point to the next, but they do not possess the Federation's capture-and-receive technology.''

''Very well.'' He turned back to the Zondarians. ''We will bring you aboard our vessel and we can discuss the matter more thoroughly.''

''How will you do that?'' inquired Killick.

''It's not very involved. Bridge to transporter room,'' Calhoun called. ''Lock onto the transmission origin and beam the senders aboard. I'll be right down to greet them.''

''Affirmative, Captain.''

A moment later, Killick and Ramed vanished from the screen in a startled dissolve of sparkles. Calhoun nodded approvingly, and then said, ''Shelby, Soleta, Si Cwan, Kebron—with me. Mister McHenry, you have the conn. And no evasive maneuvers while we're gone.''

''Aye, sir.''

''Come, people: Let's see what our new friends have to say.''

''You are the Savior.''

They were in the conference lounge: Calhoun, Soleta, Shelby, Si Cwan, and the Zondarians seated around the table. Kebron had taken up position directly behind the Zondarians, just standing there with his massive arms folded across his chest, his hard-to-see eyes glittering from deep within his face like diamonds with attitude. Clearly he was waiting for evidence of even the slightest false move on the part of the newcomers, and if they provided him with that opening, he would strike quickly and with finality.

Calhoun was staring at the Zondarians in disbelief. ''I'm sorry, Killick, I didn't quite catch that, or even understand it. I am the what?''

''The Savior,'' repeated Killick, sounding extremely reasonable. ''Our Savior. You are He. You are come. Just as was prophesied five hundred years ago.'' He looked to Ramed for verification, and Ramed nodded agreeably. ''You see?'' he said as if that constituted the final, rock-solid proof. ''If there is something that even Unglza and Eenza can agree upon, then it must be so.''

''Far be it from me to dispute the indisputable,'' said Calhoun, ''but may I ask how just how, precisely, you came to this conclusion? That I am your Savior?''

''Yes,'' Ramed nodded emphatically. ''There can be no mistake.''

''May I ask how you can be so sure?'' Shelby inquired.

''It is in the lore of our greatest prophet, Ontear, and his greatest acolyte, Suti,'' Ramed told them, and now it was Killick who was obediently bobbing his head in affirmation. ''Ontear predicted your coming.''

''Was the captain mentioned by name?'' asked Soleta.

''Well . . . no,'' admitted Ramed.

''Well, then,'' Soleta continued, ''unless this prophet said something to the effect that you should be on the lookout for a starship captain with a scar who will show up shortly after a giant flaming bird puts in an appearance, I'm afraid I don't quite see the logic in believing that Captain Calhoun is your anointed one.''

Killick and Ramed looked at one another, and then Killick sighed. ''You're the Eenza; it's your right. Go ahead and say it.''

Ramed slowly stood, and he seemed so consumed with excitement that he could barely keep his legs still. His fingers rested on the edge of the table as if he needed it for support. " 'Look to the stars,' he intoned, 'for from there will come the Messiah! The bird of flame will signal His coming! He will bear a scar, and He will be a great leader! And He will unite our planet!"

"That was written by the great Ontear, on his last day upon our world, five hundred years ago," Killick informed them.

As one, the others turned and stared at Soleta. She shifted uncomfortably in her chair. "A lucky guess," she said in an offhand manner.

"It really says all that?" Calhoun asked in disbelief.

"They would not lie about the predictions of Ontear, Captain," Si Cwan said. "It is a subject they take most, most seriously. To even joke about such matters is the equivalent of consigning your soul to . . . well, whatever passes for oblivion in Zondarian theology."

"Is that specific enough for you, Captain?" asked Killick.

"I have to admit, it's a fairly impressive set of coincidences," Shelby agreed. "Perhaps too many to be considered 'mere' coincidence, although I still don't rule out a more scientific explanation."

"Such as?" inquired Ramed politely.

"Lieutenant?" Shelby turned and looked hopefully at Soleta.

Soleta shrugged. "Nothing comes to mind," she said.

"Thanks for the help, Lieutenant."

"Not a problem, Commander."

Calhoun leaned forward, and there seemed to be mild amusement in his eyes. "All right. Just for the sake of argument, let's say I am your Savior."

"Which we are not saying, most emphatically," Shelby quickly put in. She looked to Calhoun for confirmation of that, and was a bit disconcerted when she didn't see it.

"As I said," he repeated calmly, "just for sake of argument. If that were the case, what would you expect of me?"

Killick glanced at Ramed, who nodded silently, and then turned back and said, "It is our hope that you would come to Zondar. Your return has long been associated with peace among our people. Were you to come to our world, as a vehicle for peace, we know that they would listen. Both the Eenza and the Unglza are building up arms in preparation for a resurgence of the violence that has dominated our relationship for centuries. But leaders of both groups have agreed to set aside differences for the purpose of sitting at a negotiation table with the Savior Himself. Who, after all, could possibly turn down such an honor?"

"Who indeed?" Si Cwan affirmed. "Captain, in my opinion, it would be foolish of you to deny your obvious heritage. The beliefs of these good people should be—must be—honored."

"You are our Savior," Ramed said with quiet conviction. "Save us, anointed one. Save us . . . from ourselves."

The Zondarians had returned to their ship, impressed by the power of the *Excalibur*'s transporter, and Kebron—the possible threat to security now gone—had returned to his post on the bridge. Calhoun was now meeting in privacy with the remaining officers. "It could, of course, be a hoax," Soleta pointed out. "The prophecies written only recently by those within an inner circle and then 'discovered' in order to fulfill recent events."

But Si Cwan was emphatically shaking his head. "No," he said flatly. "I spoke separately with them. These writings go back half a millennium, as they said. There's no chance of forgery."

"You can't intend to go along with it, Captain," Shelby said.

Calhoun was scratching his chin thoughtfully. "Why not?"

"Why not?" She couldn't quite believe she had to spell it out. "Captain, you cannot go to these people and present yourself as their . . . their messiah!"

"Why?"

"Because it's a clear violation of the Prime Directive! You're interfering with the development of their society!"

"With all respect, Commander, I disagree," Si Cwan replied from across the table. "The captain has not inserted himself into their society. Their society has reached out to encompass him."

"Some men seek out greatness," Calhoun said sagely, "and others have greatness thrust upon them."

Shelby kept her voice level, endeavoring to explain that which, to her, seemed crystal clear. "Captain, you do not seem to be regarding this situation with the gravity that it quite clearly demands. To set yourself up as some sort of ruler for these people, even if they demand it—even if the title seems yours by some sort of prophetic right—it's against everything that the spirit of the Prime Directive stands for."

"I'm not an idiot, Commander," Calhoun said, a bit more sharply than he might have intended to.

"I never meant to say, or imply, that you were, sir," Shelby replied stiffly.

"I know what you're concerned about. I know the regs. What I also know is that these people stand on the brink of almost certainly heading back into a civil war, now that the Thallonian Empire's influence has ceased."

"There is no 'almost' about it, Captain," Si Cwan affirmed. "The grudges are long-standing, the hatred beyond any rational discussion. They are not able to look beyond their squabbles and stereotypes of one another. But the one thing upon which they do agree, which cuts across all of their hatred, all of their hostility, is that their Savior will reunite them. Indeed, perhaps it's their conviction in that regard that has given them license to attack one another all these centuries. They believed that they were destined to do so. But now their Savior is here."

"He's not here!" said Shelby firmly.

"What would you have me do, Commander?" asked Calhoun reasonably. "Go to the Zondarians and say, 'Sorry, you've got the wrong guy. You're on your own.' And leave? Turn my back while men, women, and children are slaughtered?"

"No, of course not."

"You wouldn't want to take the Thallonian route, I presume. Go in and threaten them with force of arms? Cow them into submission?"

"That is also, obviously, not an acceptable alternative." She sighed. "Captain, I want peace for these people, the same as anyone else. And aiding in peace negotiations is well within the mandate of our mission."

"If that's the case, then I think I have a simple solution," Calhoun said. "In fact, from the look in your eyes, I suspect you have it, too."

"To neither confirm nor deny?" suggested Shelby.

"Precisely."

"I'm not quite following, Commander, Captain," admitted Si Cwan.

"I will not go to the Zondarians and put myself forward as being the fulfillment of their prophecies," Calhoun said. "By the same token, if they ask me, I will not deny it either. I will simply nod, smile, and say something vague such as, 'Who am I to argue with prophecies?' I'm not going in there for the purpose of self-aggrandizement. I'm going in to try and convince a race that seems hellbound on destruction that there are better courses for them to follow. If they want to think of me as some sort of 'Savior,' let them. Let them think I'm God from on high. Let them think I'm J'e'n't, the Three-Headed Xenexian God of Lightning, for all I care. As long as it gets them seated across from each other at a negotiation table, talking with one another, then my job is done."

"The end justifies the means," commented Soleta.

"Of course it does. Always," Calhoun readily agreed.

"Captain," Shelby said cautiously, "I know that your motives are pure and well intentioned. And I agree that this seems to be the most expeditious manner in which to proceed. But expediency doesn't always equal wise. We have to tread very, very carefully. We're walking a fine line here between right and wrong, both from a Starfleet standpoint, and the standpoint of morality."

"I know that I can count on you, Elizabeth, to keep me on that straight and narrow line and warn me lest I fall off."

She smiled wanly. "I'll certainly do my best, Captain."

The door to the conference lounge slid open, and Doctor Selar entered. "Captain, you wished to see me?" she asked.

"Uhm . . . yes. I believe we're done here, then?" There were nods of affirmation from all around. "Commander, kindly inform the Zondarians that we will indeed proceed directly to their homeworld, there to meet with their senior advisors to try and map out some sort of permanent peace between the Eenza and the Unglza. Have Mister McHenry bring us there at warp two. That'll give them some time to build up anticipation over our arrival. Lieutenant Soleta, work with Ambassador Si Cwan, if you will, and dig up any other information you can on this reputed Savior of theirs. Anything I can use to my advantage to pull this off will be of great help. All right, people," and he clapped his hands briskly. "This all sounds like a plan."

Everyone filed out, Shelby the last, and she hesitated just a moment as she passed Selar. A significant look passed between them, one that was not lost on Soleta, who was very aware of the mating urges that Selar was dealing with. She'd heard the rumors flying around the ship regarding the captain and Selar, and had known what aspects to dismiss—also which aspects to take seriously.

There was something else going on, however; some sort of odd dynamic between Selar and Shelby that Soleta could not quite understand. Feeling a need to come somehow to the aid of her fellow Vulcan, Soleta—who was already out in the hallway—said questioningly, "Commander?"

"Yes. Coming," said Shelby, shaken from the spell that had momentarily distracted her. She walked out behind Soleta as the door slid shut behind her, leaving Selar and Calhoun alone in the conference lounge.

Selar waited expectantly.

"I've given the matter a good deal of thought," Calhoun said.

"You mean the matter of having sex with me."

He wanted to say, *No, the matter of whether or not there is a God,* but he wisely decided that that would not be the best course. "That's correct. I've consulted Starfleet regs on the matter, and they seem rather vague on how to proceed in this instance."

"Since this is a condition that we generally like to keep to ourselves, even though others may tend to broadcast word of it"—and she glanced with a clearly annoyed manner in the direction of the departed Shelby—"it does not surprise me that it would not thoroughly be covered in literature."

"Be that as it may, it seems to me that the wisest course might be to say no, simply to avoid the possible entanglements such an encounter might engender. Besides, there may be other possibilities. Have you considered the option, Doctor, of simply returning to Vulcan? Of finding a mate there? I could arrange for transport."

"I am very aware of that, Captain," replied Selar evenly. She looked down at the toes of her boots, and for the first time she actually looked vulnerable to Calhoun. Even a little scared, although he was quite sure that she would never admit to it. "Captain, I find the entire concept of *Pon Farr* to be most onerous. My duties as chief medical officer of the *Excalibur,* on the other hand, give me great satisfaction. It does not seem proper or just to me that I must dispense with the latter in order to accommodate the former. Furthermore, I—"

She hesitated. He thought of prompting her, but he knew that she would tell him in her own time.

"I . . . have no one on Vulcan, sir. No one I would be . . . comfortable with."

"Comfortable? Doctor, the bottom line is you hardly know me, and vice versa."

She returned his gaze, and it seemed to him as if she were dissecting him with her eyes. "You are a good man, Captain. A proud man. Clever, inventive. I have not known many men whom I would classify as heroic, but you would certainly fall into that category. I would be," she began, and it seemed to him—although he might have been imagining it—that she had to make the slightest effort to keep her chin from trembling. ''I would be most proud if you were to sire my child.''

Calhoun smiled, actually feeling embarrassed, although he'd believed that couldn't possibly be the case. He felt his head nodding even before he said anything. ''All right, Doctor. If that's what you want, I'll accommodate you.''

''Thank you, Captain,'' she said with clear relief.

They were standing about a foot away from each other, and the moment seemed to call for some sort of physical contact. They each moved their hands in a vague manner, and Calhoun even thought to hug her except he felt that it would be wrong somehow. They settled for a brisk handshake.

''So, judging by the fact that you're not knocking me onto the conference lounge table, I can take that to mean that you're still in 'remission,' as it were,'' he said.

She nodded. 'Yes, that is correct. However, the mating urge will resurface, probably within the next week. I will inform you when I will need you. I will endeavor to time it at a point where your duties and requirements are minimal.''

''I appreciate your consideration for my schedule.''

''It's more than that, sir. You see, as I go more deeply into *Pon Farr,* I will . . . link with you, psychically. You will become as driven by the impulse to mate as I am. You will be consumed by, and be able to think of nothing else but, sex.''

''Sounds like fairly typical male behavior,'' Calhoun observed. Then he grinned at the seriousness on her face. ''It was a joke, Doctor.''

''Ah. I see. Humor is a difficult concept.''

They stood there for a moment, uncertain what else to say.

''Captain.''

''Yes, Doctor?''

''If you would like, you may call me Selar.''

He nodded appreciatively. ''And you may call me Mac, if you wish.''

She seemed to roll the name around in her mouth for a moment, and then she said, ''If you will not be insulted, I think I would prefer 'Captain.' ''

''As you wish, Selar.''

''Thank you, Captain.''

7

The High Priest of Alpha Carinae did not like what he was hearing.

The Alphans were relatively recent converts to Xantism. They were a somewhat barbaric race, really. Large, muscled, fairly savage of mien, yet living with a rather healthy fear of the Redeemers, which was naturally how the High Priest preferred matters.

Different High Priests handled their positions of power in different manners. High Priests on some other worlds, for instance, chose to keep themselves in seclusion, learning of the world through various "eyes" and "ears" among the populace who were loyal to the way of Xant. But the High Priest of Alpha Carinae was far too outgoing an individual to stay hidden away somewhere. He insisted upon moving among the populace, to hear their words with his own ears. To know what they were thinking, to look into their eyes and see whether their love and belief in Xant was sincere.

The High Priest was becoming concerned.

It seemed to him that the Alphans were not looking at him in the same, comforting manner of fear that usually possessed them. Usually, if there was a crowd of Alphans, they would part to make way for him. Recently, however, they'd been slower to do so. Not only that, but when they did get out of his way, they made a major show of doing so as if to draw attention to themselves, as if to make mockery of the High Priest.

And as he walked away, if he strained his ears he could hear muttering. Hear the name of the Redeemers mentioned with what sounded like contempt, and other names murmured as well. Names he had heard bandied about with greater and greater frequency these days. Names such as "Calhoun" and "*Excalibur.*" The names, in and of themselves, did not mean a great deal to him. But it was enough to cause a stirring of concern in the pit of his stomach.

He did not yet consider himself to be in any sort of danger. The person of a High Priest of the Redeemers was sacrosanct, and he was certain that none of the Alphans would be foolish enough to transgress in that respect. They knew the consequences. At least, he thought they knew the consequences.

However, he needed to find out more for himself. So, during one of his daily perambulations, he chose at random a cluster of Alphans standing at a streetcorner, talking and arguing with what seemed to be tremendous enthusiasm. Something had them rather worked up, and the High Priest reasoned that only two things could get a group of young males quite that excited: sex, or a stimulating religious discussion.

Slowly the High Priest moved toward them. One of the young males had his back to him and so didn't see him approaching. The others' discussion and chatter quickly trailed off as they spotted him coming, and the one whose back was to the High Priest slowly trailed off, looking and sounding rather puzzled until he turned around and saw the High Priest standing directly behind him.

"Saulcram, isn't it?" asked the High Priest. He tapped the young man's chest with his staff.

Saulcram nodded fretfully. The others began to back up as if conspiring to make a getaway, but the High Priest froze them with a glance. He slowly turned his attention back to the first young man. "I would be interested to know that which you are discussing, Saulcram."

"It's nothing, my lord," Saulcram said nervously.

"If it is nothing, then it is of such little consequence that you should not hesitate to tell me what it is. Correct?" He made it sound so pleasant, so simple. He prodded Saulcram under the chin less than gently with his staff. "Now you will tell me, yes?"

Saulcram looked to his friends, and then back to the High Priest. "We're just . . . just discussing, well . . . what everyone is discussing."

"Odd," said the High Priest. "I don't recall discussing it. Why don't you share that which apparently should already be common knowledge, hmm?"

"Well, it's . . . it's about . . . you know . . . the Second Coming."

"The Second Coming." The High Priest nodded approvingly. "You refer, of course, to the Second Coming of Xant."

"Yes. Yes, that's it exactly. Can I go now?"

The end of the staff had a curve to it. The High Priest twisted it slightly so that the curve snagged Saulcram's upper forearm, keeping him serenely in place. "Well, I find this a bit odd, Saulcram," the High Priest told him. "If that was indeed all you were talking about—the Second Coming of Xant—then why did you hesitate to tell me? Why were you so nervous? Why are you so nervous still?"

"I . . . I swear, I don't—"

The High Priest suddenly gripped his staff with both hands and twisted quickly. The abrupt sharp turn of the hooked end bent down and back against the arm, and there was a very audible snap. Saulcram went down, clutching at his broken arm, and there were tears already starting to well up in his eyes.

The others surrounding the High Priest took an angry step forward, and once again the High Priest glared around at them in that forceful way he had. It was a look that was usually capable of thoroughly intimidating the Alphans. This time, the High Priest made a mental note that the Alphans did not appear intimidated at all. Hesitant, yes. Unsure of whether to make a move or not. But it seemed no longer that they would hesitate to attack. Rather, it appeared that they were simply waiting for the right time, although no one seemed to know precisely when that was going to be.

Other passersby were stopping to observe the altercation. A crowd was beginning to grow, and it was not something the High Priest could particularly say he liked. He raised his voice and called out, "The person of a High Priest is sacrosanct! Do not forget that! Let none of you forget that! For to injure or kill a High Priest is to spell swift and immediate doom for your entire world! Know that!"

And from somewhere in the crowd, he heard a voice call out. And the voice said, "*Excalibur* is coming!"

"*Excalibur,*" he murmured in confusion and annoyance.

"*Excalibur,* the force of freedom, chosen of the flame bird!" someone shouted.

A third person called out, "The liberator is coming! They will destroy you, and the Redeemers, and even your precious Xant will not be able to stand before them!"

Still another person shouted out, "Calhoun! Calhoun!"

The crowd began to take up the chant, repeating it over and over: "Calhoun! Calhoun! *Calhoun!*"

The High Priest had no idea what was going on, but he knew he did not like it. Not in the least.

He stepped back away from Saulcram and his friends. Caught up in the defiance of the crowd, even Saulcram and those with him were calling out *"Calhoun! Calhoun!"*

The High Priest, maintaining as much of his dignity as possible under the circumstances, made his way back to the Alpha Carinae Central Hall of Worship. Even though things seemed calmer once he put some distance between himself and the impromptu rally, he couldn't help but feel that all eyes were upon him. He kept feeling that someone would launch himself from the shadows of a nearby building. Anything from a harsh word to a projectile might have come flying his way at any moment. As it happened, however, his return to his base occurred without incident. And so it was that—with his skin intact, albeit it with nerves somewhat strung out—the High Priest was putting through a transmission to Tulaan IV as fast as possible.

Moments later he was speaking directly with Prime One, the Overlord's good right arm. At first he had been concerned that Prime One might be upset in response to what should have been a minor problem, but instead Prime One seemed amused by it all. "I know whereof the Alphans speak, Brother," Prime One said calmly. "We know well of this 'flame bird' that was mentioned. You will be most pleased to know that the Overlord had officially declared it to be a sign."

"A sign," the High Priest repeated uncomprehendingly.

"A sign that Xant will be returning," Prime One said with a touch of impatience. He outlined the specifics of the flame bird's appearance in as broad strokes as he could, and then concluded, "This is not a time of concern, Brother. This is a time of rejoicing!"

"Rejoicing is a luxury in which you can indulge yourself, Prime One," replied the High Priest. "But the people of Alpha Carinae do not seem to necessarily share your conviction that this is a precursor to the return of Xant. They seem perfectly inclined to attribute some other cause to it."

"Other?" The thought literally had not even occurred to the Prime One. "What other could there possibly be?"

"This *'Excalibur'* they mentioned. And another name . . . Calhoun."

"Yes, we are aware of both of these," said Prime One. *"Excalibur* is a Federation vessel, Calhoun its captain. They were merely on the site when the bird signaled the return of Xant. They have nothing to do with the creature's existence, nor with the return of Xant."

"That may very well be," the High Priest informed him, "but the Alphans seem to feel otherwise. They believe in some sort of link. That, rather than signaling a return by Xant, the circumstances surrounding the creature's appearance is an endorsement of, or a precursor to, the one they call Calhoun. They seem to regard him as some sort of . . . of liberator."

"Liberator?" Prime One was thunderstruck. "Liberation from the word of Xant? From the spirit of Xant? Who in their right mind would desire to be liberated from that?"

"The Alphans apparently, sir. They have no comprehension or appreciation of all that we try to do for them."

"I will inform the Overlord of this situation," Prime One said after a moment's thought. "He will want to know of the wrongheadedness in many which surrounds this clear signal of Xant's return. He may very well want to address Alpha Carinae . . . and perhaps even other worlds which may be laboring under similar delusions. Thank you for informing me of the situation there, Brother."

"It was my honor as always, Prime One."

"May Xant light your way."

"Yours as well, Prime One."

Prime One's image blinked off the screen, leaving the High Priest to gaze out the windows at the populace below him. It was a populace amongst whom he had never hesitated to walk, but now something told him that he would be most well advised to stay exactly where he was. That perhaps now was not the time to spread the good word and tidings of Xant among the Alphans.

Because somehow, he had the feeling—a feeling that, as it turned out, was a correct one—that the last thing the Alphans were interested in doing at that particular moment in time was listening.

8

Selar was seated by herself in the team room, which was how she was customarily seated. She was carefully nursing a glass of Synthehol when she looked up to see Burgoyne 172 staring down at her.

"Somehow, Lieutenant Commander," Selar said slowly, "I suspected that we would be chatting in the near future."

"Really," Burgoyne said. "So you're saying there's something you want to talk to me about?"

"Not in particular, no," replied Selar. "However, it was my suspicion that you would desire to talk to me."

"Well, now aren't we full of ourselves," said Burgoyne, and Selar could see from the slightest waver in Burgoyne's bearings that s/he had already had a bit to drink. Selar was well aware (since Burgoyne had boasted of it on more than one occasion) that s/he had a fairly impressive collection of scotch back in hir quarters, a drink s/he had apparently developed a taste for while imbibing with a former engineer from another ship.

"Would you care to sit down, Lieutenant Commander," said Selar, "before you fall down?"

"Why don't you ask me to sit?" Burgoyne demanded.

For the briefest of moments, Selar doubted her sanity. Was it possible, she wondered, that the semidelusional state resulting from heightened *Pon Farr* was enough to cause her to lose track completely of time or a discussion? Hadn't she just asked—

She shrugged mentally. It hardly seemed worth a dispute. "Why do you not sit down?" she inquired.

"Thank you," said Burgoyne, dropping down into a chair next to

Selar. Burgoyne was leaning so far over toward Selar's side that she had to slide over a bit so as not to wind up with Burgoyne in her lap. That was a situation that certainly would not have been off-putting to Burgoyne, but was not something that Selar desired to explore at this particular moment in time.

"How may I be of service, Chief Engineer?"

"For starters, you can call me Burgoyne. Or Burgy. Most fother olks do."

It took the Vulcan a mere moment to realize that Burgoyne had meant to say "other folks," and somehow the letters seemed to have gotten away from hir, to say nothing of each other. Although the familiarity was uncomfortable to her, she opted to accede to hir requests rather than risk a protracted conversation. "Very well, Burgoyne. How can I help you?"

"Well, I thought that I could have helped you," said Burgoyne. S/he didn't seem particularly happy at the moment. "But I must have looked pretty foolish, huh? There I was, letting you know I was interested. Talking about how good we could be together. And it turns out you already have something going on. With the captain, no less."

"My involvement with the captain—whatever that may or may not be—is no concern of yours, Burgoyne. If you must know, I . . ."

Burgoyne looked up at her, hir eyes looking slightly bloodshot. "Yes?"

It was at that moment that Selar almost blurted all of it out. Not just the needs of *Pon Farr,* but the fact that she did indeed find Burgoyne attractive. Despite hir over-the-top approach, despite all of hir aggressive and devil-may-care theatrics—or perhaps *because* of them—Selar had slowly come to consider Burgoyne very desirable. So much so that she had been ready to give herself over to Burgoyne during one of the more aggressive flare-ups of her condition. But she had seen Burgoyne with Mark McHenry at the time. There had been something about the cavalier, casual way in which Burgoyne had managed to toss aside Selar and move on to someone else—of another gender, yet!—that had prompted Selar to back off from the Hermat. Had prompted her to look elsewhere for a suitable mate, one who might be just a bit more stable.

"If you must know," repeated Selar, "I find the captain . . . most attractive."

"Good for you!" said Burgoyne. S/he slapped hir hands together in loud applause, drawing looks of casual confusion from other officers sitting nearby. Selar quickly reached over, put her hands on top of Burgoyne's, and pushed them down to the table top.

Burgoyne's tapered fingers wrapped around Selar's for just a moment, holding them, and Selar felt a jolt of electricity between the two of them. It was insane. What the devil was it about the Hermat that caused hir to have this sort of effect upon Selar? Selar didn't know, and it was perhaps that very ignorance that she found the most off-putting. The captain she found suitable for a variety of intellectual reasons. That was something she could grasp. Burgoyne as a choice was totally and utterly illogical, and there was absolutely no reason in the galaxy for Selar to pursue such a relationship. None.

"I mean it," and Burgoyne sounded less blustering, more sincere. "Truly, I mean it. I want you to be happy, Selar. And if the captain is what you want, and if he's what will make you happy, then I would be the last person to stand in your way. I mean that. I value relationships too thoroughly to get between the two of you."

"I . . . appreciate that, Burgoyne. I do."

"Well, good." Burgoyne had still not released Selar's hand. And then s/he looked up at Selar with a look of mischief on hir face. "Threesome?"

"I . . . beg your pardon?" asked Selar.

"Well, I was simply curious, that's all," Burgoyne told her. "Have you ever tried a threesome?"

"I am not certain what it is you are referring to."

"I mean three people. Having sex. At the same time."

Selar stared at hir. "With whom?"

"With each other!" laughed Burgoyne. "I mean, I don't know the captain apparently as well as you do. But if that's something the two of you would be interested in exploring . . ."

"Three . . . together . . . simultaneously . . ."

"Yes, that's the general—"

"Burgoyne, that is not sex. That is a committee."

"Well, only if you start taking votes and things . . ."

"Burgoyne," and Selar began to rise from her chair, "I do not know how things are done on your world—"

"I have a book. With illustrations and footnotes."

"Keep it. We are . . . we are too different, that is all. I do not know why I even considered—"

"Considered?" The moment she'd mentioned the word, Selar wished that she could have the sentence to say over again. But that wasn't possible, for Burgoyne had quickly picked up on the slip. "Considered what? Me? You and I? Us?"

"No," Selar said flatly. "I was going to say, I do not know why I even considered the possibility of talking to you simply as one individual to another. You are—"

"Dashing? Charming? Wonderfully open?"

"I believe 'insane' is the word I was searching for."

"I'll take that as a compliment. Insane, as in crazy about you."

"Burgoyne, you are intoxicated. It is prompting you to say things that you would not ordinarily say, which is, in and of itself, surprising to me, for you have rarely shown any restraint before in saying whatever comes to mind. But I believe you have set a new standard for yourself with this conversation."

"But I'm happy for you! Can't you see that? I'm just pleased you're not lonely!"

"Lonely?" She gazed at hir with what seemed a distracted air. "Do not dismiss the concept of loneliness, Burgoyne. There is much to be said for it. There is much comfort that one can take in it. Once one adjusts to loneliness, one can never be hurt again. Yes, indeed . . . loneliness is underrated."

"I can think of no worse, or depressing state, than loneliness," Burgoyne replied. "It can be all-consuming. It can and will destroy you. I can think of no sadder state."

"And that," Selar said softly, "is why you will do whatever you can to avoid it. Cast about for bedmates, flirt shamelessly, do whatever it takes to make certain that you are not alone. I pity you, Burgoyne."

Burgoyne's face clouded. "Save your pity for someone who needs it. I'm happy. Happy. You understand? Happier than you will ever be."

"As opposed to loneliness, happiness is overrated."

Selar left her drink behind as she headed out of the team room, Burgoyne calling after her, "It's been great talking to you, too!"

S/he plopped down into the chair Selar had just occupied, still feeling her warmth from the seat cushion. Burgoyne shook hir head. "Women," s/he sighed.

McHenry had entered the team room, and now he spotted Burgoyne by hirself. He strolled over to hir, reversed the chair and straddled it. "You look lonely, Burgy."

"You look off-duty, Mark."

"I am."

"You doing anything?"

"Well," McHenry told hir, "I'm reading a quantum physics review article."

"What?" Burgoyne looked at McHenry's empty hands, then over hir own shoulder to see if there was something visible behind hir. "What are you talking about?"

"I have a photographic memory," McHenry told hir. "Some new articles came through the ether this morning, but I didn't have time to sit down and read them. So I kind of glanced at them and just made mental snapshots. Now I'm pulling them out and reading them while we talk. Although if you find that distracting, I can stop."

"No, it's quite all right. About how much of your brain functions does that occupy?"

"Maybe thirty percent."

"I see," Burgoyne said thoughtfully. "And tell me, Mark," and hir small tongue strayed across hir distended canines, "how much of your brain function does sex require?"

"Fifty, maybe fifty-five percent."

"So what do you do with the remaining fifteen percent?"

"Overflow space," McHenry told hir. "In case some of the rest of it gets used up unexpectedly quickly."

"Well, I have an idea," Burgoyne told him. "Why don't we go back to my place and see if we can fill up the unoccupied space, okay?"

"Sounds like a good deal to me," McHenry grinned.

And later, when they were together, their clothes strewn about the floor, McHenry moving atop hir with easy grace, Burgoyne's fingers traced the curve of McHenry's upper ear, and s/he inadvertently whispered the name "Selar."

Fortunately, McHenry was engrossed in a particularly riveting footnote in the article and so didn't hear.

And in the meantime, several decks away, Selar tossed in her sleep and dreamt of a tongue gently caressing canine teeth . . .

Calhoun was sound asleep when he heard the buzzing of his room bell. From long habit, he snapped to full wakefulness. Calhoun had never been one for waking up slowly. Why give an opponent an opportunity to stick a sword between your ribs while you're busy rubbing the sleep from your eyes?

"Who is it?" he called, no trace of grogginess in his voice. He had already stepped from his bed and pulled on his robe.

"Shelby," came the reply.

"Shelby," he muttered. "How did I know. Lights. Come in."

The room lights flared on as the door slid open, and Shelby entered. She looked as if she hadn't been to bed yet, and had a great deal on her mind.

"Let me guess," he said, his hands shoved deep into his pockets. "You've suddenly realized that faster-than-light travel is an impossibility, and we should head home immediately before someone realizes and we all get in trouble."

"I can't agree with the decisions you've made lately," she said, the words coming out all in a rush.

"None of them? I mean, I was thinking about changing the part in my hair. Perhaps now I'd better reconsider it."

"I think this Messiah business is fraught with danger."

"Fraught? Eppy, it's"—he glanced at a chronometer—"it's oh-one-thirty hours. It's the wrong time of night to use words like 'fraught.' "

"I don't want you to be flip with me."

"Neither do I. I'd rather be flipping with my pillow, but you seem to have precluded that." He dropped down onto the bed. "Eppy, I thought we had this settled . . ."

"I've been thinking about it—"

"Obviously."

"And I think we have to set them straight, right at the beginning. Tell them no, tell them this Savior business is pure fiction on their part."

"How do we know that?" Calhoun replied.

"How do we *know?* Mac, you're not their Savior!"

"No man knows his destiny, Eppy. Perhaps I am. Perhaps their predictions got it right. If that's the case, then I'd be violating the Prime Directive by refusing to fulfill that destiny, since I'm already a part of their culture rather than something on the outside interfering with it. In any event, we'll see when we get there. Now if there's nothing else, don't let the door hit you on the way out." He pulled the blanket over himself, even though he had his robe on, and tried to find escape in the pillow.

"There's also the matter of Doctor Selar."

"*Grozit.* Here we go." He sat back up, stared at her for a moment, and then stood with his hands placed firmly on his hips. "You know what your problem is? You're jealous."

"Jealous! Oh, get over yourself, Mac."

"I'm over me, but you sure as hell aren't. Why should you care whether I become Selar's lover or not?"

"Because there's questions of protocol! And because she's not thinking clearly!"

"She seemed quite lucid when she came in and asked me."

"She said herself that the *Pon Farr* can affect the way she thinks, affect her perceptions. I think that's the case here."

"Why? Because no woman in her right mind would consider me a suitable father?"

"And what about that?" she challenged him. "What's going to happen when she has the child, huh? Is she going to remain aboard the *Excalibur?* We're not set up for families the way other vessels are."

"I suppose we'll face that situation when we come to it," replied Calhoun. "There are always possibilities."

"And are you going to participate in the raising of the child? Or are you going to walk away from this one, too."

Calhoun's brow darkened. "That was uncalled for."

"Well maybe something is called for, just to get you to think about some of the things you're doing! To think about the damage you might inflict on Selar, or on the people of Zondar!"

"I'm providing a woman with relief for a medical condition, and I'm giving a race of people a shot at freedom. That sounds pretty laudable to me."

"Oh, Mackenzie Calhoun, the selfless martyr," retorted Shelby. "Admit it. This all appeals to your ego. The educated woman who picks you as the main stud on the ship, the race of people who think you're the second coming of God. It inflates your ego."

"No," said Calhoun, raising his voice slightly. "The only thing I'm getting any ego gratification from is the knowledge that you are so totally jealous of Selar and me that you're willing to come in here and make a complete jackass of yourself rather than stand by and watch me become involved with another woman."

"You have no idea what you're talking about." She threw her hands up. "I tried. God knows, I tried. I tried to make you see the error of your ways. I tried to make you realize the danger in what you're doing. If you don't want to listen to me, fine. If you want to risk exacerbating situations under the delusion that you're making them better, that is likewise fine. I don't care. I don't care anymore. I really, really—"

"Don't care. Yes, I get the picture." He tried to put his hands on her shoulders but she pushed them away. "Eppy, I know that look in your eyes. The sleep-deprived look. Once you leave here, you're going to go back to your quarters, and you're going to fall asleep, and when you wake up in the morning you're going to hit yourself in the side of the head and say, Oh God, what an idiot I made of myself last night."

"You just dream on, Calhoun."

"The moment you leave, that is precisely what I intend to do."

With an annoyed huff, Shelby turned and stomped out of the room, leaving an amused Calhoun behind shaking his head and wondering just what exactly he'd gotten himself into by taking command of this vessel.

"I've seen more stable nuthouses," he said as he flopped back into bed. "I bet Picard never had these problems."

9

The home of Ramed, as was typical for a Zondarian home, was heavily fortified. One never knew when there might be stray missiles flying, or when pieces of hurtling shrapnel would suddenly present a danger to life and limb. Nor was anyone there desirous of any intruders. The wandering packs of Unglza raiders were well known to all of the Eenza, and anyone who had the wherewithal to protect his family did not scrimp in the least little bit.

Most of the furniture was heavily curved, symbolizing the Zondarian belief that all was eternal. That what began had no end, and vice versa. Furthermore, most of it was bolted to the floor, so that vibrations from nearby explosions would not send them tumbling all over the place.

It was early in the morning, and Ramed's wife, Talila, had already prepared breakfast for herself and their young son, Rab. For the first time in a long time, she had moved about the house without the perpetual cringing in her shoulders, an involuntary spasm that haunted her most of her waking hours as she prepared herself for the sound of another shell dropping or another bomb exploding in the middle to near distance. There was a cease-fire throughout Zondar, and thus far it seemed to have taken hold. It was as if the entire planet was awaiting the coming of the Savior.

Talila felt so close to the actual event, particularly because it was her husband who was part of the inner circle. He who had studied the sacred writings of Ontear and Suti, probably with greater detail and scrutiny than virtually anyone else on the planet. When he had told her of the possible coming of the Savior, she had been unable to find words. Instead she had simply begun to cry, tears of joy pouring down her face so effusively that she couldn't begin to control them. Nor was she interested in trying.

Since Ramed had joined with Killick of the Unglza (whom she did not particularly trust, but Ramed seemed tolerant enough of him) to go to the Savior and convince Him to come to Zondar and fulfill His destiny, Talila had not known what to do with herself. Little Rab had asked every day since his father's departure when he would be coming back, and she had never known what to tell him. "A few days," Ramed had told her, but who truly knew what that constituted?

Talila had just cleared the breakfast dishes away, and was now preparing to teach Rab his morning lessons. Like most children in their particular sphere, Rab was home taught. It was not an unreasonable course of action. Both Talila and Ramed were, naturally, highly educated. And it saved Rab from having to make that potentially treacherous journey to school every morning. Instead she kept him safe and sound in their home, teaching him the wisdom of the Zondarians while protecting him from the foolishness of those very same peoples.

She heard Rab cry out, and immediately a chill cut through her. A woman in her situation automatically assumed the worst when hearing her child sound a cry of alarm, and she immediately went to the main foyer . . .

There to find Rab wrapped around the leg of his father.

Talila went to him quickly and embraced him with all the fierceness that her small frame commanded. "It seems as if you have been away for ages!" she said.

"I feel the same," he said, stroking the back of his wife's gleaming head. "It is good to see you, wife. Were there any . . . problems in my absence?"

The pause before the word was painfully significant. It was his understated way of inquiring as to whether there had been any threats to the safety of his wife or son.

"None, Ramed," she was happy to reply. "The cease-fire remains in force. It is as if our whole world is . . . is holding its breath. Tell me," and her eyes widened, "tell me what . . . He was like."

"He?" For a moment, Ramed didn't understand what she meant, and then, of course, he did. "The Savior."

"You saw Him, father?" asked Rab.

"Yes," and he embraced both wife and son. "Yes. I did."

"Did He have a . . . glow about Him?" Talila asked. "Did power crackle from His eyes? Did He perform any miracles for you?"

"He was . . . different than I expected."

"Different? How so?"

"He had power about Him. It was a quiet power, however. Almost an . . . an aura. A sense of command, of inner strength."

"As if He wanted to keep His true power hidden?"

"That could be," he agreed. "Yes, that would definitely be one way to look at it." He strode thoughtfully around his living room. "As if mere mortals such as ourselves should not—would not even want to—look at Him in display of His full glory. It might be too much for us."

"Did He know that He was destined to be our Savior?" she asked.

"No. No, it was completely a surprise to Him." He shrugged. "All of us have our places in the grand scheme, my wife. Sometimes we are aware of them, and sometimes we are not. Nonetheless we fulfill our purpose."

"I suppose you are correct. It's so amazing," she breathed. "To think that this would happen within our lifetime. Is He with you? Has He returned with you?"

"He is on His way," Ramed assured her. "We raced ahead to make preparations."

Talila turned to Rab and knelt down to face him. "I want you to begin keeping a journal, my dear. You are young yet, and the events might not be as clear to your recollection when you're older. So you should be able to look back at your words of this age as a sort of tunnel back through time."

"Yes, mother," Rab said agreeably. "Will you help me start it?"

"Of course. Let me just spend some time with your father first—"

"But I want to start it now," Rab protested. It was not an atypical reaction for a child. An idea that had not even occurred to him mere moments before had suddenly become the single most important thing in his world.

Ramed put a gentle hand on his wife's shoulder. "It's all right, wife," he said gently. "Be happy that the boy has embraced the notion. I need a short time to myself to collect my thoughts anyway. I shall be in my study for a bit."

"As you wish, husband." She brought his knuckles to her lips and smiled at him affectionately. She touched his face and whispered, "I have never been more proud of you."

He smiled in response as she went off with Rab to help him set up his journal. But then the smile faded as he retreated into his study.

He knew that Talila would not have entered it in his absence. She respected his privacy; indeed, she might even have been a little afraid of the room. Talila was a sweet woman, a good wife, a superb mother. But she was not the scholar or philosopher that Ramed was. When Ramed and the others in his clan would gather to discuss various fine points of Eenza law, or go over the predictions of Ontear and Suti to see how they applied to the modern world, she was a bit intimidated by it all. She would stand on the outskirts of the group, dart in and out of the room and pick up snatches of conversation, but she did not pretend to understand any of it. Nor did she have need to, really. She was married to a great man. In truth, that alone was really enough for her.

But because of the slight intimidation factor, she kept her distance from such places as Ramed's study. For any number of reasons, he found that preferable, although it was not as if he had ever given her explicit instructions not to enter. It was simply an unspoken understanding between them.

He stood in the middle of his study, drinking in the presence of the words. The shelves were lined with scrolls of knowledge dating back to ancient times, carefully preserved. There had been a movement to transfer that information to more modern, computer-oriented means of information storage, but the Eenza inner circle had fought that notion. There was something pure and sacrosanct about the preservation through writing, through that physical connection to those scribes who had taken the time to write down the words of wisdom those many centuries ago. It was more of a living history in this manner.

His eyes skimmed the repository of Eenza written tradition, each carefully preserved in their cylinders, but he did not focus on any one of them in particular. Instead he went to one cylinder in particular set in the lower right-hand section of the shelving. Unlike the others, however, it did not slide loose from its place in the rack. Instead he pulled on it and it pivoted on a hidden hinge. A moment later, a small section of the nearby wall swung open. Ramed reached into the hole in the wall and pulled out a scroll, older than any of the others on the wall. He unrolled it carefully on his reading table, clipping the upper and lower ends down so that he could read it flat and uninterrupted.

It was not as if he didn't have it memorized already. He had read it so many times that every word, every syllable was seared into his consciousness. Yet for some reason he derived some degree of affirmation, perhaps, by seeing the original writing once more. Words written by the divine Suti himself, as told to him in turn by the sacred Ontear at the time when the mysterious Great Wind had come down and whisked Ontear away to whatever his reward would be.

Words that had only partly found their way into the sacred texts of Zondar.

Ramed had never been entirely certain just how the original, unexpurgated text had wound up in the hands of his family. It had been given him by his father, who had in turn been given it by his, and so on. It was not as if Ramed was a direct descendant of Suti himself; to the best of anyone's knowledge, Suti had never married, never produced any offspring. The words of Ontear and the spiritual well-being of the Zondarians was the sum and substance of his entire life. He had never seemed to need anything more than that.

Perhaps he had passed the complete text to a trusted disciple, and he had held onto it until his passing was near, and in turn had given it to a trusted individual. It was nothing short of miraculous, really, that the scroll had found its way through the centuries to Ramed without word of its full contents filtering outside of the sphere of its caretakers.

There was something else that was in the same secret compartment as the scroll had been. It was a cylinder, about a foot long and made from wood. One side was closed off, the other end open. On the handle, a small emblem that looked like a flame was carved on it. He ran a finger over it lightly, as he had so many times before.

He extended the cylinder straight out in front of himself and pushed in firmly on the flame. And with a quiet *shak* noise, a sharpened rod snapped out of the end of the handle. It was telescoped in three places and extended to about a yard in length. As always, it felt incredibly light. Ramed swung it about him experimentally, satisfied at the whistling sound it made as it passed through the air. Then he lunged forward once or twice, and wondered what it would be like to drive it through the chest of a living, breathing being. Would it be possible? When the time came, would he have the intestinal fortitude to do what had to be done?

He thought of what he had just said to his wife. "All of us have our places in the grand scheme, my wife. Sometimes we are aware of them, and sometimes we are not. Nonetheless we fulfill our purpose."

He had his purpose. He had his own role that had been handed down to him. How would he be viewed, he wondered? As one of the great heroes of Zondar? As one of the most memorable traitors? Would he be a martyr to a great ideal that he, and only he, knew to be the truth? What would they say to his wife? What sort of torment would his son be subject to?

Perhaps the course upon which he was embarking was the wrong one.

He began to tremble. Whether it was in fear, in excitement, or in religious zeal over the rightness of his actions, he couldn't begin to say. All he knew was that he was trembling so violently, he couldn't even hold on to his weapon. It clattered to the floor, although the noise was minimal since the staff was so lightweight.

He dropped to his knees, waiting until the spasms passed. And all during that time, he prayed. Prayed to the shades of Ontear and Suti. Prayed for guidance.

"Please," he whispered to them. "Please . . . help me do the right thing."

He paused a long moment, then picked up the spear. He envisioned the Savior standing against the opposite wall. Standing there strong, confident. Ramed then drew his arm back, as he had so many times before, and hurled the spear. It flew lightly through the air and thudded into the far wall, the shaft quivering, the point squarely in the heart of the Savior.

"May the fates help me," he whispered. "And may the Savior, even in His death throes, have mercy on my soul."

10

Burgoyne sat in hir office in engineering and studied the reports compiled by Ensign Beth, looking over them again and again until it felt as if the numbers were blurring in front of hir. S/he became aware that Beth was hovering nearby, probably looking rather concerned. S/he couldn't blame her, because the information that s/he'd been handed was less than useful. "So let me see if I understand this," Burgoyne said slowly. "We not only do not know what is causing this energy wave, but now it's causing a *drain* on the engines."

"Not exactly a drain, Chief," Beth said. "Look, follow the power curves. The energy reserves begin to build up exponentially. They reach a maximum point of somewhere around eighteen percent above the norm, and then they drain off, reaching standard levels. As if someone were topping off a glass of water and then sipping off the top so that it doesn't overflow. Bringing it down to a more reasonable level."

"But what's causing the overage?" asked Burgoyne in frustration. "And when it's being drained off, where is it going? You don't think . . ."

"Think what?" asked Beth.

Burgoyne sat back, studying the readouts with just a touch of visible apprehension. "What if we've some . . . thing . . . living in there? Something sentient."

"A sentient energy creature?"

"We ran from one not too long ago," Burgoyne pointed out. Beth was forced to agree with that reminder. "If this is somehow connected with that . . ."

"Is there any way that we can determine it?"

"I'm not quite sure," said Burgoyne. "At the very least, we keep observing it. Also, we'll probably want to bring Soleta in on this. She's the science officer, after all."

"How about medical?" asked Beth. "If there's a living creature rooting around in our energy transfer ducts somehow, then maybe Doctor Selar can—"

"Let's leave Doctor Selar out of it for the time being," Burgoyne said after a moment's thought.

"Are you sure? Perhaps if we—"

Burgoyne turned, and hir canines were extended as s/he said, "Are you questioning my orders, Ensign?" Hir voice was very sharp, hir eyes narrowed and genuine anger was flashing within them.

"No! No, sir!" said Beth quickly.

There was such clear alarm in her voice that Burgoyne immediately felt chagrin. "Sorry, Ensign," Burgoyne said, the ire passing as quickly as it had made its presence known. "It's not your fault."

"I was hoping it wasn't." Beth paused a moment, and then said, "Chief . . . I hope I'm not overstepping myself here, but is everything okay between you and the CMO?"

"Okay?"

"It's just that any time she's mentioned for some reason, you seem to tense up. Personality conflict?"

Burgoyne considered several possible answers, but finally said, "You could say it's something like that."

"I know how it is," Beth said by way of commiseration. "Sometimes you just meet someone, and for absolutely no reason you can think of, you just connect on a negative level. You take an instant dislike to them. It's as if you have a bad history that goes back before the two of you even met."

"That is an . . . interesting way to look at it."

"Sometimes two people just click—like Christiano and I did," admitted Beth with a grin. "And other times, well, two people can't even work together without getting on each other's nerves."

"You're very likely correct, Ensign. It would probably serve us best if we didn't discuss it anymore." S/he went back to the energy wave readouts. "Look at this. This is interesting."

"What do you see, Chief?"

"During those periods when the energy drain slows down, it occurs when the *Excalibur* speeds up. The faster we go, the slower the energy drain. And when we go in excess of warp five, there's never any drain at all. Those are the points at which the energy wave indicates growth.''

''That's right,'' Beth said slowly.

''Of course that's right,'' Burgoyne said archly. ''I said it. Therefore, by definition, it's right.'' S/he drummed hir fingers in annoyance. ''I should be able to figure this out more expeditiously,'' s/he said. ''I've just got to get my mind clear.''

''What's on your mind, Chief?'' asked Beth.

And for just a moment, Burgoyne allowed hir thoughts to stray to a face that had a perpetual stoic pout, framed by the loveliest pointed ears.

''Just someone I can't work with,'' Burgoyne said with a trace of sadness.

On the bridge of the *Excalibur,* Calhoun leaned forward in the command chair and said, ''ETA at Zondar?''

''Three hours, eleven minutes, sir,'' McHenry said crisply. As always, he didn't even bother to check his instruments. The first several times, it had been a bit disconcerting to Calhoun, and extremely so to Shelby, but by this point they were accustomed to it.

''Keep her steady on course, Mister McHenry,'' Calhoun told him.

''Steady on, sir.''

Lefler glanced at the captain, who seemed to become involved in conversation with his first officer. Then, very casually, she sidled over from her post at Ops and murmured, ''Haven't seen you around much after hours.''

''Hmm?'' He looked up at her, apparently surprised that she had come over. ''What?''

''I said you're something of a stranger off-duty these days. Don't see you in the team room, or any of the usual haunts. What have you been up to?''

''Oh, that,'' said McHenry. ''I've been busy.''

''Busy . . . how?''

He shrugged as if it was no big deal. ''I've been spending a lot of time with Burgy.''

'' 'Burgy,' is it? Very friendly nickname to be using.''

''Is it?'' McHenry seemed unimpressed. ''I didn't think so especially.''

''So what do you guys do? Talk?''

''No, we have sex,'' McHenry said matter-of-factly.

Now, Lefler didn't fancy herself as a prude, but nonetheless she was still caught a little flat-footed by the frankness of his response. "Oh," was all she could think of to say.

"That's what you wanted to know, isn't it?" He seemed rather amused by her expression. He leaned toward her and said, "Robin, I may seem distracted all the time. I may seem in my own little world. But I'm not stupid. I know what you want to know. What's it like? What's s/he like? Right?"

Lefler squirmed slightly, suddenly feeling that she should be elsewhere. Anywhere else, in fact, which was odd considering she usually was the most frank and open of people. She made vague gestures in the direction of Ops and said, "I, uh . . . I should really get back to—"

But he put a firm hand on her wrist, and she was surprised at the forcefulness of it. The cheery manner never left his face, but there was strength in his grip that seemed at odds with the lackadaisical demeanor. "S/he's amazing, Robin," McHenry told her. "Very free, very open with hir body. Very eager to please, and also eager to be pleasured. The fact that s/he is both male and female probably adds to hir expertise, because s/he knows what men like and what women like. S/he sees life, love, and sex from all angles."

"That's . . . uhm . . ." Lefler found herself completely tongue-tied. She'd always considered herself something of a free spirit, a "party girl" who was open to all manner of experimentation. "And, you're, uh . . . you're not distracted by the, uhm . . ."

"The what?"

"The, uh . . . hir . . . *male* aspect? That doesn't, you know . . . give you navigational difficulties?"

"Not especially. It's nice to have someone who knows what a man wants."

"Oh? And what does a man want?" Lefler said challengingly.

McHenry looked her straight in the eyes. "If I tell you," he said, "will you be sure to jot that down so it can be in the next newsletter?"

They laughed together at that point, and then Lefler said, "Lefler's Law number fifty-two: Never underestimate a man's ability to make you laugh."

"Laughing at a man is okay," McHenry said. Then, as an afterthought, he said, "Unless, of course, you're pointing while you're doing it. Laughing and pointing . . . bad combination."

Lefler laughed more loudly at that. She took care, however, not to point.

And then she said, very softly, "Do you love hir?"

"Love?" For the first time, McHenry looked uncomfortable. "We . . . haven't discussed that."

"Why not? Don't you think that's important?"

"To some people, yes. Not to me. I'm not interested in falling in love. I'm not sure how Burgy feels about it; I haven't asked hir."

"Why aren't you interested in falling in love, Mark?"

He stared at her. "Tried it once. It didn't take."

"Didn't take? Why not? I mean, if you don't want to tell me . . ."

McHenry seemed to stare off into space for a time. This was not atypical for him, but there was a different feel to it this time. "Mark?" she prodded gently. "Why didn't it take?"

He returned his gaze to her and smiled a sad little smile.

"She tried to kill me," he said.

Lefler's jaw dropped, and she tried to find a way to frame a follow-up question. But then from behind her she heard Shelby's voice. "Lieutenant, is there a problem? Something I should know about?"

Lefler stood up, smoothing the front of her uniform. "No, sir," she said briskly, all business. "Just consulting with Mister McHenry on some crosschecks."

Shelby nodded, apparently satisfied, but there was clear curiosity in her eyes. Lefler quickly crossed back to her station and sat. Several times for the rest of the shift, she glanced in McHenry's direction. Not once, in all that time, did he meet her gaze again.

Doctor Selar had taken a brief break, returning to her quarters to get some rest. She lay on her bed, able to feel the slow percolating of her hormones within her. She knew that the *Pon Farr* would be back in full phase before very long. However, she didn't wish to deal with it immediately. She knew that the ship was on a mission, heading for the world called Zondar. She knew that the captain was some sort of focal point for these people, and he had to keep his mind clear and focused. It would have been irresponsible for her, she felt, to pull Calhoun into the world of the Vulcan mating ritual at this particular moment in time. She had warned him of how all-consuming the interest in sex became once the Vulcan and her selected mate were in the throes of *Pon Farr,* but the fact that he had joked about it led her to believe that he did not fully grasp the reality of the situation. Since she herself knew what was to be expected, therefore, she felt the onus was upon her to try and act in as responsible and intelligent a manner as possible.

She decided to meditate a bit, to give her mind and body some time to calm down. However, a chime sounded at the door in the midst of her musings, disrupting her, throwing her off-balance. She had been reclining, but now she pulled herself to sitting, her legs securely folded. "Come," she said.

The door slid open, and to her surprise she saw Burgoyne 172 standing there.

"Doctor," s/he said, nodding hir head slightly in acknowledgment. "They said you were here in your quarters. It's nice to see that they spoke truly."

"Yes. I came here for the purpose of being alone."

"Ah. I see," said Burgoyne, stepping in so that the door slid shut behind hir.

"I do not think you truly do see," Selar pointed out, "considering the fact that you have entered my quarters, thereby precluding my being alone." She hesitated. "If there is a matter that you wish to discuss, Lieutenant Commander, then kindly do so and be done with it."

"I was just interested in . . ." S/he cleared hir throat. "I just wanted to congratulate you."

"I see. And why would that be?"

"Because of you and the captain," Burgoyne said. S/he felt a little odd that s/he had to explain it to Selar. Didn't she know the details of her own affairs? "It is my understanding that you and he are . . . involved."

"Very delicately put," Selar said with an ever-so-slight hint of surprise. "That is unusual, to say the least. You are not generally known for your delicacy. Rather, bluntness seems to be your stock in trade."

"You seem to be someone who prefers delicacy. I just . . ." S/he seemed to have trouble phrasing what was on hir mind.

"You just what?" prodded Selar, curious in spite of herself to see where the conversation was going.

"I just wish you had been honest with me."

"Honest?" Selar was far too controlled or thorough-going a Vulcan to allow outright astonishment to creep onto her face. Nonetheless, her surprise was evident if one knew where to look. "I have not lied to you, Lieutenant Commander."

"You asked me to leave you alone, without telling me why," Burgoyne said with ill-concealed annoyance. "Had you simply informed me of your involvement with Captain Calhoun, I could have avoided potentially making a fool of myself. Instead I pursued you, spoke to you of gentle relations, told you that I felt we were destined to be together . . . and all that time, you had an understanding with the captain.''

Selar could have corrected hir, of course. Her relationship with the captain was, after all, a fairly recent development. It had purely been Burgoyne's misinterpretation, a mistaken assumption that Selar and the captain were involved with one another at the time that Burgoyne was making advances upon Selar.

Selar's discouragement of Burgoyne had had nothing whatsoever to do with the captain. She had simply found the Hermat so brazen, so aggressive, so over-the-top, that her gut reaction had been to keep Burgoyne at more than arm's length. And when Selar's position had softened, she had seen Burgoyne arm-in-arm with McHenry. At that point, Selar saw little reason to try and pursue Burgoyne in return. She did have her pride, after all. Something about her didn't want to give Burgoyne the opportunity to stand there with hir smirk and say, ''Ah, now you want me.'' Nor did she want to feel like an also-ran to McHenry.

But Selar, who just wanted Burgoyne out of her quarters already, saw no reason not to take advantage of Burgoyne's perception. She had no desire to lie outright. It cut against her Vulcan grain. But she saw no harm in selective revelation of the truth.

''We have an understanding, yes.''

''And may I ask what that understanding is?''

She cocked an eyebrow. ''You may ask. But no answer will be forthcoming, since I owe you no explanations and since it is none of your business.''

''Had a feeling you'd say that,'' s/he said ruefully. ''I suppose, on some level, I agree. But you and I, Selar, we operate on a different level.''

''Lieutenant Commander, *you* operate on a different level,'' Selar replied tartly. ''I operate on the level of one who wishes to keep her private affairs private, despite all the best efforts of this ship's personnel to make it the business of the entire crew complement. I would ask you to respect that privacy.''

''I do,'' sighed Burgoyne. ''Believe it or not, I do.'' Burgoyne strode across the room to her and hunkered down opposite her. S/he smiled, displaying hir canines. ''Selar, believe it or not, I wish you all happiness.''

''Do you,'' Selar said, her voice inflectionless.

''Yes, I do. I want the best for you, and if you feel the captain represents the best . . . well, truthfully, I'd be hard-pressed to disagree. He is quite a man. And you are quite a woman.''

''And you, Burgoyne,'' Selar said with attempted diplomacy, ''are quite a . . .'' Then she hesitated and finished with a mental shrug, ''A person.''

''I appreciate that. And I want you to know something: I still feel a connection to you, even though you obviously do not share it.''

I do. But you are completely wrong for me, went through Selar's mind unbidden. Her face, however, remained inscrutable. ''I do not . . .'' She found it hard to say. She licked her lips, which were suddenly extremely dry, and continued, ''I do not wish to cause you any pain.''

Burgoyne waved off the notion. ''Don't worry about that. I'm fairly resilient; takes a lot more than that to hurt me. But I want you to understand something.'' S/he took one of Selar's hands in both of hir own. Hir long fingers intertwined with Selar's. ''I will always feel the attachment to you, whether you want it or not. Whether you like it or not. I will never do anything to cause you harm, and you will always be under my protection.''

''I appreciate the sentiment that you—*ow!*'' Selar was startled as she felt an abrupt prick of pain in the top of her hand. She pulled the hand away from Burgoyne's grip to find a small bit of green blood welling up on the top. There was a minute scratch there, and Selar looked up at Burgoyne. Despite her Vulcan training, surprise registered on her face as she saw a trickle of green blood on Burgoyne's fingernails. Selar had never really noticed before, but Burgoyne's nails were rather long, almost conical.

Burgoyne brought hir right hand up to hir face and daintily licked the blood off with hir tongue.

''What are you *doing?*'' demanded Selar, rather put off by the entire business.

''Consecrating my promise to you,'' replied Burgoyne. The green liquid was already gone from hir right fingers. There was a small spot of the Vulcan's blood on Burgoyne's left hand as well; Burgoyne brought that up to hir nose and passed it under, hir nostrils flaring slightly, and then s/he licked that clean as well. ''I hope I didn't startle you.''

''To be blunt, you did. And I would prefer that you do not puncture, wound, or lacerate any other parts of my body unless you have been granted specific permission for that activity.'' She shook her head. ''It is my desire to, at the very least, be able to tolerate you,

Burgoyne. You are not making that simple, and such stunts as these do not endear you to me.''

"They may someday,'' said Burgoyne, and then, with a lazy wink, s/he walked out of Selar's quarters, leaving the doctor shaking her head.

11

The excitement had spread throughout Zondar as the *Excalibur* drew closer. Statues were being erected to Him. However, since descriptions of Him varied tremendously, one statue would look very different from another. That really didn't matter, though. It was, truly, the thought that counted.

Festivals were held. Parades were staged. There was a general air of euphoria upon the entire world. And, most importantly of all, the Eenza and the Unglza did not launch into immediate battles whenever any members of the two groups happened to run into each other. The cease-fire was in force, of course, but that was only part of it. The cease-fire, after all, was imposed from above by the respective ruling bodies of the Eenza and the Unglza. The true desire to get on with one another, however, had to come from the people themselves. And that seemed to be exactly what was happening. The people seemed to be viewing each other with a new eye, as if trying to contemplate what it would be like to be able to live side-by-side with their "enemies." And the speculation itself did not seem so intimidating once they were faced with the prospect. They began to envision a new age for Zondar, one in which they did not perpetually have to watch their backs against attacks from rival groups. An age where the Eenza and the Unglza would actually be able to work together, perhaps to develop something greater than either of them could accomplish on their own.

These possibilities were being discussed in all sectors of Zondar, including in the home of Ramed. There, Talila bustled about with tremendous excitement as Ramed watched her go about her business with a paternal sort of smile. ''You are a one-woman hive of activity, Talila,'' he said, amusement in his voice.

She was unable to avoid saying what she had sworn she wouldn't say. ''Am I going to meet Him, husband?''

''Him? You mean the Savior?''

''Is there any other 'Him' worth discussing these days on Zondar?'' she asked reasonably, and he had to admit that she had a valid point. ''At the convocation. Am I going to meet Him?''

He paused a moment before answering, as if preparing to discuss something that he knew was going to be very unpleasant. ''You will not be attending the convocation, my wife.''

She gaped at him, not quite willing to believe what she had just heard. ''I am not going to come with you? But . . . but I have already prepared—and Rab! I told Rab that he would be coming as well! Husband! You are one of the foremost speakers of the Eenza! It cannot be that you—''

''This is my decision, Talila,'' he said flatly. ''I must be focused on the matter at hand. I cannot be distracted by—''

''Distracted!'' She made no attempt to keep the bitterness from her voice. ''After all these years together, after all my time as your helpmate, aiding you wherever and whenever I could . . . is that all I am to you in the final analysis? A distraction?''

''That is not how I meant to . . .'' He sighed and put his hands on her shoulders, but she pulled away from him. He stood behind her, looking saddened. ''My wife, there are things I must accomplish at the convocation. Difficult, involved matters. I must be able to devote myself solely to the work that must be done for the purpose of saving Zondar. I cannot act in the capacity as husband, as father. I simply cannot. Talila,'' he said, not without compassion, ''you have trusted me all these years. Trust me in this. If you never trust me in any other matter again, trust me on this. I know what I am doing.''

Slowly, with clear frustration, she nodded. Obedience to her husband was ingrained as to be second nature, so she found that he couldn't quite help herself. But she was not happy about it. ''I feel,'' she said softly, ''as if you are being selfish, Ramed. Or perhaps you are simply embarrassed to have me as a mate.''

''Embarrassed!'' he said in surprise.

''I am not as wise as you. Not as learned. Perhaps you are ashamed to have me meet the Savior of Zondar. You feel that I am not good enough, or will reflect poorly on you.''

Again he took her by the shoulders to turn her around, and this time she did not resist. "Your assumption could not be farther from the truth," he said firmly. "You must trust me on that as well. No Zondarian could be prouder of his mate than I."

He embraced her then, and she held him tight. And as he held her, he could not help but wonder if he was ever going to see her again.

The exact location of the convocation had been hotly debated, and had been solved in a rather unique manner. There had been no question that the convocation should be held in a temple, but naturally both the Unglza and the Eenza were at odds over whose it should be. With time ticking down and no immediate consensus apparent, an intriguing idea was suggested and immediately adopted. A special temple would be built that would represent the first co-venture between the two groups. Contractors, architects, builders had all assembled their workforces and thrown the temple together in what was not only record time for Zondar, but possibly for the entire sector of space. It was nothing fancy; more utilitarian than anything else. There wasn't time to do something with a lot of flourishes. It was spherical to represent the entirety of the world of Zondar, and two large hands were intertwined on the front—one presumably Eenza, the other Unglza.

At the appointed time, as the *Excalibur* moved into orbit around Zondar, the assemblage began. Killick was there, as was Ramed, of course. From the eastern territories arrived the Clans of Sulimin the Planner, Arbora the Unseen, and Freenaux the Undesirable (who showed up despite popular demand to the contrary). From the northern plains came the offshoot group of the Unglza known only as the Dissuaders, an arbitrarily negative group who intended to spend much—if not all—of the convocation trying to convince everyone else that they were wasting their time. From the western tropical region came Maro the Questioner, Quinzix the Unforgiving, Tulaman the Misbegotten, and Vonce of the Many Fortunes. All of them converged on the eastern territory where the Savior was to arrive.

The Zondarians were not entirely sure just how the Savior was actually going to show up. There were rumors that He possessed transmat technology that far outstripped anything existing on Zondar. There were other rumors that He was, quite simply, a being of magic, who could come and go wherever and whenever He pleased. Walls were as nothing to Him, distances merely something to be traversed in an eye blink through force of will alone.

Nonetheless, to play it safe the Zondarians constructed the equivalent of a "landing pad." It was festooned with decorations, flowers, and greetings of welcome sent from all over the world. As Zondarians of all sizes, shapes, and castes converged on the spot, there was a festive atmosphere. Everyone felt that they were present at the beginning of what was to be a new golden age for Zondar.

The *Excalibur* had signaled down to the planet surface to let them know precisely when the Savior would be arriving, and they in turn indicated the precise spot that they desired Him to make His entrance. At the appointed time, Zondarians (some of whom had been waiting from the previous day) packed in the area. They kept a respectful distance from the appointed landing place, but were crushed in so tightly that it was believed a Zondarian could drop dead in the midst of the crowd and still remain standing just by dint of the crush of bodies all around. Unglza were pressed up against Eenza, and although the initial close contact prompted some grumbling, overall it was a fairly well-behaved throng, particularly considering that there had to be close to two thousand Zondarians crushed into an area that would have been better suited for half that number.

There was talking, there was chattering, there was singing, there was all manner of vocal discourse both loud and soft, and then slowly, as the appointed time drew near, it all trailed off into silence. All over Zondar, people began to look to the sky. No one knew quite what to expect. Perhaps the mighty vessel of the Savior might descend from the sky. Perhaps the Savior Himself would appear on a raft made of purest spun clouds. No one knew for certain.

And at precisely the appointed time, the Zondarians who were fortunate enough or highly ranked enough to be on the actual spot of contact heard a humming in the air. They looked up, looked around to see if they could determine the source. It sounded vaguely like their own transmat booths, but the sound was far more focused.

And then there was a collective gasp as Mackenzie Calhoun materialized out of thin air, his body a haze of shimmering sparkles that quickly coalesced into a human body.

There were two others, one on either side of him. One of them was instantly recognizable to many in the crowd as Lord Si Cwan, formerly of the Thallonian Empire. The other was a sight such as none on that world had ever seen. He was as wide across as any three Zondarians, and his skin was dark and leathery. He surveyed the crowd with eyes that were quite small, and yet seemed to take in everything.

And then a collective roar, a cheer, went up from the throat of the entire assemblage. The Savior's arrival had been simultaneously broadcast all through Zondar, and around the world the cheer went up as well.

It was certainly a good day for a rally. There were almost no clouds in the sky, which seemed to sparkle blue with hints of purple slathered across it, as if a painter had designed it and decided to toss in just a dollop of another color. The air was warm, even a little bit dry in his lungs.

At the forefront of the crowd were Killick and Ramed. They strode forward, bowing deeply in the presence of their Savior. They remained that way until Calhoun finally said, "Up. You can get up now."

They rose fully. "Savior," said Killick, forgetting himself long enough to genuflect, however briefly. "You will be interested to know, I think, that the prophecies regarding your coming state, and I quote: 'He will come from air and return to air.' You see? You have already fulfilled that portion of the prophecy."

"I didn't come from air, technically," Calhoun said, sounding reasonable. "I came from my ship. The air was simply an environment—"

"Savior," and Killick smiled beatifically. "You must learn not to question yourself or your destiny. Self-doubt ill suits you. The Savior will be—is—a man of character and determination who will unite the world. There is no place in that destiny for uncertainty."

Calhoun was about to debate the point further, but he saw how Killick, Ramed, and all the others were looking at him, and instead he simply shrugged graciously. "All right," Calhoun said, not wanting to sound unreasonable. "I will certainly accept your view of the events."

"Thank you, Great One." Killick seemed about to touch him on the arm, but then thought better of it, instead gesturing to the others in an encompassing sweep. "Everyone here has waited most eagerly for you."

"Greetings," Calhoun called to them, and a roar of approval went up. Truthfully, Calhoun felt a bit exposed and vulnerable with so many people packed in so tightly. His old warrior's antennae went up as he swept the crowd, trying to see some sign of danger. He knew that Zak Kebron, the mountainous security chief, was doing the exact same thing. It gave him a certain degree of confidence, but he was still duly suspicious and apprehensive of the situation. But it was hard to remain so in the face of such open and unstinting adulation.

Theoretically, this entire business should present no problem to him.

"We have private quarters prepared for you, Great One . . . and for you also, of course, Lord Si Cwan," said Killick. "And for . . ." He turned and looked at Zak Kebron, and tried to smile in amusement. "Well, I certainly hope that we have something large enough for you, sir. It is 'sir,' is it not?"

Kebron didn't bother to nod. He didn't even seem interested in acknowledging that Killick had spoken. But then he said, "I will need to remain in proximity to the captain."

"As you wish," Ramed spoke up.

They proceeded to leave, and the crowd parted before them. Many of them were bowing, or trying to reach up and ever so tentatively touch the trouser leg of Calhoun as he passed by. It was an odd sensation for him . . . and not entirely unpleasant.

"The quarters are quite nice, Commander," Calhoun said, speaking into the monitor as he glanced around. Indeed, "quite nice" understated it. They were rather posh.

From the bridge of the *Excalibur,* Shelby nodded thoughtfully, not caring overmuch what the quarters looked like but wanting to remain politely attentive. "And what is next on the schedule, Captain?" she inquired.

"They're having some sort of welcoming banquet tonight. They want me to stay here overnight. And tomorrow, the peace talks begin in this temple that they've built."

"Is it necessary for you to stay there?" she asked cautiously. "Is there any reason you can't return to the ship? Security considerations would dictate—"

"I understand what you're saying, Commander, but I think I'll be safe enough here. Kebron's hovering over me, plus Si Cwan is busily paving the way; he's already having discussions with the assorted heads of their religious castes. This may be the simplest peace anyone's ever negotiated."

"I know, I know. That may be what makes me nervous. It seems too easy."

"Very little in this galaxy, Commander, is too easy."

"Watch yourself, Captain," she said cautiously.

"I always do. Calhoun out," he said. His image blinked off the screen to be replaced by the rotating orb of the planet.

She didn't like it. Anytime the captain left the vessel, it was asking for trouble. But obviously in this instance, there was simply no choice. Calhoun the Savior was who they wanted to see. She hadn't even asked Calhoun if he was trying to be circumspect in terms of how he was presenting himself to the crowd. The entire "anointed one" business was still fraught with peril, as far as she was concerned, from a Prime Directive point of view.

She hoped like anything that Calhoun wasn't making a mistake, and worse, that she wasn't just sitting around letting him make it.

Si Cwan was becoming slightly worried.

Certainly the enthusiasm for Calhoun was remaining consistent wherever he went. After being brought to his quarters and informing the Zondarians that the accommodations were more than adequate, Calhoun was paraded around the city. Wherever he went as he was escorted about, people lined up, cheering, shouting, waving. A number sobbed openly, so overwrought were they by his mere presence. It seemed to indicate to Si Cwan that the people were doing everything they could to embrace both the concept and reality of their peace-bringing Savior.

But the leadership, on the other hand, still had Si Cwan nervous.

For the assorted clans were more than just keepers of power. They were also maintainers of petty squabbles that seemed to go back generations. Sulimin was not speaking to Maro, Quinzix seemed totally disinterested in conversing with Vonce, and so on. Si Cwan had asked all parties involved in the discussions—and it was well over a dozen people—for a list of grievances to be discussed. He had been staggered to see that the list went on for page after page. Some of the disputes were centuries old; indeed, Si Cwan was astounded to discover that one of them involved a territorial dispute over land that had been victimized by shifts in tectonic plates and had, in fact, slid into the ocean two hundred years previously. But both the Unglza and the Eenza said that they had title to it, and were standing firm on one side or the other, neither admitting that they were in the wrong.

"Gentlemen, ladies, we must reach some accords here," Si Cwan said finally. He was addressing the group that was seated around a large round table. He noticed that they had split up so that they were sitting along caste lines. He was holding the list, but was doing so with all the enthusiasm of massaging toxic waste. ''Rather than obsessing about the individual grievances, of which there are many, perhaps we might wish to get to the core of the disputes between the two groups. We acknowledge and understand that the Unglza and the Eenza have been at war with each other for nearly a millennium. But why? What began it? What set it off? I have studied your philosophies, your religious beliefs—they are fundamentally the same. There do not seem to be vast gulfs between you. Why, in short, are you not able to live in peace with one another?''

They looked at each other, scowling across the table, and then slowly Quinzix rose on somewhat shaky legs, for Quinzix was not as young as he once was. ''The Eenza religion,'' he said slowly, ''places the Eenza above all others on this world. It is their belief that, at the time of judgment, it will be the Eenza who are given preferential treatment at the hands of the one who sits in judgment over all. We of the Unglza believe that they are wrong. We believe that the Unglza will be valued most highly. And we consider it an affront to us, and a self-worshiping elevation of the Eenza, for them to think otherwise.''

There were nods from around the table, or scowls, depending upon who was nodding. Tulaman now rose, casting an angry glance at Quinzix, who had remained standing. ''He oversimplies, Lord Cwan. The truth is that once the Eenza and Unglza were as one. But individual caste and family members desired to take control of the leadership, determined to force out the Eenza leaders. To do whatever was necessary to take over the governing and land that they desired. It all comes down to territory, Lord Cwan, at its heart. That's what this dispute has always been about. Do not let them convince you otherwise.''

There was already the grumbling of rising disputes around the table, and Si Cwan put up his hands for silence. ''But this is absurd,'' he said. ''Certainly we can come to some sort of arrangement. You're speaking of leadership struggles among people who have been dead for centuries, and philosophical debates about matters that will only be pertinent after those of you at this table, and all of your constituents, pass away. In the here and now, there seems to be no reason—''

''The reason is, they are Unglza!'' shouted Tulaman, stabbing a finger at Quinzix. Quinzix for his part trembled with outrage, and seemed prepared to shout back. All around the table, participants were starting to get to their feet, and Si Cwan could feel the rage bubbling through the room.

At that moment, the doors to the chamber opened wide. Calhoun entered, Killick and Ramed on either side of him, Zak Kebron directly behind him.

"Great One," murmured the various people around the table.

Si Cwan said, "Captain, it was my understanding that you would not be joining us here at the temple until tomorrow."

"I know," Calhoun said sounding disturbingly cheerful. "But there's only so much adulation one can take before one feels the need to accomplish a bit more with the day than just shake hands and provide spiritual comfort. So, my friends," Calhoun continued, briskly clapping his hands together and rubbing his palms as if preparing to deal a deck of cards, "what are we discussing?"

The summary did not go particularly well. Si Cwan attempted to outline the disputes in as straightforward and neutral a manner as he could, but it didn't appear to help. He was interrupted no fewer than three times and, by the end of the summation, arguments had erupted throughout the room. There was pointing, there was shouting, there were accusations, there were claims and cross-claims, threats of assault, threats of retribution, threats and more threats . . .

Kebron grabbed the table.

This was not a light table. It was solid metal, having sat in the home of one of the under-bishops of the Eenza caste and having been donated to the temple specifically for the arrival of the Savior. It was ornately carved and it was massive. It had taken twenty Zondarians half a day, moving it with gravity negators which kept burning out, before they'd managed to transport the monstrosity into the conference room within the temple that had been set aside for it.

With the slightest of grunts, Kebron lifted one end completely clear of the floor. His leverage wasn't properly set for him to raise the entire thing clear, but nonetheless it was an astounding feat. There were gasps of astonishment, and the assembled Zondarians jumped back as Kebron then slammed the table back to the floor.

The clang of the metal on the floor was one of the most earsplitting things that anyone gathered in the room had ever heard. Nor was it confined to the room. The echo resounded throughout the temple and out into the street, where passersby stopped in their tracks at the sound of the massive chime emanating from the temple.

Everyone within the room was clutching their ears, save Calhoun, who simply stood there with a rather satisfied expression on his face. This was not done without effort; Calhoun's head was ringing no less than anyone else's, but he felt it necessary to maintain utter composure.

"Great One—" Killick started to say, but Calhoun silenced him with a glance. Then he looked back at the room full of assorted leaders.

"I've been out among your people," Calhoun said slowly. He circled the room, his hands draped behind his back. "While you were in here, tossing around accusations, defending a status quo built upon a legacy of bloodshed, I walked among the Zondarians, those whom you supposedly represent. And I saw faces filled with such eagerness, such hope. They offered up prayers to me, did you know that? They begged me to help them, just through my mere presence. I spoke to parents who are afraid to send their children to school, for fear that they will end the day burying the bodies of their beloved children. I spoke to people who came out of their homes for the first time in ages without fear, confident for the first time that there may be a hope for peace. There is still a great deal of suspicion out there, my friends." He stopped and put one hand on Quinzix's shoulder and the other on Tulaman's. "There is fear. There is anger. However, it's microscopic compared to the intensity and depth of hostility that I feel when I am in here. Now the people out there have bought into this 'Savior' business. I do not know that I have, especially. But if it will help your people, then you, my friends, will buy into it. You will work with me. You will work together. And if not . . ."

Suddenly the friendly hand on the respective shoulders of Quinzix and Tulaman increased in pressure, and he snapped both of them around so that they were facing one another. "If not, I will knock your heads together, with the aid of Mister Kebron here. Do I make myself clear?"

"Great One, you do not understand the difficulties—" began Quinzix.

At the same time, Tulaman started to say, "We will not simply accept, on their say-so—"

Calhoun knocked their heads together.

It was relatively gentle; he could have done it a great deal harder. But it made a very loud and satisfying thud when their skulls came into contact with one another. Both of them yelped in a most impressive manner, and Tulaman was immediately on his feet, although it was clear that the room was spinning for him somewhat. The others were looking on, aghast. "*Do you know who I am?*" raged Tulaman.

"Yes." In comparison to Tulaman's anger, Calhoun was the soul of calm. "And do you know who *I* am?"

Tulaman looked squarely into Calhoun's purple eyes, and saw the fearsome scar that seemed to be blazing a darker red than it had before. And Tulaman looked down. "Yes," he said reluctantly. "Yes, I do."

"Damn right you do," Calhoun told him. He took in the rest of the room with a glance. "This is not the first world I've brought peace to, gentlemen and ladies. When I last accomplished that, I was half the age I am now. I did it with the strength of my right arm and a refusal to see good people suffer anymore. Now I didn't ask to be your 'Savior.' You came to me. You wanted me to step in, to try and bring you a peace that has long been predicted but never really considered to be a possibility. Well, I'm here, friends, whether you still want me or not. Lord Cwan, Mister Kebron, and I, we are the negotiating team that is going to bring your dreams to fruition. I am the Savior, predicted, believed in, and trusted. Lord Cwan is the experienced negotiator, skilled in dealing with recalcitrant world leaders. And Mister Kebron here . . ."

"Breaks people in half," offered Kebron.

"Well put," said Calhoun. "We are in a life-and-death situation, my friends. We do not end this business until it is concluded to my satisfaction. Anyone who stands in the way of that . . . Well, Mister Kebron here will make certain that any man who blocks the peace process will die a man of parts. Do we understand each other?"

There was a collective numbed nodding of heads from around the table.

"Excellent," said Calhoun with remarkable cheerfulness. "That being the case, my friends, let's get to work."

The official banquet that night was remarkably festive. There was a sense of exhilaration in the air, largely because so much had been accomplished. Whether it was from a genuine desire to help the good people of Zondar, or whether from an equally genuine desire to keep all their limbs intact, the religious and caste leaders of Zondar worked with an amazing amount of effort in negotiating various treaties, agreements, and the like.

After his initial threats of violence, knocking heads, and dismemberment, Calhoun had been surprisingly quiet. It was not necessary, he felt, to be a continued intimidating presence. Rather he came to regard himself as something of a sergeant-at-arms. One who both inspired the peace and then made sure it was enforced. Si Cwan, for his part, handled the actual "dirty work," as it were. His familiarity with the long-standing hostilities of the Zondarians, as well as his own previous experience in creating an enforced peace on Zondar, served him extremely well. By the end of the day when they discontinued talks to allow for the celebratory banquet, everyone in the room felt that they might actually have something genuine to celebrate.

The dining hall was elaborately festooned with decorations. Alcoholic libations were flowing freely, and there was much laughter and polite discourse. Arbora the Unseen was spotted repeatedly as she pirouetted across the dance floor. Maro the Questioner was seen fielding questions from Vonce of the Many Fortunes. The Dissuaders, under the watchful and threatening eye of Zak Kebron, kept more or less to themselves, got quietly drunk, and wound up having to be picked up from under the tables.

Through it all, and above it all, Calhoun watched the festivities.

And felt concerned.

Calhoun had always had something of a sixth sense for danger. It was hardly infallible, to be sure, but there was something there. He'd even been tested for it at Starfleet Academy, and researchers had found nothing in particular. Calhoun's contention was that there was nothing to find because, during the research, no danger was present. Ultimately, whether they found something that they could justify or not was of no consequence to Calhoun at all. He simply knew that he had a sort of "warrior's instinct" for danger. It might have been based upon his being able to look over a situation, instinctively know that something was wrong, and act accordingly. It might have been something on a psionic level. It might have been plain old dumb luck; after all, if one was suspicious all the time (as Calhoun was) and if one faced an assortment of people who wanted to kill one (as Calhoun had) then it was only natural that one would say, "Ah-hah! I had a feeling something was up!"

Whatever the reason, whatever the cause, Calhoun was concerned that danger was present during this festive occasion. He couldn't place exactly what the source was; his instinct wasn't always that specific. But in this instance, he felt a general free-floating apprehension. He wondered if Shelby hadn't been right and perhaps the smart thing to do was return to the ship. But something in him railed against the idea. He had talked tough. He had threatened, he had badgered, he had cajoled, and, above all else, he had acted with supreme confidence. To tuck tail and run now just because he was having an attack of nerves just didn't sit right with him. It stung his pride.

Something Shelby had said to him any number of times rang in his head: "Pride Goeth Before a Fall."

He was aware of someone at his side, and he glanced over to see Si Cwan there. Cwan was regarding him with what seemed to be a mixture of disapproval and amusement. "I am not entirely certain, Captain, whether Commander Shelby would approve of your negotiation style."

"It's hardly my universal approach to situations, Lord Cwan," replied Calhoun. A server brought him a large glass of wine. He sniffed it experimentally, sipped it slightly, and wasn't thrilled with the taste. He put it aside. "In this instance, the people of this world have endowed me with a tremendous amount of power through their perception of me. There's a good deal to accomplish on this world, a lot of walls to deal with. In some cases, I try to get around a wall. Other times I try to burrow under it. In this case—"

"You're simply smashing directly through it."

"Exactly. It's direct, it's simple—"

"And it leaves rubble in your wake."

"These people need help, Cwan."

"No argument there, Captain. But Commander Shelby was right; we must tread carefully. After all, in using your strength as their savior to ramrod through needed changes, you run the risk of their becoming dependent upon you in order to do what needs to be done."

"I certainly hope you're wrong about that, Cwan," replied Calhoun. "It's daunting enough having the crew of the *Excalibur* dependent on me, and that's in my job description."

He looked out upon the celebration once more. "Look at them, Si Cwan. They're happy. They have hope. We're responsible for that. Does it matter how we get them to that point?"

"Yes," Si Cwan said immediately.

"Let me remind you of something, Cwan: Your hands aren't exactly clean in this matter. It was your people who forced a cease-fire down their throats by blowing up part of their geography. The Thallonians set the precedent. If I have to stay consistent with that in order to accomplish what needs to be done, well, I may not be happy about it, but that's what I'll do."

"I don't know about that, Calhoun."

"Don't know about what?"

"About your not being happy about it. I think you're perfectly happy about it.'' He leaned forward and Calhoun smelled the whiff of alcohol on his breath. Si Cwan was definitely speaking with a looser tongue than he usually had. ''Just between us, I think you're a bloody bastard who'd just as soon throw himself into a fight as walk away from one.''

Calhoun smiled thinly. ''And why do you think that, may I ask? That I'm a bloody bastard?''

''Because,'' Si Cwan told him, ''it takes one to know one.'' He winked heavily, rose to his feet and walked away with an ever-so-slight swagger.

A moment later, Zak Kebron was looming over Calhoun. ''Captain,'' he said softly—which, for him, was a low rumble—''do you wish to return to the ship?''

From nearby, Killick's voice shouted out, ''To the Savior!''

Everyone in the room echoed the sentiment, repeating the word ''Savior!'' or ''Calhoun!'' and his name rose in volume, thundering through the room, out into the streets beyond. And in the streets, people took up the chant, shouting, ''Calhoun! Calhoun!''

And for a moment, just a moment, he was back on Xenex. Back in his heyday, with the mobs of warriors shouting his name as he would stand there, sword raised triumphantly over his head, declaring that Xenex's oppressors would be driven from the surface of the planet, even if it took his dying breath.

He had never realized just how happy he had been at that moment. In a bleak fashion, he couldn't help but wonder if perhaps his best days weren't already long behind him. No matter what he accomplished, in many ways it would be nothing more than a mere rehash, a shadow of that which he had achieved so many years ago.

Calhoun drank it in. And for the first time in a long time, he was happy.

Shelby did not sleep well that night.

She tossed and turned, unable to get comfortable, and visions of Calhoun filled her head. Calhoun in pain, Calhoun in danger. When she awoke, she was covered with sweat, her simple white shift clinging to her body. Despite the constant, comfortable temperature of her cabin, she felt as if she were suffocating.

''Damn the man,'' she whispered. ''Damn the man.''

She called out in the darkness, cursing herself silently even as she did, ''Shelby to Calhoun.'' At the command of her voice, the computer-operated comm system immediately patched her through to

Calhoun's comm link. She knew that he would awaken instantly, as he always did. When they were together, it had always bugged the hell out of her. She couldn't so much as sneak out of the bed to go to the bathroom at night without Calhoun coming to instant, immediate wakefulness.

At this point she was prepared for the reception she knew she'd get. The confused and irritated voice, the demand to know why she had bothered him so early in the morning. He might even take offense that she had so little faith in him that she felt the need to check up on him.

What she was not prepared for was the dead silence on the other end.

Moments before she had felt mild alarm and major embarrassment over endeavoring to get in contact with her captain. Now the "mild" and "major" considerations had switched positions as her alarm swelled and her embarrassment evaporated. "Shelby to Calhoun. Captain, report in," she said more loudly, as if he'd have a better shot at hearing her from the planet's surface if she raised her voice.

Still nothing.

She had fully risen from the bed, and once more she said, "Shelby to Calhoun. Damn it, Mac, report!" She didn't wait more than half a heartbeat before switching and saying, "Shelby to Zak Kebron."

This time there was only a pause of a couple of seconds, and then Kebron's voice responded. "Kebron here. Go ahead, Commander."

"I'm trying to reach the captain. He's not responding."

"On it," was the terse reply. And then she heard what sounded like a crash, and shouting.

And barely a minute or two after that, Kebron reported back—and Shelby felt as if her life were spinning away.

Kebron had been sleeping lightly, as he usually did.

He was fully dressed, as was his custom. Furthermore he had discovered some time back that he rested best when he was on his feet. The Brikar security chief would stabilize his balance, becoming about as moveable as an Easter Island statue, and then he would consciously slow down his body functions to an even slower state than they usually were. Even in his semi–dream state, however, he remained alert and aware.

He had offered to stay within the captain's quarters, but Calhoun had told Kebron that it wasn't necessary. Kebron couldn't help but observe that the captain certainly carried his warrior's pride close to the surface. He hadn't even wanted Kebron to stand directly outside his door. "I'm supposed to be the most worshiped individual on this planet, powerful and unafraid," Calhoun had told him. "How is it going to look if I have to hide behind my security chief?"

So Kebron had settled for being in the room next door and resting as lightly as he possibly could. Consequently he had come around immediately when Shelby had summoned him.

When he learned that the captain was incommunicado, Kebron did not hesitate. He and Calhoun had had adjoining rooms, but they were not connecting. A second later, however, they were indeed connecting, as Kebron charged forward and slammed one of his massive shoulders into the wall. It bent from the impact, shuddering. Kebron backed up a few steps and then barreled forward once more, and this time succeeded in plowing directly through. Mortar and rubble rained down around him as Zak Kebron stumbled slightly, but righted himself as he entered the captain's quarters.

He wasn't entirely certain what he had expected to see, but the sight that greeted his eyes certainly wasn't it.

Assorted members of the Zondarian ruling and religious castes were grouped around the bed that Calhoun had presumably been lying in. The sheets, however, were in disarray, and there was no sign of the captain anywhere.

The smashing down of the wall was hardly subtle, and the others looked around in shocked confusion as Kebron stood there, quickly brushing off the powder and traces of dust. His eyes had narrowed to a diamond-hard glitter as his gaze focused on Killick. "Where's the captain?" he demanded, and his voice was a terrible thing to hear. The men and women assembled in that room were the cream of Zondarian society, the best and brightest that their people had to offer. The masters of their race who feared nothing and no one. And every single one of them trembled upon hearing that voice. "Where . . . is . . . the captain?" Kebron repeated.

"He . . ." Killick seemed anxious to try and find the words, and was unable to frame them. He looked helplessly to the others.

It was Tulaman who stepped forward, doing everything he could to steel himself for the purpose of facing down Kebron.

"The Savior is dead," said Tulaman.

12

Kebron slowly stared around the room before his gaze returned to, and focused on, Tulaman.

"What are you talking about?" In direct contrast to his bulk, his voice was at that point so soft that everyone in the room had to strain to hear him.

"We . . ." It was Killick who answered. "We sought the advice of the Great One on a matter of some debate—"

"At this time of morning?"

"The Savior had told us that, had we any questions, we were to ask Him regardless of time. We believed Him, for anything He told us was, naturally, true. We came here, to His room, knocked on His door, and when He did not respond to our summons, we came here and found Him—"

"Found him what? Where is he?"

"He was dead, Kebron," Tulaman said with certainty. "With my own eyes, I saw. His head to one side, eyes wide open, mouth partly open. It is my belief that He suffered some sort of seizure and simply . . . died. Heir to the frailties of the flesh, as much as any other man."

"Indeed." Kebron's voice was so flat, so monotone, that the Zondarians at first thought that he had failed to grasp the severity of the situation. "Where is the body?" he asked.

"He was removed from here, of course," Tulaman said. "None but the highest of the high in our caste—the wisest, the most holy, the most educated—would be worthy of seeing the deceased body of the Savior Himself."

"I want to see the body immediately," Kebron informed them.

"Providing it can be produced, which I am beginning to doubt. He will immediately be returned to the *Excalibur* for proper medical treatment."

"Treatment!" Tulaman was beginning to sound annoyed with statements that he considered to be beyond obvious. "What treatment is there for a dead man?"

"If he is dead, then none. If he is not, then I will go through each and every one of you until he is found. Bring me the body of Captain Calhoun, Tulaman."

"Impossible," said Tulaman with conviction.

"Wrong answer," Kebron informed him. And before Tulaman could say another word, Kebron's right hand swung around with what seemed a very slow, relaxed manner. The back of his three-fingered hand struck Tulaman squarely in the side of the head. Kebron had judged the impact quite precisely; if he'd hit Tulaman with any greater force, he'd easily have caved in Tulaman's skull. As it was, the eyes of Tulaman the Misbegotten rolled up into his skull and he fell without another word.

The others stood there in stunned silence, and then Kebron turned to Freenaux and said, "Bring me the body of Captain Calhoun, Freenaux."

"That . . . that isn't possible," Freenaux started to say. He got as far as "That isn't," however, and then his unconscious body joined Tulaman on the floor.

"Wrong answer," Kebron informed the insensate Freenaux, and then he surveyed the remainder of the room's inhabitants. "Sulimin," he said. "Bring me the body of Captain Calhoun."

"Right away, Lieutenant Kebron," was Sulimin's rather panicked reply.

This satisfied Kebron as being the right answer. Then he walked back into his quarters through the rubble of the wall and tapped his commbadge. "Commander," he said as soon as he had Shelby on the line. "This is Kebron."

"Report, Lieutenant," said Shelby, and he could tell that she was keeping her voice steady with effort.

He paused, contemplating the best way to put it, and decided that ultimately there was really only one way to say it. "Commander, Captain Calhoun is missing and presumed dead."

There was total silence on the other end, and for a moment Kebron thought he'd lost contact. "Commander?" he prompted.

"I heard you, Kebron," and there was cold fury in her voice. "What the hell happened?"

He told her in as quick strokes as he could, and when he finished, Shelby said, "Stay on post there. I'm coming down with Doctor Selar immediately. The three of us are going to find out exactly what the hell is going on. Because I'll tell you right now, Kebron, the Mackenzie Calhouns of this universe don't just die quietly in their sleep. They die with their teeth firmly buried in the throats of their adversaries."

"Understood," Kebron said.

And he waited for the advent of Commander Shelby.

Shelby steadied herself in her cabin, determined not to let the world swirl around her as it was threatening to do.

It couldn't be that Mackenzie Calhoun was gone. It simply couldn't be.

It was some sort of bizarre trick. That had to be it. It was the only thing that made sense. The Zondarians were trying to pull some sort of . . . of spectacular hoax. And she was going to make damn sure that it failed.

"Shelby to Selar!" she shouted, much more loudly than she had intended, even as she yanked her shift off and fumbled for her uniform out of the closet.

"Selar here," came the Vulcan's voice. She sounded sleepy but alert.

"We're going planetside, doctor. The captain is missing, and the Zondarians claim that he's dead. We're going to find him. Meet me in the main transporter room."

"I shall be there immediately," said Selar. There was something to be said, Shelby realized at that moment, for having a Vulcan for a CMO. There were no emotions, no histrionics, no demands to know what had happened. She knew that the moment she arrived in the transporter room, Selar was going to be standing there waiting with her medical equipment and an entirely business-oriented demeanor. She would ask no questions beyond what she needed to know in order to deal with a medical emergency. There was no excess verbiage required by her.

"Shelby to security," she continued, and upon receiving the acknowledgment, said, "I want two security officers, heavily armed, to meet me at the transporter room." She had no intention of screwing around with the Zondarians: When she went in, she was going to go in with a show of force. Shelby finished dressing, charged out of her quarters, and was at the transporter room, as it turned out, in just under three minutes. Selar was standing there waiting for her. Shelby's hair was disheveled, her manner one of barely contained anger, outrage, and confusion. Selar, on the other hand, looked calm and cool. For one moment, Shelby found that she no longer appreciated Selar's unflappable demeanor. Instead she discovered the truth of the age-old adage, namely that misery loves company. The security guards, Hecht and Scannell, were there as well. They had obeyed her instructions to the letter. Hecht had heavy-duty hand phasers strapped to either side of his uniform, looking for all the world like a cowboy. Scannell had a phaser rifle slung under his arm.

''Very impressive, gentlemen,'' she said with approval.

Ensign Watson had just taken position behind the transporter controls, and she immediately configured the coordinates for the point of transmission from which Zak Kebron communicated mere minutes before. ''Energize!'' called Shelby as she stepped onto the platform, a slightly sloppy maneuver that could have had a costly effect. If Watson hadn't been paying attention and simply activated the beams on command, the front portion of Shelby's body would have preceded her to the planet's surface. As it was, Watson was cautious enough to wait until Shelby was completely on the platform before beaming her down to Zondar.

Kebron was waiting for her when the four of them arrived seconds later. Kebron glanced in acknowledgment at Hecht and Scannell. Had he so chosen, he could have expressed annoyance that the bringing out of security guards without clearing it through him was a breach of protocol, but he didn't bother.

''Where was his room?'' demanded Shelby without preamble.

Instead of answering, Kebron led her to the quarters where assorted Zondarians were still milling around in what appeared to be barely controlled chaos. Shelby spotted Killick, the one Zondarian she recognized, and without even bothering to offer greetings, said, ''Where the hell is the captain?''

The question prompted a barrage of responses, not just from Killick but from everyone around. As Shelby tried to sort out who was saying what, she started to hear something else as well. A chorus of voices, but it was not coming from within the temple. Instead it rose from outside, high-pitched and frightening in the depth of its grief. A thousand voices, more, rising as one and giving vent to some sort of deep-seated mourning. "What is that?" she demanded, but even as she asked, she already knew.

"Word of the Savior's passing has spread to the populace," said Killick. "They are bemoaning the passing of—*urkh!*"

The last part of the sentence came as a result of Shelby's hand at his throat.

Killick gasped, unable to get air to his lungs, as Shelby pushed him up against the nearest wall with astounding force. She was unaware that Kebron had already knocked cold two of the Zondarians. It's unlikely that, even had she known, it would have made the slightest difference in how she conducted herself.

Hecht and Scannell looked at each other, and the same thought was clearly on both their faces: They weren't entirely sure what Shelby needed with additional security guards. She was turning into a one-woman army.

Through gritted teeth, she said, "Understand: I am not a morning person. And on mornings where my commanding officer supposedly dies—and vanishes—I am really, truly, not someone that *you want to* groz *with!*" she finished, her voice rising in volume. "Don't you dare stand there and tell me that Captain Calhoun is dead unless you are prepared to produce a steaming corpse. And if you can't do that, then you had damn well better be prepared to bring him here safe and sound. Have I made myself clear?"

A thoroughly intimidated Killick nodded his head. "I . . ." and his throat was so choked that the word was virtually inaudible. Shelby removed her hand and Killick tried to straighten his garments and repair the disarray that he was in. "I found the body myself. Lying in the bed, staring off into the abyss to which we are all destined."

"Some of us," Kebron rumbled, "may be destined sooner than others."

The threat was not lost on Killick or anyone of the others in the room. "We are . . . locating the Great One's body . . . even as we speak," Killick assured them, "so that you may see for yourselves the tragedy of this event."

"Very wise," she told him flatly. "And let me tell you one thing right now: God help you if there is any sign of foul play. Because I swear to you, if one of you brought harm to the captain, then I will bring you to justice or, failing that, I will bring this place down around your ears. Have I made myself sufficiently clear on that point?"

There was mute nodding from all around.

Selar, for her part, was running the medical tricorder over the bed that had been occupied by Calhoun. She checked the readings once more, and then gestured for Shelby to come over and join her. Shelby did so, leaving Killick rubbing his throat. The others gave her a wide berth as she passed. It would have been a tough call to determine at that point who was more intimidating to the Zondarians: the mammoth Zak Kebron or the smaller but extremely vicious Elizabeth Shelby.

"What have you got?" she asked.

"It is difficult to be certain, but I am reasonably sure that the captain did not die in this bed."

Shelby felt the first bubble of real hope beginning to surface in her heart. "Why do you say that?"

"The humanoid body, when it ceases function, does not generally do so in a neat or tidy manner," Selar said. "The bowels and bladder relax and evacuate any matter left in them, or there is excretion of—"

"I get the idea," Shelby said quickly. "You're saying that there's usually some sort of physical trace left behind."

"However minute it might be, yes," Selar said. "But in this instance, I find nothing. Not so much as a stray bit of spittle on the pillow."

Shelby wasted no time, turning immediately back to Killick and saying, "You're lying to me, Killick."

"I am not! As the Savior is my witness—" He stopped, realizing the inappropriateness of the statement. It was a reflexive comment, one that he had made any number of times throughout the years before there was an actual, flesh-and-blood Savior to which the invocation could be attached. "I swear to you," he amended. "It is as I described it. His body was right there. He was not, to the best of my ability to ascertain, alive."

As he had been speaking, Selar had had her tricorder focused on him. "Commander," she said, "I believe he is telling the truth."

"Are you sure?" asked Shelby.

"To a ninety-eight percent probability," Selar told her, showing her the tricorder readings. Shelby, of course, did not quite understand what she was looking at, but was loath to admit it, so she feigned thoughtful expertise as she regarded the readings. "Making allowances for the stress of the moment, his pulse and respiration remained relatively close to the Zondarian norm when he was making the statements. Either it is the truth, or at the very least he believes it to be the truth."

"What is going on in here?" came the startled voice of Si Cwan. He was standing in the doorway, having thrown a robe on, looking around in confusion at the assemblage before him. He took it all in in a glance, and then his face darkened as he said, "What happened to the captain?"

Kebron, ever suspicious, said, "How do you know that something happened to the captain?"

"In the name of the gods, Kebron, I'm not completely dim," retorted Si Cwan. "Everyone is standing here looking disconcerted, there's no sign of Calhoun, and Shelby, Selar, and two security goons have shown up. One does not have to be a detective to figure this out."

At that moment, one of the servants to Killick came running in, looking extremely concerned. He motioned for Killick to come over to him, and Killick did so. What followed was a rapid exchange of words, with Killick looking increasingly disturbed, shaking his head in what was clear disbelief. Shelby tried to listen in on what they were saying, but it was hard to hear anything—even her own thoughts—over the wailing and moaning that was coming from just outside. As this happened, Kebron quickly outlined the situation for Si Cwan. The red face of the Thallonian noble became darker and darker by the moment.

Finally, looking for all the world as if he'd rather be anywhere else, Killick turned back to them and cleared his throat apprehensively. "The Savior's body is, uhm . . ."

"If you say 'cremated,' you're next," Shelby told him in no uncertain terms.

"No, but it is . . . it is gone."

"Gone," said Si Cwan in astonishment, beating Shelby and Kebron to the punch by a fraction of a second. "What do you mean, gone?"

"It was brought to a sacred place of preparation, where only the noblest and best of Zondarians are taken for handling," Killick said. "But we have checked there now, and there does not seem to be any sign of him. It has . . . has disappeared. The only thing remaining is . . . is this," and he held up Calhoun's communicator badge.

Before any of the *Excalibur* crew could say anything, Vonce spoke up, and it was in a voice that was filled with joy and reverence. "It is a miracle!" he cried out. "It is as Ontear foresaw! A miracle, I say!"

"What are you talking about?!" demanded Shelby.

" 'He will come from air and return to air!' " Vonce explained eagerly. "Don't you see? The prophecy has been fulfilled! He came from air, via your transportation device. And now, with His passing, He has vanished into the air as well! There is no trace of Him to be found! We are dealing with the miraculous, I say!"

"Don't be a fool!" said Maro the Questioner. "We are dealing with thievery! Thievery of the most vile and depraved sort! That is what faces us! Thievery on the part of the Unglza, who are probably behind all of this!"

This immediately prompted a firestorm of protest from the Unglza representatives, a chorus of agreement among the Eenza present, and a few holdouts who agreed with the miracle theory postulated by Vonce.

Shelby pulled out her phaser and discharged it once skyward. She only had it set on stun, so the result was simply a very loud noise rather than any damage being done. It was, however, enough to immediately seize their attention.

"We," she said with great control, "are going to look for the captain. We are going to operate on the assumption that he is alive, well, and being held by person or persons unknown. We will find him, make no mistake. And when we do, if we discover that any of you had any involvement in this matter . . ."

She let the threat trail off, reasoning that whatever they might come up with would likely be far more frightening than anything she could possibly say.

"Shall we . . . shall we bring you to the last known location of his body?" asked Killick.

"That should not be necessary," Selar said. "Commander, with your permission . . . ?"

"Whatever you have in mind, Doctor, I'm all ears," Shelby told her.

Selar tapped her comm link and said, "Selar to transporter room."

"Transporter room, Watson here."

"Watson," Selar said, "I require your aid in locating Captain Calhoun."

"Yes, Doctor," came back Watson's voice. "Uhm . . . how are we going to go about that?"

"Elementary, Watson," said Selar, and she was about to continue when she was interrupted by a rather surprising guffaw from Shelby. She looked questioningly at the commander. It hardly seemed the time for any sort of levity, and she was at a loss to determine just what it was that Shelby considered so funny. Shelby waved it off and gestured for Selar to continue.

"Doctor?" came Watson's mildly confused voice.

"We have the captain's DNA records and molecular patterns in the transporter buffer files," continued Selar after one more puzzled glance at Shelby. "Use the shipboard computer medlink and download that information directly into my medical tricorder."

"Will do, Doctor. Give me a minute to pull up the pertinent data. Keep your tricorder on in order to ensure proper information retrieval."

"Understood."

While they were waiting for the information to be processed, Shelby turned to Si Cwan. "I want you back on the ship," she said.

"What?" demanded Si Cwan. "For what purpose? If I remain here—"

"If you remain here, you could wind up in the same trouble that the captain's in, whatever that may be," Shelby told him. "I'm not going to have any more dealings with these people until we know exactly what's going on around here. Nor am I going to have any non-Starfleet personnel putting themselves at risk."

"I can take care of myself, Commander," Si Cwan informed her.

"Lord Cwan," Shelby said with fading patience, "there is not a single individual in this galaxy whom I would have thought more capable of taking care of himself than Mackenzie Calhoun. He's now missing. So don't for one moment think that your protestations of your own capabilities are going to cut any ice with me. Do we understand each other?"

"Perfectly," said an annoyed Si Cwan, clearly disagreeing but realizing that he wasn't going to make any headway against the immovable object of Commander Shelby. And then he turned to face Zak Kebron. "Bring him back, Kebron. Bring him back safely. If anyone can, you can."

"A compliment?" said Kebron with mild amusement.

"No. A challenge." He tapped the commbadge that he had been issued and said, "Si Cwan to *Excalibur*. One to beam up." And, moments later, he had dematerialized in a sparkle of molecules.

"Well done, Watson," Selar was saying in the meantime.

"Not a problem, Doctor. Anything else you need, just ask."

"Understood. Selar out."

"All right, Doctor," Shelby said, her arms folded and looking barely patient. "What have you got in mind?"

''We can use the tricorder as a localized detection device,'' Selar said, after making a few adjustments. ''Lock on to traces of his DNA or molecular structure in the same way that a tricorder can be utilized to locate any other specific trace elements.''

''If we can lock on to where he is, let's just find his coordinates and have him beamed up to the ship.''

''The equipment is not quite that localized, Commander. It will indicate direction, but not the final destination.''

''Wait a minute.'' Shelby tapped her commbadge. ''Shelby to Bridge.''

''Bridge. Lieutenant Soleta here.''

''Just the person I wanted to speak to.'' She quickly outlined what it was that Selar had planned, and then said, ''Can we run the same information through the ship's sensors? Do a sensor sweep of the planet using his molecular structure as a guide?''

''Absolutely,'' Soleta replied. ''But via our sensors, it would be more of a selective process. Essentially we'd have to filter through all the biological organisms within the area of the sensor sweep and detect the captain either using his molecular patterns as a guide, or else by process of elimination. That is to say, we eliminate everyone we know is not the captain and, in doing so, eventually find him.''

''Sounds like a plan,'' said Shelby, who then almost bit her tongue since she had inadvertently blurted out Calhoun's favorite expression. The last thing she wanted to admit was that she had been influenced by him in any way. ''Do it,'' she said. ''Until I return, you have the conn, Soleta.''

''Yes, sir. I'll get right on it.''

Shelby turned to Soleta and said briskly, ''All right, Doctor. Fire up the tricorder, and let's track down the captain. Between our being on the scent down here, and the *Excalibur* tracking him on their end, we should be able to do this in no time. Gentlemen,'' and she addressed Kebron, Hecht, and Scannell, ''let's go find the captain.''

Killick quickly made his way to what he hoped would be a private communication point, deep in his own personal sanctum. Quickly he used it to contact Ramed's home and, to his concern, Talila appeared on the screen. ''Killick!'' she said, making no effort to hide her surprise. She knew of Killick, certainly, but since he was of the Unglza, she had never actually had any direct communication with him. ''This is a surprise.''

"Yes, I imagine it would be," he said, trying to remain calm. "Is Ramed there?"

"Here?" The genuine puzzlement on her face was all the answer he needed, but it would have been rude to simply shut off the link. "Why would he be here? He's there, isn't he? He . . . he left for there. He even spoke with me just the other day to tell me that he had arrived."

"Did he say anything to you, Talila?"

Talila was completely confused, to say nothing of frustrated. She was, after all, speaking with someone whom she regarded as the enemy. She knew, however, that Zondar was endeavoring to enter a new age of tolerance, and what sort of mother and wife would she be if she resisted something as positive as cooperation and brotherhood? So she put aside her immediate temptation to bite off a sharp answer and instead replied, "Did he say anything? What would he have said, Killick? I . . . do not understand."

"I'm not sure," he admitted in annoyance. "But—"

"But what?"

He took a deep breath, and said, "The Savior is dead. Dead and gone. I saw His body myself, and that body has now vanished. And Ramed is gone as well."

"Gone?" She stared at him, and he could almost see the wheels turning in her mind, almost perceive the actual thought process as it was reflected on her face in growing disbelief. "Dead and gone . . . and you . . . you are implying that Ramed had something to do with it?"

"I don't know," Killick said in frustration. "All I know is that he is gone. That makes him a suspect."

"No," Talila shot back at him.

"Talila, listen to me—"

"No!" she said again, even more forcefully. "Ramed's absence does not make him a suspect. Any one of a dozen reasons would suffice to explain that. No, what makes him a suspect is you. You and years, centuries of distrust of him and all those like him. All those like me. I resent your implications, Killick. Resent them most deeply, and you would be well advised not to be in contact with me again."

"Talila," he started to say.

"Never again!" she reiterated more forcefully, and shut off the connection.

Killick leaned back in his chair and let out a slow sigh of dread. "I dislike the way this matter is developing," he said.

Talila sagged against the wall, shaking her head and murmuring, "No, no, please, no," over and over again. From his room, Rab heard her and emerged, going to her and touching her leg gently.

"Mother?" he inquired. "What's wrong?"

She looked down at him and then, rather than say anything, she took him up in her arms and rocked gently back and forth with him, all the time praying that what she feared could not possibly, under any circumstances, be the truth. She tried to tell herself that Killick had called her up out of some misplaced sense of spite. That the conclusions she was drawing could not possibly be accurate.

She told herself so many things, but the bottom line was that she was terrified. And she had never in her life felt more helpless.

13

The High Priest of Alpha Carinae looked down from the high window in the Central Hall of Worship, and for the first time felt apprehension.

Then he quickly fought to rein in his concerns. It was absurd for him to worry, he realized. His personal safety was simply not a consideration. Everyone, even the relative barbarians of Alpha Carinae, knew his person was sacrosanct. Had they not had that reality drilled into them sufficiently when the Redeemers first arrived upon their world?

The High Priest remembered those first, glorious days. The Redeemers had a fairly standard method of operation. When they targeted a world for redemption, they would sweep in with the full force of their armada behind them. Any initial battle against the Redeemers would very quickly be snuffed out. The current religious leaders of the world were targeted for primary redemption: Either they would accept Xant as their one, true deity or, failing that, they were executed. Usually the Redeemer board of inquiry could determine very quickly whether or not there was going to be cooperation with the redemption. More often than not, there wasn't. In the final analysis, it never really mattered.

Once the world had sworn allegiance to Xant, a High Priest was left in place. One was usually all that was needed, although occasionally two would be left in place on a particularly populous planet. In the case of Alpha Carinae, however, the one had been deemed more than sufficient.

Now the High Priest was beginning to wonder if that confidence had not been misplaced.

Whereas once he had walked the streets with impunity, now he found that the hostility that was greeting him was simply too much. No one had assaulted him; no one would possibly be that foolish. But he could feel the glares, the anger drilling into the base of his skull. Everywhere he went now, he heard the name of Calhoun being bandied about. Calhoun and the *Excalibur.* He was finding leaflets being handed out, some of them being brought to him by his spies, others pasted up on buildings with an audacity he once would not have thought possible.

Part of him wanted to contact the Overlord immediately, to tell him of the further disintegration of the situation on Alpha Carinae. Prime One had certainly been polite and responsive enough when he had sounded the initial warning. But he was concerned that, should he contact them as a follow-up so quickly, it might seem that he was weak and fearful. It was one thing to apprise the Overlord of a situation, as he had already done. It was quite another to run back to him repeatedly as if he, the High Priest, were unable to attend to his own territory.

One of his more trusted servants knocked on the door and waited politely for the High Priest to turn and face him. "There is a delegation here to see you, High One," said the servant.

"A delegation?" The High Priest had been sitting, but he pulled himself to standing while leaning on his cane. "From whom, may I ask?"

"From the . . ." He paused and pulled out a piece of paper, clearly having written it down to make certain that he got it correct. "From the People's Association for Peace."

"A gentle name, certainly," the High Priest acknowledged. "A name designed to put one at ease." He tapped his staff thoughtfully. "One would almost assume that it is deceptively obvious that the name is created so as not to arouse suspicion. Nonetheless, we cannot allow our fears to govern us, can we? Send them in."

The servant nodded once and walked out of the door. Less than a minute later, a group of four male Alphans entered, looking not particularly threatening. One of them, the High Priest immediately noted, was Saulcram. He looked none the worse for wear, considering the severe banging up he had received earlier.

"Gentlemen," the High Priest said slowly, "to what do I owe the pleasure?"

The four men glanced at each other, as if needing to silently affirm one more time what it was that they wished to discuss. Saulcram took an unsteady step forward. Apparently he, the lucky devil, had been selected to serve as the group's spokesman. "We have an . . . an issue that needs to be discussed, High One."

"Indeed. And what might that be?"

Saulcram readied himself for what he felt had potential to be a major problem. As it turned out, he could not even begin to grasp the accuracy of that sentiment. "We wish to worship Calhoun."

Although he was not entirely surprised at the words, the High Priest was still rocked to hear them. He did not let his surprise show, however. He was far too much of a professional for that.

To play it safe, he thumbed a small switch on the inside of his staff. Immediately it triggered a recording device safely hidden within the staff, with a back-up copy being made deep within the confines of his private office. "You wish to worship Calhoun instead of Xant. Is that correct?" he said slowly.

There was hesitant nodding of heads from the envoys.

"And you ask my blessing to do so. Is that what this is about?"

"We . . ." and Saulcram drew himself up straighter, prouder. It was as if the fact that he had not simply been struck down by a thunderbolt from on high had given him a measure of new and increased confidence. "We are not seeking your blessing. We will do as we wish."

"My dear friends," the High Priest said expansively. "This Calhoun is not unknown to me, nor is his vessel. He is a mere mortal, dear friends. A brave one, to be sure. A staunch leader, so I am told. But a mortal nonetheless. You cannot seriously expect to forsake a god, to turn your back on one such as Xant, simply for the purpose of attending to the word of a mortal."

"You are mortal," another of Saulcram's colleagues pointed out. "We attend to your word."

"But my word is the word of Xant."

"How do we know?" came the challenging reply.

The High Priest chose not to rise to the belligerence inherent in the tone. "It is enough that I know, my friends—"

"We are not your friends!" Saulcram said sharply, pointing a quivering finger at the High Priest. Slowly he started to approach him. The High Priest's instinct was to back up, but he resisted it. Instead he maintained his ground as Saulcram advanced on him.

"You and your kind overthrew us, remember? Overthrew our belief in ourselves. Battered us down, forced your god upon us—"

"We forced nothing! We saved you. You do not fully comprehend that yet, but we—"

"You took away from us our right to choose for ourselves! To think for ourselves! You ask us to trust you when you clearly do not trust us, even for something as simple as making up our own minds about the world in which we live!"

"Stop where you are," the High Priest said fiercely, his veneer of polite patience slipping somewhat. Out of long habit, Saulcram halted in his tracks. "You are tempting a terrible punishment. Terrible beyond your ability to grasp."

"I can 'grasp' just fine, oh High One," Saulcram told him. "And what I grasp is that, for the first time, the Redeemers are wallowing in the stench of fear. You cling to your musty belief in Xant, and in the meantime a true redeemer is here! On Zondar they call Him the Savior!"

"They can call him whatever they wish, but in the end he is no replacement for Xant!" the High Priest declared. His voice had been getting louder and louder, but now he pulled it back to a low and deadly tone. "I have been more than patient with you, Saulcram. With all of you. You have taken it upon yourselves to indulge in some foolish notion of worshiping another, when we both know that the way of Xant is the one, true way. It is my very strong advice that you leave now."

"You don't yet understand, priest," Saulcram told him angrily. "We are not the ones who will be leaving. You will be the one who leaves."

The High Priest tilted his head as if he could not quite believe what had just been said. "I beg your pardon?" he said. This time there was no threat in his voice. If anything, he sounded amused.

"You will leave. Now. This day. You will pack your book, your statues, your teaching scrolls, your tools of consecration. All of it," Saulcram said. Any last vestiges of nervousness had evaporated. "You will take it and you will depart this world, and that is the only way that you will live to see another sunrise. Do we make ourselves clear?" There was silent bobbing of heads from his associates. "We have spoken to thousands of our peers, and they all feel the same way. They want you out, and the advent of Calhoun into this sector is the sign that we have been waiting for."

"A sign." The High Priest scratched his chin thoughtfully. "Let me tell you of signs. The great flaming bird signals the coming of Xant. I do not speak of some uncertain and distant future that you and your descendants may or may not live to see. I am speaking of soon, within your own lifetime. I have spoken to the Overlord himself,'' which was something of an exaggeration since he had spoken only to Prime One. ''It is his proclamation that the return of Xant is near. You would be most ill advised to ignore this very important news. How do you think Xant, and the Overlord, would feel if a previously colonized world had an uprising just in time for Xant's restoration to power and glory? An uprising, the main theme of which was that you did not believe in Xant or his message. What possible purpose could such a happenstance serve you, eh?''

And suddenly, with absolutely no warning at all, Saulcram grabbed the High Priest by the front of his robes. The very act of laying hands upon a High Priest caused gasps of surprise from the others. It took the High Priest no time at all to realize that Saulcram was acting on his own. The others had wanted to draw a hard line, but it was Saulcram who was becoming excessively physical.

''We do not believe you!'' Saulcram fairly shouted in his face. ''We do not believe you, and we do not believe *in* you! Xant is not coming! Xant is never going to come, and even if he does, then he can trot right back to the great unknown because we have no use for him! You say Calhoun is merely a man. Fine, then, if that is what it takes to survive on our world! I would sooner admire, work with, and worship a living, breathing man that I can see rather than some mysterious unknown deity who will likely never show up in this or any other lifetime!''

''You are wrong,'' the High Priest shouted back, and he pulled away from Saulcram. ''And you are dangerously close to being not only a dead man yourself, but the executioner of your entire race.''

''Again come the threats!'' said Saulcram angrily. ''We are tired of your threats, High Priest! And we are tired of you! You threaten us with the extinction of our entire race if we should so much as lift a hand against you. You have traded upon the reputation of the dreaded Redeemers. But perhaps that reputation is not so deserved! Perhaps we should not be afraid of you!''

''If you are not, then that will be your error. And a most costly error it—''

Saulcram's fist lashed out and slammed the High Priest in the face. The force of the blow took him completely off his feet, knocking the startled High Priest to his back. He lay there, momentarily stunned, reaching up to feel the blood beginning to fountain from his nose. With his free hand he was still clutching his staff. "You . . . idiot!" he yelled. "You have no idea what you've done! No idea at all! Our persons are sacrosanct! They—"

Another of the Alphans stepped forward, eager for a piece of the retribution that was being dealt out, and kicked the High Priest squarely in the stomach. The High Priest moaned, and a gurgle barely recognizable as something made by a living being, rattled around in his throat. With boiling fury, the High Priest lashed out with his staff, trying to trip up his assailants, but they were too nimble. Saulcram leaped over the hooked end of the staff, then slammed down on it with both feet, immobilizing it. The High Priest pulled on it desperately, and he muttered an imprecation as best he could, considering that he could barely form a coherent sentence.

Saulcram yanked the staff away, gripped the shaft firmly, and then swung it up and over his head. The High Priest looked up, saw what was about to happen, and managed to shake his head and mouth the word, "Sacrosanct," just before the hooked end of the staff slammed down on him, splitting his skull. His body trembled, shuddered, and continued to twitch for a moment or two more before ceasing.

His assailants stood there for a moment, barely able to believe what they had done. The first moments of nervousness crossed their faces then, for this was not exactly what they had planned. Threats, yes, they had planned threats. They had even anticipated having to use force in order to get the High Priest to leave.

But the violence . . . the violence had simply seemed to arise from nowhere.

"It was necessary," Saulcram said sharply, as if to bolster the failing confidence of his companions.

"But . . . but the person of the High Priest is sacrosanct . . ."

"Shut up!" Saulcram shouted. "That's their rhetoric you're spouting! The threats they use to keep us in line! Now that the threats have failed, we have to prepare for the inevitable attack, the attempted retribution. We have to muster our forces! We must steel ourselves for battle! We must win back our freedom from the aggressors! We must follow the way of—"

Saulcram suddenly found it very difficult to speak. His tongue felt swollen, his throat suddenly quite dry. He wanted to lick his lips and discovered that his jaw was unable to move. He looked to the others, and his eyes widened in horror as he saw that the man nearest him seemed to be rotting from the inside out. His skin was turning a dark, dusky black and sliding away from his face, his eyes bugging out, the blood vessels within bursting and trickling down his face.

Then Saulcram went blind and he realized with a fading desperation that the exact same thing was happening to him. He clutched at his throat, trying to get air to pass through, fighting desperately for life even when he knew that it was already hopeless, that he was already dead. He fell to the ground, clutching at his mouth, trying to physically pry the jaws open so that he could get some air down his throat. He gave it all the power that his fading strength had, and finally he succeeded in a manner of speaking: His entire jaw snapped off, clattering to the floor and shattering into powdery remains.

The four of them writhed on the floor and died without uttering a single sound except for a few stray gurgles that escaped their lips, or whatever was left of their lips.

So perished the People's Association for Peace, resting in not-so-peaceful a state in the Central Hall of Worship. They were not destined to be alone in their hideous deaths for very long.

The disease that spread from the body of the High Priest, triggered to life by his death, was an airborne virus that made twentieth-century Earth plagues such as the *Ebola* virus look like the chicken pox. It spread through the ventilation ducts of the Hall itself, bringing swift and violent death to all inside within several minutes. None of them had the slightest comprehension of what was happening to them. They had been going about their lives, making preparations for the evening meal, intending to cater to the needs of the High Priest. Ultimately, in a manner of speaking, they accomplished that end, for the High Priest needed them to die in order to prove a point. And so they died, just as rapidly, hideously and uncomprehendingly as the four individuals who had murdered the High Priest minutes before.

Having done its work there, the virus swept out onto the four winds across the surface of Alpha Carinae. No city, no town, no village or hamlet was spared. The virus knew no innocent blood. The very old collapsed into gasping heaps next to the very young. All over Alpha Carinae, from one pole to the other, across the face of the globe, the disease marched, more unstoppable than any army, more merciless, more pitiless. Frantic doctors fought to discover a cure, but there was no cure. The Redeemers had seen to that. They had had, after all, plenty of time to perfect it. Anything that any Alphan doctor might be able to discover or come up with had already been anticipated and attended to.

Within twenty-four hours, half the populace of Alpha Carinae had the disease. It slowed down briefly, then renewed its march across the planet, getting into the water, poisoning the air. There was no escape, no hope, no prayer, even though there were prayers in abundance. The Alphans prayed to the Redeemers for forgiveness, they prayed to Calhoun for salvation, they prayed to whatever gods, goddesses, and holy figures they could think of. And their response was nothing but the crashing silence of entities or deities who were unable or unwilling to help.

The Alphans died abandoned, they died unloved, and ultimately, they just died. Sixty-one hours after the High Priest had fallen to the ground, bleeding and dying, the last of the Alphans hit the floor. The last Alphan was precisely four years old, that very day, and she gurgled out the name of her mother by way of her last words. Her mother, who was lying in a crumbled heap on the floor not ten yards away.

And then the last living being on Alpha Carinae twitched ever so slightly, and stopped moving.

For a long, long while, not a sound was made on the entire planet.

Then a shadow was cast over it. A shadow as if the great spirit of death was hovering over the world, examining it carefully to see precisely what had been wrought.

The shadow came from a great ship, a ship that descended through the atmosphere of Alpha Carinae and did a slow fly-by over selected portions of the planet. The inhabitants of the vessel had been instantly aware of the crisis that had faced the doomed world, but had been forced to allow the disease to do the job for which it had been so thoroughly and mercilessly designed. Having thoroughly obliterated all life on Alpha Carinae, the virus had lingered another twenty-four hours in the air, land, and water, and then, as it had been created to do, the virus simply self-destructed. In no time at all, the surface of Alpha Carinae was perfectly habitable, if one did not mind stepping over all the corpses. Although, on the other hand, there wasn't that much left of them. The virus was extremely thorough in its rotting properties.

The great ship cruised over the surface, inspecting the damage that had been done, the wrath that had been inflicted upon the helpless inhabitants. Finally it hovered over the Central Hall of Worship before landing directly in front of it. In landing, the ship crushed the remains of at least fifty bodies, but this was of no consequence to the inhabitants of the mighty vessel.

A door irised open and the Overlord of the Redeemers emerged.

He looked neither left nor right, for the desiccated remains of an unredeemable race were of no interest to him whatsoever. Instead he entered the Central Hall, barely bothering to afford a glance at the fallen bodies except to step over any that happened to be in his way. Very quickly he found the room where the body of the High Priest lay.

The Overlord had not felt particularly close to this particular priest. He had not been one of those whom the Overlord had trained himself. Nonetheless, there were certain obligations upon the Overlord that came not as a result of personal closeness, but from his position and a sense of loyalty to his fellow Redeemers.

He stood over the fallen priest and mourned his passing. The Overlord's personal escort did likewise, their heads bowed and their lips murmuring invocations to Xant that the fallen priest would walk with him in the light.

Then the Overlord picked up the fallen staff and nodded approvingly to see that the recording device within had been functioning. He looked distastefully at the blood on it, and one of his entourage ripped off a piece of clothing from the body of Saulcram and used it to clean off the staff as best he could. Some of the blood was dried on and there was nothing he could do about it, but the Overlord accepted the staff as it was.

He returned to the ship without a word, removed the recording chip, and plugged it into the ship's computer. Immediately the voice of the fallen High Priest filled the control room, and the discussion that had filled his last moments. The Overlord listened dispassionately, no flicker of emotion whatsoever registering on his face throughout the entire recording. When it was done, he played it once more, as if wanting to be sure that no mistake was made.

Then he turned to his fellow Redeemers and said simply, "I want Calhoun and the *Excalibur.*"

And the Redeemers immediately set about to put the order into action.

14

Soleta was becoming extremely worried.

She paced across the bridge in an extremely un-Vulcan like fashion and then said, "Time, Mister McHenry?"

"Two minutes later than the last time you asked, sir," McHenry replied, turning in his chair. "I thought you Vulcans had an internal clock or something."

"Perhaps mine needs adjusting," said Soleta. "The away team is overdue to check in."

"Yes, it is," affirmed Lefler. "Fifteen minutes."

"They've got two heavily armed guards with them, and Kebron, who's the equivalent of five more guards," McHenry said confidently. "What can happen to them with him along?"

"I know you intended that as a rhetorical question, Mark, but I'm getting the distinct feeling that I've no desire to learn the answer," replied Soleta. "Lefler, try to raise them."

"Aye, sir," said Lefler, and she immediately set about doing so.

Soleta stared at the planet as it turned below them. It seemed to calm, so peaceful. And yet there was so much wrong down there, so much that had happened. The captain, missing, perhaps dead, and now the away team having lost touch with the *Excalibur*. She did not like how this was shaping up at all.

"Lieutenant," Lefler said, trying to keep the apprehension out of her voice, "I'm not getting a response from them. I can't raise Shelby, Selar, or Kebron."

"Can you get a lock on them at all?"

Lefler quickly checked, sending a locate beam through to their communicator badges. "There's . . ." She shook her head in frustration. "There's some sort of heavy interference. I'm not sure what's causing it. It is the same sort of interference that is impeding our sensor sweep for the captain."

"Atmospheric disturbance?"

"Negative. Seems man-made. Artificial. It's blocking my primary sweep."

"Punch through it, Lefler. I want them out of there."

"Out of there, sir?" Robin looked at her in surprise. "Without a distress call or an order from the Commander?"

"They're overdue," Soleta reminded her. "Weighing the safety of the away team against the chance that Commander Shelby might yell at me, I'll risk the latter. Now get me the away team."

"Working on it, sir," said Lefler. For minutes she adjusted the frequency of the search probe, trying to pull up a contact with the away team, and finally she called out, "Got four of the five, sir! Managed to crack through whatever the local interference is, at least for the moment!"

"Send it through to the transporter room. Bridge to transporter room, four to beam up, now!" called Soleta.

"Starting to lose them!" Lefler called.

"Transporter room, get on it!" Soleta said urgently.

"Beaming them up now, sir!" came Watson's voice. "Having trouble reintegrating the signal, but I think I've got them cl—"

There was a pause, and Soleta fancied that she felt her blood chill ever so slightly. "Transporter room, report!" she ordered. "Who have you got? Are they okay?"

"Bridge, transporter room!" Watson cried out, and there was no mistaking the alarm in her voice. "Medical emergency! Sickbay already summoned! You better get down here! They—oh, God!"

"On my way!" Soleta called out, stopping only long enough to say, "McHenry, you have the conn!" before dashing into the turbolift.

McHenry slowly turned and looked at Lefler with clear concern. "I don't know which is more frightening," he said slowly. "That something's happened to Selar and Shelby . . . or that I have the conn."

"Shut up, Mark," said Robin with no trace of amusement. McHenry, wisely, said nothing.

* * *

Soleta barreled through the corridors of the *Excalibur* and arrived just as the team from sickbay was hauling the remains of the away team out of the transporter room. It took all of her carefully learned stoicism not to turn away in horror.

Shelby and Selar looked like hell. Half of Shelby's uniform was torn away, and there were burns all over her, huge patches of charred skin on her upper body. Her head lolled to one side; she barely appeared to be breathing. Selar had not fared much better. She appeared to have been lashed by some sort of tendril, tearing away her clothing and skin in vicious strips. The tip of her right ear had been torn off, and there was blood all over the side of her face.

Hecht was dead. Soleta could tell just from looking at him. His body lay on the rolling cart, twisted at an impossible angle. As for Scannell, physically he appeared untouched. But his mind was gone. His eyes stared blankly, although whether it was into the air or into himself, Soleta could not be sure. His back was arched, and he was babbling inarticulately, shaking his head every so often as if trying to ward off something that only he could see.

Shelby seemed to be barely conscious, and Soleta ran along side the antigrav gurney as it was rushed toward sickbay. "Commander," she said urgently, "can you speak?"

"Lieutenant," Doctor Maxwell began, trying to shoo her away even as he was putting a stasis field in place, while running, in order to stabilize Shelby's condition. "Now is not the time—"

"Commander, what happened?" demanded Soleta, ignoring Maxwell completely. "Did you find the captain? Where is Kebron? What happened down there?"

Shelby's mouth moved, but no words came out. Then, with great effort, she formed a word . . . one word:

"Borg," she managed to say.

Then she lapsed into unconsciousness, leaving a stunned Soleta in the corridor as the gurneys were sent into sickbay.

Burgoyne looked up from hir work in engineering to see the ashen face of Ensign Ronni Beth. "I take it that further analysis of the energy drain—" Burgoyne started to say, but then s/he saw the look on Beth's face. "What's wrong?" s/he demanded.

"Did you hear?"

"About the captain? Yes." Burgoyne shook hir head. "I don't believe it for a moment. I know this captain. It's going to take more than—"

''Not him. He's still missing,'' Beth said quickly, ''but I mean, about the away team. The one that was looking for him.''

Slowly Burgoyne got to hir feet. ''What happened?'' s/he said slowly.

''I cannot say that I am surprised,'' Killick was saying.

He was speaking via the screen to Soleta, who was seated in the unaccustomed place of the command chair, her fingers steepled. Si Cwan was standing just behind her. ''Why, may I ask, are you unsurprised?'' inquired Soleta.

''From the coordinates you've given me, it is my estimation that your away team had trespassed into Ontear's Realm.''

''Excuse me?'' said Soleta, leaning forward in polite confusion. ''Ontear's Realm?''

''It is a sacred land,'' Killick informed her. ''It was there that Ontear dwelt. It is believed by many that he dwells there still.''

''Ontear,'' Si Cwan now spoke up. ''That would be the philosopher and seer who died five hundred years ago.''

''Ontear did not die,'' Killick said, sounding just slightly defensive. ''He was taken away to join the gods, as anyone who has read the books of—''

''Fine, then,'' Si Cwan saw absolutely no point in disputing it. ''Either way, we're agreed that it's not terribly likely he would still be around.''

''Do not underestimate the power of Ontear, or the spirit of Ontear''—and Killick's voice dropped to a level that was tinged with menace—''or the vengeance of Ontear.''

''Nor should we underestimate your obsession with saying the name 'Ontear,' '' commented Soleta. ''Are you claiming, Killick, that our away team fell victim to some sort of curse?''

''I would not have put it quite that way, but it is an acceptable summation.''

''It is not acceptable to me, sir,'' replied Soleta. ''It is, in fact, illogical. I have an away team with members that are variously injured, dead, and missing. Their intention was to find the commanding officer of this vessel—''

''If their trail led them truly, Lieutenant,'' Killick informed her, ''and your captain is within Ontear's Realm, then you will not be bringing him back. The Realm of Ontear was consecrated after the death of his greatest acolyte, Suti, and forbidden to all Zondarians. Forbidden, in fact, to all who live.''

"Even the Savior?" asked Soleta drily.

Slowly, Killick nodded. "Even to one such as He. If He is there, then He is already dead. As for you, Lieutenant, I would consider myself fortunate if I were you."

"And why is that?"

"The fact that you got any of your people back alive. That, in and of itself, is nothing short of miraculous. You should thank the spirit of the Savior for your good fortune."

"I will be certain to keep that in mind," Soleta said with more sarcasm than Si Cwan would have supposed a Vulcan was capable of.

Killick's image blinked out, and all eyes turned to Soleta.

"Now what?" said Si Cwan.

And Soleta—Soleta, who had once resigned from Starfleet when she discovered her Vulcan/Romulan breeding; Soleta, who had until relatively recently been content teaching science courses at Starfleet Academy; Soleta, who, truth to tell, would have been perfectly content never to set foot on a starship again in her life, much less suddenly find herself in a position of command upon one—said the most difficult four words that she had ever uttered in her life.

"I am not sure," she replied.

Burgoyne strode into sickbay like a force of nature. Several medtechs tried to stop hir, but were utterly unsuccessful. Burgoyne pushed them aside, with strength in hir wiry frame that surprised anyone endeavoring to get in hir way. S/he cast a quick, pained glance in the direction of Shelby. S/he had served with Shelby before, thought her a fine officer and a good person, not to mention possessing one seriously fine body from this angle at least. (the latter comment, for reasons of discretion, never having passed through Burgy's lips). But the majority of hir attention was focused on Selar, who lay nearby, eyes closed and breathing shallowly but steadily.

Dr. Maxwell stood near her, checking readings, when Burgoyne walked up. Maxwell glanced up at hir and said, "I would appreciate it if you chose to visit at a later hour."

Burgoyne fixed Maxwell with a dark stare. "Doctor, out of my way."

Maxwell drew himself up, squaring off against Burgoyne. "There is no need, Chief, to be rude."

With a flash of hir canines, Burgoyne said, "That, Doctor, depends entirely upon you."

Maxwell was prepared to say something further, but wisely decided that it would do him little-to-no good, and possibly even some serious harm. With one more quick glance at the readings, Maxwell walked away, allowing Burgoyne some time with Selar.

Burgoyne leaned over her, running hir long, tapered fingers over Selar's battered face. S/he saw a patch of Selar's head where the hair had been burned away. What could possibly have happened to her? What could have done this to her? Slowly Burgoyne felt a deep, burning anger building within hir chest.

"They will pay," Burgoyne whispered to her. "I swear to the gods, whoever did this will pay."

Suddenly Selar's eyes snapped open. She didn't seem focused on anything, her gaze instead darting around as if looking for something.

"Selar!" Burgoyne said in a harsh, amazed whisper, and then s/he called, "She opened her eyes! She—"

Burgoyne's hand was on Selar's temple, and then Selar's eyes snapped into focus on Burgoyne's. Her hand, down at her side, wrapped around Burgoyne's free hand, snapping on to it and grasping it like an infant reflexively holding on to anything thrust in its palm.

Burgoyne gasped as sickbay fell away from hir, and suddenly there was sand and dirt beneath hir feet, hot air burning in hir lungs, and a roar from all around, roaring in hir ears, in hir mind. S/he became aware of the fact that s/he was no longer perceiving things solely through hir own mind, but s/he was having trouble distinguishing hir own state of mind.

And the roaring . . . no, it was howling. Like a massive wind rushing, except the wind was alive somehow. It burned into hir, and s/he felt something angry and ancient flailing at hir, trying to beat hir away.

And Burgoyne would not be intimidated. Instead s/he snarled back, hir canines fully exposed, ready to rend and tear, and s/he howled defiance and swore an oath of bloody vengeance. S/he saw caves and cliffs, and the aged evil bellowed a challenge that Burgoyne eagerly accepted.

And Burgoyne knew at that point, beyond any question that s/he was suddenly in a war. A war that had become very personal.

Then something seemed to insinuate itself into Burgoyne's mind, wrap itself around hir, and hir first instinct was to fight it. But then s/he realized that it was Selar. Selar in a way that s/he had never seen her. Selar, desirous, eager, hungry, wanting and striving and trying to reach out from the depths of her injuries, driven by an instinct for self-preservation and by something else as well. Something that Burgoyne didn't quite understand, but it was a need, a deep, sexual hunger consuming both Burgoyne and Selar as well. Heat seemed to pound through Burgoyne. And just like that, s/he knew Selar, knew her in and out, felt a connection as deep and as full as anything that Burgoyne had ever felt and would ever feel. Burgoyne cried out, and then the creature roared in hir head once more, splitting Burgoyne and Selar from one another. Burgoyne reached out, hearing Selar howling away in the grip of her memories of what she had faced, and then Burgoyne hit the floor.

As opposed to the subjectivity of what s/he had just seen, the floor was all too real. Burgoyne sat there, feeling rather foolish, hir head swirling even as a couple of medtechs helped hir to hir feet. Maxwell, to his credit, had put aside whatever bruised feelings he might have sustained from his high-handed treatment by Burgoyne before, saying, ''Chief, are you okay?''

''Fine,'' Burgoyne said in a voice that was much huskier than s/he was accustomed to. ''I'm . . . I'm fine. How long was I out?''

''Only a second. From the moment you said her eyes were open to when you hit the floor, it couldn't have been more than a second.'' Maxwell glanced over at Selar, checking her readings. ''Her eyes are closed again.''

''It's okay,'' Burgoyne said, sounding stunned for a moment. Then hir full concentration returned, with an intensity like a beacon. ''It's okay. I . . . know what I need to know.'' S/he headed for the door.

''Chief,'' said Maxwell. ''Did she make some sort of . . . contact with you? A meld or . . . ?''

''She did something, all right,'' Burgoyne affirmed.

''What did you see?''

''Enough,'' Burgoyne said. ''More than, in fact.'' And s/he headed out the door and down the corridor.

Soleta was in the main transporter room, speaking with Watson and endeavoring to refine the search pattern for the captain when Burgoyne entered the transporter room and strode over to the platform. Soleta and Watson both watched hir step onto the platform, whirl to face Watson, and say, ''Wherever you brought them up from—beam me down there.''

Watson and Soleta exchanged looks, and then with a shrug Watson reached for the controls.

''Belay that order, Ensign,'' Soleta said quietly.

Burgoyne's dark eyes narrowed and sized up Soleta like a hawk considering a rabbit. "Ensign," s/he said, although s/he never took hir eyes off Soleta, "carry out my order. Energize."

"Watson," Soleta told her, "I believe it's time for your break."

"It is?" asked Polly Watson, and then when she saw Soleta's expression, she quickly said, "You know, you're right. What was I thinking?" and she vacated the transporter room as quickly as she could.

"Would you mind telling me what you think you're doing?" Burgoyne said to Soleta, sounding very dangerous. "In case it's slipped your notice, I outrank you. What you've just done is insubordination."

"That's one interpretation," replied Soleta evenly. "On the other hand, Commander Shelby left me in authority. She trusted me to attend to the welfare of the entire crew complement, and that would include you."

"Soleta, we don't know each other all that well," Burgoyne said with very forced patience. S/he descended from the transporter platform and continued, "When I take it into my head to do something, I do it. This has become a *Gi'jan* to me. A quest. Something of a personal nature."

"Personal considerations have no place in deciding who is and is not to be sent into a hazardous situation," Soleta replied evenly.

"Perhaps not to you," Burgoyne shot back, "but it does to me. Now, Lieutenant"—and s/he moved briskly to the control board—"I am programming my destination. I am setting it to a timer so that I can simply walk over there, step onto the platform, and beam down. And last, I am personally encoding it, on my authority, to my own private password override, so that nothing you can say or do can prevent the beams from functioning. I believe that covers all the bases, Lieutenant, unless you intend, for some reason, to get in my way."

"That," replied Soleta, "would not be logical."

"Very wise," said Burgoyne, completing the last of the adjustments to the controls. S/he nodded in quick approval of hir work, and headed back toward the platform, walking past Soleta as s/he did so.

S/he never even felt the feather-light touch of Soleta's fingers on hir shoulder. All s/he knew was that suddenly the world was going dark and the floor was approaching hir at a depressingly rapid speed.

When s/he came to some minutes later, Soleta was standing over hir, her arms folded. ''In case you wish to keep a tally,'' Soleta informed her, ''that could be construed as assaulting a superior officer.''

''What did you do?'' asked Burgoyne. S/he sat up, hir head spinning ever so slightly.

''The Vulcan nerve pinch. I momentarily stopped the flow of blood to your brain, causing unconsciousness.''

''Heh.'' Burgoyne actually allowed a moment of self-mocking amusement, which was a fairly sporting attitude for hir to take, all things considered. ''There are some people around here who would think that kicking me in the buttocks would accomplish that.''

''That would be an acceptable fall-back technique.'' She cocked her head slightly. ''You do not seem dismayed that I rendered you insensate.''

''You got me fair and square. I can appreciate that. I don't have to be thrilled by it, mind you, but I can appreciate it.'' S/he rubbed the base of hir neck regretfully. ''Where did you grab me? Here and here?'' S/he indicated two spots on hir neck.

''Yes,'' Soleta said. ''Although non-Vulcans generally do not master the technique. Some study for years and still fail.''

''Well, I can be a fast learner.'' Then s/he paused and said, ''Look, Soleta, when I said it was personal, that . . . that doesn't even begin to cover it. Selar and I, we have some sort of . . . of bond.''

''Bond?'' Soleta said skeptically.

''I don't know how it happened. She came to in sickbay, and we, we . . . linked somehow. I can't begin to describe it. I knew what she knew, what she experienced. I felt a part of her. I—'' S/he hesitated, and then shrugged. ''I also feel an overwhelming need to have sex with her. Understand, a high sex drive is certainly nothing new for me, but this . . . this is something I can't even begin to describe.''

Burgoyne didn't notice the change in Soleta's expression. Clearly somehow Selar had established a rapport with Burgoyne, had zeroed in on hir as a mate. She might very well not have been in her right mind when she did it, lying on a med table in sickbay and reaching out for the first sympathetic mind that was in proximity. Or there might be something deeper there; Soleta had no way to be sure. Either way, Burgoyne's personal stake in the matter had definitely increased.

''I want to go down there, Soleta,'' Burgoyne said. ''I need to. It's a *Gi'jan,* as I told you. I need to find the captain, and find whoever it was that hurt Selar. They must pay. There must be justice for the crime.'' S/he shrugged. ''If nothing else, think of it as a means of utilizing all the energy I've got running through me right now. Soleta, I'm going to get down there. With or without your help, I'm going to do it. We both know it, unless you intend to try and stick the chief engineer in the brig.''

''I'd rather not,'' Soleta admitted.

''So it would be simpler for all concerned if you would just cooperate.''

''A valid point. However, Burgoyne, you must admit that it is a daunting task you are setting up for yourself. An entire, experienced away team is damaged, dead, or missing.''

''So you see what happens when you send a large number of people in. Send in one person who can take care of hirself, however—a smaller target, as it were—and we might stand a better chance. Besides, I have an advantage,'' s/he said. ''I have a link, a sense of what they faced. I'll be ready for it.''

''Was it the Borg?'' asked Soleta.

Burgoyne shook hir head. ''Not that I saw. Although from what I glimpsed—and I can't even begin to describe it—it may very well have been worse.''

''This is not encouraging my cooperation.''

''Soleta . . .'' Burgoyne tried to find the words, and then simply said, ''I've got to do this. Do you understand? I have got to do this. Give me twenty-four hours—''

''Twelve,'' Soleta counter-offered. ''And you will have to bring someone with you. I will not have you down there alone.''

''Let me guess: You.''

Burgoyne was quite surprised when Soleta shook her head. ''I am needed here,'' she replied, ''to endeavor to coordinate the sensor search for Captain Calhoun. Besides, what you need is someone from the security force.''

''I'm going to be moving pretty quickly,'' said Burgoyne. ''You have to understand, Soleta, there are various aspects to me that you never see in day-to-day life here on the *Excalibur.*''

''That may very well be, but as my ability to render you unconscious indicates, you are in need of someone to watch your back. Furthermore, I am quite aware of your more . . . feral attributes,'' Soleta informed hir. ''I have someone in mind who I believe would be capable of accompanying you on this quixotic quest of yours. Someone who will be able to 'keep up with you.' ''

''Who?'' And then Burgoyne realized even before Soleta said it. ''You can't mean—''

"Ensign Janos."

"Soleta, be reasonable," Burgoyne started to say.

"I am being most reasonable. Janos is ideally suited."

"Janos makes me nervous," protested Burgoyne. "He makes everybody nervous!"

"So do you," shot back Soleta.

"That's not exactly fair," Burgoyne said, although s/he did allow a small smile. "Janos works the graveyard shift by popular demand. He prefers it that way and so does most of the crew."

"Granted," agreed Soleta. "But the bottom line is that he's a formidable security guard, incredibly strong, remarkably intelligent. If you want someone to be watching out for you, Janos is your—"

"I hope you weren't going to say 'man.' "

"You, of all people, Chief Engineer, should not find amusement when a crewmember eludes easy categorization."

"All right, all right, point taken."

"Good. Then we have an agreement. Twelve hours, with Ensign Janos as your back-up."

"You drive a hard bargain, Lieutenant," Burgoyne told her.

Soleta tapped her commbadge. "Transporter room to Ensign Janos." They waited, and when no response was forthcoming, Soleta tried again. Still no answer. "I was afraid of this," Soleta admitted. "He's off shift, so he's likely asleep. He is sometimes difficult to awaken."

"All right. I'll do it." S/he shook hir head as s/he walked out of the transporter room.

The door slid shut behind hir, and Soleta said calmly, "I'll be certain to change my door lock code."

Burgoyne stood outside Ensign Janos' quarters and rang the chime once more. There was no reply from within. Not wanting to waste any more time, Burgoyne tapped in the security override code that was known only to hirself and a handful of other ranking officers. The door beeped in acknowledgment and slid open.

Burgoyne stepped into darkness, hir eyes adjusting with preternatural speed. She was able to pick out a bulky body hanging upside down in a corner of the room. "Janos," s/he hissed. "Ensign Janos . . ."

Suddenly the bulk was gone. S/he tried to refocus and then, right in hir face, something large and bulky roared at hir with deafening volume. The breath was not especially pleasant either. Even with hir excellent night vision, s/he sensed rather than saw the behemoth raging in front of her.

"Ensign, it's Chief Engineer Burgoyne! Burgoyne one-seventy-two!" s/he said loudly. "You weren't answering the comm! You're needed for a special assignment!"

The mass in front of hir paused, and s/he heard the deep rasping slowly fade, to be replaced by normal, if heavy, breathing. "Special assignment?" came the thick-voiced reply.

"That's right. The captain's disappeared, the away team was slaughtered, Lieutenant Kebron is missing, and you and I are going down alone."

"Why?"

"Why? To show everyone else how it's done, that's why."

There was a pause. "Lights to half," said Ensign Janos. The lights in the cabin obediently came to half illumination.

Burgoyne immediately saw that Janos was unclothed, which was not particularly unusual for him. He preferred a state of undress, considering it more natural, although of course he did follow Starfleet constraints and wear a uniform when he was on-duty. Even so, no one would have found it particularly disconcerting since Ensign Janos was covered, head to toe, with thick white fur.

Janos, as did others of his species, also had a general ape-like appearance, and was likely the only other individual on the ship, aside from Burgoyne, to sport fangs. However, that was where his resemblance to others of his kind ended, something that became immediately clear the moment he opened his mouth.

"Sounds brilliant," Janos said. "A real rip-snorter of an escapade. I appreciate your thinking of me for it."

Wasn't my idea, thought Burgoyne, but rather than admit that, s/he said, "Not a problem."

"Hope I didn't startle you overmuch. I have that sort of killer-instinct thing on when I'm slumbering. Anyone who startles me, well, you get the idea."

"Oh, definitely. How long will it take you to get ready?"

"Half a mo'. Just need to pull on a clean pair of woollies and then we're off to the races!" Ensign Janos, the mugato security guard, didn't grin. His face wasn't built in a manner that allowed him to. But he did seem exceedingly chipper about it. "You can wait here if you wish, Chief. Not as if I have anything to hide, and besides, I hear you're somewhat the frisky one when it comes to matters of sexual orientation, eh? Watching a fellow like me get dressed shouldn't be too much of a shocker for you, I'd surmise."

Burgoyne considered it for a moment, and then said, "I think I'll wait outside, if it's all the same to you."

"As you wish. Pass up the thrill of a lifetime, if that's your pleasure."

Burgoyne stepped into the hallway, waited until the door shut behind hir, and then muttered, "Soleta, I'll get you for this. I'm not certain how or where, but I will get you for this. And Captain, if you're alive, I certainly hope you appreciate this."

15

Across the beleaguered world of Zondar, arguments spilled over into feuds. Skirmishes became outright battles. Accusations ricocheted, counteraccusations flew. Mourning took hold of the entire populace as they came to feel that a golden age of growth, a time of peace and prosperity, had been snatched away from them. It seemed to many that night and day became filled with nothing but ululations of grief, cries that could be heard from one side of Zondar to the other.

Mackenzie Calhoun was deaf to all of them.

He lay inside the cave, unable to move, barely even able to think. Slowly he felt his strength starting to return, but when he tried to move his arms and legs, nothing seemed interested in functioning. It took a massive amount of effort just to be able to open his eyes, and when he did, the entirety of his reward was darkness. Slowly he started to be able to make out things, except all he was making out was cave walls. There was no chill in the cave, however; instead he felt a distant warmth, leading him to believe that he was in a fairly arrid area.

He tried to call out, but his mouth was dry and raspy, his throat not much better. He cleared his throat, took another stab at it, and this time managed to get out, "Hello?"

He didn't get an immediate response, and he wasn't entirely certain if that was a good thing or not. He felt the bonds at his wrists and ankles, tested his strength against them, and found that they were more than capable of standing up to his best efforts. That didn't stop him from trying to pull his wrists clear, but after several minutes that only resulted in severe abrasions, he stopped to reconsider the matter.

He tried to remember how he had arrived at his present situation, but his memory was hazy at best. He recalled the banquet, and the vague sense of danger. He remembered retiring to his room. Beyond that—nothing. He looked down at his chest and noticed that his communicator was gone. Well, whoever had made off with him was thorough, he would certainly give him that.

Slowly he surveyed his surroundings. Definitely a simple cave, fairly unremarkable. Now if he could just figure out what in hell he was doing there. Who could possibly have done this to him, and for what possible reason?

Then something flickered over near the wall. He looked up at it, squinting, trying to make it out.

It was some sort of light emission, that much he could see. And it appeared to be taking some sort of form, coalescing into . . .

A Zondarian.

But it was not one that Calhoun had seen before. He was hairless, with the same glistening leathery skin that the rest of the people shared, but he seemed older somehow.

Calhoun sat up, propping himself up on one elbow, and said to the image, "Who are you?"

He wasn't entirely certain if he expected an answer, but was rather startled to receive one, although it wasn't much of one: "I know who you are," replied the image. It had only partly materialized; Calhoun could still clearly see the cave wall behind him.

"Oh?" was all Calhoun replied. It wasn't the most useful of responses; after all, Calhoun knew perfectly well who he himself was.

"I watched you," said the new arrival. "I watched you arrive. I watched you hailed as the Savior. That is what I do, much of the time. I watch. Watch and record."

"Would you be kind enough to tell someone where I am?"

"They will know," replied the image cryptically. "I have already seen that. That is what I do, you see. I notice certain moments, and then track them to see how they develop. I have already seen what will happen to you. Now, for curiosity's sake, I am studying to see how you got to that point."

"I'm flattered I'm of such interest to you." He felt his arm becoming numb and shifted his position. "Since you seem to be so cognizant of what's to come, would you mind telling me if I get out of here?"

"You will be saved by neither man nor woman," replied the image, and then slowly it began to fade out.

"I appreciate the encouraging words!" Calhoun called out. "Get back here!"

But the image was gone.

Insanely, Calhoun sensed that the floor was warm directly beneath where the image had been, as if it had been generating body heat. But that was impossible. It had been nothing more than a hologram . . .

For, for all Calhoun knew, it had been a complete delusion. Perhaps he was simply losing his mind. Now there was a cheery thought. The image had vanished and he'd been left with more questions than answers.

And then it appeared that his questions were going to be answered in very short order, because he heard a soft footfall approaching him. Rather than immediately tip off the fact that he was conscious, Calhoun laid his head down and narrowed his eyes to slits so that he could still see. He slowed his breathing down as best he could to try and simulate an unconscious state.

He saw someone approaching him, and this, in contrast to his previous visitor, was very much a flesh-and-blood Zondarian. His captor stopped several feet away from him and said, "Feigning unconsciousness is rather pointless. I heard you talking to yourself before, so I know you are awake."

Slowly Calhoun lifted his head. "Ramed, if I'm not mistaken."

"I am honored that you remember me, oh Great One," Ramed said with a slight inclination of his head. "You have, after all, met a great many of us. It is flattering to know you can keep track of who is who."

Ramed's comment about "talking to himself" had immediately struck Calhoun as odd. Ramed had apparently been oblivious to Calhoun's visitor from moments before. Calhoun decided to keep that information to himself. He wasn't sure if that was going to be of any use, but when one is in a hostile situation, any knowledge one possesses that is not shared by one's opponent is inherently some sort of advantage, even if the details of that advantage are not readily apparent. "So, what did you do to me?" asked Calhoun. "To get me here. To knock me out?"

"A simple drug in your food."

"But I ate and drank the same as everyone else. You couldn't have singled mine out."

"I did not have to. I put it into everyone's drink. However, a drug that can reduce your bodily functions to simulate death can also be completely harmless to Zondarians.''

So much for my vaunted sixth sense, Calhoun mused. He rationalized to himself that perhaps he hadn't realized specifically where the danger was coming from because, to so many people in the room, it presented no danger at all. Or, more likely, he just wasn't perfect. That was something he definitely hated to admit.

''And then I simply brought you here after your body was taken to the sacred place of preparation. I am somewhat stronger than I may appear to you, oh Great One. I admit, you did become a bit heavy the last mile or so, but it was nothing I could not handle. I have, after all, the strength of my convictions.''

''Would you mind telling me what the hell we're doing here? I take it that this isn't something being sanctioned by your peers.''

Ramed shook his head. ''No. No, not at all. At the moment, in fact, there is great consternation among my people. You made quite the impression upon them in a fairly short time. Although admittedly, you did have help. We told the people of your coming, we told them that you were the fulfillment of prophecy. Naturally they could not help but love you. See you as a symbol of something truly great.''

''And you, for some reason, feel the need to undo all that?''

Slowly, Ramed sank down to the ground near him, as if he were commiserating somehow. ''I have no choice,'' he said simply. ''My part in these matters is as predestined as your arrival was. As your death is.''

''You are so certain, then, that I am going to die.''

From the folds of his clothes, Ramed pulled out a wooden handle. He pushed on it and a long and sharpened point snapped out. ''Neither man nor woman will save you,'' Ramed said.

The words immediately struck a cord within Calhoun. It had been the exact words of his ghostly visitor from earlier. But Ramed had made quite clear that he had not heard the exchange; unless, for some reason, Ramed was endeavoring to completely confuse him. But that didn't seem likely. Ramed might be deluded, even demented, and certainly bent on Calhoun's destruction, but remarkably subtle he most definitely was not.

They stared at each other for a time. Then Ramed said, ''Are you not going to beg for your life?''

''Am I supposed to?'' Calhoun asked sarcastically. ''You seem to be rather cognizant of what's to come. You tell me.''

''I do not claim to know *every* detail,'' Ramed replied.

"Ah. Well, thank you for clearing that up." Calhoun's eyes narrowed. He struggled to bring himself up to a fully sitting position and managed by dint of pulling his back up against the wall. "Why do you think I'm going to beg for my life?"

"Well, that is a natural action for one who is destined to die."

"We're all destined to die, Ramed. Beg for my life? I've been prepared to die since age fifteen. I never expected to live to see twenty. Every day beyond that, I've considered to be something of a gift. So if you're expecting to see me grovel and crawl now, if that's what this is about—"

"No, that's not what this is about. This is about saving my world."

"I thought that's what my presence here was doing."

"You have no say in the matter either, oh Great One. You are as caught up in all this as I am."

"Caught up in all *what?"* Calhoun said slowly, as if addressing a child. "You have yet to tell me what the hell this is all about."

"You truly desire to know?"

"No, Ramed, it's always been my goal to die in ignorance. Yes, of course I want to know."

Ramed rose, walking away from him and disappearing into the inner recesses of the cave. This, to Calhoun, did not seem the most straightforward manner of answering a question. Moments later, however, Ramed returned with a scroll. It was carefully preserved within a tube, and Ramed removed it from the cylinder with extreme delicacy. He began to read from it, and Calhoun could tell from the way that Ramed wasn't even truly looking at it that either he was making it up as he went, or else he had read it so many times that he more or less had it memorized.

" 'Look to the stars, for from there will come the Messiah,' " Ramed said. " 'The bird of flame will signal his coming. He will bear a scar, and he will be a great leader. He will come from air and return to air. And he will be slain by the appointed one. The appointed one, who will be privy to great knowledge. The appointed one, a great spiritual and religious leader, one to whom many will look for guidance, who will hear these words and know, within his heart, that he is the one who is chosen to slay the Savior. He and no other. There will be a great festival to celebrate the Savior, from which the Savior will disappear. And he will then live for three days and three hours exactly after that disappearance. There will come a great confrontation within the place that was once my home. The Savior will be saved by neither man nor woman, and he will die, impaled on the great spear passed down by my descendants. And in that slaying, the Messiah's death will unite our planet. And . . .' " Ramed's voice trailed off.

"Oh, don't stop now," Calhoun said drily. "This was just getting interesting."

" 'And if he does not die in the appointed way, then the final war will destroy all? All. All!" he added for emphasis.

"That was truly riveting," Calhoun told him. "And what am I supposed to learn from that?"

"You are supposed to understand," Ramed said in genuine confusion. He waved the spear around for emphasis. "This is prophecy. These are the words of Ontear himself. Most of it has not been made known to the good people of Zondar. Only that the Savior would one day come. That is all they know. But it was the wish of Ontear—a wish carried out by his greatest acolyte, Suti—that only the innermost circle know of the true, full details of what was to happen. After all, who would willingly wish to become known as the Savior of the Zondarian people if he knew that his destiny was to die in order to obtain that unity?"

"I can see where that would be a problem."

"Suti kept the sacred knowledge within his own family, and that knowledge was handed down, from one generation to the next. The secret scroll, passed down, the information waiting for the time that was to come."

"And you're certain that I am the Savior," Calhoun said. "You're so certain of that. And that you are the appointed one who is supposed to kill me."

"Of course," Ramed said in clear confusion. "How can you possibly dispute it? The prophecy is clear—"

"Is it? How do you know?"

"It could not be more clear!"

"*T'han*chips. I think you're looking for an excuse," Calhoun told him. "I think you're just a deluded, would-be murdering bastard who's looking for any excuse—"

Ramed was literally trembling with rage. "How can you say that? You know nothing of me! *You know nothing!*" He drew closer to Calhoun. "I have a wife! A son! I am a good man, a decent man, who has never harmed a soul in my entire life! Do you think I wanted this task? Do you? I lived in dread of being the appointed one! As did my father, and his father before him! You have no idea what it was like, Calhoun! No idea of the burden my family has carried!

Every day, for generations, Zondarians have hoped and prayed that the Savior would come! And every day, for generations, my clan has dreaded that moment, for we knew that the knowledge we possessed ensured our damnation! If I lived my entire life and never set eye on the Savior, I would have died in peace—no! I lie, for I would have had to pass the knowledge on to my son, thereby condemning him to a life of apprehension! I have spared him that, at least. For that, I suppose, I should be grateful. I must do this thing, Calhoun. I have no choice, no free will. My people, the fate of my very world, depends on my next actions! I must do that which I find personally repugnant in order to ensure that my planet is united! For if I do not, if my will is weak, if I fail in the endeavor, then there will come a great war which will destroy everything! How can I condemn my people, my world, to that?''

''Your destiny is no more and no less than what you make of it,'' Calhoun said. ''Letting your every move be dictated by vague prophecy . . .''

''There is nothing vague about it!''

''There sure as hell is.''

''It speaks of your coming from the stars, with the flame bird as your avatar!''

''The flame bird merely speaks of the timing of it. Even if you judge that this is the time, that doesn't mean I'm necessarily the one you're expecting. All our worlds orbit stars, or suns. We owe our lives, our existence to them. We all come from the stars, Ramed. All of us. Singling me out simply because I come from a starship is folly.''

'' 'He will come from air and return to air!' You materialized out of the air itself!''

''You're a spiritual individual, Ramed. Don't you believe in the ephemeral nature of the spirit? We are plucked from nothingness, and to nothingness we return.''

Ramed shook his head and pointed accusingly at Calhoun, coming to within a foot of him. ''This is absurd,'' he said. ''In most cultures, prophecies are vague, and those with something to gain try to find the specifics that will serve them. Here the prophecies could not be more specific, and you seek to dilute them.''

''I'm simply pointing out that maybe they're not as precise as you thought. You could just as easily be the savior as me. You're a great leader, after all.''

"Oh really?" Ramed smiled patronizingly. " 'He will bear a scar.' What of that? I have no scar."

That was when Calhoun lunged forward.

He'd slowly been positioning himself, maintaining what seemed a casual sitting position. The moment that Ramed was close enough, however, Calhoun made his move.

His intention was to slam into Ramed with such force that he would knock him cold. He would then grab the sharpened pike and use it to cut through the ropes that were binding him. For a spur of the moment plan, it wasn't bad.

Unfortunately the ground betrayed him.

There was a thin layer of gravel. Had his feet been free so that he could properly maneuver, he would have easily been able to vault it or maneuver around it. But with his feet tied up, it was impossible for him to move with his usual agility.

Consequently his bound feet went out from under him, and he collided with Ramed in a totally off-balance fashion. Ramed staggered back, spinning away, and his face smashed into the cave wall. He slid to the ground, momentarily dropping his spear, and Calhoun tried to angle around to get it. But Ramed was too quick, snatching it up and holding it between them, point directly aimed at Calhoun's chest. Calhoun lay on the ground, his purple eyes focused pitilessly on Ramed.

"What did you think you were doing?" Ramed gasped out. Blood was pouring down the side of his face from where he'd slammed it against the wall.

"Trying to make my own destiny, you pathetic idiot," Calhoun snapped at him. "Just as I've been doing all my life. You—you're a slave to yours. But I'll shape my own. By the way, congratulations. That's going to leave a rather impressive scar."

Ramed was trying to staunch the bleeding. He tore off a portion of his sleeve and used it to put pressure on the wound. "Very amusing, Great One," he said, with as heavy sarcasm as he could muster. "Very, very amusing. You're trying to confuse matters. To confuse me. But it's not going to work, do you understand?"

"I understand perfectly. You're obviously the one who doesn't understa—"

He didn't have the opportunity to complete the sentence, because a chime began to sound from within the cave. Calhoun looked around. "What's that?" he asked. "An alarm clock to tell you that now's when you're supposed to butcher me?"

"No. It's a proximity alarm," Ramed told him. He pulled the cloth away and saw that it was soaked with blood, but also could see that the flow had slowed down appreciably.

"An alarm? We're in a cave in the middle of nowhere. What kind of alarms and technology do you have in a place like this?"

Ramed stared at him. "You'd be amazed," he said.

"If someone's coming," Calhoun told him, "particularly if it's my people, I assure you, they'll get past whatever it is you've got prepared."

"Your confidence in your crew is most heartening, even though it indicates an unwillingness to accept the hopelessness of your situation. This area has been prepared, you see. Prepared for centuries by my ancestors, who have known that this would be the place where the Savior would be taken to meet His destiny. There is technology here that is undreamt of, even by your standards. It's one of our other great secrets. Anything that your people might have prepared has already been considered and guarded against."

"I was unaware that you were that technologically advanced a race."

"We're not," Ramed smiled ruefully. "That is both our blessing and our curse. Your people have already made a foray to find you. They were rebuffed."

"Rebuffed?" This caught Calhoun's attention. He started to sit up, but Ramed held the spear out in a vaguely threatening fashion and Calhoun stopped moving. "What do you mean, rebuffed? What did you do to my people?"

"I? I did nothing. They did it to themselves, just as these newcomers will. And once they are disposed of, well, the third hour of the third day beckons, oh Great One. That which will be your last hour."

"Or yours," Calhoun replied.

Ramed looked at him sadly. "Poor, sad Savior. Still hoping to be rescued. Still refusing to believe that neither man nor woman will save you."

And Calhoun smiled. "Believe me, Ramed, with my crew, that isn't necessarily as much of an obstacle as you might think."

16

It was late at night on Zondar as Burgoyne stood on the rocky outcropping, hir nostrils flaring, feeling more alive than s/he had in ages. The moons of Zondar were full, providing a healthy dose of light. Nearby Ensign Janos—looking cramped, as always, in his Starfleet uniform—cracked his knuckles with a sound that seemed like a cannon shot.

The area around them did not seem particularly inviting. It was fairly mountainous, with a myriad of caves. Burgoyne realized that there was any number of hiding places where the captain and his captor could be. S/he held up a medical tricorder, packing the same information that Selar's had held, as a means of tracking down the captain. But a quick readout of the immediate area revealed a problem. ''We're getting some sort of interference,'' Burgoyne said. S/he tried adjusting the tricorder but had no success with it.''

''Which would lead us to assume,'' Ensign Janos observed, ''that someone is actively trying to discourage us from locating the captain.''

''Obviously. This must be one of the things that caused the other away team to run into problems. So,'' and Burgoyne snapped the tricorder closed, ''we're just going to have to go about this the old-fashioned away. How's your sense of smell, Janos?''

''My olfactory abilities are exceptional, as befits my race, if not necessarily my breeding.''

''All right, then. Start sniffing around. You take east, I'll take west.''

No words were exchanged for some minutes after that. Burgoyne prowled the area, paying little attention to Janos at that point. All of hir senses were extended, trying to pick up some physical trace of the captain. S/he sniffed the air, s/he scented around rock and rocky trails, trying to detect some sort of lead, some vague hint as to where the captain might have gone to.

"Chief!" called Janos. Janos was approximately a hundred yards away, but Burgoyne crossed the distance quickly and efficiently, moving with a grace and ease that would have startled any onlooker with the possible exception of McHenry. Janos was down on the ground, sniffing around one particular section, and he grunted, "I think I've got something."

"The captain?"

"No. I think it's Kebron."

Burgoyne quickly dropped to the ground next to Janos. It would have been a strange sight, had anyone been around: two Starfleet officers, crawling about on the ground, sniffing. Fortunately enough for decorum and the image of the fleet, no one was around at that particular moment.

"I think you're right," Burgoyne said after a moment. "Let's go."

They stayed low to the ground, on the scent. Burgoyne quickly took the lead, moving on all fours across the rough terrain, hir arms and legs bending at joints usually covered by hir uniform. S/he hit an incline at one point, and hir hardened nails dug into the rocky ground with efficiency. There was no unnecessary chatter between the two of them; they were moving entirely on instinct, and Burgoyne came to the reluctant realization that Soleta had known what she was about when she insisted on pairing Burgoyne with Janos.

And as s/he moved across the terrain, as all of hir tracking senses came to the fore, subtle changes came over Burgoyne. Hir lips drew back to reveal hir canines, but it was not in the teasing or slightly threatening manner in which s/he usually displayed them. Rather, it was as if s/he was prepared to use them—indeed, couldn't wait to do so. Hir normally dark eyes had clouded over completely as s/he tapped deeply into hirself, into an essence that was hir natural state but one that s/he normally did everything s/he could to keep hidden away. Hir claws—for that was, indeed, the best way to describe them, since "nails" somehow didn't do them justice—clicked against the rocky surface as s/he made hir way across it. S/he sensed rather than saw that Janos was directly behind hir, smelled his thick fur and distinctive scent.

There was a deep crevice just ahead of them, and Burgoyne—

disdaining to scamper the rest of the way—coiled and then leaped, clearing the distance of fifteen feet in one vault. Cautious of a possible booby trap, Burgoyne tentatively stuck hir head over the edge and peered down.

Wedged in, far below, was a familiar dark-skinned form.

"Kebron!" called Burgoyne. "Kebron, it's me! Burgoyne one-seventy-two! Kebron!" A moment later, Janos appeared at Burgoyne's side. "Kebron, can you hear me?"

There seemed to be a slight appearance of movement on Kebron's part. He tried to angle his head upward, but since his neck was virtually nonexistent, this was somewhat problematic for him. He had to try and tilt his entire torso back as best he could, and was only partly successful. His voice strained with the effort. "I . . . hear you," he said slowly.

The crevice had to be at least twenty feet down. "Kebron, we'll get you out of there!" called Burgoyne.

"Can't," he told them, and he'd never sounded so tired. "Grav generator . . . out . . . can barely . . . move. . . ."

Immediately Burgoyne knew what had happened. Zak Kebron was so massive, that the only way he was able to move in a non-Brikar gravity field was with a small portable gravity generator that he wore in his belt. It was virtually impossible to break the generator through conventional means. Something had managed to short it out, however, and Kebron was clearly finding it impossible to do anything.

Burgoyne tapped hir commbadge in an endeavor to raise the *Excalibur.* Hir reasoning was simple: Beam Kebron up out of the crevice. This intention, however, was quickly thwarted when all s/he could get over hir commbadge was static. And the idea of Burgoyne and Janos going down and trying to pull Kebron out was simply an impossibility. Even between the two of them, and the considerable strength that Janos possessed, there was just no way that they could possibly haul Kebron out from the crevice.

"Kebron!" Burgoyne called down to him. "You'll have to wait there until we find some way to get you out!"

"Wait . . . fine . . . not planning on . . . going anywhere . . ."

"What happened, Lieutenant?" Janos called down. "What did this to you? How many of them are there?"

Kebron didn't seem to hear at first. He appeared stunned, and Burgoyne realized that it was a condition beyond anything that the simple deprivation of the field generator could have caused. Kebron was in shock.

"Hundreds of them . . ." Kebron said. "Thousands . . . couldn't stop them . . ."

Burgoyne and Janos looked at each other. "That sounds pleasant," Janos observed.

"Kebron, be strong," Burgoyne urged him, although s/he wasn't sure just exactly how much good that was going to do. "We'll be back for you as soon as we can."

No reply came back.

Quickly the two officers vaulted the crevice, sniffing the air, the dirt, anything they could. And this time it was Burgoyne who picked up the scent. S/he had been crouched on the ground, running the crumbling dirt under hir fingers, and s/he detected something that became stronger as s/he moved off to hir right. "Got it!" Burgoyne called. "Got the captain!"

"Brilliant!" crowed Janos.

"It seems as if—" S/he prowled the area, trying to confirm what s/he already suspected. "Yes. Whoever took the captain was likely carrying him, and then became tired and started dragging him. This way."

"I'm with you, Chief."

Quickly they set off across the terrain, moving with amazing speed. The scent grew stronger the farther along that Burgoyne went, and within moments s/he was no longer running in anything that vaguely approximated humanoid manner. S/he was sprinting on all fours, a satisfied growl low in hir throat, and there was no concern whatsoever about what s/he might run into. S/he was completely focused on the hunt.

And it wasn't just about finding the captain, either. S/he was eager to track down the person or persons who had abused Selar. S/he wanted to wrap hir fingers around their throats, s/he wanted to sink hir teeth deep into their flesh, to rend and tear . . .

There was a faint buzzing in hir head that began to grow louder and louder, but s/he wasn't fully aware of it. Instead s/he was completely wrapped up in the thoughts of what s/he was going to do to Selar's assailants when s/he got hir hands on them. S/he could almost taste the sweetness of their blood pumping into hir, could savor the screams for mercy that they would utter. But there would be no mercy. There would only be slaughter, and blood, and Burgoyne's laughter combined with a triumphant roar . . .

S/he took another step, then another, and the buzzing was becoming louder still, and finally s/he became aware of it in a distant manner, wondering what it was . . .

And suddenly s/he was on the *Excalibur.*

S/he looked around in confusion, not entirely sure how the devil s/he'd gotten back there. The corridors were empty. S/he began to run, calling out names of various crewmembers, trying to find someone. S/he didn't even think to hit the commbadge on hir chest. S/he just yelled, becoming angrier as hir cries were ignored.

S/he ran into engineering, and everyone was there. Everyone. Everyone s/he'd ever known, everyone s/he'd ever encountered. Hir parents were there, and others from Hermat—not friends, certainly, for s/he'd had no real friends on Hermat—and the engineering crew, and the command crew. There was Calhoun standing there, arms folded, shaking his head in clear disdain, and Shelby's face twisted in contempt, and the others were all pointing, shouting at hir.

"Freak!" they called out. Over and over came the word, "Freak, freak!" spoken with derision, cried out in a hundred different voices that combined as one.

A freak to hir own people, for the outgoing and sexually joyful Burgoyne had never truly fit in with other Hermats, who tended to prefer their own kind. Freak to the people of the *Excalibur,* who had never known a Hermat before and didn't at all know what to make of hir. All the suspicious glances, the scornful looks, all aimed at hir. S/he tried to back out of engineering, but the door had closed behind hir and refused to open.

"Get away from me!" shouted Burgoyne. "Get away!"

Instead, they advanced, and there was McHenry in the forefront, shaking his head and saying, "You were just an experiment! An exercise in weirdness! I never found you attractive, never!" and there was Selar, as burned and battered as when s/he'd last seen her, and Selar was sneering, "Even on my deathbed I'd never want you! You vile, bizarre thing! You sickening, perverted monster!"

Burgoyne roared in fury. The hackles on the back of hir neck rose, hir eyes went completely dark, and hir claws were fully extended. All of the playfulness, all of the confidence, everything that made hir what s/he was, had vanished. All s/he knew were those who feared hir, hated hir, despised hir either behind her back or to hir face.

"I'll kill you!" s/he howled, and with uncontrolled frenzy s/he leaped forward . . .

And crashed squarely into Ensign Janos.

Janos, who was surrounded by mugatos, his own kind with whom he had as much in common as he had with an amoeba. Mugatos jumping around, snarling at him, picking at him and poking at him in the midst of the jungle on Tyree's World to which mugatos were native. Janos had never set foot, paw, or anything else upon Tyree's World, but he had known it just the same. They prodded at him with their horns, they tore at him with their poisonous fangs, which were not toxic to him, but could rip him up and injure him just the same. He cried out as they came at him from all directions, and then the carefully cultivated personality that he'd worked so long to develop evaporated, and Janos bellowed, a truly frightening sound of a mugato in full rage. A mugato seeking an enemy to rend limb from limb.

It was in this state of mind that Burgoyne and Janos slammed into each other.

And nearby, something formed of coalescing energy took shape and started to advance upon them.

17

The long range sensors gave the *Excalibur* her first warning that there was danger imminent.

Boyajian, the tactical officer filling in for Kebron due to the security chief's absence, called out to Soleta, who was in the command chair. "We have an incoming vessel, Lieutenant. And it's big."

"Put it on screen," Soleta said calmly.

"Not yet possible, sir. Hasn't emerged from warp space yet." He paused and then said, "Orders, sir?"

Soleta considered the situation a moment. Unknown territory, an unknown vessel coming toward them, intentions unknown. She didn't like to take an immediate defensive posture with a new encounter, since it could make them look as if they were combative or spoiling for a fight. Nonetheless, not doing anything would be tempting fate, particularly if the other vessel dropped out of warp space with all weapons blazing.

Lefler and McHenry were both looking at her expectantly, as were the other members of the bridge crew. Soleta began to feel, once again, the gnawing doubt of someone who believed that she was in way over her head. But there was absolutely no way that she was going to share that sentiment or concern with the rest of the crew.

"Yellow alert," Soleta said after a moment. "Raise shields. Bring weapons and targeting systems on line, but do not energize weapons."

"Do not—" repeated Boyajian.

"No. The chances are that their scans won't be able to detect that we've got them targeted, but would be able to determine that we're running weapons hot."

"So we're hedging our bets," commented Lefler.

"Precisely, Lieutenant. Our bets are significantly hedged. Continue sensor sweeps for the captain."

"Lieutenant," and McHenry leaned back in his chair to address Soleta. There was a trace of worry in his voice. "We haven't heard from Burgoyne or Janos."

"I didn't expect to, Mister McHenry," replied Soleta. "The area that they are exploring is in the heart of the interference zone. That's the territory that we're having difficulty scanning or getting any communications from. The likelihood that they would be able to keep us apprised of their progress is fairly slim. It is my assumption that if we do hear from them before the end of the twelve-hour period I've given them—of which eight hours, fourteen minutes remains—it will be because they have accomplished their task and emerged from the zone." She hesitated and then added, in as close to an understanding voice as she could muster, "I'm sure Burgoyne is fine, Lieutenant. S/he is a rather resourceful individual."

"Believe me, I know," McHenry said.

Boyajian suddenly looked up from tactical. "Lieutenant, she's coming out of warp."

"All departments report confirmation of yellow alert status," Lefler confirmed.

"Ship coming in at nine-hundred-thousand kilometers, bearing two-eleven mark three."

"Bring us about, Mister McHenry. Let's keep some distance between us," Soleta said.

"Aye, sir."

"Bridge to Ambassador Si Cwan," she added after a moment's consideration.

"Si Cwan here," came the brisk reply.

"Ambassador, your presence on the bridge would be most appreciated. We seem to have visitors."

"On my way."

The *Excalibur* angled out of orbit and came around to face the newcomer. The vessel's warp drive bubble evaporated as the ship entered normal space and came to a halt approximately 850,000 kilometers from the starship. The ship was pyramidal, powerful-looking, and half again as large as the *Excalibur*.

"Hail on all frequencies, Mister Boyajian," Soleta said, drumming her fingers gently on the armrest. ''Let them know we're not out to start a fight.''

''I am hailing them, sir, but they're not responding.''

''That could be unfortunate.'' She leaned forward, studying the ship's configuration. Soleta was not entirely unfamiliar with Sector 221-G; she had spent some time exploring the once-Thallonian Empire at a time when outsiders were not only unwelcome, but more often than not, put to death. She had acquired some knowledge in her travels, and she had the suspicion that she recognized the ship's configuration. If she was correct, then the situation with which they were faced was a fairly incendiary one.

The turbolift doors hissed open and Si Cwan strode onto the bridge. Immediately his gaze went to the front screen, and he slowed to a halt. Then he spat out a word that Soleta immediately recognized as a rather extreme Thallonian profanity. ''I take your reaction,'' she said slowly, ''to be an indicator that our new arrivals are, in fact, who I think they are.''

''The Redeemers,'' Si Cwan nodded. ''Just what we needed.''

''I take it that's not good,'' Lefler surmised.

''Not in the least. Boyajian, sensor scan?''

''They are heavily armed, Lieutenant. They have not as of yet activated their weapons array. Their shields are likewise in place.''

''In other words, we're both suspicious, but neither of us wants to provoke the other.''

''An accurate assessment, Lieutenant.''

''Lieutenant, these are Redeemers we're talking about,'' Si Cwan told her. ''They are missionary zealots, and if you do not accept their particular deity—Xant—then they will have no use for you.''

''Meaning they'll leave us alone?'' McHenry suggested optimistically.

''Meaning they will endeavor to blow us out of space,'' replied Soleta.

''Oh. Well, that's not quite as good.''

''Let me try to talk to them. We've dealt with them before. The royal family has always managed to avoid Holy Wars with the Redeemers; perhaps I can continue our run of good luck.''

''Be my guest, Ambassador,'' said Soleta.

''Put me on a hailing frequency,'' Si Cwan said to Boyajian, and when the latter nodded confirmation that he was on, Si Cwan said, ''Attention, Redeemer vessel. This is the *Starship Excalibur.* This is Ambassador Si Cwan speaking. Perhaps you remember me; you've had dealings with both myself, and my ancestors, for many years. We have always managed to have mutual respect for each other's concerns, and I see no reason that that has to change now. Please inform us of your concerns, and we will endeavor to answer them." He stopped and turned back to Boyajian. "Did they get that? Did they hear me?"

"I broadcast it, Ambassador," said Boyajian. "Whether they actually listened, I couldn't tell y—" Then he paused, checking the readings on his board. "Lieutenant, we're getting an incoming hail."

"It would seem they indeed heard you, Ambassador," Soleta said. "Well done."

"Let us save the congratulations until we see whether they are saying anything we wish to hear."

"A valid point. Put them on, Mister Boyajian."

The screen rippled and, a moment later, the ebony face of a Redeemer appeared on the screen. He gazed at them with eyes that seemed to glow a deep and frightening red.

Lefler immediately felt a chill at the base of her spine. Her impulse was to look away, but she didn't want to appear weak or faint of heart. She glanced over at McHenry and took a small measure of comfort in seeing that he appeared to have the same reaction. It appeared as if McHenry would rather be looking anywhere else than directly at the viewscreen. But he couldn't take his eyes away from it: Not just out of a sense of duty, as was the case with Lefler, but also out of a deep fascination. He found the Redeemer just too compelling, in a negative away, to look away from him.

Soleta, for her part, remained impassive. As for Si Cwan, he had seen enough Redeemers in his life not to be put off or intimidated by their frankly frightening air.

"I am Prime One," said the Redeemer. His voice was an odd combination of deep but brittle. "I am second only to the Overlord in the Redeemer hierarchy."

"Greetings, Prime One," said Si Cwan. He made a small hand gesture that Soleta surmised to be some sort of ritual greeting. "We have not met, but I know of you. I am Si Cwan."

"I know of you, Thallonian. I have heard many positive things about you. Also"—and his eyes seemed to glow more brightly—"some rather negative things."

"That is the way of all things, is it not, Prime One? Even in the light of Xant, there must be darkness."

Prime One inclined his head slightly to indicate that Si Cwan had a point. He glanced around the bridge from his vantage point. "We desire to speak to the captain."

"The captain is not available," Soleta said, rising from her chair. "I am Lieutenant Soleta. You may address me in any matters pertaining to this vessel."

"Where is your captain? Where is the one called Calhoun? Is he on your vessel?"

"The captain," Soleta repeated guardedly, "is not available. If you have business, it can be discussed with me."

"Our business is not with you," Prime One said. "It is with Calhoun. The one whom those on the world below call 'Savior.' The one whose name and reputation spreads from one world to the next, like a plague."

"I'm not quite following," admitted Soleta.

Prime One let out an irritated sigh, as if he felt he was speaking to someone who wasn't worth the effort. "We have been preparing the worlds under our sphere of influence, plus other worlds that may be worth our while, to prepare for the return of Xant. Xant, the one true god. Xant, the one true Savior of all worlds."

"I see," said Soleta. "And why would this be pertinent to us?"

"Do not be coy with me, Vulcan. It ill befits you or your eminently logical kind. We both know that various planets—including, most conspicuously, the one directly below us—are espousing the opinion that Calhoun's arrival is tantamount to, and even more important than, the return of Xant. Calhoun is working to supplant Xant's rightful place in the galaxy."

"Captain Calhoun is doing no such thing," replied Soleta.

"We have information to the contrary," began Prime One.

But Si Cwan stepped in quickly before Prime One could continue. "Your information, I must tell you, is faulty," he assured Prime One. "I will grant you, the people of Zondar seem to have elevated Captain Calhoun to some sort of god-like status. But that was the decision of their world, and one that was not supported by Captain Calhoun himself."

"From our understanding, he presented himself as the Savior of Zondar."

"He was endeavoring to save a race from destroying itself," Si Cwan pointed out. "Further, he presented himself as nothing. They believed him to be their Savior. What matters what a race believes when one is trying to save it? You know of the civil war that grips the Zondarians."

"Yes, we were aware," said Prime One. "It was, and is, a tragic situation that brother should slay brother."

"You see, we are in agreement then."

"About the situation, yes. But we had every intention of attending to Zondar in our own way."

That comment, and the implied threat, were unmistakable. "Are you saying that you intended to . . . redeem Zondar?"

"It was a planet ripe for redemption. And with the demise of the Thallonian Empire, all agreements between ourselves and your family are, obviously, in abeyance."

"Even so," Si Cwan said, "you cannot feel that Mackenzie Calhoun has undercut the divine Xant simply because he was doing his job. He is here to help. To aid a belligerent people in setting aside their differences. What matter the method?"

"It matters to us," Prime One told him flatly. "What Calhoun has done is nothing less than pose a threat to the entire structure of the Redeemers. At least you Thallonians did not trespass into the realm of the theological. Yours was a straightforward environment of warfare and business. You conquered and controlled, not out of a sense of divine right, but out of a belief in your own intrinsic strength. We believed it to be shortsighted and limited, but it was a mind-set with which we could co-exist. Calhoun, on the other hand, is being perceived as some sort of Savior."

"Mackenzie Calhoun cannot control how he is perceived by others."

"Granted," said Prime One. "We, however, can."

McHenry turned to Lefler and in a very low voice, said, "I do *not* like the sound of that."

Nor did Si Cwan. "May I ask," he said slowly, "how you would propose to exercise that control?"

"By destroying both Calhoun and his vessel," said Prime One matter-of-factly.

And now Lefler murmured to McHenry, in an equally low voice, "Yup. That would do it."

Soleta now took a step forward before Si Cwan could reply. "I must warn you, sir, if you fire upon this vessel, we will take retaliatory action. Furthermore, bear in mind that this is a Federation starship. To fire unprovoked upon us is to risk direct confrontation with the Federation itself."

"Unprovoked?" Prime One retorted. "We have endeavored to save the souls of the races in this sector before your Federation had even assembled its meager membership. You come in here, on your supposed mission of mercy, when in fact the Redeemers consider it nothing less than trespass. And then to foist one of your own off as a major religious figure . . .''

''We have been over that, Prime One,'' Si Cwan said. ''The primary mandate of this vessel is to save lives, and Captain Calhoun—''

''And our primary mandate is to save souls!'' shot back Prime One. ''And how is that to be accomplished if Xant is to return, only to discover that he has been forsaken in the name of some upstart Starfleet captain?! A world already lies in ruins because of him.''

''What do you mean?''

''Alpha Carinae, Lord Cwan. The people there came to believe in the influence of Mackenzie Calhoun. In so doing, they attacked and killed the High Priest of that world. You know the consequences of such an act.''

For a moment, Si Cwan felt the strength draining from his legs. He reached back and gripped the upper rail behind him. Soleta looked to him questioningly, standing with her back to the screen so that they had a fraction of privacy despite the height difference between them.

''High Priests are equipped with a sort of fail-safe device,'' Si Cwan said, after he'd taken a moment to steady himself. ''A particularly virulent strain of virus. It's contained within their bodies, in a device that is keyed to the heartbeat of the priest. If the priest is critically injured or killed—in short, if they die of anything save natural causes—the virus is released. Within seventy-two hours, no one is left alive on the world.''

Soleta's eyes went wide.

Si Cwan then looked to the screen, his face hardening. ''And you would blame this . . . this tragedy on Calhoun?''

''On whom else, Lord Cwan?'' demanded the Prime One.

''On whom else? And on whom did you place the blame when there was revolt on Oxon Three, eh? And your little plague-retaliation lay waste to that race? Or what about the brutal beating of a High Priest on Lesikor, eh? That time, you intervened quickly enough so that merely half the population of the planet was destroyed. And where was Calhoun then, eh? No, no, Prime One. Look elsewhere for your precious blame. Look to yourselves. Your converts balk against your restrictions and your oppression. They rebel against you. You try to redeem them when the only thing they need saving from is you yourselves! So if the people of Alpha Carinae latched onto the legend building around Calhoun, what of it? Sooner or later they would have seized upon someone or something else. They were not turning toward another. They were turning away from you, and that's the truth of it! Rather than seek out Calhoun to punish him for your own shortcomings and oppression, look on this as an object lesson in the danger of domination!"

Very quietly, Prime One replied, "I hardly think that you, of all people, are qualified to spout lessons on the danger of domination, oh fallen Lord Cwan."

Si Cwan's face darkened slightly, and he said, "Actually, I beg to differ. I think I am eminently qualified. After all, who knows better of the hazards of dictatorship than a fallen dictator?"

Through the distance of space, the two of them stared at each other for a long moment.

"Calhoun is no threat to you," Si Cwan said at last.

"Perhaps you are right," Prime One said.

Several members of the bridge crew let out sighs of relief.

"But then again, perhaps you are wrong," continued Prime One. "We cannot take that chance."

Boyajian looked up from his sensors. "Lieutenant, they're going weapons hot!"

"Red alert, sound battle stations," Soleta said, icy calm descending upon her. She was now faced with a worst-case scenario, and she had absolutely no choice but to try and see it through. In a way, it was almost a relief. Now she knew what she had to face. "Prime One," she said as she took one more try at the screen, "I must warn you once more: We will defend ourselves if fired upon."

"I would hope so," replied Prime One.

"Calhoun is not aboard this ship!" Si Cwan called above the klaxon of the red alert. "You're accomplishing nothing!"

"The ship is doomed anyway, for we would hardly want the vessel of a martyred captain cruising the spaceways, spreading word of his great deeds," reasoned Prime One. "If you are lying and the captain is on the vessel, then we have accomplished our mission. If not, and he is on the planet surface, then we will either redeem the planet or—if it is irredeemable—obliterate the populace as well. The infection of Calhoun worship will end, here and now. May Xant light your way to the next life." And the screen blinked out.

"At least he gave us his blessing," McHenry commented.

"Incoming!" called Boyajian. "High energy concentration plasma torpedoes! Locked on and tracking us!"

"Evasive maneuvers!" called Soleta.

And McHenry promptly slammed the *Excalibur* into reverse.

At high speed, increasing with every moment, the *Excalibur* hurtled backward on full reverse thrust, the torpedoes in hot pursuit.

"Thirty thousand kilometers and closing!" called McHenry.

"Locking on counters!" Boyajian said. "Keep us steady, McHenry! Just need another few seconds!"

"Maintaining course and speed!"

"Counter torpedoes locked on! Firing!"

Photon torpedoes leaped out from underneath the ship, hitting the plasma torpedoes squarely. The explosion rippled outward, but the *Excalibur* gracefully sailed around it.

"Redeemer vessel in pursuit," called Boyajian. "Orders, Lieutenant?"

Soleta hesitated, unsure of exactly how to proceed.

And at that moment, she heard the hissing of the turbolift door and a strong, if struggling voice, say, "I'll take this one, Lieutenant."

Everyone on the bridge turned and reacted with similar astonishment, except for Soleta, who was well-trained enough to mask not only her surprise, but a vague sense of relief.

Shelby was standing in the doorway. She was still clearly injured, and she was laboring to keep herself standing. Skin grafts had been attached to replace the areas where her face and body had been lacerated, but the healing process had only just begun. Nonetheless, Shelby forced her legs to carry her forward.

"Commander?" gasped out Lefler.

"I heard a red alert. We're in trouble. If you think I'm going to lie around in sickbay, you can forget it." She staggered, gripped the command chair, and eased herself in.

"Commander, are you sure—" asked Soleta.

"No," Shelby told her. "No, I'm not sure. But I'm here, much to the chagrin of Doctor Maxwell, who's still on the verge of apoplexy that I walked out. So . . . status report."

"We are under assault by a warship belonging to a race known as the Redeemers. They are heavily armed and shielded, and have a stated intention of destroying us and, after that, Captain Calhoun. Orders, sir?"

Shelby leaned forward. "Prepare to kick 'em to hell, Lieutenant."

And Soleta came as close to smiling as she ever did. "All prepared, Commander."

18

With a snarl, Burgoyne ripped a chunk out of Ensign Janos.

Janos roared in fury as his thick white fur quickly became bloodstained around his ribs. Burgoyne sank hir canines squarely into Janos's upper shoulder and, bracing hir feet against his upper chest, did everything s/he could to rip Janos's arm out of its socket.

Furious, Janos grabbed Burgoyne by the back of hir uniform and pulled hir off him, losing some more fur in the process. He hurled Burgoyne across the rocky terrain, and Burgoyne slammed into an outcropping, momentarily stunned. Without hesitation, Janos lowered his head and charged, driving his horn straight at Burgoyne's chest. Burgoyne had been momentarily stunned, and hir vision cleared just in time to see the horn bearing down straight at hir. Just before Janos made contact, Burgoyne took a quick step forward and leaped high, somersaulting through the air and over Janos's head. Janos, unable to halt his charge in time, crashed into the rocky wall, chipping off some of the rock and some fur off his head as well.

Janos spun, baring his fangs and howling his fury at Burgoyne. He charged after hir, the ground shaking under him. Burgoyne, had s/he been in hir right mind, would have run. Instead s/he maintained her ground to meet the charge. It was nothing short of suicidal, for the fangs of the enraged ensign were poisoned, and the slightest scratch from those frightening weapons would kill anyone: even a Hermat chief engineer.

Janos lunged, sweeping his right claw through the air. Burgoyne ducked under it, not even moving hir feet. S/he snarled derisively, and the move further enraged Janos. He swung a left, another right, just trying to get a grip on Burgoyne, but the Hermat was too quick. S/he maneuvered as if Janos were moving in slow motion. Quickly becoming fed up, Janos charged forward with his entire body. Burgoyne darted between his legs, taking a moment to sweep with hir talons across the upper portion of Janos's thigh. The ensign went down, howling, clutching at his leg. He didn't know how lucky he was. Burgoyne had been moving quickly, and if s/he hadn't had to hurry hir thrust and had, in fact, hit where s/he was aiming, Janos's scream would have been considerably higher-pitched.

Burgoyne started to scramble to hir feet, and suddenly Janos hurled himself backward. He did so blindly, but he had a general sense of where Burgoyne was, and the move caught hir by surprise. All four hundred and fifty pounds of ensign landed squarely on top of hir, knocking the wind out of hir and pinning hir.

Janos tried to reach around, find a part of hir that he could grab, get to his mouth, and chomp down on. The moment he accomplished that, the battle would effectively be over.

Moving quickly, fired by desperation, Burgoyne swung hir talons around and raked the side of Janos's face. Janos let out a yelp and Burgoyne quickly squirmed out from under the massive fury body, pulling hir legs clear and rolling frantically away.

They faced each other, both crouched, their respective teeth bared, and they circled warily. Burgoyne's talons were poised, ready to strike again, and Janos was maneuvering around to try and find a suitable terrain so that he could charge again with his horn.

And then something sounded within Burgoyne's mind. A voice . . . of someone who wasn't there.

In sickbay, Selar's eyes snapped open. She moaned, trying to sit up.

Maxwell saw it out of the corner of his eye and immediately summoned medtechs over. Selar was babbling incoherently, and Maxwell tried to make out what she was saying. Something about Burgoyne, something about monsters, and she spoke as if someone were standing right there next to her whom only she could see.

"Sedate her!" called Maxwell.

"No!" Selar said with what sounded startlingly like a growl. "*No! Leave me alone! S/he needs me!*"

Burgoyne felt her. Felt her in hir mind, in hir heart. Felt her connection to hir.

For just a moment, Burgoyne's mind cleared. The *Excalibur* evaporated, the assailants vanished, the laughing stopped . . .

And there was Ensign Janos, charging toward hir with an undiluted roar of fury.

"Oh, hell!" Burgoyne cried out, and s/he backpedaled rapidly as Janos came at hir. Realizing that Janos was going to catch up if s/he continued to run backward, Burgoyne whirled and dashed at breakneck speed, arms pumping furiously.

Dead ahead of hir was a solid wall of rock.

Right behind hir was the infuriated mugato.

Burgoyne picked up speed, ran as fast as s/he possibly could. Janos was right behind hir, propelling himself forward even faster with the aid of his knuckles.

And the second that Burgoyne reached the rock wall, s/he ran right up the wall, hurling hirself up and over. As s/he cleared the top of Janos's head, s/he grabbed the horn. The mugato reached around, trying to get at hir, as Burgoyne landed, allowed hir momentum to carry her, and twisted forward and down with all hir strength. Janos was hauled back and over in a flip, slammed down to the ground.

For just a moment, Janos was immobilized. With the blood lust upon hir, Burgoyne would have taken the opportunity to try and tear out Janos's jugular vein. But hir head was clear, and Burgoyne's hand stretched out, clamping onto the mugato's shoulder. Hir long fingers moved in perfect imitation of the way that Soleta had dropped hir with the nerve pinch.

Janos let out a startled yelp. His body trembled for a moment, and then pitched forward. Burgoyne stepped back, still cautious, in case Janos was pulling some sort of trick. But s/he quickly realized that that wasn't the case; Janos wasn't budging.

S/he felt heat beginning to build beneath hir feet, as if some sort of massive machinery was functioning beneath the ground. For a moment s/he considered picking up Janos and trying to lug him along, but quickly dismissed the notion as unworkable.

"Good thing you were here to watch my back," s/he said, before allowing him to slump to the ground.

Then s/he felt it again: that same sensation that caused the hair on the back of hir neck to stand up. S/he spun . . .

And saw it coming toward her.

It was massive, hundreds of feet tall, and all s/he could make out was its outline. It seemed to shimmer and coalesce in the darkness, and it appeared to fill not only the air all around, but the area within

Burgoyne as well. It seemed to have some sort of massive mouth, and a hundred eyes, every one boring its way into hir soul. S/he began to feel the same fears, trepidations . . .

"Get that way from me!" shouted Selar, all thought of Vulcan control tossed aside. She was sitting up in bed, struggling to shove aside the stasis field.

Maxwell came at her with a sedative, but he never had the opportunity to inject it into her. Her hand whipped around and she smacked the hypodermic out of his grasp, sending it clattering to the floor.

"Burgoyne!" she cried out, reaching into thin air. "Come back to me! Come back!"

And then s/he shook it off. The creature raged above hir, and at first Burgoyne backed up, intimidated, afraid. But s/he felt something else within hir mind, something that was helping hir to brace hirself against the beast . . .

And s/he realized what it was doing.

"I am not alone," whispered Burgoyne. "I am not alone, and you have no power over me."

Selar did not understand what was going through her mind. She was operating purely on instinct. She shoved aside the stasis field, and stumbled off the medtable, hitting the ground heavily. She wasn't remotely aware of her surroundings. All she knew was the instinct that was pounding through her, the need for her mate. The need to feel completion. The need to share herself.

She could feel hir. She had no clear idea of how s/he had gotten into her mind, but she was beyond caring. Medtechs approached her, tried to haul her back to the medtable. They made the mistake of doing so by hauling her arms up onto their shoulders. Her instinct in overdrive, she knocked the two of them cold with deftly placed nerve pinches. They slid to the floor and she went down with them, her legs skewed, her eyes staring into nothing and something all at the same time.

"Burgoyne," she whispered.

Burgoyne started forward with slow, measured tread, tapping into the ferocity that rampaged through hir. Ferocity that was born not only of hir own inner nature, but of carefully channeled sexual energy . . . energy that s/he wanted to expend with Selar, but instead focused with the intention of avenging the calamities that had been visited upon the Vulcan doctor.

The creature loomed over hir, and s/he was reminded of the truism that any science, sufficiently advanced, would appear as magic to races that didn't understand it. S/he didn't pretend to comprehend the nature of the being that faced hir. Whether it was biological, whether it was the creation of unseen machines, whatever—s/he didn't care. All s/he knew was that s/he was in another place, another mental realm where nothing was going to stop hir, least of all some static-filled, snarling mass of electrons.

"Take your best shot!" shouted Burgoyne. S/he made no effort to dodge, didn't try to run or maneuver around the energy creature. Instead s/he plunged straight into it, bellowing hir defiance. "I know what you're doing! I know what your design is! We are born alone, and we die alone, all of us! And we spend a lifetime running from that fact! Taking solace in relationships, making children to follow in our footsteps, all to avoid any contemplation of the fact that we are always alone! Always separated by our very natures! But I'm not alone, creature! I'm not!"

S/he shoved hir way squarely into the beast, and was immediately buffeted by high energy emissions that threatened to flay the skin from hir body. But there was more than physical punishment. One had to be battered down mentally in order to succumb to the beast, that much s/he had already figured out. It was the classic divide-and-conquer strategy. Separate the intended victim from all that he or she holds dear: from friends, from loved ones, from self-esteem, from the belief that good ultimately triumphs, and that life has any purpose. Leave all that behind and discover that all you have remaining to you is emptiness and hopelessness, and no point whatsoever in trying to continue one's existence. Flood the mind with that which is most frightening. Or overwhelming, like the Borg imagery for Shelby.

But that wasn't working with Burgoyne, for Burgoyne had drawn into hirself the essence of Selar. S/he held it close to hir, nursed it, drew warmth and confidence from it. The creature roared in fury all around hir, and s/he felt it descending upon hir. It was like trying to walk step by slow step through a tornado, feeling it flailing at you and trying to rend you limb from limb. Burgoyne, however, would not be stopped, would not be slowed.

Shelby, Selar, Hecht, and Scannell, even the mighty Zak Kebron . . . they had all endeavored to enter this realm, and all had failed. All had somehow been battered into submission, had been made to feel small and alone in a hostile galaxy. Not Burgoyne. Burgoyne felt the closeness of the link with Selar, and not only that, but s/he felt the eternal company of hir own nature. Male and female, yin and yang, the two eternal parts kept close with one another. Not only was Burgoyne joined with Selar, but furthermore, Burgoyne was at one with hirself. And as such, s/he would not be stopped.

"Get out of my way!" s/he howled once more, as loudly as s/he could, and then s/he pushed completely through the creature and suddenly felt relief swelling through hir. Relief and a sense of dizzy light-headedness. S/he spun and saw that the beast was raging behind hir, infuriated at hir ability to get past, and then it started to reach for hir.

With a snarl, Burgoyne kept going, no longer moving in anything vaguely resembling something humanoid. In hir four-legged, miles-consuming stride, s/he came across as something akin to one of the great cats of Earth. S/he charged up an incline, gravel rolling away beneath hir, hir nostrils flaring as the scent became stronger and stronger with every passing moment.

And so did hir killer instinct as well. S/he sensed that s/he was drawing close to the individual who was to be held accountable for the injuries to Selar. S/he knew now, beyond a doubt, that it was the energy creature that had been personally responsible for the state of Selar and the others, but something in turn was behind the creature, either having activated it or brought it to full life. Either way, Burgoyne was there to dispatch justice, no matter what it took.

And then, toward the top of the ridge, s/he saw him.

He was standing there with some sort of short spear, about a yard long. He was tapping the pointed end gently into the palm of his hand, as if he were tapping out a tune that only he could hear. He was shaking his head in apparent amazement of Burgoyne's arrival.

"You," he called down, "are going to have to die."

Burgoyne said nothing, but instead scrambled up the side of the hill. Just beyond the man waiting for hir was a cave, and she was positive that the captain was held within, presuming that the captain was still alive.

"I am Ramed," he told her. "You arrive at a propitious moment. It is the third hour of the third day. It is time for the Savior to pass on. Have you come to bear witness?"

Some feet away, Burgoyne had come to a cautious halt. S/he had hir talons extended, and there was a dark and fearsome look in hir eyes. When s/he spoke it was in a low and guttural voice that was barely recognizable as hir own. "Did you . . . do it?' s/he asked.

"Do what?" Ramed seemed only mildly interested.

"Did you hurt Selar?"

"Who is Selar?"

"The Vulcan. The Vulcan doctor." Burgoyne was having trouble focusing on the words; all s/he really wanted to do was leap forward and tear his throat out. But s/he had to be sure.

"Ah, yes. The Vulcan. Not directly, you understand. It was not my hand that inflicted the injuries upon her. However, I did bring into existence the rather devastating creature that attempted to stop you earlier, and that laid waste to your previous rescue attempts. How did you get around that? I must know. Because your friends were so utterly unable to—"

Burgoyne had heard enough. S/he crouched and let out a bellow akin to the roar that a lion used when endeavoring to freeze prey in place in preparation for a charge. It shook Ramed to his core. To his credit, he tried not to let it show. "Most impressive," he said. "A pity that you will not be saving the captain, however. That is impossible."

"Why?" Burgoyne managed to get out.

"Because it is written that the captain will be saved by neither man nor woman. And what does that leave?" Ramed said reasonably.

Burgoyne took another step forward, hir fangs bared. "I am a Hermat. I am both man and woman. No individual, as your prediction might indicate, but rather a merging of both. So it would seem to me that I'm not covered by whatever it is that's written."

It took a moment for this to sink in for Ramed, and when it did, a slow burn of uncertainty began to spread through him. Again, however, he tried to cover it up as best he could. "That is mere semantics," he replied. "Trickery. Word games."

"Perhaps. But nonetheless, it's true. Give me the captain."

"No." Ramed gripped his spear more forcefully.

"Give me the captain and perhaps I'll let you live," Burgoyne said. S/he had dropped to all fours once more. S/he padded toward him. It was a most disconcerting thing to see: S/he spoke with the barely controlled voice of a humanoid, but hir every move and gesture was evocative of a great cat.

"Don't you understand? It's not up to me! This isn't even about me! What I'm doing, I'm doing on behalf of my world! He has to die! You wouldn't understand, because you don't believe! It is from where I draw my strength—the strength that enables me to stand up to you, and do what must be done!''

''I have my own beliefs,'' Burgoyne told him. ''My own religion, which means as much to me as yours does to you. It's where I draw *my* strength from.'' S/he had stopped hir approach and was starting to circle, trying to find the best angle from which to charge. ''I believe in the sacred merging of male and female. Creatures such as yourself go through life as half one or half the other. You always remain separate. Always. I am complete. I am the embodiment of the sexual union. All strength, all power derives from that union.''

''That's ridiculous.''

''Is it? No single act is more powerful. A merging of body, and of spirit. A sharing of all aspects of what you are. A uniting of purpose. The creation of new life, and the reaffirmation of one's own. A letting down of shields and barriers in the pursuit of that one, pure, undiluted moment of ecstasy. The most powerful symbol in nature, and my people are a living embodiment of that symbol. Great power is drawn from that. A strength that you, with your enslavement to the scribblings of others, cannot possibly stand up to. Ultimately your faith will fail you.''

''My faith is complete unto itself,'' Ramed said, his anger building. He swept the spear back and forth in an arc, and it whistled through the air. Burgoyne approached cautiously, aware that Ramed seemed rather adept with the weapon. Clearly, he'd been practicing with it. ''Don't think to challenge me on the strength of faith, because you will surely lose.''

''You've already lost,'' retorted Burgoyne. ''I have faith that I will win. Faith drawn from my unity and holy purpose, my quest that I know I will fulfill. You . . . you have no faith at all. I can tell. I can smell it on you. I can smell the fear radiating off you, oozing through every pore. The fear, the uncertainty. You don't believe in what you're doing. You act out of some misbegotten sense of obligation. But you don't have the stomach to kill. To do what must be done.''

''You know nothing! I am a good man! A decent man! And I can kill if I have to!''

And Burgoyne laughed. It was not a pleasant sound. S/he tossed back hir head and a contemptuous snicker erupted from hir throat. ''You idiot,'' s/he told him. ''You're not fooling anyone, least of all me.''

''I can kill him! I can do what needs to be done!''

''Oh, can you?''

And slowly Burgoyne stood. It took effort, for hir instinct was still to pounce. S/he stood there for a moment, and then gestured. "Come on. Do it. You have that pointed stick of yours. Test yourself out on me. Kill me."

Ramed stood there, the spear wavering uncertainly. "This is—what do you think you're—"

"One of us here isn't afraid, and I guarantee you that it's not you. Take a shot. Go ahead. I won't stop you. Stab me. Stab me to the heart. Here. I'll make it easy for you." Burgoyne tapped the area directly between hir small breasts. "Right here. That's all you have to do. Strike right here. I'll offer no defense." S/he closed hir eyes, hir arms comfortably at hir sides. "Go ahead. Practice on me. Am I not an easy enough target for you?"

"Why . . . why are you doing this?" demanded Ramed.

"Because I have faith that I will win. That my gods will help me. That you do not have what it takes to be a stone cold murderer. That you lack the conviction of your beliefs. Well? Make your move, Ramed. I haven't got all night. Do what you need to do . . . presuming you can do it."

S/he said nothing more, merely stood there, hir eyes serenely closed, hir entire body posture relaxed. Clearly s/he did not believe for a moment that he would try to kill hir.

He gripped the spear with both hands, holding it as tightly as he could. This was his whole life, he realized. His entire existence, boiling down to this moment. He had to do something about hir. If he simply tried to turn and run back into the cave, s/he would surely pounce on him and bring him down. His only chance was to fight. And why shouldn't he? Was he such a coward that he could only kill a helpless victim, tied up?

What had he become? In the final analysis, what had he become? A coward? A murderer, but one unable to commit a simple murder?

In his mind's eye, he saw his wife and child. He saw the faces of Zondarians everywhere, depending upon him to do what had to be done, and he felt his faith beginning to waver. Here, at the final hour, at the moment for which he had prepared his entire life—a moment that his ancestors had prepared for—his nerve was starting to fail him. All thanks to this . . . this creature who stood before him, so contemptuous, so convinced that he did not have the necessary inner strength to do what had to be done.

He would show them. He would show them all.

In the name of eternal peace on Zondar, in the name of the Savior, who had to become a martyr if there was going to be an end to warfare, Ramed would find the inner strength. He would cling to the rightness of his actions. He would do the job that needed doing.

And gripping the spear—the spear of justice—he charged forward, driving the point straight toward Burgoyne's breast.

19

The *Excalibur* barreled toward the Redeemer vessel, shields on maximum, all weapons fully targeting the ship.

Si Cwan had just finished, in as expeditious a manner as he could, describing for Shelby exactly who the Redeemers were and what their problem was with the *Excalibur.* Shelby nodded repeatedly, seeming to take it all in, and then she ordered, "Lay down a phaser barrage. Let's see what their shields have."

The phasers of the *Excalibur* lashed out, pounding the Redeemer ship. The opposing vessel twisted away, backing off as the starship drove toward it, firing relentlessly.

Shelby pounded the arm of her chair. "Yes! Yes!" she crowed, drawing looks from everyone on the bridge. "Damage report! Did we hurt them?"

"Not to any measurable degree," reported Boyajian. "Their shields seem unimpaired. Commander, they're firing."

The Redeemers' phaser weapons blasted at the *Excalibur,* targeting the engineering and saucer sections. The ship trembled under the pounding as, throughout the vessel, crewmen who weren't belted in to their stations tumbled to the floor.

"Shields at seventy percent and holding!" said Boyajian. "Whatever they've got, it packs more wallop than our phasers do! They're not as maneuverable as we are, but with that kind of shielding and weaponry, they don't have to be."

"Damage reports coming in from all over the ship," Lefler informed her. "Life support Systems out on Deck fourteen. Rerouting power now to restore systems."

"Fire photon torpedo spread and phaser barrage. Double-barrel," Shelby said grimly.

The Redeemer ship didn't budge, didn't even engage in any sort of evasive action, as the starship fired upon them. Their shields sparked under the assault, but otherwise held firm.

"We're not getting through their shields, Commander," Boyajian said. "Still no appreciable damage."

"They're firing again!"

"Evasive maneuvers!"

McHenry tried his best, but the *Excalibur* was slowed by the damage she'd sustained. He avoided two blasts, but a third struck at the upper right nacelle.

"Shields at forty percent and falling!" Boyajian warned. "We cannot sustain another direct hit!"

"Mister McHenry, bring us around at one-four-two mark three. Concentrate all remaining shield power to the rear deflectors. Get us out of here. Full impulse."

"We're running, sir?" McHenry asked.

"Simply changing strategy." She rose and said, "Engineering. I want a full-power magnetic burst channeled through the deflector array, on my order. Then prepare to give me warp power, and we're going to need it fast."

"Acknowledged," came Torelli's voice from engineering, although clearly he didn't understand the reason for the order.

Nor did McHenry. However, he was aware of another situation, which he felt was necessary to bring to Shelby's immediate attention. "Commander," he said. "The course you've ordered . . . it has us on a collision course with the Zondarian sun in just under two minutes."

"I'm fully aware of that."

This pronouncement brought concerned looks from everyone on the bridge, and someone would have said something to Shelby had they not received an incoming hail from the Redeemer ship. "Federation vessel," came the voice of Prime One. "Stand down and surrender. Throwing your vessel into a star will accomplish nothing."

"We'll be just fine, thanks," Shelby shot back, her voice rising, "because the great god Calhoun will protect us! And Calhoun can wipe up the floor with your god any day of the week! Catch us if you can, you posturing fool! *Excalibur* out!"

A stunned Boyajian cut off the signal as Soleta and Si Cwan stepped forward. "Commander," Soleta said slowly, "is it possible that you released yourself from sickbay too early?"

"This is erratic behavior, at best—" began Si Cwan.

"I didn't ask for your opinion, Ambassador. If you've nothing to contribute of substance, then get the hell off my bridge. Lieutenant, are you challenging my authority?"

Soleta looked long and hard into Shelby's eyes. She felt as if the entire crew were looking to her, waiting on her judgment. She tried to see some indication of whether Shelby was operating in some sort of diminished capacity, or whether she truly had a plan.

She saw craft and cunning and even a sort of demented anticipation in Shelby's eyes. And there seemed to be nothing of unsteadiness about her.

"No, sir," said Soleta.

"One minute, thirty seconds to Zondarian sun, commander," McHenry said. He was trying to put his worries aside as he saw the star dead ahead, apparently waiting for them.

The ship trembled once more under a blast from the Redeemer ship, but it was a glancing blow, and with all power to their rear shields, they were able to sustain it with minimum problems. The *Excalibur* did not slow down as it tore through space, heading straight on what appeared to be a suicidal course.

"One minute to sun," McHenry told her. The ship, shields down in the front, was beginning to feel the heat. "The Redeemer vessel is still in pursuit."

"Of course they are. It's a matter of pride now. They have to show that their god will protect them as well as ours will. When dealing with fanatics, count on their fanaticism," Shelby said.

"Fifty seconds to sun . . . forty, Commander." McHenry, to his credit, didn't sound nervous. He seemed resigned, even interested in what it would feel like to plunge into a star.

"Give me a countdown, McHenry. Bridge to engineering, ready on deflector dish."

Sweat was pouring down the faces of everyone on the bridge, except for Soleta, who handled the heat better than most. The sun was now completely filling the screen, which had automatically dimmed to spare viewers the intensity of the light.

"Thirty . . . twenty-nine . . . twenty-eight . . . twenty-seven . . ."

Shelby seemed to be counting down with him, making rapid-fire calculations in her head, her lips moving soundlessly as if she were talking to herself. The bridge crew gripped their seats, bracing themselves, wondering what in the world they were about to die for.

"Redeemer ship?"

"Two hundred thousand kilometers and closing."

"Maybe they want to be able to kiss us good-bye," Lefler guessed.

"Twenty-one . . . twenty . . . nineteen . . . eighteen . . ."

The star was everywhere. The heat was overwhelming.

And as if shot from a cannon, Shelby leaped to her feet and shouted, "Engineering! Full magnetic burst, on my mark, five seconds' duration! McHenry, same mark minus five, forty five degree down angle, full reverse thrust! *Mark—now!*"

The deflector dish flared to life, driving a full bore magnetic burst straight into the corona of the Zondarian sun. It struck the corona, disrupting the magnetic lines of the star's turbulent surface. Like a vast giant being stung by a hornet, the star slapped back at the irritation . . .

In the form of a gigantic solar flare.

The *Excalibur* screamed into reverse, the ship's structure howling in protest over the abrupt change in direction, pulling against the gravity of the sun that was already starting to take hold of them. For a moment that stretched into infinity, it looked as if they would not be able to break free, and then the starship tore loose of the star's magnetic field and slammed backward and down, away from the sun.

The Redeemer ship was not quite as fortunate.

Unable to turn or handle as deftly as the *Excalibur,* the Redeemers couldn't get out of the way in time. The last thing they saw was the solar flare belching up at them from the sun's surface, and then the spectacularly erupting discharge, leaping five hundred thousand kilometers from the star and pumping heat approximately twice as hot as the surface of the sun, enveloped the Redeemer vessel. Even the formidable shielding of the Redeemer vessel was unable to stand up to an all-encompassing flare in excess of twenty thousand degrees Fahrenheit. The Redeemer ship was immediately obliterated as the *Excalibur* frantically put as much distance between herself and the momentarily angered star as it could. The flare continued, as if pursuing them, as the starship hurtled backward, but the flare topped out at sixty hundred and fifty thousand kilometers. It continued to erupt for another fifteen minutes, but by that point the starship was safely out of range.

Shelby was on her feet, her fists above her head in triumph. "Hah!" she crowed. "Spectacular! Engineering, great job! You too, McHenry! Excellent all around! Oh! Look!" She pointed to midair.

"Look at what, sir?"

"The colors!" Shelby called out excitedly—and then she pitched forward, Si Cwan just barely catching her before she hit the floor.

20

Burgoyne stood there, chest bared, eyes closed, a look of serene peace on hir face, as Ramed lunged forward with his spear at hir unprotected breast.

The point slammed toward hir—and stopped two inches from impact.

It did not do so at Ramed's behest. He'd been ready to plunge it through hir. It was because Burgoyne had caught the point, hir hand moving so quickly that Ramed had never even seen it coming. Ramed's full strength from both arms was pitted against Burgoyne's single hand, and still he couldn't make any headway.

"You . . . said you wouldn't defend . . . against me," grunted Ramed.

"What do you think, I'm stupid?" snorted Burgoyne.

Ramed redoubled his efforts, and Burgoyne grabbed the spear with both hands, putting hir full weight against his. They shoved against each other, Burgoyne snarling deep in hir throat. To hir surprise, Ramed displayed greater strength than s/he'd given him credit for.

And then something caught Burgoyne's eye.

It was a Zondarian, an older one, and he was materializing like a ghost. He was looking at hir with unfeigned surprise.

It startled Burgoyne. Not much. Just enough, however, for Ramed to shove hir back. S/he stumbled and suddenly realized that s/he was treading air.

Ramed's momentary look of triumph quickly faded, however, as Burgoyne's legs scissored around his middle. The two of them plummeted down the side of the incline, hitting the side once or twice.

Burgoyne, nude from the waist up, was the more vulnerable, as hir torso was lacerated by the dirt and rocks as they rolled down, down, tumbling one over the other.

They hit the ground at the bottom, separated from one another, and miraculously Ramed had still managed to hold on to the spear. He leaped, trying to drive the point straight through hir, but Burgoyne was too quick, hir rage too towering. S/he dodged to one side, brought hir foot up and smashed him squarely in the stomach. He tried to get to his feet and then s/he swung hir talons, slicing through his upper arm, drawing blood. S/he tried to get closer, to go for his throat, but he warded hir off with the spear point, catching hir just under the ribs and drawing a thin line of blood.

They parried, thrusted, bobbed, and weaved, each jockeying for position, and Ramed fell back, back . . .

Burgoyne covered the distance between them in one jump, twisting in midair and avoiding the point of the spear. S/he gripped the spear firmly, and there was murder in hir eyes, and this time Ramed knew that s/he wasn't going to let go until one of them was dead. He steeled himself.

Suddenly they both felt the energy enveloping them.

The creature, the being of energy, the being of magic, of science—whatever it was—they had drawn within range of it, and now it enveloped them.

Burgoyne was ready for it. S/he still had the peace, the joining of Selar deep within hir. The creature insinuated itself through them, seeking weakness, trying to determine whom it could hurt.

It cascaded through Ramed, enveloping him, searching out all his weaknesses, and Ramed cried out in fear, for it was everywhere, the creature was everywhere, giving him no peace, giving him nowhere to hide.

And he knew his life for the sham that it was. Knew that he was supposed to be someone in a position of power, someone who was wise and knowledgeable and a leader. But everyone had found out, everyone had discovered the truth, that he was just one scared little man who had no true feelings of his own save what he'd been told, no real belief in himself, no confidence. He was alone, all alone, and there was Talila coming toward him, and Rab, and all of the Eenza were crying out that he had betrayed them, and all of the Unglza knew that he was a fool and that they would eventually triumph.

The knowledge tore at him, emotionally eviscerated him, and the creature flailed at him, feasting on his weakness.

And Burgoyne sensed it, sensed all of it, and suddenly, despite hir ferocity, despite hir anger, despite hir eagerness to complete hir blood quest, all s/he felt was pity for this poor, pathetic lost soul who was clutching the spear as if his life were wrapped up in it.

"Let go!" shouted Burgoyne over the howling of the energy being.

Cuts, slices began to appear on Ramed, his clothing becoming torn. He began to sob wildly, calling out names like "Talila" and "Rab," names that meant nothing to Burgoyne. "Let's get out of here!" Burgoyne shouted, and began to drag Ramed, not releasing hir hold on the spear but instead using it as a means of hauling Ramed away from the creature's influence. S/he felt it trying to get in at hir as well, but s/he steeled hirself with hir own security, and with the image of Selar that s/he held dear to hir, and s/he resisted its power.

"I can't!" Ramed howled. And suddenly Ramed began to wrestle with the spear with renewed effort.

Burgoyne braced hirself. "Let go! Let it go! It doesn't mean anything!"

"It's everything I am! It's the only thing I am!" Ramed cried out, and with all his weight, all his desperation, all his loneliness, all his hatred of himself and what he had become, he yanked on the spear. He did so with such force and fury that he actually tore it from Burgoyne's grasp.

He was unprepared for the sudden shift in weight. He stumbled forward, and the spear punched through his chest and out his back.

Ramed looked up at Burgoyne with what appeared to be confusion. He reached out a hand to Burgoyne, his fingers flexing on nothing, and then he slid to his knees, running down the length of the spear and coming to a halt as the handle bumped up against his chest.

"Failed . . . failed . . . all my fault . . ." he sobbed, but Burgoyne could not hear his last words over the howling of the creature.

And then, slowly, Burgoyne became aware that the noise was abating. All around them, the creature seemed to be dissipating. S/he couldn't tell whether it was from the creature's own volition, or if some outside force was acting upon it. All s/he knew was that, within moments, it had stopped. The creature was gone as if it had never been there.

Burgoyne crouched over the fallen form of Ramed.

Ramed looked up at hir, the life light flickering out of his eyes. His body spasmed, and he gripped Burgoyne's arm with the last of his strength. "Save . . . my world . . . ask the Savior . . . somehow . . . save my . . ."

"This . . . this didn't have to be," Burgoyne said, unable to contain hir frustration. "What a foolish, foolish waste."

And Ramed smiled.

"Better . . . this way . . ." he whispered. "Better to be . . . a mere fool . . . than a damned fool."

And as the phantom shade called Ontear looked on from a point hundreds of years in the past, Ramed passed into a history that was yet to be.

21

"And that is how I know that I am not your Savior."

Mackenzie Calhoun was circling the large table, as the most holy men of Zondar looked in astonishment at the parchment that he had given them. The parchment, unmistakably in the hand of the holy Suti, that detailed all that had happened. "Ramed," he continued, "was your promised Savior."

Near Calhoun stood Zak Kebron, his arms folded, his gaze baleful, and Ensign Janos, who was eyeing the assemblage with no less suspicion than Kebron. And to the side stood Si Cwan, watching the proceedings.

As voices of protest began to rise, Calhoun raised his voice to silence them. "Read it for yourself!" he said. "Everything that is in those scrolls fits Ramed as well as it does me. And the final proof: Ramed is dead. Slain by the ancient and sacred spear that he and his clan, in their sacred duty, had maintained for just that purpose. In his name, for his sake, in the name of the sacrifices that he made, now is the time to set aside the differences that have wracked this planet with strife for centuries."

"Your people want it, and you want it," said Si Cwan. "When the golden age of peace beckoned you, you could taste it, couldn't you? All of you could. Like honey on your lips, like the sweetest wine filled with the promise of intoxicating peace. It was yours to take. Ramed sacrificed himself to show you the way. You must follow his sacrifice."

"You're suggesting we kill ourselves?" asked Killick in disbelief.

"You've been killing each other long enough, it's almost appropriate," Maro commented drily.

"True enough, but no, that's not what is being suggested," said Calhoun. "It is our recommendation that the Unglza immediately surrender to the Eenza."

This, as Calhoun anticipated, brought a chorus of protest from the Unglza side of the table. "Why should we?" demanded Quinzix.

"Because the Eenza will then promptly surrender to you," replied Si Cwan.

This brought another broadside of objections, but Calhoun steamrolled over them. "You don't understand!" he said angrily. "This is not a request! This is not a plea! I'm telling you that this is what's going to happen! I'm telling you that Ramed lay down his life to show you the way, and you will follow that way! He died for your sins! He died for his people! He martyred himself because he believed that self-sacrifice was the only way that there would ever be peace on this planet, and so help me God, you will follow that lead or you will spiral into the pit and I will make sure that I'm there to give you the swift kick that helps you along!"

There was shaking of heads, there was disbelief, there were loud arguments and objections, there was fury, there was hostility, there were threats and more threats, there was a fistfight, there were sobs, there were pleadings, there was blustering and anger and vituperation . . .

. . . and ultimately . . .

. . . there was acceptance.

The crowds were massed outside the burial site, but for the moment, Talila was the only one allowed in. She stood at the gravesite of her husband, staring at the dirt, as if she could somehow will him back to life.

She became aware of a presence next to her, and she looked around to see a rather odd-looking individual in a Starfleet uniform.

"Who are you?" she asked.

"I am Burgoyne one-seventy-two. Chief engineer. I . . . knew your husband," s/he said. "I was there when he died."

"Did you kill him?" she asked, her voice surprisingly even.

"It was as much at my hand as his," Burgoyne admitted. "He was trying to kill me and I defended myself. But ultimately I don't think his heart was in it. I think he was searching for a way out—and found it."

"Found it in the comfort of the grave," she said hollowly. She shook her head. "Pointless. Pointless and foolish."

"That is what I thought, at first. He . . . he spoke your name at the end. Yours and, I believe, your son's."

"How kind of him," she said icily, "to think of us at the end. To think of those he was leaving behind. The wife with no one to love her, the child with no father to raise him."

"He was trying to save your world," Burgoyne told her.

And her hand snapped around, as s/he knew it would, and caught Burgoyne across the cheek. Burgoyne took the slap and didn't even reach up to rub the redness.

"Then the world can burn," said Talila. "And so can you." And she walked away, leaving Burgoyne at the gravesite of the martyr of Zondar.

"Si Cwan?"

Once again, Lefler felt as if she were talking to thin air as Si Cwan stared out his window. This time, however, rather than looking into space, he was gazing upon the planet Zondar, turning below them.

She was about to start lecturing him again on how the time she was spending as his liaison was somewhat limited. Then again, part of her didn't mind just sitting and staring at him, admiring the rippling muscles, sleek build and remarkably strong chin. But as she wrestled with her priorities, he broke the silence. "I don't know if they're going to make it," he said.

"The Zondarians?"

He nodded. "There are many who want peace, who are so hungry for it that they readily accept Calhoun's interpretation of events. But there are others who are calling Ramed the false Savior. There are others still who, having read Ontear's unexpurgated predictions, not only believe that Calhoun should have died but, in failing to do so, has doomed the entire world. At a time when they should be uniting, we're seeing factions. I just do not know if we're going to be able to pull this off."

"If anyone can, you can," said Lefler.

He turned and smiled at her. "You truly believe that?"

And Lefler, who had just been mentally kicking herself and demanding of herself, *My God, did you just **say** that? You sound like a love-struck nitwit,* immediately swtiched gears and said, "Absolutely."

"Thank you. I appreciate your vote of confidence."

Then his computer beeped at him and he glanced at it. ''Another incoming message,'' he said. He looked at it more closely. ''Well, now *this* is interesting.''

''Who's it from?''

''The Momidiums, over in the Gamma Hydrinae system. They have someone they wish to turn over to us.''

''Turn over?''

''Yes,'' he said slowly. ''A human being, apparently. Female. She was on some sort of exploratory mission there. The Momidiums felt she was a spy, but they're very reverential of life, so they didn't execute her. Nor did they turn her over to us because they felt that we would execute her.''

''Would you have?'' asked Lefler.

He looked at her evenly. ''Do you truly wish to know the answer to that, Robin?'' When she didn't reply, he took that as her response. ''In any event, they simply locked her away. They've kept her there for approximately four years now. However, they wish to embark on solid relations with the Federation since the *Excalibur* is now in the area, so they're interested in turning her over to us in exchange for certain guarantees.''

''What sort of guarantees?''

''Look for yourself.'' He turned the computer screen around so that she could read it. The various conditions were spelled out on the screen, lined up next to a photograph of the human woman.

Si Cwan frowned. ''Robin, are you all right?''

Lefler had gone dead white. Her jaw was hanging down to somewhere around the floor.

''Robin?'' he asked again.

And she looked up at him and whispered, ''That's . . . that's my mother.''

''What?'' He swung the screen around, as if he would actually recognize a total stranger. The woman had long black hair, a long face, and eyes that seemed to blaze with quiet intelligence. ''Are you sure?'' he asked.

Lefler nodded wordlessly.

''This is . . . this is incredibly fortunate for you, then!'' said Si Cwan. ''The Momidiums claim this is a recent photo of her, so apparently she is in in good health.''

''Remarkably good health,'' said Lefler, her voice sounding very distant. ''Considering that she died ten years ago.''

* * *

Burgoyne returned to hir quarters, feeling heavyhearted and despairing. S/he sank into hir overstuffed couch. The computer was beeping at hir, indicating a message was being held for hir.

"Computer. Message."

The screen came on and Calhoun's face appeared on it. "Chief," he said, "we've received permission from the Zondarians to explore the caves and machinery on their world, in Ontear's Sacred Realm or whatever it's called. There seems to be tremendous potential there for discovery. And hopefully it will provide some answers to some outstanding questions we have. When you get in, coordinate with Lieutenant Soleta."

Burgoyne nodded, as if Calhoun could see hir.

"And Burgoyne, thanks again for saving my ass. I owe you one, Burgy," added Calhoun.

The screen blinked out.

Burgoyne sighed. It was clear that s/he wasn't going to get a break. There was still that bizarre energy situation in the engine room that s/he had to explore. And now there was this mysterious alien machinery, which did hold some fascination, but still . . . Burgoyne felt tired. Wrung out.

"A quick rest," s/he said to hirself. "Five minutes won't kill anyone."

S/he rose and entered hir bedroom.

Selar was waiting for hir.

Burgoyne blinked in surprise to see the doctor standing there. She looked fairly recovered, although there were still bruises on her. Reconstructive surgery had repaired the damage to her ear. Her gaze was steady, her manner calm and collected.

No. No, it wasn't. Her body started trembling the moment that Burgoyne walked in.

"Doctor? What are you doing here? Are you all right?"

Selar tried to speak, but couldn't get words out. Instead she took two steps forward, grabbed Burgoyne, and kissed hir forcefully, swept up in *Pon Farr,* caught up in her need, and knowing, finally, for once, exactly what she wanted.

No words were required.

And Burgoyne never did get that five minutes' rest.

FIRE ON HIGH

ELSEWHERE . . .

The only sound on the planet Ahmista is the sound of a woman singing.

Oh, there are a few other sounds as well, but they are merely the sounds of the planet itself. The gentle breeze glides across the plains, moving the ashes through the air with subtle urging. (The ashes have been there for quite some time, but they dwindle in quantity with every passing day and every vagrant breeze, to say nothing of the cleansing provided by the occasional storm or downpour.)

There are also the normal grindings of tectonic plates, and a continent away there's an island of volcanoes that can raise a particularly impressive racket. Birds flap their wings against the wind; waves lap against shores, occasionally leaving a film of ash decorating the beaches.

But other than that . . . nothing.

The noise is rather conspicuous in its absence. No noise of a living, breathing population. There are none of the sounds of industry. Nor are there the sounds of people laughing or talking, or children crying out to be tended to. There are no sounds as subtle as lovers whispering in the dark, or as officious as bombs whistling through the air.

Nothing but her singing.

It is an odd song in that the tune seems to vary from one moment to the next. She lilts her way through it, never stopping except at those times when her fatigued mind and body require sleep. She does not like to give in to those urges, because it interferes with her vigilance, but every so often her head simply droops forward of its own accord and sleep steals into her head. Hours can pass with her in that condition, but then she snaps awake and is neither conscious nor caring of how much time has genuinely passed.

Even if there were sounds of any living beings on Ahmista, it is unlikely that she would hear them. She lives upon a mountain, if such a term as "lives" can be applied to her existence. It is not the highest mountain on Ahmista, but it is a fairly nice one, as mountains go. She is not quite at such an altitude as to feel a significant chill . . . not that she would even if it were subzero temperatures, because her lover keeps her warm.

In fact, her lover does more than that. Her lover keeps her company, her lover keeps her close. Her lover is the be-all and end-all of her existence on the planet, of her existence in the universe. She feels her lover in her mind, and she is content.

Her lover is sleek and gray, vaguely cylindrical in shape but with a variety of sections branching off in an assortment of directions. Its sections are inserted directly into her nervous system at a dozen points. In a way, her lover looks like a great thorny bush with limbs trailing off and intertwining with one another. And ultimately, all the branches come back to her, and she comes back to it, for together they are one. Together they are a whole. They complete one another.

She is singing to her lover more than she is to herself.

Her lover never tells her what it thinks of her songs. That's okay, really. She doesn't need to hear her lover's approval, because she knows she already has that. How could she not? After all, she has given her life over to her lover. She neither needs, nor wants, anything else. Her lover gives her so much. Gives her nutrients, gives her life and the ability to live. And all she need do is make her lover her entire reason for living. That she has managed to do.

It suddenly pulses in a different manner beneath her fingers. She has been drifting slightly, but the alert manner of her lover snaps her back to full focus. She reaches out with her mind, reaches out through her lover.

There is a creature.

It has just hatched from an egg, approximately twenty miles away, deep in a forest that is otherwise devoid of life. It is small, covered with fur, and looking for a mother who is long since dead. It has no claws, not yet. It's fairly helpless, really, at this point. Without its mother, it might very likely die on its own. However, it might be resourceful enough to survive, to grow and thrive. And possibly someday be a threat. Birds . . . birds have never been a threat, and for some reason she has always considered the sounds of their wings comforting. This, though, she cannot chance. She knows that. Her lover knows that. Or at least, she knows it now that her lover has told her, but she is—of course—in complete agreement.

At her urging, her lover reaches out with a crackle of energy, shudders slightly in her grip, and belches out an energy ball. It's nothing particularly large, because none such is needed. The energy that her lover is capable of disgorging is directly proportionate to whatever job is required. In this instance, it's fairly insignificant.

The energy ball covers the intervening distance in no time at all. The newborn creature senses something coming, looks up, and feels a source of light and heat. Its little eyes are still blind and so it cannot see what is approaching, but nonetheless makes the false—if understandable—assumption that it's about to meet its mother. It opens its mouth wide and makes a small *yeep* sound.

A second later, it's enveloped by the energy. The creature didn't really have time to have a full sense of its own existence before it didn't have an existence anymore. Instead it is reduced, in no time at all, to little more than a pile of ash. There is a hint of a tiny claw in there, and a few stray tufts of fur flutter away, caught in the breeze that quickly stirs the ashes into nothingness. Otherwise, though, there's no sign that the creature was ever there.

Back on the mountaintop, she begins to tremble. She wraps herself more tightly around her lover than before, for she knows that it has acted to protect her. The knowledge is exciting to her, stimulates her, and she begins to tremble.

She runs her hands along the surface of her lover. She has stopped singing. Instead she is beginning to quiver in anticipation, for this is how she always feels when her lover shows its strength on her behalf. And her lover knows that it has pleased her, and that knowledge excites it in kind.

She gasps out a name . . . a name known only to her and her lover. A name that has never even been spoken aloud, but is instead something communicated without need of clumsy speech. It is something deep within their mutual soul, for her lover was soulless until she had joined with it.

It had been so long since she felt the fire within her, that for the briefest of moments she entertains the notion that her lover had sought out something to kill for her. Something to obliterate, because that was the only way that it could possibly find sufficient stimulation to give her, and itself, what it needed.

But then she quickly dismisses the idea from her mind. Her lover would never do that, would have no need to do that. Her lover is not the embodiment of destruction. No. Her lover is the giver of light, the provider of joy.

The heat fill her mind, radiates from throughout her lover, and she can feel her heart speeding up, thudding against her chest with such abandon and power that it threatens to burst through her rib cage. If that were to happen, of course, then she would die, but she is not concerned. She trusts her lover implicitly. She knows it would not hurt her.

Her lover, though, is not mortal. She realizes that on some sort of base level. Her lover is something else, something special. Something beyond anything that she has ever known before.

And she comes to the realization, even as its love floods through her, that she can never return to anything that once was.

Her lover prefers the silence, for it makes it that much easier for it to hear her as she starts to sob with the pure joy she derives from their bonding.

It used to come much more frequently, back when there was more life on the planet. As each thing threatened her, her lover dispensed with it, and each demise would fill her with orgasmic pleasure. Such encounters now are few and far between, but that is all right with her. She has her memories, and she has her lover to keep her warm, safe, loved.

Slowly, so slowly, she tries to steady the pounding of her heart. She sags against her lover, clutching it even as her fingers open and close spasmodically. Deep in her chest she laughs softly to herself, enjoying the warmth her lover has given her and the sense of security and safety.

"Thank you," she whispers, which are the first words spoken on the planet in some time. "Thank you . . . for that. Thank you for being mine. Thank you . . . for choosing me."

Her lover does not reply, nor does it need to. It simply continues to pulse against her, and if it is pleased that it has given her pleasure, or displeased at her reactions, or completely uncaring, it's really impossible to say. It just sits quietly, unchanged, unreacting. She strokes it once more and she feels her consciousness drifting. She wants to stay awake, unwilling to surrender to a hazy sensation of bliss that threatens to carry her away to slumber. "Not . . . tired," she moans like a petulant child being shunted away for a nap, and she does her best to resist.

Ultimately, however, she fails. Her eyes flutter closed, her head sags forward and thumps gently against the metal sheath that is the exterior of her lover. Moments later, still warm from the gentle pleasures of her lovemaking, she falls into a peaceful sleep. She does not snore, does not make any extraneous noise. And so, for a time at least, there is no vaguely humanoid sound on the planet Ahmista aside from her soft breathing as she sleeps. Sooner or later, though, she will awaken once more. At that point, she will begin singing again in that odd, aimless way she has, remembering what her previous lovemaking was like and wondering when the next opportunity will come along. . . .

1

Commander Elizabeth Shelby ran the video log of the bridge of the *Excalibur,* not quite able to believe what she was seeing.

Nearby Dr. Maxwell was watching her with an apologetic expression on his face. Behind him, sickbay personnel were going on about their business as Shelby sat in the private office usually used by Dr. Selar, studying the last moments of consciousness she had known before keeling over several days ago. She had been certain that she was fully recovered but now, watching the video log with a growing sense of doom, she was wondering if perhaps she should take a permanent sick leave.

Through her off-the-cuff strategy, she had just managed to dispatch a warship belonging to the dreaded Redeemers by using, literally, the power of a sun to do so. But she had come on to the bridge still suffering from head injuries sustained during a disastrous landing expedition to the planet Zondar. All she remembered was that she had passed out right after saving the *Excalibur* from destruction, but now she was watching the immediate aftermath.

She watched herself leap to her feet, her fists exuberantly pumping the air over her head. She called out triumphantly, "Hah! Spectacular! Engineering, great job! You too, McHenry! Excellent all around! Oh! Look!" She pointed into midair.

"Look at what, sir?" McHenry was asking.

"Colors!" Shelby called out excitedly—and then she pitched forward, Si Cwan just barely catching her before she hit the floor.

But that wasn't the worst of it.

She wasn't unconscious, oh no. No, that would've been too merciful. Instead she had stared up into the air as Si Cwan had said with concern, "Are you all right, Commander?"

"They're all different colors!" Shelby had said. "Blue, green, pink . . ."

Si Cwan looked with confusion at the others on the bridge, who seemed equally perplexed. "What are, Commander?"

"The colors!" Shelby had said again, joyously. And then she had passed out.

In sickbay, separated from the event by several days, Shelby clicked off the video record and tried not to display the pain she was feeling. She was not especially successful, unfortunately.

"You said you wanted to see it, Commander," Maxwell reminded her as if concerned she was going to be angry with him. "I advised against it, remember."

"I remember," she sighed.

"It's not important, Commander. It was just a . . . a stream of consciousness comment. Dreaming with your eyes awake. I guarantee you, no one's going to think about it or even remember it by now. And I'm certain that absolutely no one is going to kid you about it."

She looked up at him bleakly. "On *this* ship? No way are they going to let it go," she said as if she were awaiting her turn to step into the cart that would bring her to the guillotine. She put her face in her hands. "Face it, Doctor—I'm a dead woman."

"She looks rather healthy for a dead woman."

Mackenzie Calhoun, captain of the *Excalibur,* scratched his chin thoughtfully as he studied the picture that was staring back out at him from the computer screen. On either side of the table, Ambassador Si Cwan—former head of the Thallonian ruling class—and Lieutenant Robin Lefler, the ship's Ops officer and part-time assistant to Cwan, had just heard him make this pronouncement. Although Lefler generally had a very ready smile, it wasn't on display at that particular moment. Si Cwan, who customarily had something of a deadpan, didn't look any different than he usually did.

Calhoun leaned forward thoughtfully as if closer examination might yield some bit of information that he'd previously missed. The picture on the screen was of a woman with long, dark hair, a square chin, narrow nose, and a steady gaze that appeared to have a piercing, intensely intelligent air to it. Not an easy thing to project over a mere photograph made for computer identification, but somehow she had managed it. He could only wonder what she was like in person, if that was how she came across in a simple photo.

"So let's see if I've got this straight," he said after a moment, meeting Lefler's gaze. "The Momidiums, out in the Gamma Hydrinae system, claim that this woman was rooting around on their planet about five years ago. This would have made her a trespasser as far as both the Momidiums and the overseers of the Thallonian Empire"—and he gestured suavely to Si Cwan—"were concerned."

"That is correct."

"If the Momidiums had turned her over to the Thallonians, they likely would have executed her."

"I dislike the term 'execute,' " Si Cwan said. "It sounds distasteful to me. Cruel and most impersonal."

"Your pardon, Ambassador," said Calhoun. "How about 'killed'?"

"Much better."

"As you wish. They likely would have killed her." He watched Si Cwan nod his head in agreement and continued, "However, they had no desire to overlook the crimes of trespass and perhaps spying, so they imprisoned her. Have they given any indication as to precisely what they have to hide that they thought was subject for a spy's interest?"

Si Cwan glanced at Lefler, to whom the question seemed addressed, but she made no reply and he came to the realization that she was barely listening. He lightly tapped her shin under the table while stepping in himself to say, "No indication at all, Captain. They have been fairly circumspect in that regard. As with most sentient beings, they like to have their secrets."

"Fine. We needn't dwell on that at the moment. But now," he said thoughtfully as he drummed his fingers, "they want to make nice to us, so they offer to turn this female over to us. One Morgan Primus by name." Even though he knew the name he nonetheless glanced at the computer screen for reaffirmation, much as someone who has just looked at his watch will look at it once more if someone asks him the time even a second later. "They offer her in exchange for certain promises which you, *Lieutenant Lefler,* feel are not unreasonable."

He said her name with sufficient emphasis that it appeared to jolt her from her slightly dreamy and distracted state. "I'm sorry . . . ?" she said as she realized she wasn't focused on the question.

"The Momidiums," Si Cwan gently cued her. "About their demands . . ."

"Oh. Not unreasonable at all, sir," she said quickly. "They are a fairly simple people, actually. They desire some advice from any agricultural specialists on designs for a new irrigation system they've developed for their farmland. Oh, and they have a flu epidemic in one of their outlying provinces. They believe that they've managed to synthesize a cure, but it will take them approximately two weeks to finish running tests on it, and they want to know if our facilities could possibly cut that time down."

"And—?"

"I've already run it past Dr. Maxwell, sir. He assures me that our labs could test the effectiveness of the cure through cross-matching and molecular analysis within three hours of receiving it."

"Good. And if the good doctor finds flaws in the formula, I imagine it would not be overly demanding for him to correct those flaws, now, would it."

"Bordering on Prime Directive violation, isn't that, Captain?" inquired Si Cwan.

"Bordering but not over the line, Ambassador," replied Calhoun. "However, in this instance, Starfleet agreed to give us some latitude. So, Lieutenant, in exchange for these agreements, the Momidiums will present us with this human female."

"That's right, sir."

"A female whom you claim could pass for your mother's twin."

"No twin, sir," said Lefler and she tapped the screen with a knuckle. "That is my mother."

"The mother whom you said died in a shuttle accident about ten years ago."

Lefler squared her shoulders, pulling herself up straight, for Calhoun had made no effort to hide the disbelief in his voice. "That's correct, sir. Morgan Lefler. At least, that's the name I always knew her by. 'Primus' wasn't even her maiden name, so I don't know where that name came from."

"And was the shuttle accident anywhere in this vicinity?"

"No, sir. Actually, it was in New Jersey. She was on vacation, visiting family there. She was flying a private shuttle and it went out of control and crashed into the Atlantic Ocean."

"You'll excuse me if I don't seem properly sympathetic to your, uhm . . . loss," he said, leaning back in his chair, "but do you have any theories or guesses as to how your late mother managed to get all the way from a watery grave to the Gamma Hydrinae system?''

''I believe,'' she said promptly, for naturally she had given the matter no small amount of thought, ''that she never died in the accident.''

''Well, that would certainly follow.''

''Her body was never recovered after the crash. They found the shattered remains of her personal transport shuttle, but it was cracked open and there was no sign of her. Since there were no traces of transporter energy or any other intelligent agency that might have rescued or abducted her, we had always assumed that some . . . some oceanic form of life had simply made off with her body and, uhm . . .''

''Eaten it?'' Si Cwan supplied after she was silent for a moment.

She fired him an icy look. ''Yes, thank you,'' she said, although she didn't sound especially appreciative. ''That was the phrase I was searching for.''

''You're welcome,'' replied Si Cwan graciously, sarcasm being totally lost on him.

''It is my belief,'' continued Lefler, ''that she allowed us—my father and me—to believe that she had been killed.''

''She could have been kidnapped.''

''She had been.''

''But I thought you said . . .''

''She had been, to my knowledge, abducted at least eight times in my lifetime. She was not a stay-at-home kind of mother. Each time she escaped within hours and returned within days. After the accident, my father and I held out hope for a long time. Hope that she would just walk in the front door. In the end, we had no choice but to assume she was dead.''

''Were your parents getting along? Happy marriage and all?''

''To the best of my knowledge, yes, sir. Certainly nothing my father said to me indicated otherwise. He, uhm . . .'' She looked down. ''He . . . passed away several years later, shortly after I entered Starfleet. He was never quite the same after she was killed, and it was like he just . . . just drifted away from life, and was only waiting until my life was on track and settled before he . . .''

Si Cwan reached over and put a hand upon one of hers. The contrast could not have been greater, for his hands were large and red, while hers were small, pale, and rather delicate. Under other circumstances, the physical contact between her and Si Cwan would have sent a secret little thrill of pleasure through her, but as it was she was simply grateful for the gesture. She squeezed his hand tightly in acknowledgment and he nodded slightly as if to say that he understood.

"I'm sorry for your loss, Lieutenant," Calhoun told her. "But that still leaves us with the question of why she would vanish without a trace ten years ago only to show up in Thallonian space."

"I don't know!" Lefler cried, her voice raised, and she quickly realized that her tone was inappropriate for such a response, particularly considering that she was addressing her commanding officer. She looked at him nervously, but he simply put up a calming hand, indicating that she shouldn't get too concerned over the breach of etiquette. "I don't know," she repeated, far more calmly this time. "I suppose that's why I'm rather eager to find out. When can we leave, sir? Our mission on Zondar is concluded, but we're still in orbit here. We could easily depart immediately for—"

"In case you haven't noticed, Lieutenant, our science officer is still not aboard."

"Yes, of course I noticed, sir," Lefler said. "She's on the Zondarian surface exploring some sort of archaeological dig. Can't that be concluded another time, sir? Or perhaps we could come back for her?"

"Lieutenant, as much as I appreciate your anxiety here, this is simply not an emergency."

"Captain!"

He shook his head, a grim smile of amusement playing across his lips. "If it's really your mother, Lieutenant, and you've believed her dead for the last ten years—and she's been stewing on Momidium for the last five—then a few more days isn't going to cause the total collapse of the galaxy as we know it."

"Then let me go on ahead."

"Negative, Lieutenant. The last time I sent any members of this crew 'on ahead' in a shuttle, it was with the best of intentions with the most cataclysmic results."

"Captain, this is hardly the same situation," Si Cwan said. "I know what you're referring to: When the science vessel *Kayven Ryin* informed us that my sister was aboard, it turned out to be a trap set for me by an old enemy. But the situations are hardly analogous, Captain. It's not as if the lieutenant has enemies in this sector."

"I'm not saying she does, Ambassador," replied Calhoun. "The point is, the moment I send any of my people away from the *Excal-*

ibur, I'm sending them into potential danger. I won't hesitate to do so if I feel it's necessary. In this instance, I don't feel it is."

"But Captain . . ." began Lefler.

He looked at her levelly. "Lieutenant, are you under the impression that my decision is open for debate?"

She opened her mouth a moment, then closed it and looked down. "No, sir," she said quietly.

"Good. The fact is that Lieutenant Soleta's investigations are potentially very important for our ongoing mission, and I'm not going to put a phaser to her head and tell her to hurry it up. Nor am I going to abandon her on Zondar so we can head off to retrieve your alleged mother."

"Yes, sir," sighed Lefler.

Calhoun tapped his commbadge. "Calhoun to Soleta."

After a moment, the science officer's voice came back. "Soleta here."

"Lieutenant, I'm not trying to rush you, but a matter has come up that may require our attention. Can you give me a rough estimate of when you'll be completing your investigation of Ontear's cave and the surrounding vicinity?"

"Nineteen hours, twenty-seven minutes, Captain."

He blinked in surprise. "Nineteen hours, twenty-seven minutes?"

"Yes, sir."

"I'm surprised you didn't pin it down to the exact number of remaining seconds."

"You *did* say a rough estimate, Captain," she replied.

"So I did," admitted Calhoun. "All right, thank you, Lieutenant. Calhoun out." He turned to face Lefler and Si Cwan. "Ambassador, I would like you to contact the Momidium government. Let them know that their terms are acceptable if they are indeed as described. I respect the fact that there is a time pressure regarding the illness they are trying to combat, but we won't be able to set out for about a solar day. I assume they can hold on until then."

"I imagine they will have to," said Si Cwan.

"Lieutenant, follow up with Dr. Maxwell. Inform him that we will indeed be needing sickbay's assistance in this matter and that they should have some lab time set aside to accommodate us."

"Yes, sir."

He thumped his palms on the table. "Sounds like a plan," he said briskly and rose. "Unless there's anything else then . . . ?"

Si Cwan and Lefler looked at each other questioningly. "No, I think that is more or less all, Captain," Lefler said.

"Good." He rose, and then paused and added, "Lieutenant . . . for what it's worth, I truly am sorry over the personal difficulties you've had with your parents."

"Thank you, Captain."

He nodded, turned and walked out.

Lefler sat back and sighed. "That didn't go as well as I'd hoped."

"He agreed to make Momidium our next port of call," replied Si Cwan. "Considering the number of worlds that are vying for our attention, that alone is something of an accomplishment."

She sat forward, propping her chin up in her hands. "It's insane, Si Cwan. I feel like Alice."

"Alice?" His brow furrowed. "What is an 'Alice'?"

She sighed. "When I was a little girl, one of my favorite books was *Alice in Wonderland.* My mother introduced me to it, in fact."

"I can't say I'm familiar with it."

"I wouldn't imagine it made the Thallonian bestseller list," she said, speaking with an amusement she didn't really feel. "It was actually somewhat subversive in its time. It was created to be a satire of Brit—of a particular Earth government. But functioning in and of itself, it's the story of a young girl who falls down a hole burrowed by an animal called a rabbit and discovers herself in a strange and mystical realm in which no one and nothing makes any sense. It has maintained its popularity for centuries."

"I can easily understand why. Entering a realm that makes no sense? My dear Lieutenant, the technical term for that is 'birth.' Or are you under the mistaken impression that life as a whole makes sense?"

"I guess not, but damn it, Si Cwan, you'd think some things would be a given, wouldn't you?"

"A given?" He looked at her quizzically, and then he rose from his chair and slowly circled the room, never taking his eyes off her. They had that piercing quality that she found so attractive in him, but somehow at that moment, she wasn't really paying attention to them. "What things?"

"Losing my mom . . . it was . . ." She took a deep breath and then said, "Look . . . this isn't stuff we really have to discuss, okay? I mean, it's kind of personal. And you and I . . . we don't really know each other all that well, when you get down to it. I mean, we've known each other for a little while, but not enough for me to feel comfortable discussing it with you.''

''Are you certain?''

He was behind her then, and he placed a hand on her shoulder. She felt the strength in it then, even more so than when he had rested his hand atop hers earlier. Part of her wanted to embrace him, to just flee from the turmoil going through her mind by disappearing into his large and powerful arms. But she was feeling vulnerable at that moment, more so than she could recall in quite some time. Her gut reaction was to keep her distance from him, and after another moment's thought, that was exactly what she decided to do.

She stood quickly, gently brushing his hand away as she did so. ''I'm sorry,'' she said, sounding more brusque than she would have liked.

''No need to apologize,'' he said mildly. ''This is a very difficult time for you.''

''I should be glad,'' she told him, although it was as if she were speaking more to herself than to him. ''Really, I should be glad. I mean . . . if it's her, if it's really her . . . I get a second chance. Whatever the reasons, I get a second chance with her, and that's really the important thing, isn't it?''

''Is it?''

''Yes,'' she said firmly. ''Yes, it is, and everything's fine, and we don't have to discuss it anymore. I appreciate your help, but I'm going to be fine, okay?''

''Okay.''

''And I shouldn't be looking for things to be wrong with what should be a joyous moment. Lefler's Law Number Thirty-two: If life hands you lemonade, don't try to make lemons out of it. Do you agree?''

''If I knew what lemonade was, probably.''

''Good. Good.'' She seemed about to say something else, but instead she quickly exited the room, leaving a more-than-puzzled Si Cwan wondering if there was something else he should have said.

2

In sickbay, Ensign Ronni Beth lay back on a medical table, her wavy hair surrounding her face like a corona of curls. As she did so, Dr. Karen Kurdziel checked the scanner readings and nodded approvingly. Kurdziel was a trim, blue-haired woman with an apparently endless amount of patience and a keen sense of the absurd. Both of those were serving her well at that particular moment.

"I'm gonna kill him," Beth said for what seemed the hundredth time.

"I know you are," said Kurdziel. "You've made that painfully clear." She ran her tricorder over Beth's ankle. "That's healing up nicely. Look, do me a favor and stay off the slopes, okay, Ron? Even holodeck slopes are tricky for novice skiers."

"Yeah, yeah, yeah," Ronni said impatiently. "Can I sit up?"

Kurdziel nodded and Beth sat up, pulling on her boot gingerly. "He was supposed to be with me," she fumed. "Did I tell you this?"

"Yes," Kurdziel said.

As if Kurdziel hadn't spoken, Beth continued, "Christiano was supposed to meet me on the slopes. He promised me. Then he's running late, and I figure, no problem, so I start a trial run because I figure, you know, how difficult can this be?"

"And you found out." Kurdziel was trying to remain sympathetic, but even her infinite patience was beginning to flag. Beth had been involved with Ensign Christiano, who was in Engineering same as she was. But that relationship had apparently just crashed and burned, as Beth was quick to tell anyone who was stationary for longer than five seconds.

"Yeah, but that was nothing compared to finding out he was with another woman. And after the ring I gave him!"

"Ring?" This was news to Kurdziel. "What ring?"

"Got it off a dealer on space station K-Nineteen. Picked it up just before being assigned here. I was . . . I dunno . . . I was saving it for just the right guy. And I thought sure Christiano was him."

"So ask for it back," Kurdziel told her matter-of-factly.

"I'm not going to ask for it back!" Beth said indignantly. "It was a gift."

"If an engagement is broken off, isn't it customary to ask for the ring back?"

"But this wasn't part of an engagement. I just gave it to him because . . ." She looked down. "Because I really felt like he was the one. So I got ahead of myself and did something stupid. And now I know for next time. Live and learn."

"I'm sorry, Ensign."

"Well, it's a sorry galaxy, I guess."

She was about to say something else along those lines, but then she noticed something. She didn't want to point, because somehow it seemed rude, so instead she just angled her chin in the general direction of where she was indicating and asked, "She's up and around?"

Kurdziel looked where Beth was pointing and, by way of responding to the question, said, "Commander. You're looking fit."

Commander Shelby was striding across sickbay in her familiar confident manner. There was still some faint discoloration on her face from injuries sustained during a fairly battering excursion on the surface of Zondar, but at this point she seemed none the worse for wear from it.

"Feeling ready to get back to work?" Dr. Kurdziel asked.

"You could say that," Shelby said agreeably. She flexed her shoulder. "Still feel a little tightness, but Dr. Maxwell assures me that'll pass."

"If he says so, I'm sure it's true."

"Other than that, I've been judged fit for duty." She smiled, looking somewhat relieved. "I'm not much for sitting around and recuperating. Glad to be back in action."

"The way I heard it, you got back into action a little too . . . fast . . ." said Ronni Beth, her voice trailing off, realizing that, woozy from the painkiller she was under, she'd actually spoken aloud. Immediately she tried to figure out if there was some worse way she could have shoved her foot in her mouth. If it weren't for the pain-killer . . .

Shelby, whose back was to her, slowly turned, her smile frozen on her face. "I beg your pardon?" she said with a voice that would have frosted a supernova.

"I'm sorry, I—Oh, look at the time," Beth said quickly, hopping off the table and trying not to hobble. "I'd better get go—"

"I asked you a question, Ensign," Shelby said, taking a half step that put her squarely in Beth's path, making it clear in a fairly unsubtle manner that Beth wasn't going anywhere.

"I . . ." She looked to Kurdziel for help, but Kurdziel simply shrugged in a way that said, *You're on your own.* Looking visibly pained, Beth said, "Well, word was that you went back to the bridge during a red alert, that you put us on a collision course with a sun, and that you passed out after seeing . . ."

"After seeing what?" pressed Shelby, no less icy.

Beth said something very quietly.

"I didn't catch that," prompted Shelby.

"Colors," Beth said more loudly. "Word is that you pointed into midair, said, 'Oh look! Colors!' and fainted dead away."

"And did 'word' also mention," inquired Shelby, "that my maneuver toward the Zondarian sun saved this vessel and all aboard—including, might I point out, yourself?"

"As a matter of fact, yes," Beth admitted.

"Good. Because as long as the crew is having a laugh at my expense," said Shelby, raising her voice a bit so that it carried, catching the attention of others in sickbay, "it would be nice for them to remember that particular respect is to be accorded all senior officers of a starship. Particularly those senior officers who have, through their actions, kept everyone on the *Excalibur* in one piece. Understood?"

"Understood, Commander."

"Understood?" she said again, this time directing it to the general populace of sickbay, and she got nods from everyone there. With that settled, she squared her shoulders and walked out of sickbay.

Lefler's quarters were not especially large, but she'd never been much for anything fancy. She was more of a people person, really, and so spent very little time in her quarters. A friend of hers had once speculated that Robin Lefler had only one true fear in the galaxy, and that was of being alone. That her need to be with people was so incessant that solitude was utterly anathema. When informed of her friend's appraisal, Lefler had vehemently denied it while, at the same time, wondering to herself if there wasn't just a little bit of truth to it.

At this particular point in time, however, she wanted nothing but to be alone. Even though she was on duty, even though she should have by rights been heading up to the bridge, she had bolted into her quarters, the door sliding shut behind her. She closed her eyes, leaning against a bulkhead, and slowly shook her head. "It can't be her," she whispered. "She couldn't have done that. It can't possibly be her."

She said that several more times before gathering herself and going to one of her dresser drawers. She pulled it open, rummaged around for a moment, and then removed a holotube. It was a cylinder about six inches tall, and inside was a carefully preserved hologram of her mother, the late Morgan Lefler.

She remembered the day she had gotten it. It had been the day before her mother had died.

She recalled how the irony had weighed heavily upon her. How her mother had had the hologram produced as purely a spur of the moment thing. A gift to send off to her beloved daughter, a keepsake with no particular meaning other than that her mom was thinking about her. No . . . no, there had been another meaning, Lefler now recalled. She and her mom had had a big fight the night before. Her mother had made it clear that she had matters to attend to and that she absolutely had to go off and visit relatives the next day, and so she had left her daughter—for the last time, as it turned out—with things still unsettled between them. Robin racked her brains, trying to remember what it was that she and her mother had argued about, and she couldn't for the life of her recall.

All she could remember was the guilt that she had carried with her when she'd gotten that hologram the day after her mother had died.

Not died.

Abandoned her.

With a strangled roar of humiliation, anger, and frustration, Lefler's arm drew back and she hurled the holotube with all her strength. It flew across the room and, in her mind's eye, shattered, the tiny pieces of the delicate technology littering her floor like so many precious snowflakes.

Unfortunately, or fortunately, depending upon how one looked at it, the holotube was made to last. All it did was ricochet off the wall and land on the floor with a gentle clatter. It rolled a few feet and then came to a stop.

She looked at the holotube lying there on the floor, and felt it was looking at her mockingly. Feeling anger building inside her, she moved quickly toward it and stomped down on it. But the tube shot out from under her foot, rolled up against the wall, and lay there.

Robin let out a sigh, her initial rage spent. She walked over to the holotube, picked it up and looked at it while slowly shaking her head. "You always did have a knack for bouncing back, Mom," she said ruefully before putting the tube carefully back into the drawer from which she'd removed it.

Shelby was convinced that everyone was looking at her.

Stop it! You're being paranoid! she scolded herself as she made her way down the corridors of the *Excalibur,* but she simply couldn't help herself. Looks or nods of the head that previously would have greeted her without her thinking anything of it now seemed fraught with hidden meaning. She was convinced that the entire crew was laughing at her behind her back.

Colors?

What had she been thinking? What in God's name had been going through her mind?

Try as she might, she couldn't dredge up the slightest reason why such a complete non sequitur would have popped out of her mouth. Sure, she had been a bit punchy. When they'd carted her back to sickbay, the doctors there couldn't believe that she'd been up and around at all. Even so . . .

Colors?

What could possibly have possessed her?

This was ridiculous, Shelby realized, as she headed for a turbolift. She couldn't figure out why she was being this way.

All right, that wasn't true. She did have some inklings. It had to do with the fact that, to some degree, she had felt like, and continued to feel like, an outsider on her own ship. Her style was very different from Mackenzie Calhoun's, and although they were supposed to be working in tandem, she still couldn't help but feel a streak of competitiveness with him. That was the truth of it, really. In many ways—in *all* ways—Shelby felt as if she were not only extremely qualified for command, but more qualified than Calhoun. Yet she was playing support to him, and not only that, but it seemed to her as if the crew liked him more than her.

It's not about being liked, she scolded herself. That wasn't it at all. It was about getting the job done. It was about acting in the best interests of Starfleet. It was about routine, and regulations, and procedures, and getting back in one piece. Calhoun, damn him, could afford to be flamboyant, daring, and heroic. He had Shelby to clean up the mess for him: Shelby to run interference with Starfleet, Shelby to remind him of the way things should be done as he thoughtlessly flaunted the rules. Calhoun was busy carving himself a status that could only be considered legendary, and here was Shelby, feeling like a grunt.

Besides that, she felt extremely vulnerable in that status. And matters hadn't been helped by recent developments.

But, dammit, she *had* sustained injury. That was the thing to remember. That's what she should be thinking about.

The turbolift opened and she stepped onto it. "Bridge," she said briskly.

The lift hurtled toward the bridge, and as it did so, she continued to ponder the situation. She knew the reputation she was developing around the ship. Grim, humorless, a total hard-case.

The turbolift slowed and the doors slid open. Robin Lefler was standing there, her hands draped behind her back, looking lost in thought. She glanced up and looked mildly surprised to see Shelby there. "Oh! Commander! Feeling better?"

"Just heading up to the bridge." She gestured for Lefler to join her and the lieutenant quickly did so. As the doors slid shut and the lift continued its way upward, Shelby suddenly inquired, "Lieutenant . . . you hear people talk. You get around. You know what people around here have on their minds."

"I . . . guess I do, yes," allowed Lefler. "I am in charge of Ops, so I tend to—"

"To the best of your knowledge, does the crew lampoon me? Behind my back? Do they value my contributions and qualifications?"

The questions seemed to catch Lefler completely off guard. "I beg your pardon?"

"Am I . . ." She tried to find the best way to express it, but nothing seemed to come to mind immediately. Finally, for want of a better phrase, she said, "Am I . . . 'one of the guys'?"

Lefler stared at her as if she'd grown a third eye. "Would you want to be?"

"I . . ." She'd been looking at Lefler, but now she stared at the door. "I don't know. I don't know that fraternizing with the officers is a particularly good idea."

"But is being so rigid all the time a good idea either?"

Now she looked back at Lefler and there was a slightly pained smile on her face. "Is that what they say I am?"

The door to the bridge hissed open and Shelby strode out, brimming with new confidence. Lefler walked quickly past her and headed over to her station at Ops. Mark McHenry, at the conn, was sitting and staring dreamily at the world of Zondar turning lazily below them. He looked as if his thoughts were a million miles away, but by this point Lefler—and everyone else on the bridge—was used to him, knowing that his apparent distractedness was just that: apparent.

Calhoun was seated in the command chair, going over a report, and he glanced up when Shelby entered. It was as if he were expecting her. But she was in no hurry to walk down to his level, feeling perfectly content instead to stand on the upper deck of the bridge and look down. She found that it gave her a nice dominant feeling, like a queen on high regarding her realm. Zak Kebron, standing at the tactical station, didn't even glance her way.

The captain raised a questioning eyebrow. "It's good to see you, Commander. Planning to come down here and join us?"

"Of course, sir. It's good to be back."

She slowly walked down the ramp, and as she did so she looked over the bridge personnel. She tried to see if any of them were grinning her way, or whispering among themselves, or in any other way behaving in a disrespectful or discourteous manner that would not only have been not in keeping with Starfleet decorum, but would have been inappropriate in keeping with the respect that she was due.

Calhoun caught her eye and made a subtle "come here" gesture. She drew close to him and he said in a low voice, "Are you all right?"

"I'm fine, sir. Why?"

"You seem . . . stiff."

"I'm displaying posture and poise that is suitable for a Starfleet officer," she replied.

Calhoun had been slouching slightly in his chair, and she felt a bit of smug satisfaction as he reflexively drew himself up. Nodding slightly as if having achieved a major personal triumph, she moved around the edge of her chair and took her place in it.

"Our current situation," Calhoun informed her, "just to keep you apprised, is that we are continuing to orbit Zondar pending Science

Officer Soleta's return. We will then be setting course for the planet Momidium to pick up an individual being held there under . . . unusual circumstances.''

Lefler overheard the conversation and breathed a small sigh of relief to herself that the captain remained deliberately vague. She didn't especially feel like having the bizarre circumstances of her potential maternal reunion being broadcast all over the bridge.

''All the information,'' continued Calhoun, ''is in your duty log, Commander. You can get current on it at your leisure.''

''Thank you, Captain,'' she said formally.

And then she waited . . . waited for him to say something, to make some sort of comment on the way in which she had handled matters in his absence. It would be perfectly in character for him to make some sort of teasing comment about the ''bunnies,'' or—more appropriately—to offer even a cursory ''well done'' in regard to the way she had handled the conflict with the Redeemer war vessel that had wanted to blow them out of space.

But Calhoun said nothing. Instead he went back to studying his report, his legs comfortably crossed, his left foot waving in leisurely fashion.

She made a slow visual survey of the bridge. No one was looking at her. No one seemed particularly interested in welcoming her back other than with a quick, cursory nod. Otherwise, that was pretty much it.

She should have been happy about that; relieved even. Instead it left her feeling oddly discontent for some reason that she couldn't quite isolate.

The turbolift opened and Lieutenant Commander Burgoyne 172, chief engineer of the *Excalibur,* walked out. Shelby turned and looked at the Hermat. If there was anyone who could be counted on for making an offbeat, uninhibited response, it was Burgoyne.

''Chief,'' Calhoun acknowledged hir entrance.

''Captain,'' Burgoyne replied with a tilt of hir head. ''I wanted to run some cross-checks on the energy transfer problems we've been having. Thought I'd use the station up here since the main one's being tied up for research.''

''Be my guest,'' said Calhoun.

''Afternoon, Burgy,'' Shelby spoke up.

''Commander,'' replied Burgoyne by way of greeting, and then s/he went on about hir business.

That was it. That was all.

Shelby felt utterly crestfallen.

There was no reason whatsoever that the bridge crew should make a big deal over Shelby's handling of the crisis earlier. In her heart, she knew that. At most, the captain would make a notation of it in his log and register a commendation. But that was all. Nothing further need be acknowledged, because really, when you got down to it, Shelby had simply done her job. The fact that she had done it extremely well shouldn't really have factored into it.

Except . . .

Except that the *Excalibur* was unlike any other ship she'd served on.

She couldn't help but feel that part of it was that the crew took their cue from the captain. Calhoun was a cowboy, no question, who walked with a slight swagger, wore a look of weathered amusement, operated in unexpected and unorthodox manners, and seemed to delight in having little to no regard for the standard procedures under which other ships and commanding officers operated.

As for the situation that Shelby was in, the people she was surrounded by . . .

An ambassador who had come aboard the ship as a stowaway in the science officer's luggage; a conn officer who was . . . what *was* McHenry doing now? She glanced over at him and saw that he was moving his fingers in a manner that indicated he was making a cat's cradle with imaginary string. Okay, they had a conn officer who seemed barely there, except when he was needed. And he was having an affair with a multisexual chief engineer, who was in turn (according to the latest rumors, and since the entire vessel seemed to be powered not by dilithium crystals but by innuendo, it was probably accurate) serving to sate the mating lust of the normally staid chief medical officer. The head of security was relatively normal . . . at least as normal as a walking land mass could be, but the night-side security head was different story. A large, shaggy story. It was as if Calhoun had gone out of his way to handpick a crew designed to appeal to his eclectic and rather offbeat tastes. It was less like serving on a starship than serving on a funhouse mirror version of one. The only one who seemed relatively normal was Lefler.

Shelby glanced over her duty log, which had been kept up to date by her yeoman so that she would be able to review it handily. She took one look at her, saw that the intended passenger from Momidium was Lefler's mother, who had been dead for a decade, and moaned softly to herself. *Et tu, Lefler,* she thought.

Still, with all the quirkiness, with all the oddities that seemed prevalent through the vessel, everyone seemed to be having . . . Well, fun wasn't the right word. It was a combination of professionalism mixed with camaraderie.

That was it. That was the bottom line, really. There was an air of joie de vivre on the ship. For all the craziness that went on, for all the offbeat attitudes, everyone—from the captain down to the lowest ranking technician—all seemed to be *alive* and part of a circuit of energy.

And Shelby felt as if she wasn't a part of it. She felt wedded to decorum, a living incarnation of Starfleet rules and regulations. It was as if the ship was a party, and she was the designated pooper thereof.

It was not an attitude that made her feel particularly good about herself, but dammit, she was a trained Starfleet officer. Just because Calhoun's command style was very much a shoot-from-the-hip proposition didn't mean that she had to go along with it. She was complete unto herself, confident and sure of the rightness of her worldview.

And yet . . . she was lonely.

She hated to admit it, but there it was. She had chosen a certain way in which she desired to be regarded, and the fact was, her return to the bridge had been the test of that. If they'd teased her or lampooned her, it would have been roundly insulting, and she would have been well within her rights to light into anyone who treated her in such a disrespectful manner. But instead they treated her with the esteem to which she was entitled. It should have made her feel good about herself, but instead she couldn't help but feel as if it just underscored her outsider status . . . the status that she had been boasting of to Lefler just a little earlier.

And then she heard something: the sound of slow, steady hands slamming together. She opened her eyes and turned to see Calhoun, standing, slowly applauding and nodding his head in approval.

Then McHenry joined in, as did Lefler. When Kebron tried slamming his hands together it created an almost deafening explosion of air, so he did it more gently. But ultimately, within seconds, everyone on the bridge was applauding Shelby and cheering.

And Shelby, to her own astonishment, started to laugh.

She couldn't help it. She had clearly been set up. Calhoun had orchestrated it, of that she was positive. He'd wanted to single her out for praise and commendation, but being the maverick and relatively bizarre person that he was, he couldn't find it within himself to do it in anything vaguely approaching a normal manner.

She continued to laugh, louder and with greater delight, because she felt genuinely touched and amused and even liked. An entire barrage of emotions, one tumbling over the next.

Calhoun patted her on the back and she turned to him and said, "You always have to be different, do you know that?"

"That's what my first officer keeps telling me," he replied sanguinely.

"But what about . . ." Shelby began, "you know, what I said—"

"But nothing," Calhoun cut her off. "What you said doesn't matter. It's what you did that counts."

Looking into the solemn eyes of her crewmates, Shelby suddenly felt ashamed of herself for doubting them and her place among them.

As if he sensed her discomfort, Calhoun jumped into the silence. "Let me tell you, Commander," he said, "about the colors I saw, wounded and raving, after I won the Battle of Maja on Xenex. . . ."

3

The snoring of her security guard was beginning to get on Soleta's nerves.

The science officer had been probing every inch of the area known as Ontear's cave, displaying the customary patience that was a valuable part of her Vulcan heritage. Her streak of impatience, unfortunately, to say nothing of her more human reactions, could be chalked up to that part of her that was her Romulan heritage. She did not like to dwell on that, though. Instead she far preferred to focus her mind on the task at hand.

Ontear's cave was situated in a remote and rocky area of Zontar, many miles outside the main city. The ground was pebbly and slippery, and there were crevices that were almost impossible to see until one was practically stepping into them. Ontear, according to Soleta's research, was a seer and wise man who had lived five hundred years previously, and had been instrumental in shaping the direction of his world. He had died, or disappeared, depending upon one's interpretation, under most mysterious circumstances. According to legend, he'd literally been plucked up and away by the wrath of the Zondarian gods themselves. That was just a tad too mystical and over the top as far as Soleta was concerned. Far more likely there had been some sort of freak storm occurrence that had been responsible for hauling Ontear away to his "eternal reward."

But she was further intrigued by reports that Captain Calhoun had made to her, namely of seeing some sort of ghostly image in the cave while he had been a captive there. That was something that neither he nor she had been quite able to explain and, thus far, she had found no means of supporting its existence.

Calhoun had been very detailed in his description of the phantom being, which appeared, on the surface of it, to be the ghost of Ontear. But that was not an explanation that thrilled Soleta. What was even more disturbing, though, was that Burgoyne had likewise claimed to have encountered the phantasmic shade, and Soleta had absolutely no idea what to make of that. Group hallucination? Projection of some sort? Possibilities, but none that particularly thrilled her.

And then there had been the mental assaults. Some sort of telepathic being who had, insanely, seemed to be artificially generated, if such a thing were possible. It had acted as the first line of defense against intruders, driving them mad with fear, assaulting them, in one case even killing. But it seemed to have vanished altogether, as if its job was done or its time had passed. It all left Soleta seeking answers that did not seem remotely interested in being forthcoming.

Soleta had determined that she was going to explore the area until she had some sort of explanation for the events that had occurred in the area. However, the political climate of Zondar—although it was improving—was nonetheless in a state of flux, and Calhoun had not wanted her down there without an escort. It had been with the extreme glee, in Soleta's opinion, that Burgoyne 172 had eagerly urged Calhoun to assign Ensign Janos to the task. Since this would be a day-and-night exploration (thanks to Soleta's considerable stamina) the fact that Janos was primarily on the night shift did not factor in to the decision. Moreover, Janos had already been down to Zondar once and so at least had some familiarity with the territory. What Burgoyne did not bother to mention to Calhoun was that Soleta—while she'd been in command of the vessel—had gone out of her way to assign Janos as Burgoyne's backup when Burgoyne had embarked on a rescue mission of hir own, and this was a convenient means of payback as far as Burgoyne was concerned.

For Ensign Janos was something to see . . . a white-haired, ape-like being from a species that was generally more inclined to growl, snarl, and try to tear someone apart than engage someone in polite conversation. Janos, however, talked incessantly in an offhand, chatty manner with an accent that the British would refer to as "cut glass." In that respect he was unlike any other member of his species, although he did bear a strong resemblance to his father. Janos's background and history was unique to say the least, and Soleta found him intriguing in that respect. But she felt it was inappropriate for the science officer to consider a crewmember interesting from a scientific perspective. It was patronizing somehow, for no reason she could quite put a finger on.

Aside from his string of chattiness, though, Janos presented another problem as well: He tended to sleep if he was not actively engaged in eating, working, or sex (and considering the dearth of suitable mates for him in Starfleet, he had more or less adopted a permanent state of celibacy, which was a state of mind that did not weigh happily upon him).

Since time was of the essence, Soleta had not returned to the ship since she had arrived at the dig site. Instead she had worked steadily, probing and testing, searching for clues throughout the entire area. When she had felt fatigued, she had rested for a few minutes, fifteen at most. During all that time Janos had remained on duty, never flagging in his attention, and never shutting up. Soleta had requested a number of times that he find something else to do other than talk, and he had always oh-so-politely agreed to try and curb his normally loquacious nature. But within relatively short order he always slid back into his old habits, and finally Soleta had just developed the ability to screen him out completely.

At this point, however, languor had finally caught up with him, and he had suggested that he return to the *Excalibur* and have a replacement be sent down.

"That," Soleta had replied, "is a waste of manpower, Janos. The fact is that, truthfully, I do not even feel that your presence is required here. It seems foolish to engage the services of yet another security guard. Take yourself off-duty, and if there is any difficulty, I assure you I will alert you immediately."

"That, Lieutenant, is simply too, too considerate of you," Janos informed her with a grimace. A grimace was the closest he could come to changing his facial expression, since his species wasn't exactly geared for smiling, frowning, and other human-like actions. "I'll just toddle off for a quick one then, with your kind permission."

"Consider it granted."

Janos found a stone outcropping near the mouth of the cave and moments later was dangling upside down from his knees, as was his habit. Soleta found the quiet to be exceedingly peaceful, up until a few minutes later when Janos started snoring. She could have sworn that the vibrations were actually causing the rocks to shake.

She had initially explored the cave first, followed by the surrounding hills, cliffs, and crevices. She'd found no trace of any of the technology that she had been sure must be in the area. Technology that had generated holographic figures, mind-probing creatures, and shields that had interfered with the *Excalibur*'s scanning equipment to the degree that they had not been able to track down the captain while he was a prisoner there. Now, though, with the crisis having passed, it was as if the entire area had simply gone dead. She could find no energy emanation that might lead her to what she sought. Nothing. Nothing at all. There was nothing of any interest in the vicinity with the possible exception of Janos's snoring.

Soleta reentered the cave, the one where not all that long before, Captain Calhoun had been held prisoner by a Zondarian holy man who not only believed that Calhoun was the messiah, but that it was his duty to kill the aforementioned messiah for the sake of his world. For what seemed the hundredth time to her, she scanned the interior with her tricorder, trying to find something, anything, that might provide a clue or a lead. But once again, her tricorder told her nothing.

"All right," she said to no one in particular. "Then I will try it the old-fashioned way."

She unslung a satchel that she'd had looped around her shoulder, laid it down on the ground, and rummaged through it. From the satchel she removed a tool pouch. It had been given to her by her parents on her twelfth birthday, back when her interest in archaeology first surfaced. It was a superbly crafted and carefully maintained batch of tools. Of course, on her thirteenth birthday, her interest in astronomy drove her, and her fourteenth it was xenobiology, by which point her parents realized that she was looking at a potential career in general sciences since she couldn't seem to make up her mind as to a specialty.

Carefully Soleta extracted a small hammer from the pouch that looked as new and shiny as on the day that she had first gotten the set. Then, at the mouth of the cave, she got down on her hands and knees and proceeded to tap the floor with the hammer. She listened carefully, her sharp hearing strained to the utmost, her face a mask of concentration, as she sought to learn if there was anything on the cave floor that might lead her to something else, *anything* else.

That was how she proceeded for the next hour and a half, moving one square inch at a time, her carefully neutral face never betraying the least bit of impatience or weariness with her task. *Tik tik tik* the hammer continued, never wavering or letting up in its implacable rhythm.

After ninety-one minutes, she found something.

The difference in sound was ever so faint, so mild that the likelihood was that no one else would catch it. But Soleta's ears pricked up and her eyes narrowed as she studied the floor where she was certain she had detected some sort of mild differentiation. She ran her fingers carefully over the rocky surface, and then expertly the tips of her fingers began to probe.

She detected it almost immediately. There was a circular area, about six inches across, but the stone was inset as if it had slid over it to obscure something else. It was like a tiny trapdoor, and she wondered what it could possibly be hiding.

She tried chipping away at the rock, but it resisted her attempts. Reaching into the pouch, she removed a miniature laser carver and started to slice up the rock ever so delicately. As she cut up each section, she removed it and found that she was becoming more and more excited by what was being revealed beneath it.

It was some sort of disk, inset into the ground. A glittering silver disk with a small etching of something that looked vaguely like a flame. Soleta ran her fingers across it and she felt a warmth to it . . . a warmth and . . . and something else . . .

You . . .

She felt something.

It was ever so gentle, a butterfly's brush against her mind. The fluttering beginnings of something that seemed vaguely evocative of a Vulcan mindmeld.

From a disk? It seemed impossible. At most, the disk would be some sort of device, a machine. A machine wouldn't have mindmeld capacity in either direction.

But then she realized she was wrong. There was precedent in mindmeld techniques for merging with a machine. No one less than Spock had achieved such a blending, with a floating, threatening machine called "Nomad." And if Spock could do it, and if there really was some sort of device that was reaching out to her . . .

You . . .

She had reflexively removed her hand upon first making contact, but now she steeled herself and placed her hand squarely on the disk. She reached out cautiously with her mind while, at the same time, allowing the probe to brush against her mind.

You . . . hear us, you are . . . there . . . after all . . . this time . . .

She could feel the impulse, originating from . . . from wherever it was . . . trying to slip more deeply into her mind. But she was being understandably cautious, and she kept mental shields in place that let the other "mind" go only so far and no further.

"I hear you," was her reply. She had spoken out loud to help steady herself, but mentally projected the answer as well.

And it exploded into her mind.

The response was so overwhelming, so massive, that her shields crumbled like sodden tissue. Soleta tore her hand free from the disk, but physical contact was no longer an issue, for the thing had completely invaded her. She fell backward onto her back, twisting and writhing, trying with all her might to shove the intruder out of her skull.

She rolled over, propping herself up onto her elbows and hauling herself forward using her forearms. She was trying to get to the mouth of the cave, as if sensing somehow that once she was out of the cave, she'd be out of danger altogether. But her mind was feeling heavier with every passing moment, and her body mirrored her mind as she found herself unable to make her muscles function in concert with one another. She tried to gather enough air into her lungs to shout an alert to Janos, but she couldn't manage it, couldn't get out a single word. Her desperate fingers fumbled to touch her commbadge, but she couldn't even mange the manual dexterity required for that simple feat. Instead her convulsing, palsied hand banged against the commbadge and sent it clattering to the floor of the cave. Unfortunately, it fell on its edge and rolled a couple of feet away—not far at all, but it might as well have been in Alpha Centauri for all the good it was going to do her.

Come to me . . . it has been so long, and I deserve companionship, the same as any of my kind . . .

Your . . . kind? It was a massive effort for her just to be able to frame those words.

Come to me. . . . Yes? You will . . . come to me?

Deciding that she had absolutely nothing to lose at that juncture considering that whatever had grabbed her was perfectly capable of frying her brain into cinders, she managed to get out the single word: "Yes."

Then come to me . . . now. . . .

For no reason that she could quite discern, Soleta lunged for her satchel. It was as if she regarded it, however illogically, as the equivalent of a lifeline or life preserver. It took everything she had, every ounce of willpower, and total refusal to accept the concept that she simply could not move. Her fingers fell barely inches short, and then an additional push forward allowed her to snag the strap with the tips of her fingers. She pulled it towards her . . .

Suddenly she felt the ground opening up beneath her.

It was the most outlandish sensation. It wasn't as if the ground had gone soft beneath her, like quicksand. Nor was there some sort of trapdoor that was tilting and spilling her down to some subterranean area. It was as if the ground was just . . . just melting around her, phasing into nonexistence below her and then resealing above her. And it was pulling her down with the force of a current in the ocean. Her legs, hips, and torso all vanished below before she had time even to string together a coherent realization as to what was happening. Her arms were outstretched above her head, and at the last second she lost her grip on her pouch, the strap slipping out of her hand. She was barely aware of it, though, because the thoughts from the—the whatever it was—were still rampaging through her skull, and she felt utterly helpless to drive it away. She tried to open her mouth to call to Janos, to shout for help, but she felt as if something had paralyzed the speech center of her brain. So overwhelming were the thoughts in her head that she wasn't able to punch past it.

What was bizarre was that it wasn't images *per se* or individual thoughts. It was an overwhelming need, an urgency, and Soleta instinctively tried to pull away from it, tried to sever the mindmeld. But she was in too deep, and it had happened so quickly that she was trapped before she even knew that she was being ensnared. She tried to leave, but everything around her howled at her, *Stay with me! You can't leave now! You have to stay with me! Stay forever and ever and ever. . . .* But again, it wasn't in words. It was just her interpretation of the abiding need that had found its way into her soul and was determined to pull her down and make her a part of itself.

At the last second, just before her head disappeared beneath the surface, she suddenly realized that she had no idea where she was going or how much time she would have underground, if that was indeed where she was going. As a last-ditch measure, she took a deep breath, wondered exactly how much good that was going to do, filled her lungs with air, and then vanished completely beneath the rocky surface.

The strata seemed to melt away before her eyes, and she wondered how in the world she was actually seeing anything as she spiraled downward. There was, after all, no light. Perhaps in some way she was seeing it with her mind's eye, or maybe something was augmenting her view. All in all, though, she had no sure way of knowing.

She was corporeal, though, of that much she was certain, because she was already starting to feel the air burning in her lungs. She kept her lips tightly sealed and tried to analyze scientifically what was happening. The buildup of carbon dioxide within her was forcing her to want to blast the air out of her lungs. It was simply a matter of willpower, of explaining to her brain in as no-nonsense and reasonable a manner as she could that endeavoring to take in more air was simply suicide. It was not an option, and she was just going to have to hold on to it longer. Unfortunately for her, neither her lungs nor her brain seemed quite open to rational discussion and she knew that this was a contest of wills that she was going to lose.

She opened her mouth, expelling the contents of her lungs, quite certain that that was the last breath that she was ever going to draw.

And that was when she suddenly became aware that her legs were clear of the rock. Her feet kicked in midair, and then she was in free fall, her head and then arms coming free of the rocky strata overhead as she fell through. Fortunately enough, she only fell a couple of feet before thudding to a halt. She went limp, hitting the ground and rolling, and slapping it as she landed to absorb the impact.

The mental assault was now overwhelming, and Soleta's body shook as she was pummeled with desire, longing, loneliness . . . a cacophony of needy emotions.

Soleta gathered her mental resources, pulled them into a ball within her that she could almost visualize in her mind's eye, and then she exploded the ball in all directions as she bellowed with every thought, every fiber of her being, ***"LEAVE ME ALONE!"***

And just like that—it stopped.

But she was too wary to assume automatically that it was over. Quickly she promptly rolled to her feet, her hands poised, in preparation for a possible attack.

There was another Vulcan facing her, ready to lunge.

Janos was startled awake.

He wasn't entirely certain what had alerted him, but something most definitely had. He was more than willing to chalk it up to basic animal instinct. It was that instinct that caused him to awaken with a deep, throaty roar. He didn't simply clamber down off the rocky precipice from which he was hanging upside down. Instead he flipped off, landing on his feet, his clawed bared and his lips drawn back to reveal his fangs. He looked right, left, and behind him, reacting to something that he couldn't readily detect. But there was nothing, or at least there seemed to be nothing.

"Soleta!" he called. He waited for a response and when none was forthcoming, he said again, "Soleta!" For good measure he tapped his commbadge and said, "Janos to Soleta," just in case she was simply out of earshot. When still no reply was forthcoming, he murmured to himself, "Bloody marvelous."

His nostrils flared as he assessed scents in the area, and he quickly picked up Soleta's trail. As he tracked her, he growled angrily to himself. It was bad enough that Captain Calhoun had vanished while Zak Kebron was supposed to be keeping an eye on him. That loss had stuck deep in Kebron's stony craw, for Kebron did not take particularly well to failure. How much angrier, then, was Janos for having surrendered to exhaustion but, at the same time, unwisely heeding Soleta's expectations and confidence that she could attend to matters should something go awry. Obviously something had gone out of whack, and he had absolutely no idea what it was. But he was going to find out fast.

He saw the trail was leading him straight to Ontear's cave, and he wasn't the least bit surprised. Although they had been exploring the entire region, Soleta had kept finding herself drawn back to that one place, as if she somehow sensed that all the answers she sought were wrapped up there. And he should have known that if she was going to run into problems, that would be where they would occur. The past, and the truth, were not always prone to yielding up their secrets without demanding a high price in return.

Janos was not a big believer in weapons. He was always more comfortable using his claws and his sheer bulk. But in this case, he decided that this was the time to err on the side of caution.

He pulled out his specially designed phaser. It was an alternate model with larger key pad, controls, and trigger to accommodate the size of his hand. He thumbed the power on and carefully entered the cave, pausing at the cave's mouth to allow his eyes to adjust. He had superb night vision, so it only took a couple of seconds for the interior of the cave to be completely and easily visible to him.

He entered slowly, his claws clicking on the rocky floor, his head moving from left to right and almost turning all the way around, since his flexible neck gave him 300-degree vision. He held his phaser in a relaxed grip, and he no longer was calling Soleta's name. Instead he was trusting his own instincts to guide him to her; if nothing else, he was concerned that calling out to her at this point might alert some enemy.

His eyes narrowed as he saw the small metal device that was her commbadge. He knelt down and picked it up in one clawed hand, turned it over idly like a magician performing tricks with a coin. Then he saw something else . . . a pouch of some sort. He remembered it immediately as the satchel that Soleta had been carrying slung across her chest and over her shoulders.

He knelt down next to it to pick it up, and found, to his surprise, that he couldn't. The strap was inside the ground somehow. He was able to lift the pouch, but it jerked to a halt as if something was holding tight the strap, and he discovered that it was as if the ground had sealed over the strap.

"Bloody hell," he said thoughtfully. He tugged once more to make sure and he remained unable to pull it out. Then he crouched next to the point in the rock where the strap entered and probed experimentally. He expected some sort of sponginess, but instead the ground was, appropriately, rock solid. "Might be some sort of inverse phase transducer," he muttered. "Something that dematerialized the rock around her." He didn't feel in any particular hurry, because if Soleta had been pulled down and then the rock had reformed around her, she was already dead. Expeditiousness is rarely required in the rescue of the deceased. But if she was alive, then rushing unduly might well put an end to the one individual who was in a position to rescue her. Obviously caution was called for.

Something glittered two feet beyond. He did not approach it, though, out of concern that it might be some sort of triggering device for whatever trap had swallowed up Soleta. He decided to ignore it altogether, since obviously the main point of consideration was the place wherein she had vanished.

He rapped on the cave floor. "Knock knock," he said optimistically, and when he received no response, he added, "open sesame?" When nothing happened, he sighed and thumbed the phaser to active status. "Right, then. We do it the noisy way," he said.

4

Soleta was poised, bracing herself in preparation for the charge of the clearly belligerent Vulcan.

It was hard to make out much, because the area around her seemed thick with mist, but as near as she could tell, it was a female, like herself; ready for a fight, like herself; moving left, right, backing up, like . . . herself.

She stopped and simply stood there and waved. Her reflection waved back.

"*That* was not one of my finer moments," she muttered.

Slowly she approached the highly reflective surface, tilting her head slightly as she got closer. At first she had thought it was some sort of metal, similar to the metal disk that she had touched to first get her into this fix. But now she realized that it was some sort of incredibly polished stone, similar to marble.

She pulled her tricorder from her belt and held it up to get readings. She stared at the device, frowned, adjusted it, and tried it again. In annoyance, or as close to annoyance as she ever got, she thumped the tricorder with the base of her hand. Then she turned it on herself and the tricorder obediently began giving out readings on her. She cleared it, turned it back to the wall, and once again tried to get readings off it.

And once again she got nothing. According to the tricorder, the wall simply wasn't there.

She had been reluctant to touch the wall because the last time she had touched something, it had gotten her into a world of trouble, unleashing a torrent of communication that she had been unable to shut off. When she had hit the floor in this subterranean area, the link had mysteriously disappeared as suddenly as it had first contacted her. Coming into contact with another surface might set it off again, or unleash something even more forceful. But she felt as if she had no choice.

Tentatively she put out her hand to touch the wall. She saw the reflection of herself reaching out as well, naturally mirroring what she was doing . . . and her hand passed right through it.

Impossible went through her head, and she said out loud, "Impossible. If this wall is not here, if it is merely an illusion, there cannot be a reflection of me upon it. Light would not bounce off it, but merely pass through. Light needs something solid for a reflection to occur."

She reached forward again, and once again her image on the other side did so. Once again she came into contact with nothing, her hand passing through as if she were trying to touch fog. She withdrew her hand. . . .

Her reflection did likewise, but a few seconds later than she did.

"This is insane," she murmured. She paused a moment, considered the situation, and then stepped forward right through the wall. She moved through it without a ripple, of course, but then as she turned, she suddenly heard her own voice. . . . No, not just heard. Felt. Her voice shouting, "Leave me alone!" with tremendous volume and force.

She spun and saw—herself. She was some feet away, crouched on the ground, looking as if she were desperately trying to pull herself together. Soleta watched in amazement as herself from moments ago scrambled to her feet, saw "herself," and froze in a defensive posture.

And Soleta automatically, purely instinctively, assumed the same stance. She couldn't help it, it was completely reflex. Even as she did so, she made a mental note that she truly needed to brush up on her assorted *kata* and other exercises, because the movements of her other self seemed less than sharp to her.

Her "previous self," having ascertained that she was not, in fact, under attack, appeared to relax. Soleta did likewise. And at that point, Soleta realized what was happening: She had never seen a reflection of herself. She had seen some sort of time "phantom," an echo not of what had been, but what was about to happen. Something fatalistic within her prompted her to now make the same movements that she had seen her erstwhile reflection make only moments ago, since she reasoned that she might as well since she had already done it. She might as well keep her own personal history consistent. So she stepped forward toward herself, moved her hand when her past incarnation did, and watched the surprise flicker through her previous self upon realizing that she was not facing a hardened surface that would permit reflections. All the while her mind was racing, trying to understand exactly what it was that she was in and what she was facing.

With great scientific curiosity she watched and waited as her previous self, after some moments more, made the decision that Soleta had really already made and stepped through the wall. For a moment she wondered if a double of herself was going to step through, and wouldn't *that* be cause for conversation once she returned to the *Excalibur* with a mirror image of herself. She could already hear the snide comments. Mark McHenry, for instance, would likely say something "clever" such as, "We like your mirror version better, Soleta, but understand, that's no reflection on you."

But no copy of herself came through, and she quickly understood why. She wasn't dealing with some sort of time machine, physically casting her from one place to another. Instead it was just a sort of viewer, showing her the future on one side and the past on another. It was, in fact, rather confusing, but she didn't have the time to dwell on it further. She needed to try and sort matters out before she inadvertently found herself once more under psychic assault.

She wasn't sure if she was imagining it, but it seemed to her as if the mist around her was thinning somewhat. Slowly she made her way forward and found herself walking down a length of corridor. She started to take tricorder readings once more, and this time something began to register. It was a slow pulsation of energy a short distance ahead of her. The readings were oddly in flux, and she couldn't begin to guess what any of it might mean, but she was game enough to explore it since—after all—that was her job.

Two people were killing each other directly in front of her.

She paused a moment, but only a moment as she realized she was seeing more images. And these seemed to be from a time much farther back than the mere minutes that she'd seen in her own recent passing. It was two Zondarians, and they were garbed in a style of dress that seemed rather unlike anything that modern day Zondarians appeared to be wearing. Granted it was possible that certain sections of Zondarian society were undergoing a "retro" wave of style, but she strongly suspected that she was in fact witnessing something from many years back: two Zondarians battling it out, probably members of the two castes that had been in engaged in a civil war that had stretched back centuries.

One image after another began to flutter past her, some on the floor, others on the wall and ceiling, and still others simply wafting through the air like flights of fancy: women giving birth, people arguing, eating, fighting, dying. They seemed to occur with no particular order, no consistency. It was . . . it was almost as if she was witnessing some sort of stream of consciousness, or perhaps the reverie of a dreamer.

Oh please, she thought, *don't let this world turn out to be a sleeping giant who winds up waking up and destroying the entire place. We've been through something like that once already, and that was entirely sufficient for one lifetime.*

She turned a corner and it was everything she could do not to gasp out loud. It wouldn't have made much difference if she had, really, since she was alone, but nonetheless it was the principle of the thing. She just didn't like loud exclamations of astonishment. It wasn't proper for a Vulcan woman, even one with Romulan blood in her. That didn't always mean that she was able to prevent herself from displaying inappropriate behavior, but she restrained herself whenever she was able to.

The room she was now entering seemed to go on forever, and there was more of that marble-like material as far as the eye could see. Once again she saw herself, but this time she was quite positive that she was indeed seeing a reflection since her tricorder was giving her readings off the walls.

But there was something in the center of the room—or at least what she fancied to be the center, since she couldn't accurately determine the parameters and so make a mathematical determination—that had completely engaged her attention.

It was a column that seemed to stretch up forever. It bore a general resemblance to the marble-like walls, but it appeared softer, even porous. Perhaps even—and her heart began to race with excitement at the thought—*organic?* Some sort of techno-organism?

The columnar structure was a dark, dusky brown, and as she looked up and up, she saw that it appeared to branch off in its higher reaches. There were cross-connectors that ran off in a variety of directions.

And at its base, there were . . . devices.

They appeared attached to the structure, part of the structure but also capable of separating from it. They were a variety of shapes, made from apparently a variety of materials, and Soleta couldn't even begin to guess what any of them did. The tricorder was yielding no useful information. The alloys were all new to her, the shapes not analogous to anything was in any records.

The energy was definitely coming from within the column, but it was like nothing that she was readily familiar with.

"No," she said to no one in particular. "No, that's . . . not quite right. I've seen something like it," and she tried to remember what it was. The fact that she didn't remember immediately was extremely disconcerting to her; Soleta was not one prone to forgetting things, and there *had* been something, something that was . . .

Suddenly she was struck with a thought, and it was one that made the hair on the back of her neck stand on end. As if she had been physically hit, she spun on her heel, her head whipping around, and she called out, "What did you do to me?"

There was no response.

"What did you do to me?" she asked again, and this time she was actually driven by sufficient irritation that she tossed aside caution and strode with quick steps toward the towering column in the room. She stood before it, her arms folded, and said, "There is information missing from my mind. Information that was pertinent to what I am discovering here today. Were you responsible for its loss? Was that the reason for the connection? To see what I knew and didn't know, and then 'delete' inappropriate information from me? Well?"

Still there was no reply, which was fairly acceptable since she was not truly expecting one. She clapped her hands once and then briskly rubbed them together. "All right," she said. "Despite my earlier experience with you, I am not the least bit intimidated by the notion of a second encounter. If this is what you desire, then it will be on your head . . . or . . . whatever," she finished. And with that announcement, she placed her hands against the column.

She had no intention of forcing her mindmeld upon whatever she might encounter. The mindmeld was a delicate technique at best, and certainly not designed to be utilized as some sort of mind rape or weapon. She was, however, determined to let whatever this entity was know that it had assaulted her, and that she was none too happy about it.

The surface of the column was warm to the touch, but she was not surprised. She felt something within . . . recoil . . . as if it were surprised that she had dared to seek it out.

"Our minds are merging," she intoned slowly. "Our minds . . . are merging."

Go away.

She felt it rather forcefully, and it surprised her. Whatever the sensation in her head, it was speaking with petulance bordering on fear. Certainly not what she had expected.

You brought me here. Why do that and then tell me . . . to go away?

I made . . . a mistake . . . should not have brought you here.

Waves of concern seemed to be rolling off it. Slowly, gently, she eased her mind probe farther and deeper. She felt as if she were surrounded by blackness, falling ever farther, and all around her there were objects in the darkness skittering away, running in fear, like an army of infants seeking to avoid the advent of a stranger.

You wanted company . . . you wanted to talk . . .

Go away.

I am . . . here . . . we are here. . . . Our minds . . . are merging and we will be one . . . and you will not be afraid.

I AM NOT AFRAID!

It came at her with such force that it nearly knocked her off her feet. This time, though, she was ready for it, and she maintained her footing as she clutched the column.

Tell me . . . who you are . . . what you are.

You do not ask . . . questions of me.

We are one. . . . We are merging. . . . You cannot hold back from me. . . . You took from me . . . give back to me . . . what you took . . . and give to me . . . what you hide . . .

I do not . . . want you.

Yes you do. . . . You would not have brought me here . . . if you did not. . . . That is truly why I am here. . . . You want . . . you want . . .

"What are you *doing* here?"

The voice was loud and sounding quite upset, and it completely jolted Soleta from the concentration necessary to maintain the meld. She looked around in surprise, feeling disjointed and disoriented, which was not uncommon whenever she first withdrew from a mind-meld, and certainly understandable considering the present circumstances.

She saw a Zondarian standing some feet away, but immediately she saw that he was floating several inches off the ground. He "walked" toward her slowly, his feet moving but not touching the ground.

He looked rather old for a Zondarian, although it was difficult for her to be sure in even the best of circumstances, and these were hardly those. He was bald, as were all Zondarians, and his skin was leathery and shiny, with the customary sheen that made it look as if the Zondarians were perpetually wet. Since she was positive that she was seeing a projection of some sort, she couldn't be one hundred percent sure of such subtleties as skin texture.

The newcomer's eyes were set wide apart, and when he blinked, it was with eyelids that were clear. In real life, when Zondarians blinked, their eyelids made very soft clicking noises. They did not in this case, however; perhaps a further indication of the fact that he wasn't really there.

"Who are you?" demanded Soleta.

"I inquired of you first," replied the image. In his 'walking" manner he circled her, never taking his eyes from her. "Will you answer?"

"I am Lieutenant Soleta of the *Starship Excalibur,*" she told him.

The image stopped and appeared to be studying her closely. "Starship?" he asked.

"A spacegoing vessel."

"Remarkable," he said softly. "And your ears—are they a product of this starship? They appear rather unusual."

"I am a Vulcan," she said, "from the planet of the same name. I was exploring the upper regions of this territory, in an area called 'Ontear's cave'—"

"I know what it's called," he told her, sounding a bit arrogant about it.

"And was psychically assaulted and then dragged down here against my will."

The image seemed to look rather surprised. "Is this true?" he demanded.

"You have no reason to doubt my—"

But he waved dismissively. "I was not addressing you," he said rather archly. He paused, waiting for a reply from whomever it was that he *was* talking to.

Soleta took a step toward him, cocking her head with curiosity. "Who are you?" she demanded.

"My name is Ontear," he said in a very distracted fashion. He seemed to be listening to something as if it were originating from very far away.

''Ontear. The Ontear who died five hundred years ago, carried away at the hands of mysterious gods?''

He stopped, his attention suddenly fully back on her. ''Say again?''

''Ontear. The noted prophet and seer, lifted away into the skies by a swirling mass of air, commonly called a tornado but believed, in this instance, to be some sort of divine object.''

And with an expression of gentle sadness he asked, ''Is that what happens to me?''

Soleta had been continuing to approach him, but at that point she suddenly stopped dead in her tracks. *You may have just destroyed a time line,* her mind informed her. *You might well have informed someone from the past of their future . . . and in doing so, have virtually guaranteed he will avoid it.* ''I . . . do not know,'' she said slowly, desperately trying to figure out some way in which to salvage this awful mess that she had inadvertently stepped into. ''Not for certain. Reports are varied and conflicting, and there is no sure way to tell what truly happened. There are . . . any number of possibilities and—''

But he was shaking his head, his arms folded, and he merely looked amused at her discomfort. ''You need not worry, my dear,'' he said. ''I am too old already to worry about such matters, and my fate—even a violent one—holds no fear for me. Do not be concerned that I shall run from whatever destiny has in store for me, thereby upsetting the delicate balance of the space-time continuum. I shall embrace it, just as I have eagerly embraced all knowledge.'' He sighed. ''We do have another problem, however.''

''We do?'' asked Soleta.

''I am afraid so. You are here, my dear, due to a malfunction. As I'm sure you've surmised, you see before you a technology representing a perfect synthesis of living and mechanical technology. However, no device—even one of ours—is foolproof. The one here, I am afraid, has broken down. It brought you to itself when it should not have. It mistook you for a . . .''

''For a what?'' Soleta wanted to know.

''A lover,'' sighed Ontear. ''It then realized its mistake, but you were already down here and so . . . there it is.''

''There what is?'' She felt, not for the first time, that she was one half of a conversation and not following the other half.

''The materials you have seen, the valuable hints and glimpses of other technology, the data you have collected with that . . . device. What is that called?''

''A tri—'' She paused. She was, after all, talking to an individual from the past. She'd already made a horrible error by mentioning his fate. The last thing she was going to do was compound it by making mention of any other accurate information.

''A tri . . . ?'' he prompted curiously.

''A try-trying-to-avoid-explaining-it machine,'' she said, wincing slightly at how tortured that sounded.

''I see,'' said Ontear, and she wasn't sure but there appeared to be the slightest touch of amusement on his face. ''Very well, then. The point is, none of this was meant for you. And so something must be done about the situation.''

''Something.'' Soleta pondered the significance of this a moment and then asked, very quietly, ''Are you saying you plan to kill me?''

''That will hardly solve the problem,'' replied Ontear. ''I have no idea what information you may have already passed along to whomever you arrived with. Even if you never return to your point of origin, there may simply be more people following your lead. No, I daresay that your demise will really attend to none of the difficulties that have presented themselves.''

''That is most fortunate to hear.'' She did not, however, relax her guard for even a moment.

''No, I am afraid this entire installation will have to be destroyed. Your death will simply be an unfortunate byproduct.''

And the energy readings on her tricorder suddenly spiked off the scales. The cause was immediately, and painfully, evident, as the energy-filled column began to glow. She could feel the ground vibrating beneath her feet, and the building energy waves were so powerful that she could practically feel them pulsating against her.

''My apologies for this situation,'' Ontear told her. ''It's not fair, but then, life rarely is.''

''Stop!'' shouted Soleta, but it was too late; Ontear had vanished back into whatever ether he had sprung from.

Seeing that she had absolutely no choice, even though she hadn't a clue as to where she was going to go, Soleta ran. Her arms pumped furiously as she dashed back down the corridor, heading toward the curious wall that she has passed through. She saw something through it, something she couldn't quite make out because she was running too quickly.

All around her the place was shaking furiously. As the marble-like walls whizzed past her, she saw cracks starting to develop in them, and from overhead debris was starting to fall. It wasn't enough that she had to try and stay ahead of some sort of buildup toward detonation—she also had to run an obstacle course, dodging frantically from one side to the other as chunks of rubble fell all around her. One piece grazed her shoulder. She staggered but kept going, keeping her arms over her head to shield her from falling objects.

She made it to the wall and passed through it once more as if it wasn't there . . . which, in point of fact, it wasn't. She emerged on the other side and found herself facing a dead end. She looked up desperately, trying to find some way out, but her entrance had been through the shifting ground above her, and it now appeared to be solid rock once more. The vibrations around her became more and more fierce, and she started to hear explosions.

And, ever so faintly in her head, she thought she heard something else. Something that sounded like a faint sobbing, as if she were detecting a ghostly echo of her previous connection with the telepathic entity that had sought her out. Then, with all the substance that the wall had presented, the sound faded in her mind, leaving no more a trace than evaporated morning dew.

Then another sound replaced it. She looked up, recognizing it immediately; it was faint but growing louder. It sounded like . . .

"Phaser fire?" she murmured to herself, and then her eyes went wide as she realized its significance. And she shouted in a very loud, semi-desperate and extremely un-Vulcan manner, "Janos, here! Down here!"

But she was certain that he couldn't hear her, for the sounds of the explosions from behind her were drowning out everything. She put her hands to her ears, wincing against the overwhelming noise, trying to stay on her feet but failing and tumbling to her knees. She rolled over onto her back, and looked up . . .

She saw the ceiling, about five feet directly above her, heating up.

Realizing she had less than a second to react, Soleta desperately rolled to one side, and then there was an explosion of phaser fire directly above her as the ceiling blasted downward, leaving a pile of rubble about three feet high in the precise spot she had just vacated.

Ensign Janos dropped to the floor, landing in a crouch atop the rubble, and with great alarm he looked down at the rocky pile of fragments beneath his feet. "Soleta!" he shouted.

She ran up behind him, tapping him on the shoulder. He whirled, his teeth bared, his talons extended, and for Soleta it was another reminder of just how unwise it was to startle Janos. But then he realized who it was and said with clear relief, "This is most fortunate!" He held up his phaser. "Not precisely designed to be an excavating tool, but it'll do in a pinch, eh?"

"How do we get out of here?" shouted Soleta over the rumbling.

From a distance down the corridor there was another explosion. This one was louder, more definitive than the others, as if they'd built up to this one. There was a massive flash of light, and it felt like the air was burning around them.

"Quickly, that's how!" responded Janos. And without taking time to explain, he grabbed her arm and slung her over his shoulder. "Right! Hold on!"

She was about to register a protest over being treated as if she were a sack of wheat, but she saw something heading their way. It almost seemed like a tidal wave of energy, and suddenly the notion of getting out of there as quickly as possible, with a minimum of discussion, seemed a damn good one. The only problem was, she hadn't the faintest idea how they were evacuating the area.

Janos very quickly answered that question as he crouched and then leaped upward, his arms extended, his face set in grim determination. Soleta ducked her head, for the hole that Janos had carved wasn't especially wide, and she almost got her head knocked off as he hurtled upward into the only possible escape route.

The tunnel was perfectly vertical. For a moment Soleta found herself second-guessing Janos, figuring that the tunnel might be more accessible for her if he'd carved it at an angle. She wouldn't have to be carted around in this less than dignified manner. But then she realized that he had simply chosen to take the most direct route, not wanting to waste time. He trusted in his own strength and agility to get them back to the surface. Considering what he had gone through thus far and the manner in which things were proceeding, she reasoned that now was not the time to be critical about his strategies.

Janos climbed straight up. There was none of his conversational chatter now, none of his typical pleasantries or occasionally mordant humor. Instead he was entirely focused on the business of surviving. With impressive strength, his talons dug into the rocky tunnel around them and he pulled himself up, hand over hand. There was no sign of any strain on his part, nor focusing of his strength; he simply moved one hand up over the next, without hesitation or slowing. As soon as his body was entirely within the confines of the tunnel he put the claws on his feet to work as well, and it drove him faster, higher.

There was no guarantee that it was going to be fast or high enough as the air continued to broil around them, getting hotter by the second and presaging some massive release of energy that was already in progress below them and in the process of catching up to them. *We're not going to make it,* thought Soleta bleakly. *It is impossible, we simply cannot make it. . . .*

Suddenly they were up and clear. Janos hauled himself out of the hole into the interior of the cave, but he did not slow down even as Soleta tumbled off him. "Come on!" he shouted as he bolted for the opening of the cave. She was surprised to see that, when Janos was really hurrying, he propelled himself with added speed from his knuckles.

"Right behind you!" she replied, slowing only to grab her satchel and commbadge, which were sitting neatly placed on the floor several feet away from the hole.

And then there was an immense explosion behind them, and Soleta was lifted into the air by the force of it, hurled through the air and waving her arms in an impotent fashion. Janos, miraculously, had kept his footing and he spun to face her as she hurtled toward him at the mouth of the cave. Janos put his arms out and caught her and then, before she could say anything, he hurled himself, and her with him, off the rocky precipice that formed the entry to Ontear's cave.

They dropped through the air at dizzying speed, and then Janos's powerful legs absorbed the brunt of the ricochet off a lower outcropping of rock and angled them farther away. Soleta was pressed against Janos, looking over his shoulder, providing her a clear view of Ontear's cave in the upper portion of the cliffside.

The cave trembled for a brief moment, then erupted. An energy force blasted out in all directions, ripping off the top of the cave and then, a moment later, smashing apart the rest of it. Rock rained everywhere, a massive avalanche of rubble cascading all around. Soleta ducked her head down as several shards flew over her, close enough to have parted not only her hair but her entire skull. To the average human looking straight at the explosion, it would have been blinding. For Soleta it was extremely painful, but her Vulcan biology enabled her to withstand looking at the overwhelming whiteness for a few seconds without any significant harm. The energy seemed to whirl upward, to converge and coalesce upon itself as if forming a funnel, and then the intensity became so great that even she had to look away.

Janos thudded to the ground, seeming less light on his feet than he had been a moment before. "Get off," he murmured and she tumbled off him. There was a blast of superheated air from behind them and Janos pulled her to his chest, shielding her with his body, and he let out a roar of pain that was even more deafening to Soleta than anything she had experienced thus far. But she pursed her lips and said nothing, for the bottom line was that Janos had saved her life and she wasn't about to be such an ingrate as to complain about it, even though her head was ringing.

The roar of the unleashed energy high above them continued for what seemed an eternity, and then—just like that—it suddenly stopped. Even so, they remained in the huddled position for a time longer, as if unwilling to believe that they had really survived. Slowly, they began to rise. Soleta stepped away from him and looked up at the area of the cave. The unleashed energy had not only blasted the cave to bits, it had leveled the area.

Immediately she took out her tricorder and began surveying the area. "What are you hoping to find, Lieutenant?" inquired Janos as he dusted himself off.

"Some sign, some trace of—" She stopped as she noticed large areas of red covering Janos's back. "Ensign, you're injured. There appear to be . . . shards of rock embedded in your back."

"It's nothing to worry about. Do your job."

"Ensign—"

"Lieutenant," he said firmly, "finish what you set out to do. I'll be fine, I assure you. This is just a scratch. My pain tolerance threshold is far higher than the human or Vulcan norm. What you perceive as serious injury, I don't even feel. Really, truly, seriously, I'm completely tip-top. Right as rain."

"If you are sure . . ."

"Couldn't be more so."

Soleta nodded briskly and started to make her way up the embankment. The moment she was far enough away, Janos let out a low moan and gritted his fangs against the pain that was so overwhelming, it was all he could do not to black out. "Why do I have to be so bloody brave all the time?" he muttered.

Meantime, Soleta surveyed the area as quickly as she could, for she suspected that Janos was likely in more pain than he was letting on. Since the subterranean chamber had been destroyed, whatever it had been generating that had been blocking her earlier attempts at surveying was no longer in force. Unfortunately, there no longer seemed to be anything worth finding, since it had all been demolished.

Then she picked up something. Ten kliks to her right, there was some sort of metal being detected by her tricorder. She made her way over there and saw it glinting in the rapidly fading sunlight even before her tricorder led her to it. She knelt down and picked it up.

It was the disk. The one that had been embedded in the floor of the cave, with the unusual flame shaped symbol on it.

"After all that . . ." she muttered, but then she shrugged. At least she was coming away with something to show for her efforts. As she made her way back down the slope to Janos, she tapped the commbadge that she had replaced on her uniform jacket and said, "Soleta to *Excalibur.*"

"*Excalibur,* Shelby here. Go ahead, Lieutenant."

Soleta raised an eyebrow. "Commander. I am gratified that you have been released from sickbay."

"I certainly have. Report?"

"I have finished my survey of the area. The conclusion was somewhat . . . explosive . . . but other than that, it went relatively smoothly."

"Any answers to our little mystery?"

"I am afraid"—and she turned the disk over in her hand thoughtfully—"that we are left with more questions than answers."

"I look forward to the briefing. We'll bring you up."

"Most appreciated, Commander. Soleta out."

She quickly made her way back down to Janos and put a hand up to the joint where his wide head met his shoulder. "What are you doing?" he asked, sounding more irritated than he would have liked.

"Pressure point manipulation."

She located the area she was searching for and pressed with two fingers. Immediately Janos' eyes cleared of distraction and he looked at her in surprise. "What did you do?"

"Cut off pain impulses you might be feeling. I am, of course, aware of your very high pain threshold, but you seemed in distress and it occurred to me that you might be endeavoring to bravely endure your pain rather than allowing your discomfort to show through. So I felt it appropriate to provide assistance, even though it had not been requested. I hope I have not overstepped myself."

Janos stared at her and never had he so much wished that he was capable of smiling. ‘‘You know something, Lieutenant?’’

‘‘What, Ensign?’’

‘‘If you had claws and a thick coat of white fur, you would be perfect.’’

She sighed and, as the transporter beams shimmered around them to return them to their ship, informed him, ‘‘You have no idea, Ensign, how many times I have been told that.’’

5

Momidiums didn't walk so much as they oozed.

As a race they were relatively short. Humanoid in general appearance, but bearing more than a passing resemblance to slugs in the general shape and contour of their bodies. They had fairly pale complexions, with skin so light that once could see the thin latticework of their veins without too much difficulty. Their arms were deceptively strong since they looked so thin that one would have thought them almost useless. Their legs, however, were virtually nonexistent: vestigial stubs at most, left far behind by evolution. Instead they propelled themselves along by the thick lower halves of their bodies, which undulated along the ground. Their faces were generally round, their eyes uniformly orange. Their noses were horizontal slits, and their mouths were so narrow that they hardly seemed to move when the Momidiums spoke.

It had taken Morgan Primus quite some time to get used to them.

She had not counted, however, on having quite so *much* time.

They had not put her in a prison, at least not in the standard sense. They had not stuck her away in a cell; instead they had given her a rather nice suite of rooms, modestly furnished, although unfortunately scaled to Momidium size. She'd spent her first week there mostly banging her knees or bumping her head.

Unfortunately for her, she'd had five earth years since then to learn how to negotiate the space. She knew every foot, every inch of the place, and could pace it out with her eyes closed. Indeed, she had done so many a time, just to amuse herself, even though it was long past the point when it provided her any amusement at all.

The Momidiums had been polite enough, never referring to themselves as her captors, but rather her hosts. She was never a prisoner, but instead a guest. Nonetheless her imprisonment was quite real . . . thanks to her collar.

She fingered the thin, unbreakable band around her throat without even realizing that she was doing it. By this point she'd almost come to regard it as a permanent piece of jewelry rather than the means of her incarceration. If Morgan made any effort to stray outside the parameters of her accepted environment, the collar simply shut down all synaptic impulses. She would crumple to the floor, her brain trying desperately to fire commands to the rest of her body, and her body simply not getting any of the messages. She had tried it several times, each time certain that she could, through sheer effort of will, force herself to move, to escape.

She'd been wrong. And eventually she'd come to accept her imprisonment, although she had never resigned herself to it.

She heard a familiar noise coming toward her. There were four different primary jailers, and she'd come to recognize each of them by the individual *shlupping* sound their lower halves made when they moved across the floor. "Hail, Kurdwurble," she called before he even came around the corner.

Kurdwurble came around the corner and did that odd facial tic that passed for a Momidium smile. "Hail, Morgan," he replied. "This day finds you well?"

"This day finds me here. Therefore I'm as well as can be expected."

Kurdwurble laughed at that. Momidiums weren't in the habit of laughing outwardly—it was considered to be rather bad manners. Instead his chest simply shook in silent amusement. "Every day we say the same thing to each other, Morgan. You would think we would find something new."

"Well, Kurdwurble," she said, shifting in the recliner that she had presently sprawled upon, "if I am boring you, you always have the option of letting me go. But since it seems to be your intention to keep me here for the rest of my natural life, then I'm afraid that I'm going to have to just keep right on boring you. It's your decision, really."

He shook his head. "Not mine, I'm afraid. I am merely one of your hosts, Morgan. A humble civil servant. I'm not permitted such lofty pursuits as deciding the fate of others. Tell me, does the prospect of spending the rest of your natural life here disturb you? You have not been ill-treated, after all. Your stay has been quite comfortable, in fact.''

''It's an enforced stay, nonetheless, Kurdwurble. Whether a gilded cage or no, it's still a cage. I miss my freedom.''

''Freedom is an intangible. You have all the tangible considerations and needs you could possibly desire right here,'' and he made a wide gesture encompassing the whole of the room. ''I find myself wondering what more a reasonable person could want.''

''If you want to consider me an unreasonable person, you go right ahead.'' Her lips thinned slightly as she tilted her head to one side. ''I've certainly been called worse things in my life than that. You are a very—excuse the expression—down-to-earth people, you Momidiums. You're not among the more spiritual races I've ever encountered, and you don't have much use for ephemera. My people are built a bit differently. I'm not entirely certain why; we just are. We need something else to occupy our minds besides physical objects and creature comforts. We need spiritual matters to comfort us or guide us, we need freedom with which to move, to grow, and thrive. We need the ability to think about that which does not matter at all.''

''But why? That makes no sense, Morgan,'' he said, and he now angled his head in imitation of hers so he could continue to look at her in the same manner. ''Why would you care about that which does not matter at all?''

''Because it's only in caring about what does not matter that we are able to discover what *does* matter, Kurdwurble. Does that clarify for you?''

''Yes, I suppose, somewhat. I . . . well, no,'' he admitted.

''And in answer to your question: Yes, I'm daunted by the prospect of spending the rest of my life here, for reasons I can't even begin to go into.''

''I see.'' He sighed, which, for him, was an odd, warbling sort of noise. ''Morgan, I have never been very much of a thinker. But I have always been able to appreciate people who are, and I'm going to miss our discussions very much.''

Morgan was instantly alert. ''I'm sorry, what did you say?''

''You're going to be free of this place, Morgan.''

Slowly she rose from her chair. ''You wouldn't lie to your old friend Morgan, would you, Kurdwurble?''

''Lie to you?'' He sounded truly stricken, and he put a hand to his chest looking somewhat aghast. ''Morgan, after all this time, do you think I would lie to you? I have been many things, but dishonest has never been one of them. I have never been anything other than truthful with you, and now—as our relationship draws to a close—I certainly have no intention of changing that. Do you remember some time ago when I told you that the Thallonian Empire had fallen into disarray?"

"Yes," she said. "You made it sound somewhat routine, though. A temporary situation at best."

He shook his head. "Anything but routine, as it turned out. The very planet, Thallon, is gone. The Thallonian Empire has crumbled completely, Morgan, and it's a new galaxy that we face. And we Momidiums are seeking our place in it. We have always been willing allies of the Thallonians. Now there are new powers, new forces astride our little section of space. We would ally ourselves with them, and you, my dear Morgan, represent one of the ways that we can do so."

Her eyes narrowed into suspicious slits. "Wait a minute. You . . . you said I was going to be free."

He shook his head. "Free of this place, Morgan. Not free simply to walk away, however. But be of good cheer; for we are turning you over to your own kind."

"My own kind? What do you mean?"

"There is a starship in the sector now, representing the United Federation of Planets. We have contacted the vessel, informed them of your presence here, and have stated that we are willing to turn you over to them in exchange for several fairly reasonable considerations. They have agreed to our terms and, so I am given to understand, are on their way here even as we speak."

"A starship. After all this time." She shook her head in amazement. "Well, that is the equivalent of being free, I suppose. If it's a Federation vessel . . ." She stopped. "Which one. What's her name?"

"I believe it is called the *Excalibur,* which, I am told, is named for an Earth weapon. Rather odd name for a vessel if you ask me, but then, no one did."

"The *Excalibur*. All right, that's a relief."

"A relief?" He looked at her askance. "Should it make a difference which vessel it is?"

"No, no, not really. I just . . . didn't want it to be the *Enterprise,* that's all. I have some difficult memories attached to that one. It doesn't matter, though. If it's a starship from the UFP, then I'm as good as free,'' she said, clapping her hands together briskly in undisguised glee. ''I'm going free, Kurdwurble. I'm going free!''

''It would appear so. I have a message for you, actually.'' He held up a small recording chip. ''It came in through our comm center not twenty minutes ago. Two messages, actually. One was to our government, accepting our terms. The other was a personal message directed to you.'' He gestured to a playback unit along her wall and she turned to face it as he undulated over to it and slid the chip in. ''It is from the assistant to the official ambassador.''

''How very bureaucratic. I'm honored.''

A picture appeared on the screen. It was a young woman, with a serious expression and her hair pulled back. Morgan sat forward, her interest piqued. The young woman looked familiar. That was very unlikely, of course. This girl appeared to be in her mid-twenties, and Morgan hadn't run into any Starfleet personnel in nearly a decade.

''Hello, Morgan,'' said the young woman. ''It's me. Cheshire.''

Morgan was across the room as if she'd been spring-loaded. She punched the machine, popping out the chip and catching it in her hand. She turned to face a remarkably startled Kurdwurble, who stared at her in open surprise. ''Morgan—?''

''I want another ship.''

Kurdwurble couldn't quite believe he'd heard her properly. ''You want—?''

''Another ship, yes.''

He shook his head. ''Impossible.''

''Why?''

''That is the only Starfleet vessel in the area, Morgan!''

''Fine, then if you're of a mind to turn me loose, let me go and I'll find my own transportation off this rock.''

''It's not that simple, Morgan,'' he said, unable to comprehend what her problem could possibly be.

''Then make it that simple, Kurdwurble. You can do it. I know you can. You have friends, you have influence, you have—''

''Morgan, perhaps I haven't made myself sufficiently clear, although I thought I had. I have no say in the matter. Your release is part of a much larger picture. The *Excalibur* has offered us help and aid in exchange for your release.''

''They'll help you anyway!'' she told him flatly, pacing the room. ''That's what they do! Starships go around helping people! Just tell them that I escaped, but ask for their humanitarian assistance. They'll aid you; you have my word.''

He put his hands on his hips and looked at her in a slightly scolding fashion. "First of all, Morgan, you're asking us to take the word of someone who, if she has her way, won't be around to make good on that word should it prove to be unsupported. And second, we are people of our word. We have told the star vessel that you will be here to be turned over to them. You wouldn't wish to make liars of us, would you?"

"What I wish is . . ." But then she reined herself in, putting her fingers to the bridge of her nose and endeavoring to compose herself. "I just . . . do not wish to board that particular vessel."

"That young woman . . . she seemed to know you. What was her name? Cheshire? You seemed to react quite strongly to it."

Morgan said nothing, and Kurdwurble studied her closely. "Is Cheshire a particularly emotional name? A very rare one, perhaps, among humans?"

"It's . . . not common, no. Not as common as John or Bill or . . ." She repressed a smile, which was something she did by habit since she was not particularly inclined to display amusement. "Or Kurdwurble."

He looked at her skeptically. "Kurdwurble is a common human name?"

"Absolutely, yes," she said in such a no-nonsense tone that for a moment he almost believed it.

But then he shook his head and said, "I think you are attempting to confuse me. Yes, most certainly. I shall miss that, Morgan, as I've said. You have made my time with you . . . most interesting."

She bowed slightly in a rather gracious pose, and he returned it. He then made it clear that he was not easily distracted as he asked again, "So, 'Cheshire.' Again, your reaction was excessive. You are a very reserved individual, Morgan. You do not display emotions easily; indeed, you seem to consider them rather distasteful on the whole. I would be most curious to know what provoked your response. You know that I have found your race to be intriguing, based on your descriptions of humanity. Is there something about Cheshire that is—?"

"It simply brought back memories," she said stiffly, turning away from him. "There was a creature called the Cheshire Cat . . . in a work of fiction entitled *Alice in Wonderland.* The Cheshire Cat would speak in tantalizing ways and then would slowly vanish, one part of his body at a time, until only his smile remained."

"His smile? I do not think such a thing is possible."

"Well, it *is* supposed to be a work of fiction."

Kurdwurble looked at the blank screen where, only minutes before, the young woman's face had been. "I am not an especially knowledgeable judge of human expressions, Morgan, since I have only had yours to study. But it is my purely amateur opinion that the young woman in the message would have a rather attractive smile if she was so disposed. 'Attractive' by human standards, of course."

"Of course," agreed Morgan neutrally.

"In fact, if I were to use my imagination—which would be a problem since, as you know, I am most unimaginative—I would almost think that it would bear a passing resemblance to your own . . . were you ever to smile."

She didn't turn back to look at him for a long moment. She was trying to figure out what to say, or even if she should simply say nothing at all. Finally, though, she turned to face him . . .

But he was gone.

She looked down and saw the slight trail of slime on the floor that always seemed to be left in the wake of Momidiums. It tended to evaporate very quickly, however, and so presented minimal risk of slipping. Still, it was unusual for Kurdwurble to simply disappear that way. Perhaps he wanted to make a dramatic exit; or perhaps, she realized, he felt she simply wanted to be alone with her message.

She stared at the chip in her hand and considered grinding it into dust. But finally she realized that it would only prolong the inevitable. So she placed the chip back into the player and stepped back.

How could she not have known the face immediately? Granted it had been ten years, and granted she'd been barely a slip of a girl at the time, but even so, the face was almost entirely unchanged. A bit rounder, a bit more mature, but that was all.

What was she going to do now? What the hell was she going to do?

Steeling herself, she activated the message chip and the face of Roblin Lefler appeared on the screen once more.

"Hello, Morgan," it said just as it had before. "It's me, Cheshire. I imagine you're surprised to see me. Imagine how surprised I am to see you. Imagine my amazement upon seeing that my dear mother, who died ten years ago, is hale and hardy and in one piece on the planet Momidium, deep in the heart of Thallonian space."

Morgan wanted to look away, but she wasn't able to. She was fixated by the stare of her daughter: a bizarre combination of cold fury stoked with flames of anger.

"Well," continued Robin, "I'm sure you're curious as to everything that has happened since your . . . departure. Dad died, a little piece at a time, and finally all of him died. And I joined Starfleet, as you can see, living under the assumption that I was an orphan." She paused a moment, appearing to give the matter a good deal more thought, and then she shrugged. "That is more or less it, I guess. The *Excalibur* is on her way to pick you up, and then we'll take the opportunity to get reacquainted. I'm sure you're looking forward to that almost as much as I am. I don't know about you, but I . . . right now . . ." For a moment it seemed as if she were gong to lose her composure, but she kept her chin rock steady and maintained it. "I . . . right now . . . knowing that you disappeared . . . knowing that you abandoned Daddy and me, and that I mourned you when it was just a joke, and that the last ten years of my life have been a complete lie . . . Right now, mother, I wish I were dead. And I hope you're feeling the same way." And the screen blinked out.

Morgan slowly sank into a nearby chair, staring at the screen even though it was blank. Her fingers strayed over her chest as if she were trying to massage a stopped heart back to life, and as she did so she felt the coolness of the medallion she wore pressed against her. For the umpteenth time she wondered if it had all been worth it.

And then she leaned forward, still in the chair, and replayed the message, over and over again. And it was, of course, the last words that struck most closely to her heart.

I wish I were dead. And I hope you're feeling the same way.

"Darling," she said to the screen, "for what it's worth, I do. And I just wish to God that it were that simple."

6

Dr. Selar stretched on her bed in a manner similar to a cat, starting at her toes and slowly elongating her spine, her hands over her head and her fingers outstretched to the utmost. Then she let out a low sigh and shook herself slightly.

She simply lay there, the hissing of the shower in the next room only faintly making an impression on her as she gazed out the window of her quarters at the stars as they passed by. Not for the first time, she wished for some other view. The peaceful deserts of Vulcan would have gone down fairly well about then, or that glorious red sky. For that matter, although she had long ago become accustomed to the carefully maintained atmosphere aboard starships, there was part of her that missed the arid air of home.

She wondered if this was all part of *Pon farr.* Whether there would be some sort of internal drive that would try to get her to go home, now that she was . . .

Pregnant.

She felt a strange sensation on her face, muscles stretching that didn't ordinarily move, and there was a faint pressing together of her teeth. It took her a moment to fully understand what was happening to her, and she had to reach up to touch her face to verify the fact for herself.

Yes, there it was, big as life: a smile. A broad, beaming, totally unhidden smile wide across her face.

There was no logical reason for it, but there it was all the same. She was smiling so widely she felt as if it would split her face in half. She was relieved that no one was watching her, because it was extremely embarrassing. She fought the smile, commanding the muscles in her face to relax and smooth out, but it was there all the same. This was ridiculous. This wasn't her.

She heard the shower stop, and that immediately wiped the grin off her face. Furthermore, she suddenly felt a degree of modesty sweep over her. She had not felt that way for several days, particularly not whenever Burgoyne was around. Selar had been rather demonstrative with her lusts; in fact, to some extent she couldn't even remember everything that had happened. She could recall skin against skin, and Burgoyne looking down at her with a look of determined exhaustion on hir face, her fingernails digging into Burgoyne's back, and a lot of sweat—which was most unusual since Selar didn't customarily sweat—and heat like exploding suns that seemed to blast out of every pore of their bodies . . . and laughter. Her laughter, which was something she never heard. She realized how odd it was not to know what one's own laughter sounded like. She had no basis for comparison, really, and had no idea at all whether she had a good laugh, or a stupid laugh, or what.

But she had made love for days, having taken time off from her duties as CMO for medical reasons. That had certainly been a legitimate enough claim; the demands of *Pon farr* had been overwhelming and a medical necessity: she would have died had she not satisfied them. She had felt almost hedonistic during that time. She had wanted Burgoyne constantly, and not just on a physical level. She had bonded with hir on an emotional level as well as physical, had felt a closeness to hir that she never would have thought possible. She felt complete trust in hir, that there was nothing she couldn't tell hir, that s/he . . .

But . . . but if Selar truly did feel that way, she wondered, then why had she pulled the blanket up under her chin? Why did she now feel a certain degree of dread that any moment Burgoyne would emerge from the bathroom? Why did she suddenly not have the faintest idea of what to say?

Something about readouts of the phase generators as they interfaced with the coils. Selar didn't care, or want to listen to it. In her state of urgency, it was simply unimportant. Burgoyne had been trying to tell her about it, but Selar had been too busy pulling off Burgoyne's clothes to pay all that much attention.

In any event, Burgoyne had been essentially doing double duty over the preceding days. S/he'd been with Selar, doing hir level best to satisfy the Vulcan's seemingly insatiable needs, and when Selar had fallen into exhausted sleep, Burgoyne had somehow managed to haul hirself out and attend to engineering responsibilities. In a way, Selar couldn't help but admire hir stamina. Indeed, there was much that was admirable about Burgoyne. She'd heard about how Burgoyne, seized with righteous indignation, had gone after the individual who had been responsible for badly injuring Selar down on the surface of Zondar. It had been an amazing display of stamina, daring, bravery, and utter moral outrage. In the subsequent word-of-mouth retelling, Burgoyne's feat had only become more and more impressive. It had been the last element that had broken down Selar's resistance to Burgoyne's "charms." Selar had originally thought to have the captain serve as her sexual partner, and he had been willing if not overly enthused. But Burgoyne had been making overtures to Selar since they had first met, and between Burgoyne's incredible display of devotion and her own hormones driving her to make a choice, well . . . Burgoyne had won out.

Yes, there were a lot of positive things to say about Burgoyne 172, the Hermat engineer of the *Excalibur.* The only thing was . . .

Selar wasn't sure if she was the one to say them. She wasn't sure how to phrase it, she wasn't sure how to put across the emotions that she was feeling because her old training, her old personality were starting to take hold and the concept of emotions were, once again, anathema to her.

If her mate had been a Vulcan, this would have been understood between the two of them. Indeed, he'd probably be feeling exactly the same way. But Burgoyne . . . Burgoyne was a Hermat. Burgoyne was someone who rejoiced in emotion and displays of affection, tendencies that had been so overwhelming to Selar at first that she had tried to do everything she could to distance herself from hir. Now she had gone in the other direction, becoming so intimate with hir that there was nowhere she could hide any part of herself. She felt . . . she didn't know what she felt. She only knew that she wanted that emotional distance that would be automatically conferred upon her by a Vulcan partner. With Burgoyne, she had no idea where she stood.

At that moment, Burgoyne emerged from the bathroom. S/he was adjusting the top of hir uniform, and s/he was shaking hir head in puzzlement. S/he caught Selar looking at hir and smiled, displaying just a hint of hir fangs. "Feeling rested?"

Selar nodded, not taking her gaze from Burgoyne, her mind still racing as she tried to sort out the unwanted feelings tumbling through her mind.

"By the way, Selar . . . damnedest thing, I think I forgot to mention it . . . at least, I was going to mention it when I came by earlier, but we got a bit distracted . . ." S/he smiled at the memory, but then noticed that Selar didn't seem to be reacting one way or the other, so s/he continued. "That problem in Engineering? The one I was telling you about, with the energy wave that we couldn't figure out? It stopped. Just like that, no warning. We still hadn't quite figured out what it was, although I had some pretty far-fetched theories. And then for no reason at all, we couldn't detect it anymore. I've had my people working on it, but I—"

"I am pregnant," she interrupted.

That left Burgoyne speechless for a moment before s/he had a chance to compose hirself. "Are you . . . are you certain?" s/he finally managed to get out.

She nodded slowly. "It is curious. My mother told me that she was aware of my existence from the moment I was fully conceived and gestation was under way. She claimed many Vulcan females were capable of that. I was . . . skeptical. It seemed most illogical to me, and I did not see how it was possible to have awareness of a being so . . . so small. But she was correct. I sense it. I am aware of it as an extension of my being: separate, yet as one. It is a most *compelling* sensation."

Burgoyne couldn't take hir eyes off her. S/he strode to Selar's side, knelt down and said, "Can I . . . feel?"

"There is nothing to feel," Selar said matter-of-factly. "The infant will not be detectable to the touch for seven point five weeks. There is no logical reason for you to place your hand on my stomach."

"Maybe. I just wanted to anyway," Burgoyne said tonelessly.

Selar looked at hir with curiosity. "Burgoyne, we need to speak. There is much that we—"

"No, we don't need to," Burgoyne said. S/he rose, finishing fastening the top of hir uniform jacket. "Because I know exactly what you're going to say, because it's what I was going to say."

"I do not quite comprehend," Selar told hir.

"Well, then, I'll make it clear to you. We've had our fun, Selar. Both done what we wanted and needed to do. And now it's time to move on. So we just end it clean. Go back to being crewmates, and that's all."

"Are you . . ." Selar couldn't quite believe she was hearing what she was hearing. "Are you saying that you are not interested in pursuing any further relationship?"

"Of course not," Burgoyne replied. "I'd have thought that would be obvious. You don't know much about Hermat psychology, Selar."

"Yes, so you have told me on previous occasions," she said carefully. "What aspect of that psychology is pertinent to this moment, may I ask?"

"We're not built for long-term relationships. It's just not in our makeup. We're a free-spirited group, we Hermats. We're not especially monogamous. We prefer a variety of partners, and to savor whatever it is that life has to offer us. It would be natural for you to fall in love with me—"

"I?" She cocked an eyebrow. "I . . . fall in love . . . with you?"

"Well, you had this whole *Pon farr* thing going. You weren't thinking especially straight. You left yourself vulnerable to me. It would be natural for you to form an attachment to me, but I'm telling you right now, there's no point to it. We wouldn't have a prayer together. Not even a prayer of a prayer."

"I find it . . ." She sought the right word, since "stunned" and "shocked" expressed more emotion than she desired. "I am intrigued that you would feel this way. It is not how I perceived you."

"Perceived me?" S/he laughed curtly. "I'm not entirely sure what you mean by that."

"It means that I . . . thought I had a sense of the person that you were. And now it would appear that I was mistaken. I emphasize that it appears that way. However—"

S/he raised a long tapering finger, momentarily silencing her, and s/he said, "Was I, or was I not, there for you when you were ready to get physical."

"It is not quite that simple—"

"Was I," s/he repeated patiently, "or was I not?"

"You were," she admitted.

"And you were about to tell me that you weren't really comfortable in continuing our relationship as it was. That, in effect, you wanted to end it. Correct?"

"There is more than—" But when Burgoyne once again interrupted her with a slightly scolding gesture, she sighed and said, "Once more you are, in essence, correct."

"Don't you see, Selar?" asked Burgoyne as s/he backed up toward the door. Impressively, s/he managed to do so with something of a swagger. "That's why we were perfect together. We always know exactly what's going on in the other's mind. I was—and remain—everything you ever needed in a man. And in a woman, for that matter.'' And with that, Burgoyne touched hir forehead with hir finger in a signal of departure, turned, and walked out of the room.

Selar sat there for some time longer, amazed that it had been that simple. Burgoyne had taken it perfectly well, had not made a fuss over the situation, had even beaten her to the punch by ending the relationship before it began to get uncomfortable. She should be happy that it worked out as smoothly as it had.

Still, for some reason that she couldn't quite articulate, she suddenly felt a bit cold. She placed her hand on her stomach and felt warmth radiating upward from it.

And she looked around right and left, as if afraid that someone might somehow see her (illogical as that concern was) and when she had satisfied herself that she was, in fact, alone in her quarters, she allowed herself to smile once more.

Burgoyne's first impulse was to go straight to hir quarters, but s/he was not, by nature, a solitary individual. Besides, s/he would have felt as if s/he was hiding, which would not have been far wrong. And so, deciding firmly to take matters in the other direction, s/he headed straight for the single most populated area of the ship that s/he could find, namely the Team Room lounge.

It was busy, as it often was this time of day when the day shift had just come off duty. The noise and chatter from within hit hir like a solid wave. S/he looked around carefully, spotted Robin Lefler and Si Cwan off in a corner by themselves, and Lefler seemed somewhat intense in whatever she was saying to Cwan. Then s/he noticed the captain and commander seated at one table, involved in what seemed like a rather animated discussion. For a moment s/he considered endeavoring to join it, but then s/he spotted the person s/he was looking for. He was seated at a table by himself, calmly nursing a drink and staring off into space as he so often was. There was no one on board ship whose mind was always a million miles away quite like this individual.

S/he made hir way across the room to the bar, and then procured a shot of scotch. Then s/he headed for the table, stepping between people who were heading to or from the bar, and dropped into a seat opposite him. ''Hello, stranger,'' s/he said.

Mark McHenry looked up at hir with momentary surprise, and then he smiled in amusement. ''Come up for air, did you?''

''A very large lungful,'' s/he replied. ''So how are you? Haven't seen you around in a while.''

''Possibly because you haven't been around,'' McHenry told hir.

S/he leaned forward, dropping hir chin into hir upraised hand. ''Do I detect a tone of annoyance, Mark?''

''Not at all,'' he said easily.

''I think,'' said Burgoyne leaned forward, looking playfully at McHenry with that decided cat-and-mouse manner that McHenry frequently found annoyingly attractive, ''I think that you are jealous of the good doctor and myself.''

''That is ridiculous.''

''I think that you picture me in her arms and it drives you completely crazy nuts with envy. Yes, I do.'' Burgoyne was now grinning widely.

''Burgy,'' McHenry sighed, ''if you're wrong about that, as I assure you you are, then you're just wasting your time. And if you're right about it, then what you're saying now is kind of . . . what's the best word?''

''Sadistic? Torturous?''

''I was gonna say 'silly,' but those are fine, too.''

Burgoyne studied McHenry for a long moment, and then leaned back in hir chair, way back. ''Doesn't matter,'' s/he said. ''The doctor and I are *pffft* anyway.''

''What?'' He looked at hir in surprise. ''That one didn't come down the rumor mill yet. When did that happen?''

''Just now. It was a long time coming though.''

''A long time? You were together less than a week.''

''Really? Seemed so much longer.''

''Well, that's . . . that's really surprising, Burgy. And a . . . shame, I guess.''

Burgoyne hadn't been entirely sure what s/he expected McHenry to say, but that wasn't it. ''A shame? Why a shame?''

''I don't know. I just felt like you had wanted her, fought for her. You really seemed to like her, that's all.''

And Burgoyne ran hir tongue over hir upper ridge of teeth. ''I like you, Mark.''

He stared at hir as if he couldn't quite believe what he'd just heard. Then, with a slight laugh, he said ''Ooooohh no. Oooohhh, I get it.''

''Get it?''

''Yeah. Yeah, I do. You and Selar had some kind of fight, that's it.'' He pointed an accusing finger at hir. ''You had a fight, and because you can't stand being alone, you're coming back to me. Good old reliable McHenry. You must figure, 'Mark, he's such a flake, he probably didn't even notice I was gone.' Well you know what, Burgy? I did notice. And I'm not completely the flake you assume I am.''

''Oh, Mark—'' s/he sighed.

''Don't 'Oh, Mark' me. What am I, your life preserver? Your way of avoiding solitude? I don't think I'm comfortable with that, Burgoyne. Go off to other people, have your flings or your affairs, and then come back to me, the safe harbor, the port in the storm. I feel used,'' McHenry said indignantly.

''Aw, come *on,* Mark. What the hell are you talking about? Are you completely flutzed in the head or what?''

He was about to reply, but then stopped. ''I don't know,'' he said honestly. ''No one's ever asked me if I'm flutzed. For all I know I might be.''

''Take my word for it, you are. We had fun together, Mark! You and I, we had some great times.''

''Great times.'' He chuckled softly.

''What's so funny? We didn't have great times?''

''We had fun, Burgy. That's all we had.''

''Yes! Exactly!'' S/he thumped the table for emphasis. ''Wasn't that great?''

McHenry leaned back and shook his head. ''Burgy, you just don't understand, and I don't think you're culturally capable of understanding. So let's just leave it, okay?''

S/he shrugged. ''Fine. So you wouldn't be interested in seeing me tonight?''

''No way. You just don't get it, Burgy. Maybe I need someone who cares about more than just using me as an object to satisfy hir. Maybe I want someone who won't make me feel like a Ping-Pong ball, or a toy to be picked up when s/he feels like it or put aside when s/he finds someone else, only to be grabbed later when s/he wants another guiltless 'good time.' Maybe I want someone who cares about Mark McHenry the man. Who cares about my hopes and dreams and aspirations more than my body. Maybe I need someone who'll treat me better than you do.

''Then again,'' he said, the memory of their last interlude coming back to him, ''maybe I don't.''

''Your place or mine?'' s/he inquired, looking completely innocent.

''Whichever,'' he managed to choke out, ''is closer.''

''Mine, then.'' S/he put down the drink. ''Shall we go?''

* * *

Robin Lefler and Si Cwan sat undisturbed in a corner of the Team Room, and Lefler hadn't been saying a word for some time. Si Cwan stared at her in silence and finally he asked, "Was there something in particular you would like to discuss?"

"What gives you that idea?" she asked sullenly.

"Well, to start off with there was that rather scathing communiqué you sent to your mother."

She looked up at him, her dark eyes snapping. "How do you know about that? Were you reading my personal communications? Who do you think you are?"

"Well, when the Momidium government first got it, I was the one whom they came back to and asked whether we really wanted it delivered. I told them to transmit it back to me so that I could 'review' it. In point of fact, I hadn't seen it at all."

"It was sent as a private transmission. They had no business viewing it."

"It was sent to a prisoner. They had every business viewing it, and you should have known that, Robin. Considering the fact that I authorized its delivery to the intended recipient, and considering that I am choosing not to make a further issue out of an extremely inflammatory message, I would mind my tone a bit if I were you. Do we understand each other?"

"Yes," growled Lefler, "I understand."

"If I may make an observation, it seems to me that you have a great deal of anger toward her."

"She abandoned me! She—" She stopped and shook her head in frustration. "You wouldn't understand."

"I might."

She considered that possibility a moment, drumming her fingers on the table as she thought about it. "This stays between us?" she asked after a time. "Doesn't leave this table?"

"Yes, presuming you feel that you can trust me."

"Yeah. Yeah, I think I do. Okay," and she shifted in her seat, "you have to understand, I never really felt like I knew my mother. I never felt as if she was really there for me. There were always other things on her mind, and when she spoke to me it was like she was a million miles away. She was sad much of the time, and I never knew why. Every night—every single night of my life—she would always be outside come nighttime, sitting there and staring up at the stars. I don't ever remember her going to bed. I'm sure she did, but not so I ever saw. I always figured that something terrible had happened to her. Some sort of trauma in her childhood that made her that way. And I wanted to work past it. I mean, she was my mother. You're supposed to love your mother, right? You're supposed to do whatever it takes.

"So I made it my job to try and be her personal jester. No matter how down she was, how depressed or melancholy, I made that much more effort to be upbeat and cheerful. I'd joke with her, clown with her. Broke my back just to get a smile out of her. And she knew I was doing it, of course. She was a brilliant woman, my mother, I mean absolutely brilliant. Dad said that when she did sleep, she relaxed herself by doing complex equations in her head. He could hear her muttering them to herself. So there I'd be, her little Robin, dancing and smiling and saying, 'Let's have a party, Mom!' She called me her 'Party Girl.' 'The Walking Grin.' There was a character called the Cheshire Cat in that book I mentioned to you, *Alice in Wonderland,* and he always had this big smile. After mom read me that book for the first time, she started calling me Cheshire because I always had this big, stupid smile plastered on my face all the time. I felt I didn't dare ever let her see me sad, because I didn't want to take any risk that I might ever depress her. I'd always be looking for the upside. Laughing hyenas would have looked morbid next to me. I started doing that whole 'Lefler's Laws' thing because she seemed to think it was funny when I would just come up with these crazy rules of mine.

"But with all that, my mother never seemed to try and make any time for me. Not ever. She seemed amused enough by my antics, but she seemed to regard me as a curiosity, like she was studying me through a microscope. Like she was afraid to get too near me. I think, bottom line, she never really liked me much. I was just this pathetic little thing practically killing herself just to get a laugh out of her mother. How pathetic is that?"

"I don't think it's pathetic at all," Si Cwan said softly. "Clearly you cared a great deal for her. Certainly she must have known this. I'm sure it made a difference to her."

"Not enough of a difference to get her to change," replied Lefler bitterly. "And then, when I was still a teenager, just like that, *poof.* She's out of my life. I spent years mourning the loss, Si Cwan. Not just mourning the fact that she was taken from me, but mourning the fact that I never really got to know her. That I had been deprived of a normal mother-daughter relationship when she was with me, and that I'd never have the opportunity to try and fix things. I've carried that with me, that base sense of failure, for a decade now. And you know what the worst thing was?'' He shook his head and she continued. ''Deep down . . . waaaaay, way deep down where smart people don't go, I almost felt as if she had gotten killed because she wanted to get away from me. How is that for a completely screwed up way of viewing the world? That this was a woman who was so tired of having me around for a daughter, that she was actually ready, willing, and able to shrug off this mortal coil rather than have to deal with me anymore. The thing is, you can chalk this up to the overstimulated and angst-ridden imaginings of a teenager, but now here I am, I'm all grown up, and look what we've got. We've got my worst nightmare come true. She's alive, Si Cwan. She's alive, and it looks for all the world like I was dead right. That she went and faked her death just to find a way out. Part of me is screaming, 'Good move, Lefler. Not only did you drive away your mother, but you cost your father his wife. You cost him his life, because he died of a broken heart!' It's beyond belief! It—''

He took her face in his hands. She was amazed by the warmth of his skin, and when he looked into her eyes she felt as if she were being pulled into them.

''Now you listen to me,'' he said forcefully. It was the voice of someone who was not only accustomed to giving orders, but to having them obeyed instantly. ''Whatever happened with your mother was not your fault. Whatever happened with your father was likewise not your fault. You are carrying whatever burdens they may have had upon your shoulders. There is no point to that, no reason for it. Whatever reason your mother had for disappearing had absolutely nothing to do with you.''

''You don't know that.''

''I do not have to. I know you. I know the wonderful kind of person you are, Robin. I can see it in your eyes, in your heart. You're kind and compassionate, and if you wish to ascribe to your mother all the reasons for your most positive qualities, then that is entirely your privilege. The important matter is not how you got this way, but that you are this way. She missed you growing up, and that is your loss, but it is also hers. And she was the one who set that into motion.

''Listen carefully to me, Robin. You are being given a rare opportunity here. My entire family was slaughtered in the fall of Thallon except for my younger sister, who is lost somewhere in this gods-forsaken space sector. My relations with my family members were extremely acrimonious, and there were many points of disagreement between myself and them. There is so much that I wish I had said to them, so many pointless hours wasted in argument and vituperation that could just as easily, and preferably, been utilized for some positive pursuits. But all those hours are lost to me, as is my family. You have been blessed, Robin. You thought resolution, closure, maybe even personal growth were all lost to you. Instead, you have been given a second chance. Most of us would kill for that second opportunity. I certainly know I would. You've been given that chance, and the optimistic and bright-eyed Robin Lefler would probably have a rule to cover that. Does she?''

''Lefler Law One hundred and eight,'' she said without hesitation. ''It's not over until it's over, and sometimes not even then.''

''I'm not sure I understand it,'' Si Cwan told her, ''but you say it with conviction. The most incomprehensible pronouncements of our time have been said with that sort of conviction, and subsequently accepted. In fact, there are any number of laws that have been made that probably originated in just that way.''

''You think I'm being ridiculous,'' she sighed.

''I think you're being Robin Lefler,'' he replied. ''And that is more than enough for me. It would be nice if it could be enough for you as well.''

''You flatterer,'' she said with a shake of her head.

Suddenly he drew her face toward his, and she knew that he was going to kiss her. For a wild moment, she wondered what it would be like. Would it be soft and loving or hard and rough? Which way did she want it? Part of her wanted to be swept off her feet by this rather dashing and romantic fallen monarch. But another part wanted to take it slow, to have the relationship meet its full potential. To . . .

He kissed her chastely on the forehead.

She stared at him.

''You know,'' he said, sliding back into his seat and patting her hand warmly, ''in so many ways, you remind me of her.''

''Her who?''

''My sister. Same enthusiasm, same joy of living, same social consciousness and feeling that the problems of the galaxy are all caused by her. Being with you reminds me of her, makes me feel like we're together, just for a little bit.''

His sister. Great. I'm his surrogate sister.

''Robin, are you quite all right?''

''Oh, fine,'' she said quickly. ''I'm perfectly fine. Your sister, huh? Well, that's certainly what I was aspiring to. And you're certainly like the brother I never had. Well, the brother I never had if he'd turned out to be red-skinned and have tattoos on his forehead. That kind of brother.''

''I see.''

''I want to tell you, Si Cwan,'' she said as she started to rise from her chair, ''this has been a really wonderful, revealing chat.''

ELSEWHERE . . .

Her lover is speaking to her.

It tells her of a loss. Another of its kind is suddenly gone, just like that. It causes her, just for a moment, to cease her singing. She feels her lover's sadness, and she mourns the loss of others like it.

And then a fear begins to pervade her. She does not realize its origins at first, because she thinks it may be coming from within her. But then she realizes that such is not the case. It is, in fact, coming from her lover.

The realization is startling to her. In all this time, her lover has been her strength, her salvation. All of her own confidence and certainty comes from the protection that her lover provides her. For her lover now to feel fear, it must be a most terrible state of affairs indeed.

She reaches into her lover, probes gently, to learn what disturbs it.

She finds fear of being kidnapped. Fear of forced abandonment. Her lover senses something, senses that some change has occurred. That something new has been introduced into its personal environment. A variable, an x factor that threatens to disrupt the status quo. And once something like that has been introduced, it is impossible to determine what the outcome will be or where it will all end up.

It is possible, of course, that there will never be any disruption to her lover. That their little world of Ahmista will remain undisturbed and unaffected by whatever is happening elsewhere in the galaxy. It is more than possible, in fact. It is extremely likely.

But there is still a chance, of course. An outside chance that something could happen. Someone might come to try and take her lover away.

She will not let that happen. She knows that for a certainty. If someone should come along and try to deprive her of her lover, she will fight back with every bit of ability at her disposal. Mercy will be an alien concept to her. She will destroy anything and everything that attempts to separate her from that which she adores, that which she could not live without.

She strokes her lover gently and speaks to it with the power of her mind. She reassures it, lets it know that she will never abandon it or turn away from it. *You are mine. You will always be mine, and I yours. Nothing can ever change that. If others try to . . . I will destroy them. I will obliterate them. It will be as if they had never existed. You can trust me on that, I swear to you. I swear it.*

And her lover believes her. It knows that she is sincere, and accepts her without hesitation.

She will be one with her lover. She will stay with her lover.

She draws it tighter to her, and in her mind she calls out defiantly to any and all who might try to separate them. *Come to me,* she challenges any and all potential threats. *Come to me and I will show you what happens to anyone who would hurt me, or who would try to come between my lover and me. We are together, forever. Come to me, if you will. Come to me . . . and know my love . . . and know your death.*

And she waited eagerly for the chance to prove her love by destroying whomever might approach.

7

"It's back, sir."

Leaning over the console in Burgoyne's office, Ensign Beth tapped the readouts dancing across the screen, the energy spikes being generated by the engines. Burgoyne shook hir head in disbelief as, all around hir, the day shift in Engineering came on duty.

"You see? During a routine diagnostic, it suddenly spiked as if it . . . it . . ."

"Woke up," Burgoyne murmured. "That'll teach me to start a day with anything approaching a good mood."

"A good mood?" Beth smiled wanly. "Another wild evening with Dr. Selar?"

Burgoyne immediately fired her a look that fairly shouted to her that she'd overstepped herself. "I'm disinclined to be grist for the rumor mill, Ensign, if it's all the same to you," s/he said sharply.

"I'm—" She quickly looked around as if hoping that she could suddenly spot someplace else she should be. "I'm sorry, sir."

But Burgoyne simply regarded her as if from very far away for a moment, and then said wistfully, "No, no, it's all right, Ensign. You're just being human, with all the attendant problems that brings with it. If we could design a starship that was fueled by rumors, we could probably crack Warp Ten with it." S/he scratched hir chin thoughtfully. "I should have known it wouldn't be that easy, that the problem wouldn't just disappear."

"You were speculating earlier, Chief, about the possibility of there being something . . ." She looked uncomfortably in the direction of the warp core. "Well, something alive in there? And now you're talking about maybe something woke up. Do you really think that—"

"I'm not sure," admitted Burgoyne. "But I'll tell you one thing, Beth. If there really is some sort of energy being or creature rumbling around in the engines, this has suddenly gone beyond being an engineering problem. I'm going to have to bring in science on this." S/he tapped her commbadge. "Engineering to Soleta."

"Soleta here. Go ahead."

"We have a situation down here that I'm having trouble resolving—and you did not hear me say that, since everyone knows I have the answers for everything."

"Understood, Chief. I am about to brief the captain and commander on the details of my excavation on Zondar, but I will be down directly."

"I'll be waiting. Burgoyne out." Burgoyne turned to Beth just in time to notice that Ensign Christiano was walking past Burgoyne's office and he seemed to be trying to sneak a very nonchalant look in. Beth was pointedly looking in the other direction. This exchange, or lack thereof, was hardly lost on Burgoyne, who said, "Trouble in paradise with Mr. Christiano, Ensign?"

"Lieutenant Commander," Beth said stiffly, squaring her shoulders, "if you are permitted to keep the details of your private life private, then I would think that you would allow me the same courtesy."

"By all means," Burgoyne assured her.

"Whatever is going on between Ensign Christiano and myself, or whatever is not going on, is not something that I really wish to discuss at this time."

"I understand completely."

"I don't want to talk about him or my ring, all right?"

"I'd be happy to honor your . . ." Burgoyne blinked a moment in confusion. "Your ring? What ring?"

"Well . . ." She cleared her throat. "Since you asked . . ."

In the conference lounge, Calhoun was holding up the disk, carefully examining it front and back. Standing directly behind him, looking over his shoulder, was Shelby. "I take it, Lieutenant, that despite your time already spent in this sector of space, that you've never seen anything like this?"

"No, sir, I have not," said Soleta. "The symbol on it has no particular meaning. The material itself is not especially abnormal. An alloy with a mix of at least twelve different elements to it. No internal circuitry that I can detect; it appears to be solid throughout.''

''Looks like a metal hockey puck,'' Shelby observed.

''Since I'm unfamiliar with that device, I will take your word for it,'' Soleta said.

''And you said that it talked to you somehow? That it channeled some sort of a . . . a mind?''

''So it seemed, Captain. But to be honest, everything happened so quickly that it is difficult to know precisely what happened. It's as I described in my report: I touched it, I felt some sort of warmth, and suddenly there was this . . . this voice in my head. Events unfolded rather quickly after that.''

''Yes, so you said. Nice that you made it back in one piece.'' He sat back and said sadly, ''I just wish that there had been something left there for us to study.''

''As do I, Captain. Unfortunately, there's definitely nothing left. The force blast that blew off the top of the mountain was rather comprehensive. It was designed to obliterate everything that was there. From my firsthand observation, I would have to say that it more than did the job.''

''And you're convinced,'' Shelby said, slowly walking along the interior of the room, ''that the image you saw was Ontear. *The* Ontear of Zondarian history.''

''That is my conclusion, yes.''

''And mine as well,'' Calhoun reminded her. ''I saw him, too, when I was a captive down there.''

''You're not going to tell me this was a ghost, are you?'' Shelby warned, clearly not sanguine over that prospect.

''Far from it. I think he was all too real,'' said Calhoun.

Soleta was nodding as well. ''From your accounts, Captain, and from my own experience, I believe that what we saw was a crude form of observational time travel. Ontear utilized technology that enabled him to project himself forward in time, to observe and, if he desired, interact with whatever he encountered while never truly leaving his own period of time. Since he amassed himself a considerable reputation as a seer, I would surmise that he pursued these endeavors within his local arena of time as well. There is not all that much difficulty in being a soothsayer—''

''If you have firsthand access to the sooth,'' Calhoun said. ''Charming little deal he has worked out. He goes to the future, watches it unfold, then in his own time he predicts its coming.''

"But he had to be judicious about it," Shelby pointed out. "He had to do things in such a way that it wouldn't result in the future actually being changed. That could have jeopardized the entire time line that he was trying to observe."

"From my preliminary research," Soleta told them, "at least half of his predictions involved natural disasters. Warning people of floods, quakes, and such. Nothing that foreknowledge could possibly have made any difference in."

"I disagree," said Calhoun. "Let's say that Citizen X was destined to die in a volcano. If Ontear targets the volcano, and Citizen X knows to get the hell out of there or he winds up roasted in lava, then history could indeed wind up being changed."

"We will never know for certain," Soleta admitted. "Although I would like to think that, at the very least, he was selective in whom he dealt with and what particular moments, if any, he chose to interfere with. He might have been bright enough to target the potential focal points in time that could seriously have disrupted the path of Zondarian history."

"We can only hope," sighed Calhoun. He slid the disk back across the table to Soleta. "Check this with Si Cwan. See if he knows anything about it or has ever seen anything like it. This is supposed to be his home turf, after all."

"As you wish, sir."

With a glance at the both of them that seemed to indicate they were finished with their business, Calhoun rose and headed back to the bridge. Soleta was about to follow when she heard her name spoken very quietly, just under someone's breath. She turned, mildly surprised, to see that Shelby was whispering her name, barely mouthing it. Shelby knew that Soleta's rather sharp hearing would detect it. She hung back since Shelby's desires were clear: She wanted to speak to her privately for a moment. As soon as Calhoun had departed, Soleta turned squarely to face Shelby with a questioning eyebrow raised.

"Soleta, may I ask your opinion about a personal matter?"

"Of course you can, Commander."

"I just . . ." Shelby's hands seemed to move in vague patterns. "I . . . wanted to talk to another woman for a moment."

"Do you wish me to find one for you?" Soleta inquired.

"No, I—" Shelby laughed softly. "I meant I wanted to talk to you. You're the highest ranking woman on the bridge aside from me.

Maybe that's a silly criterion, but nonetheless I feel a sort of . . . of connection with you in that respect.''

''It is flattering that you think of me with such regard. Very well, Commander, how may I be of service?''

Shelby walked slowly around the table with a bit of a swagger to her step, as if endeavoring to bolster her confidence, as if she were discussing something that was mere silliness at best. ''You seem to be a fairly sharp judge of character, and you've had a chance to observe the interactions of all concerned fairly closely since the launch of the *Excalibur,* and I suppose that one of your strengths is analysis, which would make you an ideal person to ask about this. I fully admit, I'm not entirely comfortable discussing it, but I'm a strong believer in talking things out, getting opinions and feedback. You understand, don't you?''

''Understand what? I confess, Commander, I am still uncertain as to precisely what it is that we are discussing.''

''Love. Desire. Attraction. That kind of thing.''

She looked at her askance for a moment. ''Commander, are you propositioning me?''

''What?''

''I admit that science is synonymous with experimentation, but I—''

''No!'' Shelby put up her hands as if shoving the notion away. ''No, Soleta, that's not what I'm talking about at all.''

''I see. Then clarification might be in order if we are to proceed.''

''Look, I just want to check how something might be perceived, that's all. In your opinion, would you or any members of the crew . . .'' She shifted uncomfortably in place. ''Does anyone think that I have romantic intentions toward Captain Calhoun?''

''I do not know,'' Soleta said, sounding no less puzzled than she had before. ''Are you asking me to conduct a survey? If so, as soon as I have completed my current studies, I shall embark on a survey of—''

''No! No, I don't want you conducting a survey, Soleta! I just want to know if I come across to you as being enamored of Captain Calhoun! That's all.''

''Commander,'' Soleta said slowly, ''to be perfectly blunt, it has never even entered my mind. Your performance as second in command of this vessel has been above reproach. Your interactions with the captain on the bridge have been nothing less than professional at all times. If you are indeed possessed of some sort of intense romantic feelings for him, it is not evident to me. Granted, I am not the ideal individual to form commentary in regard to human mating or sexual habits, but I would have to say in my assessment as a Starfleet officer that, at the very least, whatever emotional feelings you may possess for the captain have not in any way compromised or interfered with your ability to do your job.'' She paused and cocked an eyebrow. ''Is that sufficient response for you, Commander?''

''Yes,'' smiled Shelby. She raised a hand for the purpose of placing it in a friendly manner on Soleta's shoulder, but then thought better of it and simply turned it into an apparently casual scratching of her own neck. ''I appreciate the time, Soleta, and I also know I can count on you to keep this discussion between ourselves.''

''Of that, Commander, I can most uncategorically assure you.''

Shelby walked out of the conference room as Soleta gathered up the disk. The science officer watched her go, then shook her head and murmured, ''Commander, you are so in love it borders on the ludicrous.''

Soleta walked up to the turbolift and the door hissed open. She was mildly surprised to see Dr. Selar in there, and she nodded her head slightly to her fellow Vulcan in greeting as she entered the lift.

''Soleta,'' Selar said after a moment as the doors hissed closed, ''I do not believe I have properly thanked you for your help with my difficulties during the time of *Pon farr.* Any discussion I had with off-worlders about the matter was most . . . difficult. Your aid, to say nothing of your efforts in mindmelding to provide diagnosis of the situation—''

''No thanks are required, Selar,'' replied Soleta. ''You were in distress and I provided assistance. To do any less than what I did would have been illogical.''

''Nonetheless, your aid is appreciated. And you will be pleased to know that the matter has been successfully concluded. I believe I am indeed pregnant, and the mating urge has passed.''

''My congratulations, Selar.'' She turned to face her formally and raised her fingers in the customary gesture of blessing. ''May your child live long and prosper.''

''Thank you.''

''I am about to see Lieutenant Commander Burgoyne on another matter. Would it be good form for me to extend congratulations to hir as well?''

Selar seemed to study her a moment, and abruptly she said out loud, ''Computer, halt lift.'' The turbolift promptly came to a halt and Soleta regarded her with open curiosity. "Soleta, may I ask your opinion about a personal matter?"

"I'm beginning to feel a bit like ship's counselor."

"Pardon?"

"Nothing. Of course you may, Doctor."

"I simply feel that, due to our mindmeld and your involvement earlier, I feel a sort of connection to you. And I am . . ." She appeared to be searching for the right word. "I am conflicted in my attitude toward Burgoyne."

"Conflicted in what way?"

"In every way," she admitted. "The bond of *Pon farr*—" Selar paused, then continued. "The point is, I am accustomed to having distance from others. Not simply physical distance, but the emotional distance not only granted me by my nature, but demanded of me by my profession. I abandoned that distance when I gave myself over to Burgoyne. I am not certain now if it is possible for me to recapture it, nor am I certain that I am even desirous of doing so."

"The gate has already been opened, Doctor. I am not altogether certain it is possible to close it."

"Perhaps it is," replied Selar.

"Selar, you believe that you are bearing Burgoyne's child. That would seem to give hir some sort of permanent place in your life. Or did you not consider that?"

"To be honest, I had not. I had many considerations driving me, Soleta, but long-term planning was oddly enough not one of them. I do not know if I subscribe to your belief that Burgoyne's presence in my life is mandated. It is not at all impossible for me to raise this child on my own. And tell me, as a Vulcan, Soleta, can you envision Burgoyne as a lifemate for me? S/he is so different, so very much the antithesis of all that we are. Let us say that I were to return to Vulcan, on a temporary or even permanent basis. There would be no place for Burgoyne within our society. Nor would I easily fit in with Hermat society. We are too different, Soleta."

"Is that your real concern, Selar? How each of you 'fits in' to your respective worlds of origin?"

Selar considered it a moment and then slowly admitted, "No."

"I did not think so. In my opinion, Selar—since you asked—I believe that you feel rather vulnerable in the presence of Burgoyne. That it is that vulnerability you consider to be the most daunting aspect of your present situation, and that might be a problem whether you were with Burgoyne or any member of our own race. The problem that presents itself is that, while another Vulcan might be equally and comfortably withdrawn, Burgoyne would require continued displays of intimacy, both physical and emotional. You are not at all certain whether you are capable of providing those. Am I correct?"

"I would have to say that your assessment is more or less accurate."

"More? Or less?"

"More," sighed Selar.

"Selar, if I may be so bold, do you love hir?"

"I do not know if that is a particularly relevant question."

"I disagree, Selar. I think it may well be the only relevant question."

Selar seemed to be staring intently at the door of the lift, as if she were capable of seeing straight through it and down to Engineering. "I do not know," she admitted.

"Then it seems to me," Soleta said slowly, "that once you have worked out the answer to that question, the rest of the answers should be forthcoming on their own."

Selar said nothing for what appeared to be a very long time, although Soleta knew internally that it was only eleven seconds. "Computer, resume lift function." Obediently the turbolift smoothly reengaged on its path as Selar said, "I believe you are correct, Soleta. I shall give the matter careful consideration and endeavor to come to a logical conclusion."

"If I may be so bold, Selar, might I suggest that, when pondering questions of this nature, logic is the very last discipline you would want to apply." And she stepped out of the turbolift and headed to Engineering.

"Soleta, may I ask your opinion about a personal matter?"

Soleta stared at Burgoyne across hir desk. They had been going over the energy readouts and mysterious percolations of the engines for nearly half an hour, and Soleta had agreed to give the matter a good deal more study, particularly searching for potential analogs to other such occurrences in assorted vessels. It had almost been something of a blessing for her, spending an entire thirty minutes dealing exclusively with matters that pertained to her job description. But now Burgoyne was seated behind hir desk, hir long, tapered fingers interlaced, and s/he was staring at Soleta with those remarkable dark eyes.

Apparently under the impression that Soleta hadn't quite heard hir,

Burgoyne repeated, "Soleta, may I ask your opinion about a personal matter? I mean, perhaps this is being a bit forward, but after our having worked so closely together when the captain was gone and the commander was out of commission, I feel that we established a kind of connection."

"If you say so," Soleta said.

"Sure," Soleta said more loudly. "Go right ahead, Chief. I assume that this is a question regarding matters of a delicate romantic nature?"

"How did you know?"

"I'm science officer and chief data analyst of this ship, Lieutenant Commander. Would this pertain to Doctor Selar?"

"Partly. Mostly, it's about Mark McHenry. That's why I was asking you. You went to the Academy together, worked closely, so I figured you would have some further insight."

"Oh." That surprised her slightly, but she took it in stride. "Very well. What is the nature of your situation with McHenry?"

"It's just that he may very well have pegged me on something, and I don't completely want to admit it. I'm very fond of him, and I just wanted to know if you thought that, in the long term, I might be doing him damage."

"Damage? Of a physical nature?"

"No, of an emotional nature."

"Ah, well, yes, as a Vulcan, naturally I would be the ideal person to voice opinions on human emotional durability."

"I'm sorry, Lieutenant," Burgoyne said, looking genuinely apologetic, and s/he started to rise from behind hir desk. "I shouldn't be dragging you into this."

"Perhaps not, but here I am in any event," said Soleta as she gestured for Burgoyne to sit down again. Burgoyne did so. "And McHenry is indeed a longtime associate, although 'friend' may be too strong a word, for in many ways he is almost as incomprehensible to me now as when we were cadets together. Still, of all humans that I have ever encountered, he has always shown a remarkable degree of resilience. Oftentimes it seems to me that almost nothing phases him. Do you wish to tell me precisely what is the nature of your situation?" and she added silently to herself.

"Soleta, you have to understand I'm a very physical person."

She stared at him. "As opposed to a being of pure consciousness, like an Organian?"

"No, I mean . . ." S/he let out a long, unsteady breath. "What's the best way to put this? I had . . . have . . . very strong feelings for Selar. From the moment I met her, I felt as if we could be something special together. But you understand, I'm hardly a virgin in these matters. There have been other women and men that I've had similar feelings for. I'm very driven by my physical and emotional makeup. I feel an attraction for someone and it's practically overwhelming. And I will do everything I can to make that attraction clear . . . until the physical aspect has been attended to, at which point I feel—what's the best word? Sated. I'm a very curious individual, Soleta."

"I would have to agree with that, Burgoyne."

Burgoyne was about to continue, but then hesitated and clarified. "I meant 'curious' as in 'inquisitive,' not 'curious' as in 'strange.' "

"Oh. Well, that, too, I suppose."

"And along those lines, I have . . . I had . . . extreme curiosity about Selar. That curiosity drove all other aspects of my personality, as it always does."

"I see. And under ordinary circumstances, having had your curiosity satisfied, you would now be moving on elsewhere."

"That doesn't seem unreasonable to you, does it, Soleta?" Burgoyne leaned forward, and it seemed to Soleta as if s/he was urgently looking for some degree of understanding. "I mean, let's be blunt: It's not as if my lovers aren't curious about me in turn. Don't try to deny it. I'm the only Hermat in Starfleet. I'm used to the looks, the speculation, the whispered discussions that suddenly stop whenever I enter a room. And I'm fine with that. It's understandable. It's even human. I always assume when I take a lover that he or she is motivated primarily out of curiosity as to what sex with a Hermat is like. My peers are Starfleet personnel. Investigation and exploration is our business. So it only makes sense that exploring each other would be a natural extension of the package. But with Selar there was . . ."

"Something more?" When Burgoyne didn't readily reply, Soleta continued, "The depth of connection that *Pon farr* can foster can be quite intense. To a non-Vulcan, it can even be overwhelming if you are not prepared for it."

"Could *anything* have prepared me for it?"

"Probably not," admitted Soleta.

"So, as I was saying, my curiosity should have been satisfied, and I . . ."

Burgoyne seemed to be having problems phrasing it, and Soleta stepped in. "You had problems moving on. Loving her and leaving her, as it was."

"Yes."

"You found you wanted to stay with her. To stay close to her."

"Yes."

"And the problem with that was—?"

"Don't you understand? I didn't know if it was real!" Burgoyne said urgently. "It might have been something forced on me because of *Pon farr.* I didn't know. I don't know even now . . . if the feelings that I'm having are genuine or fake. If I had to go based on my previous involvements, I'd have to say they're not remotely genuine because I've never felt like this before. But if they are . . . but I don't know . . ." S/he leaned forward, hir head in hir hands. "It's totally disrupting my peace of mind."

"And so you went running back to McHenry?"

"Mark is familiar. Mark is safe. I understand Mark, understand how he makes me feel. It doesn't have to mean anything with Mark."

"I see. What you wish," Soleta said, "is a succession of partners, one after the other. A variety of assignations that have no more meaning than a passing gust of solar wind. An endless parade of intrigued sexual playmates to satisfy your endless fascination with physical pleasure."

"Exactly," Burgoyne said. "Is that so wrong?"

"I'm not judging good or bad, Burgoyne. I'm not judging at all. To be honest, I'd rather be anywhere else discussing anything else."

"And besides, who are you to talk about emotional attachments? It's not as if that's something at Vulcans are particularly renowned for."

"Perhaps not in the standard human way, no. But we know love."

"That's an emotion. Vulcans don't believe in emotion."

"Oh, honestly, Burgoyne. You make it sound as if Vulcans accord emotion the same level of credibility as we would The Katha Legend. Of course we believe in emotion. Of course we possess emotion. If we didn't have emotions, our lives would be that much easier. What we do is control our emotions, to the best of our abilities. Love, like any other emotion, is something that we regulate. We do not fall in love based upon romantic and fairy tale notions as other species do. Love is a state of mind that is carefully developed. We make a decision with whom we will fall in love and then proceed in a logical, carefully reasoned fashion. Mates are selected through a conscientious process of compatibility in thirty-seven different areas, ranging from social equatability to opinions on matters of deep philosophical meaning. A relationship is built upon intellectual discourse, rational conversation, and lengthy interaction that elevates the spirit and leads toward a clearer and greater comprehension of the disciplines of logic and the many responsibilities inherent in being a Vulcan.''

''At which point your biological drives kick in.''

''It is not a perfect system. Nothing ever is.'' When Burgoyne laughed at that, she added, ''I'm pleased to see that you are amused by all this.''

''No. No, I'm not amused,'' Burgoyne said sadly. ''Soleta, what am I going to do? I went running back to McHenry because I was scared off about how I felt about Selar. Mark knows that's why I did it, I think. But he took me back anyway, and it all seemed a great game to me, but now I'm suddenly worried about hurting him. And I'm worried about hurting Selar, except I don't know that I have any basis or that I could hurt her, but it worries me. And I'm not used to worrying about hurting anyone. What do you think I should do?''

''Be prepared to hurt someone,'' she replied without hesitation.

''Thanks,'' said Burgoyne a bit sourly.

''I apologize, Burgoyne. This area is really not my specialty. Although, if this day keeps up as it is, I may wind up changing my discipline from science to interspecies romance. There's been a good deal written about that over the years. Quite a few in-depth studies done.''

''Really?'' This seemed to intrigue Burgoyne, and with hir pale blond eyebrows knit together in a puckish manner, s/he commented, ''I'd love to read them.''

''Somehow,'' Soleta told hir, ''I just knew you would.''

Si Cwan's quarters were becoming rather impressive. Soleta wasn't quite sure where he had managed to acquire the assorted thick cloths, trappings, and brocades that seemed evocative of his homeworld of Thallon, but she had to admit that it was looking more and more impressive.

At that moment, Si Cwan was studying the flame image on the disk while Robin Lefler watched him. ''Well?'' Soleta asked after a moment, her arms folded.

''I . . . do not know anything . . . for certain,'' Si Cwan said after a time. ''And all that I do know is a child's story.''

''Pardon?'' asked Soleta. She exchanged glances with Lefler, who shrugged.

''There was a book in Kallinda's library,'' he said. ''A book of tales of ancient Thallon. Originally handed down via oral tradition, spun by various storytellers throughout the centuries. There was one story I remember in particular: It was about a trickster god named Imtempho. He liked to do things to enrage and annoy the other gods, pulled all manner of tricks on them. The story went that the gods had created the Thallonians to be their playthings, their objects of amusement. But Imtempho, although he was merely a trickster, truly hated the gods and wanted to see them all done away with. But he was unable to lift a hand against them himself. So he stole something from the gods that was the property of them and them alone, and that was fire. He brought fire down to the Thallonians, and the Thallonians began using it to accomplish all manner of wonderful things. This angered the gods, who demanded that the Thallonians return the fire to them. The Thallonians retaliated by setting fire to the Great Hall that the gods lived within, and all the gods were burned up. In that way, the Thallonian people left behind their ancient beliefs and moved forward toward a time of reasoning and self-reliance.''

''That's a very charming story,'' Soleta commented. ''Is it remotely relevant?''

''It might be in one respect.'' He held the disk up. ''The book carried with it illustrations that were reproductions of the tale done in ancient times. And I could swear that Imtempho was always pictured wearing an emblem quite similar to this around his neck, like a medallion.''

''I see,'' Soleta said slowly. She considered it a moment, and then said, ''Very well, Ambassador. Thank you for your time.''

''My pleasure. I wish I could be of more help to you than simply recounting an old children's story.''

She nodded thoughtfully and headed out the door. It took her a moment to realize that Robin Lefler had fallen into step beside her and was accompanying her down the corridor. She looked questioningly at Lefler, who said, almost defensively, ''I'm heading back to Ops.''

''Of course you are,'' said Soleta reasonably.

They stepped into the turbolift, the door hissing shut behind them. ''Bridge,'' Soleta said.

''Soleta . . .'' Robin said after a moment.

''Yes?''

''May I ask your opinion about a personal matter?''

Soleta stared at her.

''Computer, stop lift,'' Soleta said immediately. The car promptly halted and she turned to face a puzzled Lefler. ''Love?''

"What?"

"Is this about love?"

"Well, yes."

"Mm-hmm. Let me guess: Si Cwan."

Lefler blinked in surprise. "How did you know?"

"Process of elimination. Marry him."

"Soleta!" Robin laughed in a very uncomfortable manner. "It's a little more complicated than that."

"No, it's not."

"But I don't think he even knows I'm alive!"

"Lieutenant, if you marry him and he still doesn't know you're alive, then you have bigger problems than I could possibly solve."

"Soleta, for God's sake! I thought you'd understand! I mean, you *were* responsible for getting Si Cwan on the ship in the first place, and you met him years ago when he spared your life, and you saved my life on Thallon, so I just felt as if you'd be a good person to talk to about this because I feel you have a, you know . . ."

"Connection, yes. That is becoming painfully apparent to me. If I had any more connections, I'd have my own subspace radio frequency. Lieutenant, look, it is not as if I am unsympathetic. Well, actually, I *am* unsympathetic by this point, but you should not take that personally."

"I'll try not to," Robin said uncertainly.

"Marry him, don't marry him. Tell him how you feel, don't tell him how you feel. Sort out your problems, throw yourself into his arms, tease him, taunt him, decide he is not right for you or that he is perfect for you. I do not care. It is not my problem. It is not my specialty. It is not my area."

"Soleta, I thought we were friends." Robin said, sounding a bit hurt.

"I am aware of that, Robin, and understand that I am not averse to the notion. However, if we are indeed friends, you will then be willing to be sympathetic when I say that I really, truly, do not wish to discuss these matters. Will you honor my request?"

"Well, sure. I guess."

"Thank you. Computer, resume lift operation."

The turbolift promptly continued on its way to the bridge, and they rode most of the rest of the way in silence. But just before they got to the bridge, Lefler turned to Soleta and said, "Are you going into that Vulcan heat thing?"

Soleta turned and stared at her with undisguised incredulity. *"What?"*

"It's just that you seem awfully testy."

Soleta tried to find words but, uncharacteristically, they eluded her. She settled for holding her tongue as she stepped off the turbolift. She drifted toward the science station, slowing only as she passed Zak Kebron. He looked at her with vague curiosity. "Problem, Soleta?" he asked in a low voice.

"Is it my imagination, Kebron," Soleta asked slowly, "or is everyone on this vessel preoccupied with romance?"

"Not me."

"No?" she asked.

"I don't need romance," Zak Kebron told her confidently. "I have goldfish."

Soleta wisely didn't pursue it.

8

The diplomatic reception chamber of the Momidiums was scaled to accommodate Momidium needs, as was indeed most of the other furniture and architectural design of the place. Nonetheless, it was still a rather impressive structure, and Shelby found the Momidiums themselves a rather pleasant people, easy to get along with . . . even if they did remind her a bit of slugs.

Once the *Excalibur* had settled into orbit around the planet, Shelby, Si Cwan, Selar, Lefler, and Zak Kebron had beamed down to the planet's surface at the coordinates provided. Kebron, as was his habit, spent most of the time looking around suspiciously and trying to determine if there was anyone hiding who might be prepared to spring out and launch a trap. Si Cwan, for his part, immediately fell into easy conversation with Cudsuttle, the head of extraterrestrial relations.

"I'll be blunt, Ambassador," said Cudsuttle. "I never had much patience with, or use for, the rest of your clan. But you were of a very different stripe, and I was pleased to learn that you had survived the insurrection. Rumor has it that you seek the whereabouts of your sister as well."

"The rumors are quite correct," allowed Si Cwan.

"I hope for the best, then, for her and for you," said Cudsuttle. "Commander Shelby, you have a good man here," he said, nodding approvingly toward Si Cwan. "You should take care not to lose him."

"We're very aware of that, sir, and have no intention of losing track of him," Shelby assured him. "So, I understand we can be of help to each other. Dr. Selar here is more than willing to get together with your medical personnel immediately to run tests on this vaccine of yours. With any luck, we'll be able to verify its fitness for use in . . . three hours, was it, Doctor?''

Selar nodded. ''I believe that is what Dr. Maxwell said. In fact, he tends to be conservative in his estimates, so we may very well be able to handle it more quickly.''

''Excellent. And you wished help from an agricultural specialist regarding an irrigation system.''

''Correct, Commander. Will that person be forthcoming?''

''You're looking at her,'' Shelby said. ''Believe it or not, Cudsuttle, I grew up on a farm. I doubt there's anyone on the ship more experienced in these matters than I am. I'll be more than happy to give you whatever guidance I can.''

''That is most kind of you. And we will be happy to escort Ambassador Cwan and Lieutenant Lefler to the Primus prisoner.''

''Why did you hold her?''

The question came from Robin and, unlike the quite cordial tone of voice that was the norm up until that point, she sounded tense, almost angry.

''I beg your pardon?'' asked Cudsuttle politely.

Seeing potential for problems, Shelby stepped in quickly. ''The lieutenant was simply asking, in a rather intense fashion,'' she noted in a warning tone that was not lost on Lefler, ''why precisely the woman, Morgan Primus, was held here, particularly for so long. Did you believe her to be a spy and, if so, what exactly was she spying on?''

''You mean are we hiding something of interest?'' Cudsuttle said, sounding rather amused at the concept.

''Something like that,'' Shelby replied guardedly.

''Would that we were that devious a people, Commander. We might have gotten farther than we have in galactic politics. No, I am afraid it's nothing quite as intriguing as that. It was simple caution. We were not concerned that she was spying on us so much as that she might be some sort of provocateur or emissary for an alien race, out to stir up trouble. We Momidiums are a peaceful people, Commander. We do not seek out problems, either within our own sphere or with powerful potential opponents such as the Thallonians. Perhaps she was an enemy of the Thallonians. Perhaps she wished us harm. We did not know for certain, and we did not desire to take the chance. All we knew is that she showed up on our world, asked a goodly number of questions regarding ancient artifacts, and violated one of the basic laws of Thallonian rule, which was: No out-worlders. Based upon all of that, we didn't so much make her a prisoner as take her into protective custody.''

''Her protection,'' asked Si Cwan, ''or yours?''

''A bit of both, I daresay,'' admitted Cudsuttle. ''In any event, that time is now gone. She is yours to do with as you will. I officially release her to Captain Calhoun, with you serving as his representative. Kurdwurble!'' he called, and from the sound of that Si Cwan momentarily thought that he had something caught in his throat. But a moment later another Momidium emerged from nearby. ''This is Kurdwurble,'' Cudsuttle said by way of introduction. ''He will bring you to her.''

''Right this way,'' Kurdwurble said, gesturing for them to follow.

''Ambassador,'' Lefler said suddenly, ''perhaps it'd be best if you accompanied the commander. I'm certain I can handle this on my own.''

''Lieutenant—'' Si Cwan began.

''I'm certain that I can,'' Lefler repeated, and her glance took in everyone in the away team, but most particularly Shelby, in a manner that could almost be considered to be challenging. It was as if she was saying, *I have to do this myself. Please don't mix in.*

As if in silent acknowledgment, Shelby nodded. ''Very well, Lieutenant. And good luck.''

''Thank you,'' she said, adding silently, *I'll need it.*

Morgan Primus was sitting squarely in the middle of her quarters, her hands resting in her lap. Except for a slight rise and fall of her chest, she might have been mistaken for a statue. At her feet were her packed bags, which didn't contain all that much since she had not arrived on Momidium with an excess of luggage. She had, after all, been trying to travel light.

She heard a soft footfall approaching the suite of rooms that had been her prison for all these years, and even though they were the footsteps of someone she'd never known as an adult, she was still able to recognize them. She braced herself, knowing that she was going to have to manage with all her strength to hold herself together. She was bound and determined not to let the slightest weakness show through.

Robin stepped into view in the entranceway.

They stared at each other. Simply stared. Morgan wanted to say something, wanted to explain. She was ready for the outpouring of anger and vituperation, prepared to handle questions although she had every intention of being as vague as possible about many of the replies. She was ready for the cold stare, the icy assessment, a bellow of rage fueled by pain, a shout of disbelief, a continuation of the earlier transmission. Hell, for all she knew, Robin would be so infuriated that she would simply pull out a phaser and start shooting. Stranger things had happened, certainly. A crime of passion, that's what they'd call it. Any board of inquiry in the world would look the situation over and simply pronounce it temporary insanity. They wouldn't immediately put her back in place on a starship, but neither would they stick her in a camp for the rest of her life.

What she was not prepared for, in all of that, was the simple flat stare that greeted her. There was no emotion in her eyes. She might just as easily have been a Vulcan meeting a total stranger for the first time.

Morgan realized that Robin was going to wait for her to say something. Stubborn little thing, that Robin. Probably got it from her mother. Well, there was no use for it. She was going to have to say *something,* or they might just stand there regarding each other for the rest of the day.

The silence was fortunately broken by Kurdwurble, who finally felt compelled to ask, "Are you a telepathic race?"

"What?" asked Morgan.

"I was just wondering if perhaps you were communicating by thought alone. We Momidiums are limited by our ability to articulate. I thought perhaps between members of your own species . . ."

She shook her head.

"I see," said Kurdwurble, who didn't quite, but he wasn't about to admit it. He shrugged, which for a Momidium was more a sense of one's head sagging down between the shoulders. "Well, none of my affair. Not anymore." He held up a small round electronic device. "Turn around please."

Morgan did as she was instructed, presenting her back to Kurdwurble, and Kurdwurble placed the device against a small panel on the collar. Morgan felt a slight electronic jolt and then the collar fell away from her, clattering onto the floor deactivated and harmless.

"You are free to go. It was good speaking with you, Morgan. In another life," he said with that odd shrug again, "who knows what we might have been to each other?"

"Who knows indeed. Thank you for making it bearable, Kurdwurble."

He looked to Robin and said, "Be good to her. She is a very special woman." And then, with no further words, he turned and undulated away, leaving the two women once more to their silence.

"You must have a lot of questions," Morgan finally said, unable to take it anymore.

"Yes," replied Robin in a voice that bordered on total disinterest. "Are you coming or not?"

Morgan stared at her incredulously. "That's it?"

No reply.

"Robin, let's not kid each other. You must have a million questions. You must have a great deal of anger in you; you certainly made that clear enough in your little love note. So go ahead." She got to her feet and stood there, braced. "Let me have it, right between the eyes. Tell me what's going through your mind."

Nothing.

"I see. The silent treatment. That's what it's going to be. All those questions, all that anger and hurt and whatever else tumbling around inside your head, and you're going for the silent treatment. Very mature, Robin," she said sarcastically.

"I like to think I'm very mature," Robin said in a voice that could have been originating back on Mars. "I had to grow up at a rather early age, what with my parents being dead and all."

"I'm . . ." She drew a deep breath. "I'm sorry about your father. I had no way of knowing—"

"Don't." Robin pointed a finger at her and Morgan could see that it was everything she could do not to let it tremble. The effort she was expending to control herself was having a massive effect on her. "Don't apologize. I can handle anything except that. Because there is no apology in the galaxy that can even begin to cover it, and if you try, Mother, so help me God, if you try, I will snap. Do you understand me? I will snap like a rotting twig. After everything else you've done to me, I would like to think that you'd at least have sufficient compassion not to do that to me as well."

Slowly Morgan nodded. "All right, Lieutenant." As she was about to leave, she accidentally stepped on the collar that was on the floor where it had fallen. She stooped, picked it up, and turned it over in her hands. "Hard to believe that this is what kept me here all these years."

"Perhaps they considered saddling you with a child, but they knew that wouldn't be enough to keep you in one place."

"Cheshire," she turned to face her, "you don't—"

"Shut up! Don't you dare call me that! You've lost the privilege, do you understand me? DO YOU?!?"

The volume, the intensity, the fury of it was so great that Morgan took a step back as if she'd been shoved. Robin had to visibly fight to pull in her fury and then, very quietly, she said, "Come. It's time to go."

Without a word, Morgan picked up her bags and followed her daughter to freedom.

Calhoun sat on the bridge, watching the planet turning beneath him, and wondered for what was hardly the first time if he hadn't made a mistake. He was so much happier leading away teams than staying on the bridge and allowing others to seize the day. It wasn't that he didn't trust Shelby to do the job; he did. But damn, he missed doing it.

Then again, he couldn't help but notice that whenever he did get involved with setting foot on planets, disaster seemed to strike. Thus far his two major accomplishments planetside had been having one disintegrate under his feet and being kidnapped while in residence on the other. Neither incident, he felt, was destined to win him any away team performance medals.

Shelby emerged from the turbolift and Calhoun turned in his chair and looked up at her expectantly. "Well, Commander?" he asked.

"All done, sir," she replied briskly. "I gave them a few pointers on their irrigation system that initial estimates show will improve their harvest yield by nineteen percent. And Dr. Selar reports that their serum checks out. I took the liberty of authorizing our synthesizing of a quantity of it, since the doctor reports that their facilities are, at best, barely adequate and we can accomplish the reproduction of the serum approximately five times faster than they can. Within twenty hours, maximum, this epidemic they're fighting will be completely under control."

"No sign of civil unrest?" he asked. "No outbreak of war? No one kidnapped? No giant flaming bird appearing on the horizon?"

"You mean none of the usual stuff, Captain? Nope. This was a horrifyingly simple assignment." She descended the ramp and walked around to her chair . . . and then hesitated a moment before sitting.

He caught the movement, or lack thereof, and saw her look at him with just a hint of suspicion. He smiled and shook his head, and said in a very low voice, "We're even, okay? Let's let it go."

She nodded and sat confidently in her chair. "Now, as to the matter of Morgan Primus—"

"Yes, I notice that Lefler isn't with you."

"I've assigned quarters to Primus—or Lefler, or whatever her name is—and Robin is getting her installed there. Kebron is running a security check on her now, but nothing seems to be turning up beyond what Robin already told us. I assume you want to meet with her."

"As soon as possible," Calhoun said firmly. "Her presence on this ship provides a mystery, and I generally like to have mysteries attended to as quickly as possible."

"Understood, sir. Conference lounge?"

"No," he said after a moment's thought. "Captain's ready room. The conference lounge seems more appropriate for an interrogation and, for the moment, let's remain friends."

"Considering what Lefler's going through," Shelby observed, "that's going to be a trick and a half."

"Captain," McHenry now turned in his chair. "We've just received word from the *Seidman.* She's on her way to the designated rendezvous point and wants to know if we're still going to make that as scheduled."

"If we're done here, then we certainly are. Set course, Mr. McHenry, warp factor three."

"Aye, sir."

Calhoun looked regretfully at Shelby, and she knew what he was thinking. The *Seidman* was a transport vessel sent by Starfleet to carry away the first two men that had been lost under Calhoun's command. Two security men, a highly dangerous job to be sure, but that didn't make the loss any more palatable. Hecht and Scannell: Hecht was simply dead, and as for Scannell, his mind had been totally destroyed. He writhed in the throes of madness, and although there was some hope for rehabilitation, to achieve that required facilities that were more than the *Excalibur* had to offer.

"So soon," he said with clear regret on his face, and she knew precisely what he meant. It seemed far too soon into the mission to lose any crewmen. And she also knew that, no matter what she might say, Calhoun would still hold himself responsible.

As much as she herself wanted command, there were times when

Shelby didn't regret in the least that she had not yet landed in that chair.

Morgan looked around her quarters, unpacking her bags as she did so. She glanced out her view window at the starscape and said, "Stars. Now that's something I didn't think I was ever going to see again." She tore her gaze away from it and looked around the quarters. "Nice to see that guest quarters are still respectable."

Si Cwan stood nearby, leaning easily against a wall. "Have you been on a starship before?" he asked.

She paused a moment, and it looked to Si Cwan as if she regretted having said anything. But then she appeared to shrug mentally. "From time to time," she said vaguely. She turned and looked him over from top to bottom. They openly studied each other, and he couldn't help but notice what a handsome woman she was. "So, what do they call you again?"

"Si Cwan. Ship's ambassador."

She was momentarily impressed. "*The* Si Cwan? Of the imperial family?"

"Formerly."

"Now serving as a Federation ambassador. My, how times change, don't they?" She sat down on the edge of the bed and looked up at him. "Why are you here, Ambassador?"

"A variety of reasons. I felt it necessary to return to—"

"No, I mean why are you *here?* In my quarters? Are you here to pump me for information?"

"You are a blunt woman, Morgan. That is a pleasant change. Very well. It was felt by Commander Shelby that you should not be unattended until such time as Lieutenant Kebron has run a full security check on you. Locking you into your quarters seemed rather hostile, and consigning you to the brig was likewise inhospitable. In point of fact, I believe that she was expecting Lieutenant Lefler to stay with you, but she declined the honor. So I offered my services."

"How very gallant of you. Do you work closely with Robin?"

"She is my part-time aide-de-camp. She graciously volunteered her time."

Morgan sized him up once more and then laughed. It was not an open laugh, but merely a short, even slightly disdainful chuckle, in the base of her throat. "How gracious indeed."

"Meaning . . . ?"

"Meaning you're rather attractive for a man with red skin and tattoos on his head."

"Lieutenant Lefler is a thorough professional, madam," Si Cwan admonished her. "And I will thank you not to ascribe any other motives aside from her interest in serving the best interests of the *Excalibur.*"

She put up her hands in an overly apologetic manner. "I offer my humble pardon, Ambassador. I did not mean to insult my daughter or you. If it's all the same to you, we'll keep my little gaffe to ourselves."

"I would far prefer that we did."

Si Cwan's commbadge beeped on his tunic and he tapped it. "Si Cwan here."

"Ambassador," came Shelby's voice, "would you be so kind as to escort Ms. Primus to the captain's ready room?"

"At your service, Commander." He bowed slightly and indicated the door with a wave of his arm. "After you, madam."

"At your service, Ambassador," she said in a deep, throaty tone. And as she headed toward the door, she stopped and momentarily ran her fingers along the curve of his beard. He blinked in surprise. "Between you and me, Si Cwan, I don't blame my daughter one bit."

Lefler was at her station when Shelby stepped in behind her and said softly, "The captain would like to see us in his ready room."

Automatically, Robin glanced in the direction of the captain's ready room and saw Si Cwan escorting Morgan through the door. Immediately Robin looked back at Shelby and said, "Commander, if it's all the same to you, I'd rather not."

"It's not all the same to me, Lieutenant," Shelby said, firmly but not unkindly. "What is all the same to me are orders from the captain, even the ones we'd rather not follow. He wants to see you. You get seen. So do I."

"But—" Then she saw the look in Shelby's eyes and sighed, "Aye, sir." She rose from her station as Ensign Scott Fogelson automatically took her place. When she stood face to face with Shelby, she said very softly, "I hate this."

"Understood," said Shelby neutrally. "Let's go."

Calhoun couldn't help but notice that Morgan Primus moved about the captain's ready room as if she felt she belonged there. He had chosen the ready room for a reason: He'd wanted to feel as if he had a psychological advantage. A conference lounge had the feel of neutral territory, but the ready room was the captain's home court. Unfortunately it didn't seem to have much relation to the present situation, and Calhoun—who was generally an impeccable judge of character—had the distinct feeling that Morgan was not someone who was readily, or easily, intimidated.

Si Cwan remained with them and, moments later, Shelby and Lefler joined them. There wasn't quite enough seating space for everyone, but Si Cwan made a point of simply standing over in a corner of the room, arms folded. Calhoun had noticed that Cwan preferred standing to sitting whenever possible. As if he wasn't tall enough, it appeared that he liked to loom. Shelby and Lefler sat in chairs opposite each other, and Morgan settled comfortably into the small couch. "So," Calhoun said amiably, "here we all are. So . . . Ms. Primus. Or do you prefer Ms. Lefler?"

" 'Morgan' will do, if that's all the same to you." He noticed she was running a finger along the back of the couch. Checking for dust. Who the hell *was* this woman? "I see little need to stand on ceremony."

"Very well, Morgan. Mr. Kebron has finished running his security check on 'Morgan Primus,' and it is very much as Lieutenant Lefler had told us. According to records, you died ten years ago. Your body was never recovered despite best efforts by the authorities."

"Well, Captain, it appears you succeeded where the authorities failed. You found it."

"And may I ask, Morgan, where you've been all this time? We can account for the last five years, obviously, but the five years intervening are something of a mystery."

"Captain," Morgan said slowly, "I believe that these questions are somewhat outside the parameters of your job."

"It's a funny thing about me, Morgan," Calhoun said with a thin smile. "I'm one for stretching parameters. The longer you're with me, the faster you'll realize that."

"That is good to know, Captain, but I do not anticipate being here all that long."

For the first time, Lefler spoke up. "That eager to get away from me again, Mother?"

Slowly Morgan's gaze swivelled toward her daughter. Her expression was very severe, her face beginning to darken as if a storm cloud was setting in. "Robin," she said, "do you wish to continue with sniping comments that accomplish nothing or do you want to just get it out in the open where we can discuss it?''

Si Cwan put a restraining hand on Robin's shoulder as Lefler looked as if she were about to leap out of her chair. He held her steady for a moment, but then she pushed his hand away and was on her feet. ''All right,'' she said sharply. ''You want to get to it? Let's get to it.''

Shelby glanced over at Calhoun, but he made a small gesture indicating that they should do nothing to interfere. She sat back and watched with concern.

''Bottom line, Mother, you ran out on me. On Dad and me.''

''Yes.''

''You faked your own death.''

''Yes again.''

She took a deep breath. ''Why?''

''It was necessary.''

And that was all she said. Robin waited for her to expand upon it, but as the silence lengthened she realized that Morgan was apparently under the impression that that was all the explanation required. ''It was necessary?'' echoed Robin. ''Ten years I think you're dead. Dad dies of a broken heart. And the only thing I'm entitled to is 'it was necessary'?''

''You're entitled to far more than that, Robin, but that's all I'm prepared to tell you at the moment.''

''At the moment?'' Lefler couldn't believe it. She started pacing around the chair, Si Cwan stepping back to give her room. ''What the hell are you waiting for? Until you're a grandmother? Until I'm on my deathbed? That's when you're going to come around and say, 'Oh, honey, by the way, I'm now prepared to explain to you why I *screwed up your life!*' ''

At that, Morgan was on her feet, her fists curled tightly at her sides, and said, ''I gave you life, child! I gave you life, and you seem to have survived my departure just fine. And I'm sorry that your father 'died of a broken heart,' but people die, Robin, that's just a statistical fact. And I miss him, but the strong survive, and that's just a fact of nature. That's natural selection. And if he wasn't strong enough to withstand my loss, then nature selected him not to survive, and that is not my fault.''

''How dare you!'' Lefler shouted, and leapt to her feet.

''Okay, that's enough!'' said Calhoun. ''Lefler, back off!''

Lefler didn't move, even though her whole body was trembling.

Si Cwan seemed about to try and draw her back away from Morgan, but Robin caught his movement with a sideways glance and froze him in his tracks. Si Cwan wisely decided to stay exactly where he was.

For her part, Morgan's face was flaming red, as if she'd been slapped hard. "Did that make you feel better, Robin?" she asked quietly. "Did that make up for anything?"

"No," admitted Lefler, looking no less angry. "I want to know what's going on, Mother. You owe me so much. At the very least, you owe me that."

"Perhaps you're right, Robin. But we don't always get everything we want, and sometimes there are some things that remain mysteries. Believe me when I say that it's far better for all concerned if we leave it that way."

"I can't."

"Well, I can. And unfortunately, if I'm not willing to say more than I have, then you are just going to have to be prepared to live with that. You've lived with my death for all these years, Robin. Live with my life for all your remaining years and let it go at that. Captain," she continued before Robin could even say anything, "it is my understanding that we will be meeting up with the transport *Seidman.* Is that correct?"

"Yes."

"Very well. I am officially asking you to put me aboard her. I'll make my own way from there."

"You're intending to leave Thallonian space?" Si Cwan asked.

"Perhaps," replied Morgan. "I haven't made up my mind yet."

"You know," Shelby said, "for some reason that I can't quite put my finger on, I don't entirely believe you. I have the sneaking suspicion that you have indeed made up your mind, Morgan. Do you agree, Captain?"

"I do indeed, Number One."

Morgan did a momentary double take. Then she cleared her throat and said, "To be honest, Commander—"

"There's a change of pace," murmured Lefler.

"I do not especially care what your opinion of me is," she continued as if Lefler hadn't spoken. "What I care about is continuing about my business. I have been delayed for five years. I have certain goals, certain things I desire to accomplish, and there is no way that I can get that time back. I would ask you to cooperate with me now by not delaying me any further. Now I am asking you for, and frankly I expect to receive, a means off this ship."

"Permission to show her the back door, sir," said Robin.

"Lefler, that's not going to accomplish anything," Calhoun said sharply. "Morgan—"

"Captain, if you give the matter some thought, I'm sure you'll see that you have no choice," Morgan said reasonably.

"I already have given the matter some thought, and until this situation is resolved to my satisfaction—in short, until I know why you faked your death and showed up in Thallonian space ten years later—you're going to stay put right here on the *Excalibur.*"

"What?" Morgan fairly exploded. "What did you say?"

"After all," Calhoun said, "we haven't received formal confirmation of your identity from the Terran data net. Until then, you could be anyone."

"At this distance," Morgan said grimly, "that will take . . . ?"

"At least two weeks by subspace. Not counting any bureaucratic problems on the other end."

"Robin," Morgan said, turning to her daughter, "tell them I'm your mother."

Lieutenant Leffler replied to her mother's request with an angry glare that said "so now you want to be my mother!"

Calhoun noted that Shelby's face had gone slightly ashen, although Si Cwan, from long years of practice, kept his face properly inscrutable. "You will be treated as an honored guest, of course," he assured her. "You will not be kept under lock and key, but given free access to the ship, within the limits imposed on all guests. But I have absolutely no intention of simply turning you loose. For all I know, you had some sort of mischief planned toward the Momidiums that you would implement the moment we released you."

"Captain, I assure you, if I never see Momidium again, it will be too soon."

He came around the desk and leaned against it in an almost avuncular fashion. "Morgan, I'm sure you understand why your assurances do not mean a hell of a lot to me. Not only have you been less than forthcoming, but you're almost proud over your ability to hide the truth. That does not sit well with me. Until such time that you are forthcoming, you can stay aboard this ship until you rot. Do I make myself clear?"

"This is extortion!"

He clapped his hands together briskly. "Yes, I'm clear, all right."

"You're blackmailing me, Captain! Blackmailing my right to privacy!"

"One person's blackmail is another person's negotiation," he said calmly. And then he took a step toward her and it was Calhoun whose face was darkening. The scar on his cheek stood out in sharp relief against it. "Now listen to me, lady," and his voice was low and intimidating. "I don't know you. You're just an object to me, a body to be transported. But Lieutenant Lefler here is a valued crewmember. I do not like the way you have treated her in her life. I do not like the aspects of her—the anger, the boiling fury—that you're bringing out in her now."

"Then let me go so I don't continue to be a bad influence," said Morgan.

He shook his head. "Ohhh no. No, Morgan. Whatever demons drove you away from her ten years ago don't matter to me all that much, but you don't get off that easily here. What you did to her was unjust, and there will be justice now. I will see it done."

"Captain Calhoun, trying to right wrongs and save the galaxy," Morgan asked, her voice dripping with sarcasm.

"Not the entire galaxy," he said tightly. "Just my little piece of it."

For a long moment the air between them seemed to crackle with energy and then, slowly, Morgan found she couldn't help but look away from the piercing fierceness of those stormy purple eyes of Calhoun's.

"Are we done here?" she asked, still looking away.

"It would appear that we are, yes. Ambassador . . . Lieutenant . . . if you wouldn't mind escorting Morgan to her quarters, she can begin her stay with us."

"So I've gone from being a prisoner of the Momidiums to a prisoner of Captain Calhoun, is that how it's to be?" asked Morgan.

"You're a prisoner of your own heart and deeds, Morgan, and of your own coldness. I'm just the facilitator."

She seemed about to respond, but apparently thought better of it as she turned and walked out. Si Cwan and Lefler followed her out, and Lefler paused for a brief moment to look back at Calhoun. The captain couldn't tell whether she was looking at him in gratitude, in anger, in confusion, or perhaps a combination of all three.

Shelby was about to speak when Calhoun quickly raised a finger to silence her as he tapped his commbadge and said, "Mr. Kebron, a moment of your time, please."

"Mac, you can't be serious about this."

"You seem to say that a lot, Commander. And you keep finding out that I'm perfectly serious. Sooner or later I think you should really stop saying that. It's making you predictable."

"Mac, for the love of—"

Kebron entered the ready room and stood there, arms casually draped behind his back. "Yes, Captain?"

"I want a level two security watch kept on Morgan," Calhoun said.

"All security personnel to keep an eye out for her at all times," Kebron said easily. "No single team or teams to watch her, but instead to trade off in pass-the-baton fashion. Check in with security head every fifteen minutes to keep me apprised of her whereabouts."

"That's it. Inform all guards. I want it done yesterday."

"Aye, sir." He tapped his commbadge. "All security units, this is Kebron. Security watch, level two, subject Morgan Primus, immediate institution. Go. All units confirm at security board," and he walked out of the captain's ready room with more speed than Calhoun would have given him credit for.

Calhoun then waited for Shelby to lay into him. His back was to her, but he was quite sure that it was gong to be coming any moment. When there was nothing but silence, he turned to face her on the assumption that she was waiting to be able to look straight at him. Sure enough, there she was, her arms folded and with a neutral look on her face that could only be covering what he was certain was a sense of complete and utter exasperation.

"Go ahead," he sighed. "Say it."

"Mac," she told him, "I think what you're doing is very sweet."

He looked at her as if she'd grown a second head. "Pardon?"

"I said I think it's very sweet."

Slowly he walked toward her with a bit of a side-to-side motion. "You know, Eppy, somehow of all the things I expected you to say, that wasn't among them."

"Look, I know you've got your heart in the right place. You see that Lefler is suffering, you feel a degree of moral outrage at the woman who's causing it, and you feel you are obliged to do something about it."

"That's mostly it," he admitted. "Oh, sure, part of it comes from the fact that she annoyed the hell out of me. That I can deal with, though. But you saw what she did to Lefler. Lieutenant Lefler is one of my people, and I won't see any one of them being abused if I can help it.''

''Within the context of the ship and her mission, Robin Lefler is one of your people, no question, Mac.'' She took a step closer toward him, looking sympathetic. ''But when it comes to dirt done to her ten years ago, and how she chooses to deal with it now, Robin is her own person. You can't make it better for her simply because you're refusing to let her mother run away again.''

''The ability of each and every crewmember to function at full capacity most certainly is my business,'' Calhoun pointed out. ''If this business with her mother diminishes Robin Lefler's ability to function, then that makes it my concern. And I will attend to the mental welfare of my officers as I see fit.''

''That's a reach, Mac, and you know it. If a couple of former lovers were aboard the same ship and were sick of each other, and one of them wanted a transfer off, would you refuse to do so because you wanted them to—''

He stared at his ex-fiancée incredulously.

''Okay, bad example,'' she admitted.

''I should say so.''

''The point is, Mac, you can't force people to get along. You have this King Arthur complex. You want to come riding on your brave white horse and right all wrongs, save damsels in distress, and make the world safe for chivalry.''

''You used to compare me to a cowboy. Now you say I'm a knight.''

''Whatever fits the moment. Mac, Morgan is right. You can't keep her here against her will on a tecnicality just because it seems like a good idea to you. She hasn't done anything. Hasn't broken any laws.''

''She broke Thallonian law by coming to Sector Two twenty-one-G. Lord Si Cwan is furious over the transgression, and has demanded that justice be done. He has requested that she be held until trial.''

''Oh, he has,'' Shelby said skeptically. ''Considering that he is a deposed lord and his empire fallen, his jurisdiction in this matter seems questionable. And when was this burst of indignation, may I ask?''

''Five minutes from now, after I tell him about it.''

''This isn't a joke, Mac. Your motives are pure . . .''

''As befits the ruler of Camelot.''

She nodded in acknowledgment and then continued, "But you don't have the right to do this. You're trying to twist the legitimate concerns a captain may possess about a crew's well being into a shape that will allow you to do anything you want. You can't just run roughshod over regulations whenever you feel like it. The rules exist for a reason."

"I know that, Commander. And I know that you're right. I should be making more of an effort to live within them. Often I consider rules and regulations to be unworkable and, to be perfectly blunt, if I can find a way around them in order to do what's right and proper, then I'll do so."

"Right and proper by your definition."

"Yes. Because I'm the one who's out here, Eppy. Not the paper pushers and nameless bureaucrats who made the rules that I'm supposed to follow. Something is going on with Morgan Primus, Commander. Something that, in my opinion, goes beyond her abandonment of her daughter and husband ten years ago. I don't know if it presents a threat to Federation security, to this ship, or to the whole of Thallonian space, but until I do know to my satisfaction, then here is where she is going to stay. I'm sorry if that upsets you, Eppy."

"No, it doesn't upset me particularly. Saddens me a bit, but doesn't upset me. You could be a great officer, Mac. One of the best there ever was, if you could only learn to live within the rules that other officers do. Mac, do you think I enjoy constantly having to be your conscience? To be the voice of reason? I knew signing on that I'd be serving that function to some degree, but I didn't quite expect it would be this much. Sometimes I think you never listen to me."

"I always listen to you, Eppy. Not necessarily doing what you say is not the same as not listening to you. Look, when it comes down to it, and if I have to choose, I'll settle for being the best man I can be rather than the best officer, and let everything else sort itself out."

"You can have that attitude now, Mac. But sooner or later, there's going to be fallout over it. You're flaunting regulations and someday you're going to flaunt the wrong one. And when that happens—"

"When that happens, then what? Tell me, Eppy, if they call you to testify, whose side are you going to be on? Would you sit there and tell a board of inquiry that you support me or that you're against me?"

She shrugged. "I don't know. Maybe I'll have Captain Binky come and testify in my stead."

"I'm serious, Commander."

"So am I, Captain."

She turned to go, and he smiled wanly as he called after her, "Besides, Eppy, you shouldn't be upset. It's appropriate, really."

"Appropriate? You lost me, Mac. How so?"

"You said I had a King Arthur complex. Well, what better ship to have me than the *Excalibur?*"

She shook her head as she walked out, and as she went she said, "Mac, I just hope to hell you know what you're doing."

He waited until she was gone, and then he said to himself, "So do I, Eppy. So do I."

9

Soleta and Burgoyne studied the readouts from the matter-antimatter reactor assembly as the *Excalibur* moved through space at warp three. "You see?" Burgoyne said, noting the energy spikes. "There it is again. Some sort of rhythmic pulse."

"And you seriously believe it could be a biologic?" Soleta asked. "That seems rather far-fetched, Chief."

"More far-fetched than a gigantic flaming bird smashing apart a planet?"

"No. I will grant you that. And the theory," she said, looking over the case history of the problem, "is that somehow it's becoming energized whenever we use the warp engines."

"That is essentially correct."

Soleta stepped away from the consoles and looked at the massive matter-antimatter reactor assembly. The M-ARA stood ten decks tall, with the matter reactant injector at the top and the antimatter reactant injector at the bottom. The core of the reactor was a series of doughnut-shaped pressure vessel toroids, surrounded by phase adjustment coils and coming together in the dilithium housing and reaction chamber in the middle. The crackling energy of ionized gas, hotter than the sun, pulsed within.

"Something existing in that?" Soleta said in wonderment. "Something feeding off it?" She weighed the situation for a moment, and then said, "Well, there is one way I can think of to test it."

"That being . . . ?"

"Well, when an infant is feeding at its mother's bosom, if you remove the food source, you get a reaction. The child demands to know where its food source is.''

''You're not suggesting shutting down the engines cold.''

''It shouldn't be necessary. We can scale the engines down and very likely generate the same reaction.''

''Yessss,'' Burgoyne said slowly, stroking hir chin and studying the reactor core thoughtfully. ''Yes, we could. And I'll have my people running scans all over the M-ARA to see if they can localize some sort of anomaly. It might very well stand out against the lessening energy and, at the very least, make its presence known. While we're at it, we can run a PPT—a pressure port test—at either end of the assembly. I'm worried that damage might have been done to the port seals during all these energy spikes. Besides, with the ports open, we'll have an easier time running scans to see what, if anything is in there, and we can only run PPTs when we're operating the engines at a fraction of normal capacity.''

''Won't you have to remove the magnetic fields in order to do that?'' Soleta said, sounding a bit concerned. ''We could flood the entire engine room with radiation.''

''No danger of that. We'll put a temporary containment patch on it. That'll be more than enough to hold everything in place. Only problem is,'' s/he said thoughtfully, ''we won't be able to run at warp speed. Impulse will have to do.''

''Do you think it wise to delay?''

Burgoyne shook hir head. ''Something is going on in my engines. The sooner we know what, the better off we'll be.''

''All right,'' Soleta said in a no-nonsense tone. ''I'll get the necessary clearances from the captain. We'll be a bit late for our rendezvous with the *Seidman,* but that's hardly a matter of extreme concern. You get your team assembled and we'll start the procedure at . . . thirteen hundred hours?''

''Done,'' said Burgoyne.

Morgan Primus sat in the Team Room at twelve-fifty-five hours, trying to figure out just what in the world she was going to do next. She had a large pitcher of synthehol on the table in front of her, and she was lifting it carefully as if judging its heft.

''May I join you?'' came a voice from nearby. She glanced up and saw Si Cwan standing next to her, looking politely interested in her.

''Be my guest,'' she replied, gesturing to the empty seat opposite her. Si Cwan took it and she couldn't help but notice how upright he sat. Ramrod straight. "I feel so loved."

"Indeed. And why is that?"

"See him?" she said, angling her head toward one side of the Team Room. A security guard was there, with a hand on a drink and an eye on her. "Followed me in here. And before he followed me, another guard was following me. I counted about eight switch-offs."

"Why would they be doing that?"

"Because that's what I would do. Security watch, level two, in all likelihood. Nicely effective way of keeping an eye on somebody if you don't want to look like you're keeping an eye on somebody."

Si Cwan fixed his gaze on the security guard. He looked up after a moment, noticed that Si Cwan was watching him, and quickly endeavored to look anywhere else.

"He's not particularly good at it, this one in particular. But he probably hasn't had a lot of practice." She swirled the drink she had in the glass and said regretfully, "Synthehol. Never developed much of a taste for it myself. Romulan ale is my drink of choice."

"I believe that is illegal, is it not?"

She put a finger to her lips and said "Shhhh" in a conspiratorial manner. Then she put her glass down and asked with grim amusement, "Are you here to plead my daughter's case?"

"I am here because you have a difficulty, and I wish to simplify it for you."

She leaned forward, her interest piqued. "Can you get me off the ship?"

"No. But you can get you off the ship."

"Oh. This again." She looked out the main window, and then frowned. "We're slowing down. I wonder why."

"Are you certain?"

"Believe me, I know. We've come out of warp and now we're reducing speed even further. I wonder why they cut the warp engines. It's not as if we're near anything."

"I don't know. I'm sure they have their reasons."

"Really." She turned to look at him. "Tell me, then: If you are so certain that the people in Engineering have their reasons for what they do, why can't you make the leap that I have reasons for what I do?"

"Because I know them and have confidence in them," Si Cwan said reasonably. "You are asking for that same degree of trust and have done nothing to earn it."

"You're saying I should go spill my guts to my daughter."

"I am saying you have a problem that is not going to be solved simply by sitting in the Team Room and complaining about the quality of the beverages served here. Talk to your daughter. Talk to the captain. Explain yourself."

Her dark eyebrows knit. "And how often did you have to explain yourself in your lifetime, Si Cwan, hmm? How often did you have to explain the orders you gave, to cite chapter and verse as to why your instructions should be obeyed. Not very often, I should think. In fact, all during your reign I would venture to guess that you never had to. You simply voiced a wish and it was obeyed."

"For one thing, you are not royalty."

She waggled a scolding finger. "Never assume."

"And for another," he continued, ignoring the reprimand, "I indeed had to explain myself any number of times to my peers. To those who were capable of judging what I had to say; people whose support I depended upon in order to get things done."

"Ahhh," said Morgan, "then that's where the problem is stemming from. You see, I have no peers on this ship."

"Oh, is that a fact?"

"Yes. More of a fact than you could possibly believe. Even if I explained it to you, it is most unlikely that you would believe me."

"I don't know about that," retorted Si Cwan. "I have seen and done quite a few things of amazing variety. You would be surprised as to what I would believe."

"Not this. You'll never believe this."

"And what precisely is the nature of this thing I won't believe?"

She seemed to be sizing him up once more, as if she were considering being completely honest with him. "I wish I could trust you. I wish I could trust someone. I can't even trust my own daughter," she said, looking rather depressed over the entire matter. "You'd think I could, wouldn't you?"

"I can be trusted, and so can Robin."

She shook her head. "She hates me. She hates me, and I can't blame her. She feels I ran out on her, and she doesn't understand. She just doesn't. How could she?"

"How could she understand what?"

And it was at that moment that the lights suddenly went out.

Immediately everyone was on their feet, looking around in confusion. The lights came back on again, but then dimmed, and there were noises of bewilderment, everyone asking everyone else questions.

Suddenly the ship shook violently, staggering everyone in the Team Room. Alarms began to klaxon all over the station.

And Morgan was already on the move.

The pitcher in her hand, she was charging for the door of the Team Room the moment the lights had gone out the first time. Si Cwan, looking elsewhere and distracted, didn't see her go. But the security guard had her firmly in his sights and, already certain that she had spotted him, tossed aside caution and moved to intercept her.

She got within two feet of him and suddenly she was swinging her arm around full speed. The guard didn't have any time to react as the pitcher of synthehol smashed against the side of his head. The pitcher was relatively unbreakable, but the guard's head was not. He went down, the world swirling around him and spinning away into blackness as blood poured from a large wound on his head. Morgan, for her part, didn't care. She tossed aside the pitcher and was out the door within seconds.

The plan was already running through her head even as she heard the alarms began to wail. She looked left and right and saw dozens of crewmen running to the positions assigned to them at times of shipboard emergency, which this most certainly was, whatever was causing it. There was not going to be any time for anyone to pay attention to one little passenger.

She noticed a medtech heading quickly down a corridor. The medtech had equipment attached to a belt looped around her waist, and Morgan saw possibilities. The techie was doubtlessly heading for sickbay. That was the same general direction that Morgan was going, and so she wouldn't need to go far out of her way at all to obtain potentially useful items.

Smoothly and unhurriedly, as if she had all the time in the world, Morgan Primus blended in with the running crewmen of the *Excalibur,* moving quickly after the medtech and hopefully, after that, toward her destination . . . and freedom.

On the walkways above the matter reactant injector, Ensign Ronni Beth was heading in one direction, energy survey instruments in hand, and looked up in annoyance to see that Ensign Christiano was coming toward her in the other direction. For a moment, just a moment, her heart fluttered at the sight of him—the tall, lanky body, the flowing brown hair, and the ready grin—and the memory of what she'd once had with him, but then she remembered the hurt that he had given her and her heart hardened against him.

Christiano didn't appear to notice her at first, because he was looking over his own instrumentation readings. But then he looked up, saw her and said cheerfully, "Beth, hi!"

She stopped a few feet away from him. About six feet below them, the top of the matter reactant injector pulsed slower and slower as the engine capacity was reduced. The core itself seemed, from the angle they were at, to stretch downward into infinity, the ionized gas within swirling around like a captured nova. " 'Beth, hi'? That's what I get? After the hell you put me through?"

"Look," said Christiano, "it's not what you think . . ."

"No, it's never what I think," she shot back at him. "You and I, we were never what I thought."

"Ron, don't be like that."

"I can't help the way I am!" she said, thumping the railing in annoyance. "And what the hell are you doing up here, anyway? I'm supposed to be running the scans on the MRI."

"No, that's what Burgy told me to do."

In annoyance, Beth tapped her commbadge. "Beth to Burgoyne."

"Burgoyne here. We've got the engine down to five percent of capacity, and the temporary containment patch is in place. You should be able to start running the pressure port tests."

"Will do, Chief. But I've got Christiano up here as well."

"What's he doing up there?" Burgoyne sounded confused and annoyed.

"That's what I was wondering. Did you intend to have us both up here?"

"No! Christiano, can you hear me?"

Making out Burgoyne's voice wasn't easy over the *thrumming* of the engine below, but Christiano was just able to manage it. "I hear you, Chief."

"You're supposed to be running the port test at the *antimatter* reactant injector. Not the MRI, the AMRI. You're at the wrong end of the M-ARA."

Christiano looked rather chagrined. It was bad enough being in the wrong place, but having made the screw up with Beth present and knowing about it . . . well, that was more than he would have liked. "Sorry, Chief. I'll get right on it."

"See that you do! Burgoyne out."

* * *

Burgoyne shook hir head in annoyance as s/he monitored the readouts. Soleta was next to hir and asked, ''Problem?''

''Crewman's in the wrong place. At least,'' s/he said, frowning, ''I think he is. Frustrating thing is, I hope it wasn't my screwup. I might have accidentally assigned him to the wrong place. Just had a lot on my mind lately, I guess.''

''Do you wish to discuss it?'' asked Soleta.

''No. No, I don't think so.''

''Good,'' Soleta said firmly. ''Because I do not believe I wish to hear—''

Then her eyes widened. ''Burgoyne!'' she said as the readings began to spike.

''I see it!'' replied Burgoyne. Hir heart was pounding against hir rib cage as hir mind fought to understand what s/he was seeing. ''Look at that! Something's driving the energy readings back up again! But that's impossible! Nothing can override the flow from the power transfer conduits! It's got twenty seven fail-safes!''

''Apparently that's one less than it needed,'' Soleta told hir sharply. ''The engines are powering up, the matter-antimatter feed is coming back on line.''

''Blast and damn!'' shouted Burgoyne even as s/he hit hir commbadge. S/he looked up at the ten stories of the M-ARA as s/he called, ''Burgoyne to Beth! Burgoyne to Christiano! Get the hell out of there! We're removing the containment patch and replacing the pressure ports! Get clear in case something else goes wrong!''

That was when Burgoyne heard the screams. Alarmed shouts coming from throughout the engine room, reacting to something that did not seem as if it could possibly exist.

And then s/he saw it.

In the heart of the matter-antimatter core, it began to take form. The ionized gas within moved about it, and whether it was feeding off it or whether the gas was actually constituting its body, s/he couldn't even begin to guess.

It didn't have eyes or any discernible feature. It seemed almost embryonic, as if it were trying to decide what shape it was going to take. Burgoyne could almost imagine that s/he heard some sort of distant roaring, although that was flat-out impossible. But then again, so was this.

''Soleta to bridge!'' Soleta was shouting over her commbadge. ''There is some sort of being in the M-ARA! Repeat, some sort of creature, possibly sentient, definitely hungry!''

"On my way!" came Calhoun's voice.

And then the alarms began to go off, systems shutting down and starting up again all over the ship. Burgoyne wasn't sure where to look first, and then s/he looked up and s/he saw something truly horrifying. Something that made the situation seem like the death throes of Thallon all over again, except this time it was the helpless *Excalibur* that found herself squarely in the middle of the situation.

Something was punching its way up through the top of the matter reactant injector. Although the magnetic patch was still in place, some*thing*—a talon, a claw, a tentacle, a roiling combination of all that and more—stretched through it and upward, toward the terrified forms of Ensigns Beth and Christiano.

Lieutenant j.g. Michael Houle never knew what hit him.

Houle, a tall, handsome, and freshly promoted flight deck officer at shuttlebay two, at that moment was trying to figure out why all the systems were going insane in front of him. One indicator said that the bay doors were open, another said they were closed, a third said that the annular force field that prevented depressurization of the bay had come on, another said no. It was as if the entire array had gone nuts, as if something was blowing out energy all over the ship and creating havoc with the systems.

He heard a footfall behind him and turned to see if it was someone who was going to explain to him what was going on. He didn't even have time to fully register that a fist was coming his way before it struck him cleanly on the chin. Houle's head snapped around and he sagged to the floor without having managed to say a single word.

Morgan stepped past him, shaking out her hand to remove the tingling from her fist. "Never hit bone on bone," she scolded herself. "I simply must remember that."

From the Ops booth, she looked down over the shuttlecraft available to her. There was not quite the assortment available as there was in the main shuttlebay; on the other hand, she knew it was considerably less guarded and more open to attack. Besides, she didn't need much. Then she spotted the ideal vehicle for her needs.

"A type six," she said briskly. "Will give me warp two for thirty-six hours, warp one-point-two for two days if I'm moving at full bore. Excellent."

Her intention had been to reroute the bay door commands so that she could activate them from the interior of the shuttle, but she quickly found herself falling victim to the systems blackouts that were devastating the rest of the ship. Clearly the unexpected distraction of the systems problems was a double-edged sword. It had caused enough confusion to allow her to slip by the security guards, but it was now impeding her intended means of egress.

''All right,'' she said to no one. ''Not a problem. I have a backup plan.''

Quickly she exited the Ops deck and headed down to the shuttlecraft that she had selected. She emerged from the stairway to the Ops level, ran several feet—and stopped.

Si Cwan was blocking her way, standing between her and the shuttlecraft.

''You left right in the middle of our drinks, Morgan,'' he chided her. ''You struck me as a woman of better breeding than that.

''One side, Ambassador, or I'll strike you in a worse way than that,'' she said. Slowly she walked toward him, her arms swinging in leisurely fashion. ''This is none of your concern.''

''Yes, so you believe. Unfortunately for you, I do not.'' He did not appear the least bit concerned about her advance. There seemed little reason for him to be. He was a head taller than she, with broad shoulders and muscular build. And he was someone who had proven himself any number of times in battle; indeed, he had even managed to fight the formidable Zak Kebron himself to a standstill. ''Do not try it, Morgan. The outcome will not be pleasant for you.''

''Yes, so *you* believe,'' she tossed back at him. ''Trust me, Si Cwan, you do not want to get between me and the shuttle.''

''I already am, and trusting you seems to be the root of our problem, doesn't it?''

''It would seem so.''

And then, with no further preamble, Morgan launched herself at Si Cwan.

He admired her form. She moved quickly, confidently, and although she didn't have nearly the reach that Si Cwan did, she more than made up for it with speed and aggressiveness. But Si Cwan's confidence never wavered. He sidestepped as she came at him with that graceful economy of movement he always displayed, and he swung his leg in a roundhouse kick that was designed to catch her squarely in the back and knock her to the ground.

But then Morgan made a sudden movement with her hand, something so subtle that he almost didn't spot it. When he did, it was too late. His leg was already in motion, and then Morgan had out the spray hypo that she had grabbed off the medtech and secreted up her sleeve. She jammed it squarely into his inner thigh and it hissed its contents into him.

"You . . . !" Si Cwan managed to get out, and then the world twisted around him. He sank to his knees, desperately trying to fight off whatever it was that she had pumped into his system. There appeared to be three of her in front of him and he made a desperate lunge toward the one in the middle. One would have thought it was the logical choice, but his hand went right through her and then the one on the right slammed a fierce kick into the side of his head.

And still Si Cwan would not go down. Instead he crawled on his hands and knees, trying to go after her even as she opened the door of the shuttle. "Oh, for God's sake," she said in irritation. Displaying amazing strength considering her size, she grabbed Si Cwan by the back of his tunic and yanked him toward a freight container that was anchored to the floor. It was exactly what she needed as she yanked it open and saw that it was empty. She hauled him up and shoved him into the container, snapping the lock shut on top. "You won't suffocate," she said. "I'll let them know you're in here after I'm safely gone. Trust me, this is for your own good, although you probably can't hear me or else don't believe. But as you said, trust has always been part of our problem, hasn't it?"

Si Cwan couldn't manage any sort of articulate response, which wasn't all that much of a problem since she wasn't listening to him. With the ambassador safely stowed, she headed back for the shuttle and climbed in.

Quickly she fired it up, bringing the engines on line with practiced ease. She had to hurry the systems check, but she was confident in Starfleet compulsion to keep everything in top working order.

For the briefest of moments she regretted taking off on Robin yet again. But she would just have to understand. "You're a big girl now, Robin," Morgan said, "and you can certainly live without your mommy. Heaven knows you've done it for long enough."

The bay doors remained sealed, but Morgan did not see that as being a problem for much longer. As the engines roared to life, Morgan brought the phaser array on line. Standard equipment for the shuttle did not include any weaponry, but Morgan had quickly spotted this one rigged with a type IV phaser array. Clearly this was a shuttle reserved for special operations. Well, she had just such an operation in mind.

She targeted the bay doors and opened fire. The phasers blasted outward, pounding into the doors and easily smashing through them, sending large pieces of the triple-layered duranium doors tumbling into space.

She prepared to lift off, but something ricocheted off the front of the shuttle, tumbling away. It caught her attention and she realized that it was the top of a freight container. Then she heard something else, something much fainter, bump against the lower section of the ship. She might not have heard it at all, for the vacuum of space and the roar of the engines was almost deafening, but the moment she saw the piece from the container spiraling away into space, she had known with hideous certainty what was going to be next. A quick exterior scan confirmed it for her.

"I don't believe it," she said.

Si Cwan was clutching the right warp nacelle of the shuttle, and he had mere seconds to live before the howling vacuum of space dragged him to his death.

10

The tentacle (for that was the shape that it had assumed at that moment) stretched up out of the matter-antimatter core. The magnetic seal reconfigured around the tentacle, preventing any of the intense radiation and heat—hot enough to blast a gaping hole straight through the side of the *Excalibur*—from escaping.

"You go this way, I'll go that way!" screamed Christiano as it snaked upward. But Beth was paralyzed, staring down at the tentacle in undiluted horror. No textbook had ever prepared her for this, no tall tale or fable of an expedition had ever mentioned something akin to a Lovecraftian monster taking refuge inside of the warp core. It was like nothing anyone had ever seen, a horrific thing composed of energy plasma, glowing and shifting, undulating hideously, and she could swear that it was letting loose with some sort of ungodly howling that was ripped from the primordial origins of humanity.

"Go!" Christiano shouted again, and he shoved her, and this time she started to move. Christiano bolted in the other direction and then the tentacle snaked out and wrapped around Christiano's leg. Christiano barely had time to let out a cry of terror and then he was yanked clear off the catwalk. The tentacle started to retract, hauling Christiano down toward the magnetic seal and, inevitably, toward the warp core itself. Through the clear containment of the core, Beth could see the being within writhing about, upset, confused, furious, trying to come to terms with its very existence in an environment that defied the ability of anything to live within it.

Christiano howled Beth's name, and Beth had no time at all to make a snap decision. She lunged off the catwalk, snagging the lower half of the rail with one hand and stretching her other hand to the utmost just as the tentacle descended past her with a frantic Christiano writhing in its grasp. The containment patch yawned wide beneath them, not letting the radiation out, but not stopping anyone from going in. The ionized gas roiled below and then Beth snagged Christiano by the wrist.

"Don't let go!" he screamed. *"Don't let go! Don't let me go!"*

The tentacle yanked downward and Beth's grasp slipped as she was jolted before she was able to get a firm grip on the catwalk railing. She snagged Christiano's hand, holding on with every bit of willpower she had, as she was hauled halfway forward and her ankles wrapped desperately around the lower strut of the railing. Now she had no support at all, forming a human bridge between the catwalk and Christiano. There was no way on Earth she could possibly get the leverage to haul Christiano back up.

Not that it mattered.

For with that abrupt yank downward, Christiano's lower body was yanked down into the warp core. Ironically, Beth's endeavors to help him transformed what would have been a quick death into an agonizing one. Had he simply fallen in, he would have been vaporized instantly. As it was, the lower half of his body was immediately incinerated, but the upper half—including a piercing and terrifying death scream—had time to register what was happening while it was happening.

There is no more horrifying sensation than knowing that one is already dead and there is nothing one can do about it.

Without Christiano to anchor her, Beth simply hung there, held only by the locked position of her ankles. She was stunned, her mind unable to accept what she had just witnessed, and then her entire body simply shut down and her legs went limp. Beth began a headfirst dive toward instant death.

And a taloned hand reached down from above and snagged her ankle.

On the catwalk overhead, Burgoyne 172 held on for all s/he was worth. S/he was only slightly out of breath despite the fact that s/he had scaled the emergency ladder along the reactor core shaft, up ten decks, in just under sixty seconds flat. S/he paused a moment to gather hirself and then pulled Beth up and out of harm's way.

And the tentacle writhed up toward them.

"Pressure port seals!" shouted Burgoyne at the top of hir lungs. "Bring engine up to seventy-five percent capacity and keep it there!"

And the emergency systems kicked in, slamming the pressure ports into place, sealing off access to the injectors.

The tentacle immediately dissipated, but not without giving off a massive blast of heat that Burgoyne feared, for just a moment, was capable of incinerating them where they stood. But after a few moments had passed, Burgoyne was happy to realize that they were still there and still in one piece.

S/he held a trembling Beth tight against hirself, displaying considerable agility as s/he made hir way down the ladders toward the main engineering room. Every one of hir people was gathered down there, looking shaken and confused. They were staring at the warp core with undisguised fear, for although the danger seemed momentarily to have passed, it was still all too present and all too real.

Trapped within the confines of a cargo container, Si Cwan fought desperately to shove away the lethargy that was seizing his mind. The drug injected into his system was a powerful one, but whatever it was, it had apparently been set to effect human physiology. Thallonian physiology, on the other hand, was made of sterner stuff.

It was not easy for him by any means. It was everything he could do to fight it off. His overpowering temptation was to sleep, to just give in to the darkness that threatened to envelop him. But he kept muttering, "No," over and over to himself, forcing himself to focus, to ignore the temptation to give up.

He began to pound on the lid of the container. It seemed solid, and the ringing of the noise he generated as he struck it seemed so loud that he thought it was going to split his head wide open. But he did not cease, did not give in, would not give up. "Won't . . . get away," he murmured. "Won't get away, won't get away." It became his mantra as he repeatedly pounded on the lid, over and over, determined not to lose. He felt the lid begin to loosen, bit by bit. Once more he started to tire but he knew that if he surrendered the momentum now, he would never attain it again. With both his fists he smashed upward, sending the lid flying up and off, and he started to clamber out of the container . . .

Just as the shuttlecraft blasted open the bay doors.

The vacuum of space howled around him while he was still hauling his numbed lower body out of the container. Instantly he let out much of the breath from his chest, because he knew that if he inhaled deeply, as was his reflex, the air would explode out of his lungs in a rather forceful fashion. The powerful suction hauled him out of the container and he skidded across the floor. Only seconds lay between him and ejection into the depths of space.

He pushed up with his powerful arms, angling himself in a desperate move, and slammed into the warp nacelle of the shuttlecraft. Urgently he wrapped his arms around the nacelle, braced his slow-to-function legs against the support strut, and hung on with all the strength he could muster.

The shuttlecraft lifted clear of the floor, and it was then that he realized that seeking salvation from death in space by clutching on to a vessel about to head into that very same void was probably not the best strategy he had ever developed. Unfortunately, by the look of things, he wasn't going to be around long enough to formulate any more.

"Damn the man!" snarled Morgan. "*God*damn the man!"

All she had to do was hit the forward thruster, and the shuttlecraft would be out and away. She would be clear of the *Excalibur,* gone to the safety of space and away from her imprisonment, and by the time they realized what had happened she would be long gone. Granted, they'd probably be able to follow her, but she had places she could get to, resources she could tap. Coolly she ranked her odds at about 70/30 in favor of making a clean getaway, and those were odds that she would happily take.

But it was going to be at the cost of a man's life; a man who had wanted nothing more but to try and patch things up between her and her daughter and obey the captain's dictates that she was not to leave the ship. Was her freedom worth killing Si Cwan for?

Hell yes! Morgan's mind screamed at her. *You don't owe him anything! Punch it and let's go!* But even as her mind celebrated her freedom, she powered up the reverse thrust. The shuttle backed up under her careful guidance, slowly and carefully bringing Si Cwan toward the door that led to the Operations control booth. She knew that if she could get him to that point, and if he could just hold on until she did, he could worm his way through the door and to safety.

And the drug in Si Cwan's system picked that moment to release its full potency.

Si Cwan suddenly felt his arms and legs go completely limp. He retained consciousness, but commands from his brain to his limbs simply didn't go through. He slid off the nacelle and didn't even have the opportunity to thud to the floor as the suction of deep space picked him up and hauled him toward the void. And there was absolutely nothing that Morgan could do about it.

So it was with complete astonishment that she saw Si Cwan slam to a halt just as he was about to plunge into space. An invisible barrier had sprung into existence, and Si Cwan slid off it and fell to the ground, looking somewhat stunned.

Up in the Ops control booth, Lieutenant j.g. Michael Houle had come to when he heard the phasers blast open the doors. Forcing himself to full consciousness, he had desperately tried to reroute the malfunctioning systems for the purpose of activating the forcefield, which was the normal backup when the bay doors were open. With seconds to spare, Houle had managed to bring the systems back on line and turn on the forcefield.

Instantly the suction of space's vacuum had been thwarted, although Si Cwan still looked somewhat amazed to discover that he was, in fact, alive.

Morgan, however, was left with a problem. If she tried to open fire on the forcefield, she might or might not be able to punch through it. But if she did, she'd be faced with the same problem she had before: Si Cwan, who in this case was lying in stupefied confusion, still trying to sort out what had happened, was now smack in the way. Her hasty exit meant his untimely death.

She had already faced that decision once, and she knew what it was going to be.

With the frustrated grunt of one who knows she has lost, Morgan settled the shuttlecraft back down into its place. Then she opened up the side hatch and stepped out to see if Si Cwan was all right.

What she discovered instead was half a dozen security men with phasers drawn and leveled at her.

"Hi, boys," she said with a cheerfulness she didn't feel.

A medical team had been dispatched immediately to Engineering. Aside from some minor radiation and heat burns as a result of the strange, energy plasma tentacle that had extended from the heart of the warp core, the single greatest injured party seemed to be Beth. She sat in one corner of Engineering, trembling uncontrollably, her arms drawn close together and her legs drawn up in an almost fetal position. Dr. Karen Kurdziel was administering a sedative to her as Burgoyne stood nearby, looking on and feeling more helpless than s/he had ever felt before.

"There you go," Kurdziel said. "Now come on, relax. Just relax."

And slowly she forced open Beth's arms, which were still frozen in a sort of rictus.

Something wet and fleshy plopped to the floor, causing several crewmen who were nearby to jump back, startled and repulsed. It was Christiano's right hand. Even to the end, Beth had not let go of it. She'd been clutching it even beyond the point where she was aware that she was doing it. Then the sedative fully kicked in, and she slumped over. Moments later an antigrav gurney had carried her away.

Burgoyne watched it go, and then Calhoun was at hir side, a hand resting on hir shoulder. "Nice save of Ensign Beth, Chief," Calhoun said.

"Not nice enough to save Christiano as well, though."

"You did the best you could." He raised his voice to address the other members of Engineering. "All right, people. I know this was a rough one. And I know our neighbor there"—and he indicated the warp core within which something completely unknown seemed to be lurking—"is somewhat disconcerting. But Lieutenant Soleta assures me that we can keep it under control for the time being, so we shouldn't have to evacuate the ship. I'm asking you now to be the professionals I know you are, and carry on your duties with the efficiency that I've come to expect from you as the crew of the *Excalibur.*"

There were still nervous stares, and fearful glances at the core, but slowly the Engineering staff went back to their assigned posts. Calhoun, meantime, immediately went with Burgoyne to hir office, Soleta accompanying the two of them. The moment they had seclusion, Calhoun said flatly, "You're not going to tell me I misspoke, are you, Lieutenant? You *can* control the thing."

"Yes, I believe so, at least for the time being. We can supercool the matter-antimatter mix, basically slow down the thing's metabolism, whatever that may be. It will still receive energy from the ship's engines, so it won't have another fit. But it'll be sluggish and, with any luck, unable to cause any damage."

"Did you have any idea that it would retaliate in the way that it did when we cut the energy consumption?"

"No, sir," said Soleta flatly. "But I should have allowed for that possibility. The responsibility is mine and I accept full consequences for the outcome."

"Now wait a minute," Burgoyne contradicted her. "This is my engine room, the final decision mine. If not for me—"

"This was a scientific mishap, Chief. Mine was the oversight that might have prevented—"

"Shut up," Calhoun said sharply, silencing both of them. "It doesn't matter whose fault it is. The responsibility is mine . . . and always is. And that's all. Besides, all the placed blame in the world doesn't bring back a single life. Are we clear on that?" When they nodded silently, he said, "All right. What the hell have we got in there, anyway?"

"In simplest terms," said Soleta, "something planted by the energy creature that we encountered during the destruction of Thallon. Possibly an offspring of the creature itself. I've compared the energy resonance of the bird-like energy creature we encountered with the entity that's in the warp core. There are variances, but sufficient similarities to indicate that there is some sort of relation. It is my belief that it is presently in the natal stages. But once it 'hatches,' its birth will very likely destroy the ship. And as it continues to grow, the effect it will continue to have on us is unpredictable."

"When does it hatch?"

"Unknown. It could be days, months, perhaps years. Its progenitor, if such it is, took centuries. There is simply no way to tell at this time."

"All right. And how do we get it out of our engine?"

"We don't know that either."

"Great. What *do* we know?"

"That we're screwed?" suggested Burgoyne.

Calhoun looked tiredly at Burgoyne. "Yes, Chief. I think we figured that one out all on our own."

11

Si Cwan stood outside the brig and looked at Morgan inside of it with more than a little sadness. ''I did my best, Morgan,'' he told her. ''I pointed out to the captain that you could easily have made your escape at the cost of my life, but you chose not to. I thought that would weigh in your favor. Unfortunately the captain did not choose to view your generosity in the same manner as I did.''

From within the brig, Morgan shrugged. ''That's all right, Si Cwan. You tried. And to be honest, I can see your captain's point of view on this one. There's just something about having someone blast open a door in one of your shuttlebays that makes you less than likely to think kindly of that person.''

''That's a very philosophical way to look at it,'' Si Cwan noted. Then he stopped speaking, apparently noticing someone coming his way. ''Why, Morgan, I believe you have visitor.''

Morgan knew perfectly well who it was going to be even before Robin appeared in view, for the tread tipped her off. She realized belatedly why she was able to pinpoint it so easily. It was because it sounded just like her own step.

''Hello, Robin,'' she said.

Lefler stood on the other side of the forcefield door, her hands behind her back, simply staring at her mother. Judiciously, Si Cwan said, ''Perhaps you'd prefer that I left so that you ladies could have some time alone.''

''No, that's quite all right,'' Lefler said. ''Mother, I know about the circumstances that resulted in your being here, and although I know that you were in the process of committing a crime . . . a crime for which you deserve to be punished, and frankly, I don't care if you're left here until you rot, and . . ."

"Robin, is there going to be something remotely uplifting in this dissertation anytime soon?" asked her mother. "Because if—"

"Mother, just be quiet, okay? I just . . . I wanted to thank you for not killing Si Cwan. God, I can't believe I said that. Thanking someone for not committing a murder, as if that shows any sort of incredible moral character. No one was ever thankful to me because I didn't kill anyone."

"Our tenth anniversary," Morgan said promptly.

Robin stared at her in confusion. "What?"

"Our tenth wedding anniversary, your father and me," Morgan explained. "You were five years old. And you decided that you wanted to make us breakfast. You were very excited about it. You couldn't decide what to make, so you made everything. While we slept, you destroyed the kitchen. You made eggs, pancakes—peanut butter pancakes, as I recall—French toast, cereal, bacon that was fried so tough you could have chipped a tooth on it, fresh-squeezed orange juice that still had the pits in it, and some other things. I think I've blanked them out. You brought the whole thing up to our bedroom on a tray," and she demonstrated, imitating the proud walk of a five-year-old confident that she has just performed the greatest service of her entire young life. "You woke us up, showed us how you had made breakfast for us, and then sat there and expected us to eat it."

"My God, I vaguely remember this," said Robin, putting her hand to her mouth. She looked completely embarrassed, and Si Cwan was happy to see it. It was the first time he had seen her looking anything other than angry in days. "Your hair was all standing every which way because you'd just woken up."

"That's right. And you were so adorable in this little white nightgown you had then. So you marched over and put the tray down and then plopped onto the floor with that Cheshire Cat grin and waited. And your father and I, we had absolutely no choice. So we plastered smiles on our faces and we ate everything. Every damn thing. And then we spent the next few hours taking turns running to the bathroom. It was the single most hideous meal we'd ever eaten."

"Oh, my God," laughed Robin. "I'm so sorry."

"It's okay," Morgan assured her. "In many ways, it was also the best. You were such an adorable child, the best, you . . ."

And then she saw that Robin's lower lip was trembling. "Oh,

Ches',' ' she said sadly, invoking that childhood nickname of days gone by.

''Why did you leave me, Ma?'' Her voice sounded very small and very defenseless.

And Morgan walked toward her, her arms outstretched, and Si Cwan barely had time to shout a warning before she would have hit the forcefield.

She fought to keep tears from her eyes.

''Ma, are you okay?!'' asked Lefler.

Morgan fought to bring herself under control. ''Oh, fine. Just fine. A little shaken. Nothing I can't handle.''

''I'm sorry, Mom. That was . . . unprofessional.'' She forced the tears to stop flowing from her eyes, drew her arm across her face in a large and rather dramatic smear.

''That's . . . quite all right, dear,'' Morgan said, feeling as if her teeth had been severely rattled. ''I probably had that coming. That and a good deal more, I should suspect. Look, Ches', tell me what happened before. When the whole place was going crazy. No one's speaking to me about anything.''

''There's nothing you can do about it, Mom. They're handling it in Engineering.''

''Well, honey, I don't quite believe that's all of the story. I'd very much like to know more of what's going on, and I'd appreciate it if you would bring me up to speed. And maybe—just maybe—I can solve some of your problems if you help me solve some of mine. You know me, Ches'. You know I've got some serious brainpower, if you must force me to boast of myself.''

''We have top minds working on it right now, Mom.''

''Then what's one more? Go ahead, you've nothing to lose. Tell me.''

So she told her. She laid it all out for Morgan, the entire story as Lefler had managed to hear it in bits and pieces. As the narrative went on, Morgan's face became more and more serious, and her eyes seemed to come into even clearer focus as if the only way that she could possibly view the world were through the prism of a problem that required solving.

Robin was silent for some time after she finished, and still Morgan said nothing. Finally, though, after having apparently given the matter considerable thought, she said, ''I need to see your captain.''

''Whatever for?''

''Because,'' Morgan told her with a hint of impatience, ''I think that I can actually get this mess settled. I think I may—just may, mind you—be able to save this ship. But I'm going to have to discuss it with your captain first, and I don't think I'm exactly very high on his list.''

Now it was Robin's turn to appear to ponder all that had been said. Finally she said to Morgan, ''You have to understand, Mom, you're asking me to crawl out on a limb here. Not only, as you say, are you not high on the captain's list, but you're asking me to risk my own status on that very same list. Because if I crawl out on that branch along with you and then it winds up getting sawed off behind us, there is going to be a very considerable crash when it hits the ground. I have no desire to be on it.''

''What are you saying?''

''I'm saying, Mother, that you're going to have to be forthcoming this time.'' She leaned forward to the very edge of the forcefield, resting with her hands on either side of the door frame. ''Before you're given the opportunity to convince the captain, you're going to have to convince me. Do you think you can do it?''

''Do I have a choice?''

''Not that I can see.''

This time Morgan didn't have to give it any thought at all. ''All right,'' she said without hesitation. ''I'll tell you. Not everything, mind you, but enough to get us started.''

And she told her.

The narrative took a few minutes, and as she spoke the eyes of both Lefler and Si Cwan grew wider and wider. By the end of it, they had turned and looked at one another with conviction on both their faces. ''The captain,'' said Si Cwan, ''has definitely got to hear this.''

''Do you think he'll believe it?'' asked Morgan.

''If you were in his position, would you?'' Si Cwan asked her reasonably.

Morgan pondered it a moment and then said, ''No chance in hell.''

''In that case, he probably will. Because if there's one thing I've noticed, it's that whenever one tries to second-guess Mackenzie Calhoun, one inevitably finds oneself squarely in the wrong.''

''I don't believe it,'' said Calhoun.

''Captain, I'm deadly serious,'' said Morgan as Calhoun paced the conference lounge. As opposed to Morgan's earlier meeting with him, when he had appeared utterly unflappable and relaxed for the vast majority of the meeting, this time around he seemed tense and cool. She couldn't blame him, really. He had a creature living in his warp core. That would be enough to put anyone on edge.

Also present in the conference lounge were Shelby, Soleta, and Burgoyne, as well as Lefler and Si Cwan, who had organized the meeting. They likewise seemed preoccupied, and every so often Burgoyne would, as quietly as s/he could so as not to disturb anyone else at the table, receive reports from Engineering. S/he had demanded that s/he be updated every ten minutes as to any changes that might have occurred with the creature. In a uniquely odd endeavor to lighten the situation, Burgoyne had named the creature, for no discernible reason, Sparky. When Soleta had asked, "Why Sparky?" he had retorted that the creature had to be called something, and Sparky was as good a name as any. Soleta hadn't quite understood exactly why the creature needed to be called anything other than the creature, but she didn't see much point in arguing.

"Your skepticism is understandable, Captain," Morgan said. "But I'm telling you that your only hope of solving this problem lies with a race of beings—the same beings who are the reason I wound up coming here in the first place."

"Yes, so you said," Calhoun replied. "Since you are the one who's making this rather outrageous claim, Morgan, I will thank you either to try and prove it, or else stop wasting the time of everyone concerned here."

"Captain, if you'll just listen . . ." Robin began.

"I believe, Lieutenant, that I've done more than enough listening to this woman."

Morgan sat in the chair nearest the captain and leaned forward, her fingers interlaced. Speaking with a newfound urgency, she said, "Whatever they call themselves, I couldn't begin to say. I call them the Prometheans, a highly advanced, technologically superior race. I came to Thallonian space in the company of a friend named Tarella. We'd been tracking these mysterious Prometheans, and the research trail led us to Momidium. What we found there led us to believe that the Prometheans could be found on a world called Ahmista. But before we could set off, the Momidiums wound up capturing me. Tarella got away, however, and I half expected that she would come back for me. In fact, I spent my entire first year in captivity waiting for her to return and free me. But she never came back. I don't know whether she was killed, or whether she found something so incredible that she . . .'' Morgan shrugged. ''It could be anything. Any of a hundred reasons why she didn't come back.''

''And we're supposed to go searching for your friend, is that it?''

''I don't come to this party offering a lot of guarantees. The only thing I know is that we were heading for Ahmista. What has happened to her since then, I couldn't even begin to tell you. If I had to guess, I'd say that the odds of her still being on Ahmista are pretty slim. Chances are that I'm going to have to start from level zero to try and pick up the leads to the Prometheans.''

''How do we know,'' Shelby asked, ''that this isn't simply another ploy to try and escape?''

''Don't kid a kidder, Commander. We both know that if you don't do something about junior in the warp core, there isn't going to be a ship left to escape from. You can't survive indefinitely. You might not even survive into next week.''

''Considering the gestation period of the last energy creature we encountered, we might survive into the next century,'' Soleta said.

''True enough, Lieutenant. Are you willing to risk your life, and the lives of everyone on this ship, on that possibility?'' fired back Morgan.

''None of us are,'' cut in Calhoun. ''But neither are we willing or interested in committing resources to a false lead to a race of beings so mythic you don't even have a definite name for them. We could be chasing fairy tales for all we know.''

Si Cwan stepped forward. ''And yet these fairy stories have a ring of familiarity to me, Captain. I described earlier the tales of my youth, of the gods and the firebringers. Morgan's own naming of her mystery race is after a similar fire-to-humanity story that exists in our own mythology. Don't you find it curious that both of our civilizations share a mythology having to do with the acquisition of flame?''

''That is not at all unusual,'' Soleta replied. ''There are many core concepts that prompt similar myths. Many cultures have end of the world scenarios, flood scenarios, and different mythologies explaining different aspects of nature. No, it is not uncommon at all, and hardly proof of any connection. Unless you are about to claim that these mysterious Prometheans were responsible in some way for technological advancement on the part of mankind.''

''Anything is possible.''

''But not probable,'' said Calhoun. ''We could use some sort of proof about this race aside from your suppositions and guesses. Otherwise my assumption will be that this is merely an elaborate ruse that, for some reason, Lieutenant Lefler and Ambassador Si Cwan have bought into.''

Si Cwan glance down at Morgan and said simply, ''Show him.''

''Now is the time, Mom,'' agreed Lefler.

She nodded and reached under her shirt, sliding something that was round and hard up toward the collar. And then she pulled out, mounted in a black casing, a small amulet with a raised image of a flame on it. ''We came upon two of these through a trader on Momidium who didn't realize what he had,'' she said. ''Tarella and I believed that they were markers of some sort. Perhaps even beacons, a means of summoning the Prometheans, although we were not entirely sure how they would function.''

There was stunned silence in the room for a moment.

''Look familiar?'' Morgan asked drily.

Calhoun turned to Soleta and said quickly, ''Go get it.'' Soleta was out of her chair like a shot.

This prompted a confused look from Morgan, who turned and stared up at Si Cwan and Lefler, who were standing nearby. ''What am I missing?'' she asked. ''You told me they'd be interested in the medallion. You didn't go into any detail beyond that. Is there something I should know?''

''Perhaps,'' said Robin. ''But you've been so busy being mysterious and hard to comprehend, that I thought it only fair to give you a bit of mystery right back. Seems equitable to me, don't you think?''

''Yes,'' Morgan said slowly, and clearly slightly amused by the situation. ''Yes, I suppose it does at that.''

Moments later, Soleta had returned, and to Morgan's utter astonishment, she placed down on the table a disk that likewise had a flame emblem on it. Slowly, her hand trembling, Morgan reached toward it.

''Captain . . .'' Shelby said warningly, but Calhoun decided to go with his gut and waved Shelby off, indicating that they should let Morgan touch it. She picked it up, turned it over in her hands, and ran her fingers along the flame symbol engraved on it. She noticed immediately that, as opposed to the medallion she herself bore, the flame emblem was indented on this one.

Burgoyne, for hir part, seemed unimpressed. ''We're wasting our time with this, Captain,'' Burgoyne said urgently. ''The smart move is to try and get back to a starbase out of Thallonian space. Some sort of facility that can help us in extracting Sparky from the warp core.''

"There is no guarantee that any facility short of the shipyards in San Francisco would be capable of accomplishing such a feat, nor do we know if even they could do so," Soleta said reasonably. "Furthermore, we do not know the full abilities of this creature. Can you imagine if the efforts of unknowing Starfleet engineers should cause the creature—"

"Sparky," Burgoyne corrected her.

"The creature," continued Soleta, "to flee the containment of the *Excalibur* only to take up residence within the core of Earth itself, as the energy creature did on Thallon? That scenario would be catastrophic, to say the least."

"You're saying we're stuck out here?"

"I am saying, Chief, that if there are other options it would be wiser to explore them first, no matter how far-fetched."

"Captain," Morgan said cautiously, holding the faces of the medallion and the disk opposite each other. "Do you have any objections if . . . ?"

Her intention seemed self-evident and Calhoun weighed the possible consequences. "From where I sit," he finally decided, "I don't see as that we have a lot to lose. Go ahead. Let's see if rubbing the lamp will pull the genie out."

With a deep breath, Morgan slowly brought the two metal disks together. She couldn't help but notice that the diameters were a perfect match. And not only that, but with the slightest of turns to adjust, she clicked the flame emblem of her medallion into the recess of the disk handed her by Soleta.

She wasn't sure what she had expected. A flash of light, perhaps, or a sepulchral laugh. A surge of energy or a massive telepathic bolt that would cut straight to the very core of her soul and bond with her at a spiritual level. A Chinese gong. She had no idea, really.

Unfortunately, what she wound up getting was nothing.

She simply sat there, the disks in her hand. Nothing trembled, nothing vibrated. Nothing, in short, happened.

"Are we rescued from Sparky yet?" Calhoun asked drily.

"I don't understand it," Morgan said. But then, with more firmness of tone, she added, "But then again, I didn't necessarily expect to understand it. There has to be more to it than this, Captain, and with any luck at all, the answer is on Ahmista."

"Any luck at all is something we haven't had in abundance." He sat back in his chair, considering the matter a moment. "Ambassador, do you know anything about this Ahmista?"

''Not really,'' replied Si Cwan. ''A fairly small population, the planet had no particular strategic value, and the residents were not especially advanced. It was never considered a worthwhile use of Thallonian resources to have much to do with them. We knew of them, but we never bothered with them.''

''Fair enough,'' said Calhoun. ''Do you know where Ahmista is?''

''I'm not McHenry, Captain,'' Si Cwan said with slight amusement. ''I don't carry these matters around in my head. If I could see a starmap and our relative position on it . . .''

''Soleta?'' prompted Calhoun.

Soleta punched it up on the computer terminal next to her and, moments later, the desired information appeared on the conference lounge viewscreen. It displayed all the known information about Thallonian space that they had, and a blinking spot that marked the *Excalibur*'s location. He studied it for a moment, and then pointed to a system that was not especially detailed. ''Right here,'' he said. ''This is it.''

''There's no indicator of any planets there,'' Soleta noted.

''I think you'll find that the Federation is not in possession of any complete starmaps of Sector Two-twenty-one-G,'' said Si Cwan, using the Starfleet designation rather than referring to it as Thallonian space. ''My people tended to be circumspect about such matters, even after the point that such circumspection was of any use to the greater good. Nonetheless, it is most definitely here. Three planets, with the outermost being the one she refers to as Ahmista.''

Shelby leaned forward, studying the location. ''At warp nine, it's still three days' journey from here. That's a best guess on my part; McHenry could probably tell you down to the second. But that seems about right.''

''Can we afford to go to warp nine, Burgy?'' asked Calhoun.

''I think so,'' said Burgoyne slowly, although s/he didn't appear all that enthusiastic. ''As near as we can tell, increased warp activity makes Sparky more active. Doesn't make him more hostile though. The only hitch is . . . well, it could accelerate his development or growth. In trying to track down someone who can help us with this situation, we may be exacerbating it.''

''This entire business is a long shot at best, Captain,'' Shelby observed.

''Are you saying we shouldn't do it, Commander?''

''No. I'm just saying it's a long shot.''

Calhoun considered the matter for a moment, drumming his fingers on the table in thought. And finally he said, ''I don't want to have to give up this ship, people. Abandonment remains an option, but it's not one that I accept gladly. To say nothing of the fact that, if we do abandon, we have no guarantee that once we shove everyone into the saucer section and cut the Engineering hull loose, Sparky might not come out of the warp core and take up residence in the saucer section impulse engines, and then we'll be worse off than when we started. A long shot is better than no shot. Commander, have McHenry lay in a course for Ahmista. Burgoyne, monitor Sparky even more closely than you are now. Eat, sleep, and breathe in synch with his cycle if you have to, but stay on top of him. Understood?''

''Aye, sir.''

''Captain,'' Lefler asked, ''may my mother leave the brig?''

He studied Morgan appraisingly for a moment. And then he said, ''Your mother, Lieutenant, blew a hole in the door of shuttlebay two and almost cost Si Cwan his life, her subsequent actions notwithstanding. I don't trust her yet.''

''I'm right here, Captain,'' Morgan commented. ''You don't have to speak of me in the third person.''

''I don't trust you yet,'' amended Calhoun. ''And until such time that I do, if ever, you can take up residence back in the brig where I don't have to expend any security forces for the purpose of keeping an eye on you.''

Lefler started to protest, but Morgan was already on her feet and nodding her head in acquiescence. ''I understand fully, Captain. Were I in your position, I would likely be doing the same thing. And I find that I have a fairly good track record at this point in noting what you will and will not do. Robin, Ambassador, I appreciate your efforts on my behalf. And now I believe my escort is waiting for me. Captain, may I keep this?'' she asked, holding up the joined medallion.

''I would rather you didn't,'' he told her. ''Keep your half if you wish, but return the other to Lieutenant Soleta, please.''

She nodded and, with a slight effort, pulled the two apart. She handed the indented side back to Soleta and then said to Calhoun, ''I appreciate your indulgence in this matter, Captain.''

''May I ask, Morgan, why you are suddenly being cooperative?'' Calhoun inquired.

The others looked to her, clearly interested in the answer. ''I wish I had an easy answer for you, Captain. Perhaps I simply see more advantage in cooperating than not cooperating. Perhaps I think we can actually be of help to each other. Or perhaps . . .'' She looked at

Si Cwan. "You know, I thought, for all the time that I was incarcerated on Momidium, that I would do anything, absolutely anything, to achieve my freedom. And I discovered that, no, that wasn't the case. There are some things that I wouldn't do to gain freedom. And I found that to be . . . heartening. Does that answer your question, Captain?"

"Not completely, no."

"Well, you may just have to live with that, Captain. We all do to some degree or another."

He nodded in agreement, finding himself liking her in spite of himself, which was more than a little annoying.

12

Si Cwan, in his office, studied the picture of Morgan Primus that remained on his computer screen. There was a slight flicker of power, but then the couplings righted themselves as the rerouted systems Burgoyne had cobbled together righted themselves. By this point, Cwan was barely noticing such fluctuations. Like victims of any war-torn environment, difficulties that would once have seemed oppressive now had faded into mere background inconveniences.

He studied the woman's face carefully. Damn, but she was a striking individual. There was something within her, though, something that seemed to cry out of secrecy. Some deep and unending mystery at which he could only guess.

"She has old eyes," he said at last. To a Thallonian, that was a comment that had deep meaning. To have old eyes meant that one had an old soul, and was a rather experienced and spiritually elevated individual. Either that or it made a great pickup line when one wanted to compliment a female that one was interested in bedding.

He hadn't entirely made up his mind which it was for him yet.

There was a chime at the door. "Come," he said, leaning back in his chair.

To his utter surprise, Zak Kebron was standing there. As always, the massive Brikar seemed to fill the doorway.

Si Cwan's first thought was to wonder what sort of trouble he was in. He and Kebron had had a mutual antipathy, underscored by a sort of grudging respect for each other's personality and accomplishments. The closest they had come to a true understanding was the realization that they would both far rather have each other as allies than enemies. Consequently they endeavored to minimize their conversation, limiting it to missions at hand, missions in the past, and missions in the near future. It made for fairly succinct discussions that consisted mainly of the imparting of specific data. This was a relationship that worked fine for both of them.

So it was with great surprise that Si Cwan saw Kebron standing at his door. "Is there a problem, Kebron?" he asked without hesitation.

"There is," Kebron said slowly. Kebron was the mortal enemy of the term "gregarious," likely to try and eliminate it from any dictionary in any language. When he spoke it was with short, spartan sentences, although he was occasionally capable of a fairly morbid wit that even Si Cwan had to admit that he admired. "A problem that has to be addressed."

"A problem with me?" asked Si Cwan.

Kebron nodded. Since Kebron had virtually no neck, one of his nods more or less consisted of a slight bow.

"All right," said Si Cwan, slowly rising from behind his desk. "What is the nature of the problem? If there is anything I can do—"

"There is. When I point, say 'You're welcome.' "

"What?" Si Cwan stared at him. "I don't understand."

"I don't need your understanding. Just your cooperation." Kebron hadn't moved from the doorway. "Can you do it?"

"Well, yes, of course, a child could do it."

"Very well." Kebron paused as if steeling himself and then said, "Thank you." And he pointed.

"You're welcome," said a bemused Si Cwan on cue.

Kebron turned and walked away, the door sliding shut behind him.

"Now hold on a moment!" called Cwan, not about to let it go at that. He followed Kebron out into the hallway. He didn't walk right next to him, because Kebron's size, stride, and general swing of his arms as he walked usually precluded that. So Cwan hung about a foot or so back and to the right. "What was that all about? You can't just come in, say 'Thank you,' and leave."

"I just did." As was not unusual when he was walking with a purpose, the floor under Kebron rumbled slightly under his footfall.

"You didn't say why you were thanking me."

"Unnecessary."

"Not to me it's not," and he grabbed Kebron by the arm.

The massive Brikar stopped and, without looking at Si Cwan, rumbled, "You so very much do not want to do that."

Si Cwan released Kebron's arm like a fiery briquette, but he took the opportunity to step around Kebron and stand squarely in his path. This could, of course, have backfired somewhat since Kebron could had walked right over him without too much difficulty, but he was hoping that wouldn't happen. "Kebron—Zak—what's going on?"

Kebron made a sound in his chest that came across like rocks tumbling around in a clothes drier (although neither of them had ever seen, or even heard of, a clothes drier, so the comparison would have been lost on them). "I feel constrained to thank you . . . for your help."

"My help?" Si Cwan said blankly.

"You prevented Morgan Primus from escaping the ship. That was not your job. It was my job. Mine, and my people. We fumbled it. You recovered it. So I am thanking you because I feel it is the right thing to do." It was rare that Kebron ever uttered that many sentences together, and the significance of it was not lost on Si Cwan.

"No one blames your security force for losing track of Morgan. The ship was going haywire at that moment. It was—"

"Inexcusable. I owe you, Cwan. And I do not forget my debts. So thank you."

"You're welcome," said Si Cwan. "And who knows, Kebron. I've made mistakes in the past, I admit that. I don't pretend to be perfect. Perhaps we've gotten off on the wrong foot, you and I. Perhaps this is the beginning of a new and improved relationship between us. Perhaps we can put aside our differences and genuinely build a basis for a true and lasting friendship." And he stuck out a hand for Kebron to shake.

Kebron stared at the open, outstretched hand, and then he looked Si Cwan squarely in the eyes. "I don't owe you *that* much," he said, and walked away, leaving Si Cwan shaking his head in amusement.

Dr. Selar glanced across sickbay and saw someone unexpected. Mark McHenry was there, talking to Dr. Maxwell and touching his back with a pained expression. Maxwell actually seemed to be smiling as McHenry spoke, then nodded and indicated that McHenry should get up on a med table. McHenry did so and proceeded to remove his shirt while sitting up, as Maxwell stepped over to a rack of instruments. As Selar approached the two of them, while McHenry was sitting with his back to her, she could see that Maxwell had taken the neodermic applicator off the wall. The applicator was designed to create a graft of new skin, and was primarily used for quick and easy repair of abrasions. In short, it was a high-tech Band-Aid.

Maxwell saw her coming and looked at her questioningly. Selar, for her part, was looking at McHenry's back. There were scratches across it, as if he'd been clawed. She casually gestured for Maxwell to hand her the applicator, which he promptly did.

Upon closer inspection, she could see that the cuts raked across his back. There were five of them, each running parallel to one another in a diagonal path. Being a fairly bright woman, it did not take Selar long at all to figure out just exactly how those cuts had come into being. Without a word she began to run the applicator across them. Automatically disinfecting the wounds, it left a trail of pink new skin behind it.

McHenry let out a low sigh. "Ahhhhh . . . that feels good. Magic hands, Doc." Selar said nothing, and McHenry continued, "I have to tell you, that Burgoyne . . . s/he's a wild one."

"Mmm," Selar said noncommitally.

"I shouldn't. I mean, I really shouldn't. I know that. I'm kinda weak-willed when it comes to that department. Guess I don't have to tell you about what that's like, right, Doctor Selar?"

Selar was taken aback. She had been caught off-guard by McHenry's affect of inattention.

"Only problem is," admitted McHenry, "I feel like . . . like I'm taking advantage of hir, you know? Because I'm not what s/he wants, I know it. I'm not who s/he wants. But I think s/he's afraid of how much s/he wants who s/he wants, because s/he's never felt like that about anyone. I wish I were a strong-willed enough man to insist that s/he do what's right for hir, but I'm not 'cause I'm having too much fun. So I go along with it, even though I know that what s/he really wants is to be with . . . someone else. This . . . someone, hell, I figure she'll never admit that she wants to be with Burgoyne as much as Burgoyne wants to be with her. They're going to have a baby, for crying out loud! I mean, I'm a modern sort of guy. It's not as if my mind or morality is stuck in the twenty-second century. But these people have a bond, both emotional and familial. You'd think that would mean something. You'd think they'd want to work together, not be so petrified of intimacy or commitment that they'd give each other a wide berth." He sighed again, but this time it wasn't with pleasure. "I knew Christiano, y'know. We used to hang out. Decent enough guy considering he wound up as just a hand. If I learned anything from that, it's that life is just too short not to go for something that you really want.''

Selar had absolutely no idea what to say. She had wanted to have a talk with McHenry, to ask about Burgoyne. She had heard about what had happened in Engineering, heard of Burgoyne's heroics in saving Ensign Beth. The entire experience had been a terrifying one overall, and although Selar was far too stoic to actually be terrified, she still felt a great deal of concern for Burgoyne. She had wanted to go down there, to ask personally if s/he was all right, to say something . . . try to make some sort of connection, even though she wasn't sure what to say and was even less sure whether Burgoyne wanted that connection.

And here she had wound up having a talk with McHenry, or a listen at least. Except she felt as if she were an eavesdropper. Selar was a highly moral individual, and this entire business now seemed sneaky and wrong to her. She stepped back and then saw Dr. Maxwell watching out of the corner of her eye. She gestured for Maxwell to come over, and handed him back the applicator and quickly slipped away. He watched her go, shaking his head, and then leaned over to finish the skin application on McHenry's back. Selar, for her part, retreated to her office.

''Everything okay back there?'' asked McHenry.

''Certainly,'' Selar said. ''But Dr. Maxwell will continue your treatment.''

''So . . . so what did you talk about?'' Maxwell asked, after Selar had left.

''Nothing,'' McHenry said easily. ''Nothing important at all. Trust me, Maxie, it's nothing that you have to know.''

''I have to know.''

Robin Lefler had entered the brig and was now standing opposite her mother, leaning against a corner of the wall. Morgan wasn't even looking at her, though.

''Mother, did you hear me?''

''Yes, I heard you. You said you have to know.''

''Mom . . .'' She tried to find the right words. ''The other day, when Engineering went haywire . . . we could have died then. All of us. Now, I'm not afraid of dying, Mom. I'm really not. It's not like I'm eager to, you understand. And it's not like, if someone tries to take me down, I won't go kicking and screaming. Believe me, given the choice, I'd rather be dancing on the dirt than lying under it, you know? But I . . . I don't want to die in ignorance. For years I thought that my life was simply unfair and tragic, but at least I was used to that. Now, though, I find that it makes no sense. I don't know why it makes no sense. I don't know why anything anymore. I backed you up when it came to talking to the captain. You have no idea how difficult that was for me. No idea at all. But I did it as a gesture, to show you that I was capable of trusting you. Now . . . now I need you to trust me, Mother. I need you to tell me what's really going on. The truth of everything. Will you do that for me, Mother? Will you please do whatever you can to try and help my life make sense again? I want . . . I want to go back to being the woman I was. I was happy once. I can't be happy, ever again, until I know and understand this. Please. Please do this for me. If you've ever done anything for me in your life. If you've ever really, truly believed you loved me: Be honest with me."

"You won't believe it," Morgan said quietly.

"I will."

"You won't." She looked up at her sadly. "Your father didn't believe. Not at first. At first he thought I was just crazy. And then, when I . . . when I proved it to him . . . he was afraid of me."

"Afraid of you?" Robin couldn't quite believe what she was hearing. "How could he be afraid of you? You were his wife! The mother of his daughter! He adored you, he—"

But Morgan was shaking her head vehemently. "I'm telling you that you will react in exactly the same way, Robin, and I just can't bring myself to risk doing that to you . . . and to me. Not again."

"Mother, I'm in Starfleet. My life is risk. I can handle it. I swear to you I can."

"You won't understand—"

"I'm not a child, dammit!" Lefler fairly howled in frustration. "Don't you get that? Don't you understand that—"

And then Morgan was on her feet, and in a cold and deadly voice, she said, "And don't you understand that I'm not who, or what, you think."

"What are you saying, that you're not my mother?"

"No. No, I am. I have been many things over the decades, but you know, the fact that I'm your mother is probably the thing that I take greatest pride in."

"Over the decades. Mother, what are you talking about?"

Morgan took a deep breath. "I am . . . older than you think."

''Okay, fine,'' Robin said, throwing up her hands in frustration. ''Fine, don't tell me. I don't know why I bothered. I don't—''

But then Morgan grabbed Lefler's arm and spun her around to face her, and there was fire in her eyes. ''You wanted the truth, little girl?'' she said in a voice so dark, so frightening, that it was barely recognizable as that of her own mother. She was speaking with an odd accent, one that Morgan couldn't even begin to place, although it sounded very faintly like a cross between Scot and British. ''You wanted it? Here it is, and you will listen to every damned word. I was born centuries ago, reached maturity, and discovered that I did not age any further . . . and did not, *could not,* die.''

''That's . . . that's impossible,'' said Lefler, trying to pull away. ''No one can live that long.''

''No human, but not no one. While I was raised on Earth by human parents, I soon realized that I was from somewhere else. I was very adept at creating identities for myself, living in them for a time, then faking my death and moving on. I even joined Starfleet for a time, at first hoping to find my people, then thinking that misadventure would do what the years would not.

''But it didn't work. I have an . . . an aura about me that protects me from mortal harm.''

''An aura,'' said Lefler tonelessly.

Morgan nodded. ''I tried a phaser at full disintegration; it didn't harm me. I thought of setting a transporter to disperse my molecules through space, but I'm afraid that, somehow, I'll retain consciousness in a demolecularized form, floating like a ghost—an even more terrifying state than my current one.''

''I should think so.''

And Morgan—Morgan, who did not lose her temper, Morgan who was the epitome of coolness and control—slid into a white hot fury and faced Lefler, shouting, ''Stop it! Stop patronizing me!''

The sound of her voice was like a rifleshot as Lefler went down. A security guard was immediately at the door, prepared to go in and stun Morgan for the purpose of hauling Lefler out, but Robin put up a hand. ''Stay where you are!'' she shouted. ''I'm fine!''

''The hell you are, Ches'. The hell you are, you are light-years away from 'fine,' '' retorted Morgan. ''Don't you get it? I was tired! Tired of watching loved one after loved one die while I went on and on and on! You would think that after centuries of it I'd get used to it, but no. Every single loss was like a knife to my heart. I couldn't take it anymore. I just wanted to end. And my body wouldn't let me

. . . except in ways that would be so high risk that I was terrified to try them for fear that they'd leave me worse off than when I started. I wanted something safe, certain. Don't you get that?''

''I get it, I get it,'' said Robin. She watched her mother from as far away as she was able to get from her. ''You're not human. You've been around forever.''

Her immediate anger spent, Morgan sagged down onto the bench. ''I wandered the galaxy for a time, slowly despairing,'' she said, sounding as much as if she were talking to herself as to Robin. ''Then I returned home, met your father, and fell in love. And after we married, for the first time I knew enough love that I saw a future for myself. I had you. And as I watched you grow, my love, I realized I couldn't stand to watch you get older . . . grow up. I've lost so many people that I loved, but every day I watched you get older, it was . . . it was more than I could take. So I faked my death earlier than I would normally have and left. I left because I was selfish, and determined to find a way to put an end to my miserable existence. Are you happy that you know, now, Robin? Are you happy?''

''Mother,'' Robin was shaking her head. ''Mother, look, I . . . I know what you said about Dad . . . and how he didn't believe . . . but I . . . This is so much to try and handle. This is . . . It's . . .''

''Preposterous?''

''Yes.''

''Absurd?''

''Completely. I think . . . I think maybe you should see someone. There are people who can help you.''

''Would you like to see something?'' she asked.

''Uhm . . . sure. If you want me to.''

''All right. I'm going to show you a trick.''

She turned around away from Lefler's view, and there was a sound like a snap. When Morgan turned back, she was holding up a knife. The blade, three inches long but extremely sharp, glinted in the light.

''Mother, what—''

And very quickly, very efficiently, in one smooth move, Morgan held out her right wrist and drew the knife down it. She slid it lengthwise down her forearm, opening up the vein, and blood began to well out, thick and red.

''Oh my God!'' shrieked Lefler. Immediately she sent an emergency call to sickbay.

''Don't worry,'' Morgan said calmly. ''I've done it before.''

''Mom, oh my God, Mom!'' Lefler cried out as she leaped toward her mother, clasping her hands frantically around the fountaining forearm. She tried to apply pressure, to stop the bleeding, but the blood was leaking out between her fingers. "Mom, how could you? How could you?!"

"About five seconds," Morgan said calmly. "Four . . . three . . . two . . . one . . . let go. You can let go."

"I can't let go! You'll bleed to death! You'll—"

With an impatient noise, Morgan pushed her daughter aside. She called to the guard, who was still outside as he awaited backup from the sickbay medics. "Do you have a towel on you? A cloth?"

"A . . . a cloth?"

"Never mind," she said, utterly calm. She lifted up the cushion that they were sitting on and used it to wipe away the blood. "Just send for a new one of these, okay? This stuff stains."

"Where's the medical team!?" Lefler fairly shouted. "Where the hell is the—?"

And then Morgan extended her arm, practically under Lefler's nose. Robin looked down . . . and couldn't believe what she was seeing.

The blood flow had completely stopped. Where there had been a vicious cut only moments ago, there was now simply a thin pink line standing out against the tan of her skin. And even that was already disappearing. Lefler looked in stupefaction as the pink skin of the freshly healed wound changed color and matched the tan of the rest of her arm.

At that moment the medical team came charging up. They saw the blood collected on the floor and staining the mattress, and they looked around in confusion to find the person who was apparently bleeding in such copious quantities.

"Thank you for coming by, gentlemen," Morgan said calmly, "but I'm afraid it was a bit of a false alarm. I was just showing my daughter here a magic trick—a rather sanguinary one, I'm afraid—and the dear guard here overreacted to what he was seeing. I'm terribly sorry to have wasted your time. Although if you gentlemen would be so kind as to send someone to clean that up"—and she pointed at the blood—"I would be most obliged. Robin," she said, taking Robin by the shoulders, "you look somewhat shaken. Perhaps you'd best go on about your business now. Don't you think that would be wise?"

"Yes," Robin said, clearly still in shock. "Yes, that would be . . . be wise."

The guard shut down the forcefield long enough for Lefler to leave and for a cleaning crew to come in and attend to the mess on the floor. And Lefler put as much distance between herself and the brig that was holding her mother as she possibly could. She paused only briefly to glance over her shoulder, and caught a glimpse of her mother, looking rather serene in her cell as if, all of a sudden, she didn't have a care in the world.

13

They're here. . . . They're here. . . .

Her lover cries the warning to her, and she strokes it for the confrontation that is to come.

"There's no one here."

Calhoun rose from the command chair and walked over to Zak Kebron's tactical station as the world of Ahmista turned beneath them. "What do you mean?"

"I mean preliminary sensor sweeps indicate no humanoid life-forms."

"None?" Calhoun asked incredulously. He turned to Soleta, who was already at work at her science station. "Soleta?"

"Scanning. At this point, confirming Mr. Kebron's analysis. Although the ecosystem is capable of supporting life, and there appears to be some minimal animal life, there are no humanoid organisms."

"It's the wrong planet," Shelby suggested.

"But it's right where Si Cwan said it was," McHenry pointed out from the conn.

"Could there have been some sort of . . . of war? They wiped each other out?" Calhoun said.

"There are no traces of lingering radiation, no burned areas, no pollutants from toxins or germ warfare; none of the usual indicators that a war sufficient for the annihilation of all life upon a world has occurred," said Soleta. "Furthermore, Si Cwan described the populace of this world as being fairly low on the technical scale. They very likely would not possess the type of armament necessary to do away with every man, woman, and child on the planet."

"Well, *grozit,* Lieutenant, where are they, then?"

"Unknown at this time, sir."

"Perhaps they're all hiding somewhere and waiting to pop out so they can say 'Surprise,' " Calhoun said humorlessly. "Soleta, I want you to scan every square foot of that planet if necessary. If there's so much as a campfire burning, I want to know about it. Bridge to Si Cwan."

"Si Cwan here," came back the ambassador's voice quickly.

"Mr. Cwan, kindly join us on the bridge. There's a question or two that could use your attention. Calhoun out." Without missing a beat, he turned to Kebron and said, "Have security escort Morgan Primus up here as well."

Robin Lefler turned at her position at Ops. "My mother?" she asked.

"Unless there's another Morgan Primus on the ship, Lieutenant, yes. Why, is that a problem for you?"

"No," Robin said quickly, suddenly becoming incredibly engrossed in her instruments. "No, that's no problem for me at all."

Moments later, both Si Cwan and Morgan had emerged from the turbolift onto the bridge. Calhoun noticed that Robin was carefully endeavoring not to meet her mother's gaze. Something had happened between the two of them, something since the time that Robin had appeared to be making inroads with her mother. He knew that there had been some sort of odd incident in the brig. The report he had received had been extremely confused and confusing: An attempted suicide, except that, although there was blood everywhere, there was no sign of any sort of wound on either Lefler or Morgan, who had been the only occupants of the cell at the time. It made absolutely no sense at all. It was just one of a number of matters that needed addressing.

"We have a bit of a curiosity," Calhoun said, circling them. "You, Morgan, told us that the trail of the Prometheans indicated that this world was the place where you might be able to connect with them. I notice that you never told us how, precisely, you knew this. Would you be so kind as to enlighten us now?"

"Comments we heard in our investigations. Writings buried in assorted rare texts. A long process that—" Then she saw the way he was looking at her, and for the first time since he'd met her, Morgan actually seemd less than certain of herself. "Ultimately," she admitted, "what it came down to is that Tarella and I . . . we just . . . knew."

"You just knew."

"Yes."

"That's the best you can do. You just knew."

"It's not impossible, Captain," Soleta commented, never taking her eyes away from her scanner. "Remember my experience with the similar disk. There may be some sort of connection to a greater whole."

"You're saying they're like the Borg, but little disks?" Calhoun said skeptically.

"Well, that's certainly less threatening in any event," said Shelby.

"Ambassador," Calhoun turned to face Si Cwan, "do you have an estimate as to the number of people in residence on Ahmista?"

"I couldn't say for sure, no," Si Cwan replied. "Five . . . maybe six billion, I suppose."

"Would you like to know how many there are now?"

"One."

The reply came from Soleta, which naturally captured the immediate attention of everyone else on the bridge. Calhoun crossed quickly to her station. "You found someone?"

"Took a while longer since the population was so sparse—well, sparse being a generous term, I suppose. I have managed to detect a single humanoid life-form down there."

"A single one?" Si Cwan asked, sounding appalled. "That's . . . that's absurd! Where is the rest of the population?"

"That," Calhoun said, "is what we're going to try and find out. Commander," he turned to Shelby, "I want an away team composed of yourself, Si Cwan, Lieutenant Soleta, and Mr. Kebron to head down there and see just who or what it is we're dealing with. I want everyone armed on this one, because we have no idea what it is you'll be facing."

"Even me?" asked Si Cwan.

Calhoun paused only a moment, and then he nodded. "Even you." He heard a dissatsified growl from behind him indicating that Zak Kebron was registering a complaint about his captain's decision. He judiciously chose to ignore it.

"What about me, Captain?" Morgan asked.

"What about you?"

"I brought us to this planet," she said. "If anyone is entitled to go down there and see exactly what's going on, it should be me."

''Perhaps in the way you see matters, yes, but that's not the way I see it,'' replied Calhoun. ''I'm afraid I don't have quite enough confidence in you, Morgan, to send you down there while my people have to be watching their backs. For all I know, they may have to watch their backs where you're concerned as well.''

''What about the old saying, Captain? Keep your friends close and your enemies closer.''

''I'm not altogether sure we're enemies, Morgan. Still, you raise a valid point. I will keep you here, where I can keep an eye on you.''

''That's not what I meant.''

''Yes, I know, but it's what we're going to do anyway.'' He nodded to Shelby. ''You have your orders.''

The named away team headed for the turbolift and, as they left, Morgan calmly walked to Shelby's chair and, with utter confidence, sat in it. Calhoun eyed her coolly. ''I did not say you could sit there,'' he said.

They stared at each other for a moment.

''Would you care to sit there?'' he asked.

''I'd be honored. Thank you for the consideration.''

''You're welcome,'' he replied as he returned to his command chair. And he was unable to help but notice how completely comfortable Morgan looked in the position of second in command.

Burgoyne had never felt quite as frustrated as s/he did at that particular moment.

S/he had been going over file after file, experimenting with dozens of scenarios using the computer to plot out the likely outcome of each one. And not only was s/he unable to find any direct reference to having such a creature firmly ensconced in one's warp core, but every single plan s/he designed for the purpose of getting the damn thing out of the engine ended in there being a likelihood that the ship would wind up being destroyed. It wasn't a consistent likelihood. Sometimes it was as high as ninety-nine percent, but other times it was as low as eighty-three percent. Somehow, though, s/he didn't think that even the low-end odds were going to go over too well.

S/he looked at the warp core and could see the thing pulsing slowly within the clear tube of the core. In what could only be termed a desperate measure, s/he stared at it with a very, very angry glare in hope that Sparky would sense the overt hostility and flee in terror.

Sparky did not appear to notice.

''Burgoyne.''

Selar walked up to hir, looking as efficient and removed as ever. "Doctor," Burgoyne said neutrally.

"I thought you might wish to know. I have taken several tests and I am most definitely pregnant. I felt it was not wise to rely solely on my inner instinct for such matters."

"Well, that's . . . that's great, Selar. I'm very happy for you."

"I am . . ." She took a deep breath as if plunging into something. "I am . . . happy for us."

It took a moment for the comment to sink in on Burgoyne, since s/he was still rather distracted by Sparky. But slowly it penetrated, and Burgoyne turned and looked at her with clear surprise on hir face. "I'm not sure which I find more surprising, to be honest," noted Burgoyne. "The part about being happy, or the part about us. I was unaware that there was an 'us.' "

"Do you find that thought attractive? Or do you wish to avoid the prospect of an 'us'?"

"I know that you're not interested in an 'us,' " Burgoyne said, sounding rather defensive.

Selar drew herself up. "Do not presume to speak for me, Burgoyne. You do not even know your own mind. Do not think you know mine."

"Know your mind!" Burgoyne said. "I can't even *find* your mind!"

"Oh, now you insult me. How very typical. How very emotional. I should have expected as much."

"Yes!" said Burgoyne, more loudly than s/he would have liked. When s/he realized that others were taking notice of the increasingly loud discussion, s/he started to pull Selar in the direction of hir office while saying in a low tone, "Yes, you should have expected it, because the rest of the galaxy is populated by people who laugh and cry and get really really angry, unlike Vulcans, who think they have a complete handle on emotions simply because they never use them! I—"

Selar had stopped. She was no longer following him. Instead her legs had become practically anchored to the floor and when Burgoyne tried to pull her along, s/he was completely unsuccessful. "Selar?" s/he said in confusion. "Selar, what're you—"

Selar wasn't hearing hir. Instead all of her attention was focused on the warp core. And inside the clear tubing, the energy being—whatever the hell it was—began to stir.

Slowly, one step at a time, Selar began to approach the warp core.

"Where do you think you're going?" demanded Burgoyne. Selar didn't respond. Instead she continued toward the core, as if hypnotically pulled. Suddenly Burgoyne began to feel extremely apprehensive for her. "Selar! Listen to me! Back away from that thing, right n—"

S/he grabbed Selar's arm, and Selar stiffened it and shoved hir back. Burgoyne was strong and agile, there was no denying it, but the abruptness and strength of Selar's gesture caught hir completely off guard. Burgoyne hurtled backward, slamming up against a wall array and sagging to the floor, stunned.

And Selar moved unceasingly toward the warp core, beginning to stretch out her hands as she did so.

The first thing that Shelby heard was singing.

The moment that the sound of the transporter beams faded, the lyrical singing floated through the air. It seemed an aimless tune; whoever was singing it appeared to be making it up as they went. Shelby looked around to see that Si Cwan, Kebron, and Soleta heard it as well.

There was a steady breeze blowing that was carrying the singing to them, and it appeared to be just up ahead. They had materialized on a pathway that led up the side of a small mountain, which gave Soleta a bit of stomach cramps considering that she had more than had her fill of mountains recently. But there was no helping it.

"What is that?" asked Shelby.

Soleta listened a moment more and then said, "Off-key."

"Thank you for your opinion, Lieutenant." She gestured for the others to follow and they slowly made their way up the moutainside.

As they got nearer, however, the aimless song—which had seemed lighthearted at first, almost playful—became darker-sounding. The singer went to a voice that sounded more base and—if Shelby were to judge—more ominous.

They came around a curve in the path and suddenly the music stopped. And so did they.

They weren't quite certain that what they were seeing was real: a woman, so skinny that she seemed, more than anything, like a skeleton wearing a skin suit. She might have been someone released from a labor camp, or who had been tortured for a year behind enemy lines before being returned to her loved ones. She appeared to be human, or at least she had been. Her eyes were sunken, her hair somewhat stringy and unkempt. Her clothes, what there were of them, were in tatters.

And she was wrapped around something that looked rather daunting, her arms and legs clutching it as a drowning woman would a life preserver.

If Shelby had to guess, she would have said it was a weapon of some kind. It was hard to tell, however. It was cylindrical with what could very easily be a muzzle at one end. It appeared to be at least two yards high, and a foot in diameter.

"Is that . . . a weapon?" Si Cwan asked softly.

"If so, it is a big one," replied Shelby.

The weapon pointed straight up. The woman had stopped singing altogether, but she didn't seem to be completely aware that the away team was approaching her. "Hello," Shelby said in as quiet a voice as she could, for something in the air around her made her feel as if a hushed tone was required. Although she was armed, she made sure to keep her hands clear of her phaser. She didn't want to give the impression that she was hostile. Putting aside that she had no desire to frighten the woman, if that thing was indeed a weapon and the woman suddenly aimed it at her and fired, there would be nothing left of Shelby's upper body with the possible exception of a few fond memories. "I'm Commander Shelby, *U.S.S. Excalibur.* This is Lieutenant Soleta, Lieutenant Kebron, and Ambassador Si Cwan."

Si Cwan bowed slightly. "You're looking fit, madam."

Kebron looked at him incredulously. Si Cwan shrugged at him in a sort of *What did you expect me to say?* manner.

"Would you like to tell us your name?" Shelby said.

The woman said nothing. She merely rocked back and forth, ever so slowly, and she looked into midair and appeared to see nothing.

"Would you . . ." Shelby took a few more tentative steps forward, and didn't seem to get any particular reaction out of her. "Would you like to tell us where everyone else went? In case you didn't notice, this planet is fairly deserted. Was it deserted when you came here?"

And she spoke.

It was a frightening voice, a voice that sounded like the lid to a coffin slowly creaking open. It was difficult to determine just exactly how old or young the woman was, but her voice sounded like the voice of one who had been dead for centuries.

"They wanted to take away my lover," she told them.

"Oh," Shelby said sympathetically. "That's . . . that's too bad. Who would 'they' be?"

"Them." She started to hum once more in that odd tone of hers. "All of them. But my lover, it's strong. It protects me. It protects us."

"May I ask who precisely it protected you from, ma'am?" Soleta inquired. "There doesn't seem to be anyone around."

For the first time, the woman seemed to focus on them. She looked at Soleta and there was something approaching demented amusement in her face.

"Not anymore," she said.

They looked at each other, and it was Si Cwan who said, with as much control as he could muster, "Are you saying that . . . your lover . . . got rid of all the people who wanted to separate the two of you?"

"It protects me. That's why it's a good lover."

"Listen," Si Cwan said. "Madam, you know, this would be easier if we knew your name."

"Should I tell them my name?" She was whispering to the large cylinder, talking to it as if it were a close friend. "Should I—yes. Yes, you're right, of course. It doesn't matter." She looked at them and said, "I am Tarella."

Immediately the name was familiar to Shelby. That was the name of the friend who had accompanied Morgan on her search for the Prometheans.

"Tarella," said Si Cwan. "Tarella, we have a very complicated situation here. But I am certain that we can work it out in such a manner that—" Then he paused. "Why do you say it doesn't matter if we know what your name is?"

"Because," said Tarella, "we're going to kill you now."

"You had to ask," muttered Kebron.

And he unslung his rifle.

Zak Kebron wasn't a big fan of phasers. He generally preferred to rely on his own strength and bulk. However, the captain had ordered that they go armed, and he had obeyed the captain's instructions. Normal-sized phasers, however, were even more problematic for him than they were for the large and hairy hands of Ensign Janos. He could operate a normal phaser, but it wasn't easy for him. So when he went on away missions, he generally preferred to carry a Type III phaser rifle. It was slung across his back and looked fairly impressive hanging there.

Now the phaser was in his hands, leveled at Tarella, and he

thumbed it to a high setting as he warned her, "Do not move or take any threatening physical action."

"You want to take my lover," Tarella said, her voice rising. "You want to take it away. But I won't let you. It's mine. I won't let you take it away."

"Tarella," Shelby said urgently, "there's someone back on our ship that you should really see. It's your friend, Morgan."

The name seemed to have an effect on her. Her body trembled slightly and she clutched the weapon more tightly than before. And from her cracked and dry lips hissed out the words, "Morgan is dead. Don't you say her name."

"But—"

"Don't you say her name!!!"

And the weapon erupted.

"Down!" shouted Kebron, knocking the others back with a wave of his huge arm as he fired off a shot from his phaser rifle. The blast from the phaser rifle struck the energy ball disgorged by the weapon, by the lover, and it roared forward but off its intended flight path, deflected ever so slightly by Kebron's phaser blast.

The energy ball roared through the air. It missed them—but just barely—barreled through a clearing, and struck a mountain range.

And destroyed it.

The mountain range exploded on contact. The main brunt of the hit caused the range to be reduced instantly to ashes, but the rest of it erupted skyward, showering the entire area with pulverized debris. It rained down everywhere, including upon the stunned away team who had taken up refuge some feet away behind a wall of rock. Seeing, a half mile away, the complete demolition of a mountain range with one shot of the weapon that Tarella was clutching was enough to make the away team realize that their temporary shelter was going to shelter them from precisely nothing.

Shelby hit her commbadge so hard she wound up leaving a bruise on her chest. "Away team to transporter room! Get us the hell out of here!"

Then they heard Tarella howl, "I don't want you! I don't want Morgan! And I don't want your ship!" And with that pronouncement, she unleashed the power of the weapon straight up.

The shields came on automatically before Boyajian at tactical realized that they were under attack. The computer also sent the *Ex-*

calibur into immediate red alert. ''Captain, incoming!'' shouted Boyajian. ''Some sort of energy plasma! Readings off the scale!''

''McHenry, evasive maneu—'' was all that Calhoun was able to get out as the energy ball smashed into the *Excalibur.* For all the good that the shields did, the ship might as well have been protected by plastic wrap. The energy ball slammed amidships into the vessel, and anyone standing throughout the entire ship was thrown to the ground.

Calhoun had been standing and moving toward the command chair when the ball hit. He was sent flying, crashing into Morgan and tumbling to the ground. Morgan clutched the armrests of her chair desperately and managed to maintain her place, but the impact of the ball was the least of the problems.

McHenry's station nearly exploded as a concussive buildup blasted him back and out of his seat. McHenry smashed his head against the upper rampway and went limp, blood trickling from his mouth. The conn station was in complete disarray, flames starting to shoot out. Overhead extinguishing systems were out of commission, and Morgan desperately grabbed an emergency hand extinguisher in a wall compartment, staggering across the bridge to get to the conn and put the flames out.

The bridge filled with smoke. She tried to make out her daughter and saw that she was slumped forward at the Ops station, a huge swelling already appearing on her temple. She was barely conscious and trying to pull herself together. ''All stations, report!'' she managed to get out. ''This is Ops, report status, all stations!''

The ship lurched, and Morgan managed to snag on to a chair and prevent herself from tumbling over. But then she saw the viewscreen, saw the planet lurching toward them . . . No. No, they were spiraling down toward the planet.

Morgan dropped into place at the conn station, tossing aside the extinguisher, and looked at the distressed readouts. If she was at all thrown by the calamitous nature of what she was facing, she gave no hint of it. As if she'd been doing it all her life, she began rerouting controls, trying to restore helm control so that she could pull the ship out of her dive . . . before it was too late.

Burgoyne, for all hir cat-like reflexes, was nonetheless knocked off hir feet as the ship was hit hard.

And Selar stumbled forward and struck squarely the exterior of the warp core.

And deep within the warp core, the entity residing in there—whatever it was—seemed to move down toward Selar. She clutched the warp core tube as it coalesced within around the area that she was touching.

Burgoyne scrambled to hir feet, stumbled over toward Selar, and tried to pull her away. To hir surprise, s/he had absolutely no success at all. It was as if Selar were suction-cupped to the warp core and under no circumstance was she about to let go.

Her eyes were glazed, and her lips seemed to be trying to form a word, or words, but Burgoyne couldn't make any of them out. All s/he knew was that somehow, in some way, Selar was in direct connection with whatever the hell it was in the warp core. Since Burgoyne didn't know precisely what was going on, s/he wasn't sure if it was safe to try and pull her away.

On the other side of the bridge, Calhoun could barely hear himself over the screech of the red alert bell as well as the sounds of exploding equipment all around the bridge. *This is going to take forever to fix,* he thought bleakly, and then he saw that they were heading for a crash landing. He looked toward the conn . . . and was astounded to see Morgan at the controls. He staggered across the bridge, fighting the rolling motion of the floor beneath him, as he shouted, "What are you doing?!"

She looked at him with a cold, fixed, and utterly calm gaze. "Saving your ass," she informed him, her fingers flying over the controls.

And the *Excalibur* suddenly pulled out of her dive before she fully entered the atmosphere, avoiding any further strain on the shields due to reentry.

"Helm restored," called Morgan as the ship arced upward and away from the looming planet surface. The ship moved slowly back into orbit, having barely withstood the assault and not knowing if another was forthcoming.

"Shield status!"

Lefler was rubbing her forehead, trying to see straight. "Shields at eighty percent and holding, sir. Structural integrity is holding; most of what we experienced was purely impact."

"Meaning that if we didn't have shields at all, we'd have been smashed to bits."

"Yes sir. Captain, transporter room reports a call from the away team to be beamed aboard just before the attack."

"We can't bring them up with our shields up, and we don't dare lower shields. Comm system?"

"Just back on line, sir."

"Calhoun to away team." He brushed some debris from his uniform as he helped McHenry to his feet. McHenry clearly looked confused and there were burn marks on his uniform shirt. Chances were that there were burns on his chest to match. For a long moment, Calhoun was convinced that he wasn't going to hear a word from the planet surface.

But then Shelby's rattled voice came back. "Away team, Shelby here."

"Commander! What's going on down there? Our readings didn't indicate any sort of massive weapons array, but somebody shot at us and damn near took us out!"

"It's a woman, sir. A woman with a gun."

Everyone on the bridge, sitting up bruised and battered and trying to staunch bleeding wherever they could, exchanged looks of utter incredulity. "Did you say *a* woman with *a* gun?"

"That would be correct, sir."

Robin Lefler had seen the captain in a variety of moods and reactions. But she couldn't recall having seen him looking quite as stunned as he did at that moment. "How could one woman with a gun almost knock us out of orbit?!"

There was a pause and then, apparently, because she couldn't think of any other way to explain it, she said, "It's a really big gun, sir."

Calhoun didn't know what to say to that aside from, "Oh." McHenry, for his part, was looking in puzzlement at Morgan, who was at his station. Morgan quickly rose and eased him into his seat.

"Furthermore," Shelby said, "it appears to be in the possession of the woman whom Morgan described as her former associate."

"Tarella?" Morgan called over the comm system.

"That's right."

"Captain," Morgan turned to him, "please let me go down there. I'm the only one who can possibly get through to her."

Calhoun did not like the odds of the situation, but he didn't see a lot of choices. "All right. We're going to have to risk this. Mr. McHenry, bring us back to maximum transporter range. Let's try and put as much distance between ourselves and that . . . big gun . . . as possible. Morgan, get down to the transporter room. We'll drop our deflectors for just the length of time it takes to beam you down there, and then we'll bring the shields back on line. Shelby, what's your read on the situation? Shall we bring you back up when we send Morgan down?''

''Negative,'' Shelby said after a moment's thought. ''From our vantage point, it seems as if Tarella is just sitting there now. It's almost as if she's forgotten that we're here. She seems to fade in and out of reality.''

''I can relate to that,'' McHenry said.

''Captain,'' Lefler suddenly said. She rose to her feet, slightly unsteady but determined. ''I would like to accompany Ms. Primus to the planet . . . if that's all right.''

Despite the disarray on the bridge, Calhoun managed to force a smile. ''Somehow I had a feeling you were going to say that,'' he said.

14

Morgan and Robin shimmered into existence on the planet surface a few feet from the away team, which was still crouched behind the shelter as if it provided them with any protection at all. Shelby gestured for them to approach, which they did as quietly as they could. She immediately noticed the banged up condition of the newcomers, but there was no time to discuss it. "I was so worried she'd open fire on the ship while you were coming down," she whispered.

"Do we have a plan, Commander?" asked Robin.

"Yes. It's called 'not getting killed.' "

"Good plan," said Si Cwan. "Is there anything beyond that?"

Slowly Shelby turned in her crouch to face Morgan. An eternity of time seemed to pass between them. "You really think you can get through to her?" she asked.

Morgan weighed all the possibilities, all the unknowns, and finally admitted, "I don't know. Not for sure, I don't know. At least I can distract her."

"Good. An honest answer. What did you do up there that caused the captain to trust you down here?"

"I saved the ship," Morgan said evenly.

Shelby turned and looked at Robin, who nodded confirmation. "All right, Morgan. Take it slow, take it careful . . . and take it over there," she said, pointing several feet to the right.

As Shelby had indicated she should, she stepped several feet to the right. She took a deep breath that seemed, for a moment, to be a bit unsteady, and Robin realized that her mother was—at the very least—apprehensive. Looking back over her life, she came to the realization that she had never, ever, seen her mother in any way other than completely composed and confident.

But why? If her mother was truly immortal, as she claimed, what was she so nervous about? Then Morgan cast a glance to her, gave her a quick "thumbs up," and Robin realized why she was reacting that way. Morgan was anxious about Robin's safety. She wasn't concerned about getting out of this herself. She was worried that Robin wouldn't make it.

Robin returned the gesture, and then Morgan slowly pushed herself out into the open.

Very, very tentatively, Morgan approached the woman that she had known, in happier times, as Tarella. It was all she could do to suppress the shock of what she was seeing. Tarella was humming softly to herself in a very sing-song manner, an idle and aimless tune. "Tarella?" Morgan softly called her name.

"What did you say, lover?" Tarella wasn't looking at her at all. Her thoughts seemed to be otherwise occupied, and considering the way she seemed to be moving her body up and down against the weapon that she was clutching to her bosom, it was not hard to guess exactly whom she was addressing.

"Tarella, it's me. It's Morgan. Remember? I'm . . . I'm out. I'm back. I'm here to finish what we started." She waved her hand to try and get Tarella's attention. "Tarella, that is a . . . a very impressive piece of hardware you have there. Want to tell me where you got it?"

Tarella seemed to focus on her, but her eyes were dark and fearsome things, and she held the weapon even tighter. "Morgan."

"Yes. Morgan."

"You're dead." She paused and seemed to be readjusting her position slightly. "My lover," she continued, "says we should kill you."

"If I'm dead, then you can't kill me," Morgan pointed out. "Why waste your lover's bounty on a ghost?"

It was a long shot at best, and not for one moment did Morgan expect her to go for it. To her surprise, though, Tarella seemed to be considering the notion very carefully. "I hadn't thought of that," she said, every other word going up in pitch, making her sound like a small child, or an adult cooing to one.

All the while, Morgan was drawing closer and closer to Tarella, one very careful step at a time. "Tarella," she said as unflappably as if they were at a cocktail party together, "would you mind introducing me to your lover? Does he . . . it . . . have a name?"

"No name. We don't need names, no we don't, do we?" and she stroked the weapon affectionately. And then in that same bizarre singsong voice, she said with an undercurrent of danger, "You're going to try and take my lover away from me, aren't you? That's what my lover is telling me. My lover wants to kill you, right here, right now. But I'm holding it back. Me. I'm doing that. Because I miss talking to my old friend, Morgan, even if it's just a ghost of Morgan. That makes my lover jealous. But that's okay, isn't it? It's okay to make your lover jealous every so often. Helps the relationship to stay fresh."

"I've always thought so," Morgan agreed. She almost stepped on a place where the footing wasn't as sure, and she very delicately moved her foot around it so that she would be on more solid ground. She had no desire to slip and possibly startle Tarella out of whatever psychosis-induced stupor she had fallen into.

It was difficult for her to believe that this was the same woman who had been her best friend and partner. An adventurer, a person full of joy and life. Virtually unrecognizable now, drained dry of life and love and spirit by a sick relationship with an engine of destruction that had aspirations to sentience.

It took all that she had to keep the revulsion from her voice as she asked, "Where did you meet your lover? How did you two get together?"

"The Prometheans were here," she said. "You remember them, right? They were here, just like we thought they'd be. It was as if . . . as if they were waiting for us. For me."

"That sounds like them, all right," agreed Morgan. "Master chess players, master manipulators. It was probably like a Möbius strip. They knew we were searching for them, and arranged for us to find them. Our quest created the quarry."

"That's very clever, Morgan. You always were oh-so-very clever. But not clever enough to get off Momidium, were you?"

"No. No, I wasn't."

"I waited for you. Do you have any idea how long I waited for you?" Her voice was starting to rise, her hands trembling, and Morgan was becoming increasingly concerned that she was about to fire. "Do you have any idea how long?! I've been here for three hundred years!!"

Morgan stared at her, shaking her head. ‘‘Tarella, it’s only been five. Five years. Not three hundred. Five.’’

And this announcement seemed to surprise Tarella greatly. She ran her fingers through her stringy hair and said in quiet wonderment, ‘‘Only five? Are you sure?’’

‘‘Yes.’’

‘‘My God . . . it . . . it seemed so much longer.’’

Her thoughts were starting to drift, and Morgan knew it was important to control the direction in which they went. ‘‘Tarella, your lover. You didn’t tell me . . . how did—’’

‘‘The Prometheans gave my lover to me,’’ she said. She laughed at the recollection. ‘‘They thought it was just a weapon. Silly Prometheans. A weapon that responds instantly to the thoughts of its lover. Whatever I want, it wants. And whatever it wants, I want. We are one. We are together. We are . . .’’ For just a moment, her mind seemed to flutter, and as if pulling straws from the past, she said, ‘‘The Prometheans said they wanted the Ahmistans to have it. So they could better defend themselves against possible enemies. They gave it to me . . . to give to the Ahmistans. But I realized that it was a mistake. That the Ahmistans couldn’t possibly handle it. They weren’t ready for this kind of technology. They weren’t right for it. And they didn’t love it. That’s the most important thing.’’ Tears were starting to roll down her face, her voice choking. ‘‘I knew that I was the only one who could take care of it, who *should* take care of it. The Ahmistans, they came for it. They wanted my lover. They wanted to take my lover away. I couldn’t let them do it. I had to stop them. You see that, don’t you, Morgan?’’

‘‘Of course,’’ Morgan said firmly, even as her soul recoiled at what she was hearing. ‘‘If I were in your position, I’d have done the exact same thing. It had to be that way. You did the right thing.’’

She was close now to Tarella, so close that she felt as if she could reach out and touch her.

‘‘And my lover wanted to stay with me as well. I was protecting it. I didn’t want anyone getting near it. My lover didn’t want it either. But you . . . you can stay, Morgan. It upsets my lover, but you can stay. Because you’re my friend.’’

‘‘Yes. Yes, I am. We closed out bars together, and made plans together. Did everything together. You’re Tarella Lee; you know that, don’t you? Your favorite color is blue, your favorite season on Earth is winter.’’ She was speaking faster and faster, trying to find the woman within this husk of a being. ‘‘You like white wine, but not red. You dress mostly in black. When you laugh, it's not a dainty laugh, but a big horsey bellow from your diaphragm. You remember all that, don't you?"

"I remember Tarella Lee," she said with what sounded like wonderment. "Amazing. I haven't thought of her in so long . . ."

"You look so tired, Tarella. You do."

"I am." Her body sagged against the weapon. It seemed as if it was everything she could do to stay conscious. As if all the strain that she had been through, for who knew how long, was catching up with her all at once. "I am so tired."

"Tell you what: That looks so heavy. Let me hold it while you take a rest—"

The moment she said it, Morgan wished she could call the words back to her. For the merest mention of it pulled Tarella forcefully and fiercely out of her distracted state. She clutched the weapon with redoubled fury and howled, "You want to take it away! You're just like all the others!"

Knowing that she couldn't clear the distance between herself and Tarella before Tarella fired, Morgan backed up, trying to recapture the moment of trust. "No, Tarella, see? You're wrong. I'm way over here now, and I'm not at all trying to—"

But Tarella wasn't buying it as she howled, "You're trying to take it away!" It was a fearsome howl as if torn from her soul, and she started to bring the weapon around.

And suddenly Robin was out from behind the rocks, shouting, waving her arms and calling out, "No! Don't do it!" Morgan couldn't believe it as Robin interposed herself between Tarella and Morgan, continuing to cry out, "Don't do it!"

Morgan tried furiously to shove her out of the way, but Robin wouldn't go. She clung tightly to her mother as she repeatedly shouted, "Don't do it! You don't want to! Leave her alone! Leave her!"

The shouting and commotion seemed to distract Tarella for a moment as the tormented woman blinked in confusion, trying to comprehend what she was seeing. And there was something . . . something in her eyes, in her face, and for a moment—just a moment—Morgan saw a hint of the woman that she had once known peering at her from within those haunted and sunken eyes.

"Morgan, help me." she whispered.

And it was at that moment that Si Cwan leaped in from the other side. Tarella's attention seemed torn, and by the time she was focused on the assault from the Thallonian, it was too late. He slammed into her from behind, and even though she had been wrapped around the weapon, there was no real strength in her arms or legs. The jolt was enough to send the weapon clattering from her grasp. She started screaming frantically, completely out of control, and she lunged for the weapon, which had fallen to the ground. But Si Cwan scooped her up with one arm, and he couldn't believe how light she was. It was literally as if he were lifting nothing at all.

"Let me go!" she howled. "Let me go! Let me go to my lover, it needs me, it's terrified, can't you feel it? Can't you feel it!?"

Shelby, Kebron, and Soleta were emerging from behind their refuge, and Shelby said briskly, "Kebron, get her secured. Cwan, good work. Morgan, you too."

"Don't touch it! It doesn't want you! It wants me! We are one! We . . . we . . ."

And then, slowly . . . ever so slowly . . . something started to fade from her eyes. Something that she hadn't quite realized was there until it began to dissipate. It was as if a cloud were lifting from her, and in a low and confused voice, she said, "Mor . . . gan . . . ?"

"I'm here, Tarella. I'm right here." Morgan took Tarella's face in her arms, and couldn't believe it. Once Tarella had had the softest skin, but now it felt papery, dehydrated. What in God's name had the thing done to her? "Everything's going to be all right now."

"All the people . . ." Her memories seemed to be flooding back to her. "The people . . . there were people here . . . millions . . . ashes . . . ashes to ashes . . . my God . . . Morgan . . ." She began to quiver. Whether it was from fright, or horror, or self-loathing, Morgan couldn't even begin to tell. "Morgan, what . . . what did I do?"

"You didn't do anything."

Kebron had lifted the weapon carefully, wary of any mind games it might start to play with him. "It seems almost hollow," he said in rare wonderment. "How is that possible?"

Tarella wasn't listening. Not to Kebron, nor to Morgan. Instead she heard something else, something only she could detect. "Do you hear them, Morgan? Do you?"

"I don't hear anything," Morgan said.

"The people . . . the people are screaming. . . . I can hear their voices," and she started to become completely unraveled, the last throes of a slow descent into what would likely be complete and utter insanity. "Hear their voices calling me, begging me to stop, but it won't let me. . . . I don't want it to, good God in heaven, what have

I done, all those people, bodies are ashes, floating on the wind, get it off of me . . .''

Shelby tapped her commbadge. ''*Excalibur,* this is Shelby. Prepare to beam us directly to sickbay, we have—''

And in a voice filled with more pain than she had ever thought she could feel—filled with more pain than Morgan had ever heard in all her lifetime—Tarella Lee howled with all her heart and soul, with ever fiber of her being: ''I WISH I WERE DEAD! I WANT TO DIE!''

The weapon in Kebron's arms responded, one final time, to the impassioned wish of its lover. It almost leaped out of his grip as it belched out a ball of energy plasma that had, only moments before, leveled a mountain range. This ball was smaller, much smaller, but no less devastating. It streaked across the clearing before anyone could make a move . . . not that it would have done any good.

Tarella saw it coming, knew what was about to happen, and she spread wide her arms, threw her head back, and sobbed with the joy of release. ''No!'' screamed Morgan, but it was too late, as the ball struck home and blew Tarella to ashes. There was a burst of heat that left them feeling almost crispened and then, seconds later, the last remains of Tarella were lifted up onto the winds of Ahmista and carried away to join the final remains of all her victims.

Kebron immediately upended the gun and shoved the muzzle down straight into the ground. He sank it in a couple of feet and then nodded approvingly.

There was dead silence as the away team tried to take in what they had just seen, and then Morgan lifted a fist and shouted in fury, ''Damn you! Damn you, you all-seeing bastards! You think it's funny, don't you? You think it's so damn funny! You're laughing at us, I know it! Come down here! Come down here so you can laugh at me in person and I can push your teeth into the back of your head!''

''Mother, calm down!'' Robin urged her. She faced Morgan, hands on either arm, as if she were trying to brace her. ''Calm down, for God's sake!''

''Calm down! Calm down!'' She was trembling with rage, unable to control herself, but she looked into Robin's eyes, saw the concern there, then slowly, very slowly, she managed to pull herself together. She nodded, as much for herself as for Robin's benefit, and then drew her daughter to her and embraced her tightly. ''Okay,'' she said softly. ''Okay, I'm . . . fine now.''

"Commander, take a look at this," came Soleta's voice.

Shelby had just been updating the *Excalibur* as to the status of what was happening on the planet surface. She now said, "Stand by, Captain," and walked over to the fallen weapon, which Soleta was examining closely.

"Look here . . . and here," said Soleta, touching different points on the weapon. Shelby knew at that point that she should have been surprised, but by that point in the state of affairs, virtually nothing was surprising her anymore.

Inset into the side of the weapon was a disk, identical to the one that Morgan had shown them on the ship. And next to the disk were two shallow holes in the metal, each of them looking as if they were designed to accommodate another disk. Soleta tentatively reached into the shallow holes, examining them by touch. "One of these," she said, "has a sunken flame emblem inside it, as if it's designed to fit into the medallion that Morgan possesses. The other," and she felt inside the next one, "is raised. It will most certainly fit mine." And from a pouch in her belt, she removed the disk that she had found on Zondar.

"You brought it with you?"

"It seemed a logical precaution, Commander."

"Captain," Shelby said, tapping her commbadge once more.

"Calhoun here, standing by."

"Captain, there appear to be receptacles for the disks possessed by Soleta and Morgan, inset into the weapon itself. Shall we insert them?"

"Very well. But I'm keeping the transporter on standby. First sign of danger, we beam you right out of there."

"Roger that," said Shelby.

"Commander," rumbled Kebron, "I suggest you allow me to do it—and all of you stand significantly behind me."

"Kebron," began Shelby, but then she realized the wisdom in the suggestion. She turned to Morgan and indicated that she should hand her medallion over to Kebron, which she did . . . albeit with a look of reluctance.

Kebron took the medallion in one hand and Soleta's disk in the other. They both looked tiny in his huge hands as he crouched down next to the weapon. The others hung back as Shelby said, via her commbadge, "Captain, about to insert the disks."

"We're standing by and monitoring for any trace of a power surge that would indicate a trap,'' Calhoun assured her. ''We'll have you out of there within a second of any danger signal.''

''I appreciate the repeated assurances, Captain, but frankly I wish you'd stop because you're starting to make me nervous.''

She could almost see him smiling at that, even though he was in orbit. ''Understood.''

''Preparing for insertion,'' Kebron announced. ''Three . . . two . . . one . . .''

He clicked them into place.

Sixty seconds later, all hell broke loose.

15

The med team, led by Dr. Maxwell, looked helplessly at Selar as she clung to the side of the warp core. "Heart, respiration are all remaining within Vulcan norms," he announced as he ran the medical tricorder over her. "Brain wave functions remain stable. Whatever's happening, it's not hurting her."

"You don't know that for sure," Burgoyne said angrily as s/he pulled once more on Selar's hand. It did no good. It was as if she'd been fused to the exterior of the structure. "This is insane! What if she never comes out of it? What are we supposed to do? Work around her?"

When he saw Burgoyne's look, Maxwell said in frustration, "I don't know what to tell you, Chief! The Vulcan mindmeld is something I've only read about, never seen. I could bring in instruments, hook her up to them, and send electricity jolting through her. That might disrupt the telepathic connection, tear her loose, but I don't know for certain if it would and I sure as hell don't know if we should! We need to get Soleta up here; she's the only other Vulcan on the ship, and maybe she can—"

And suddenly alarms started to go off all over the ship.

"Perfect," grated Burgoyne. "Just perfect."

At first the insertion of the disks had no effect at all. Kebron was braced for something, but nothing appeared to happen. Shelby turned to Morgan questioningly and said, "All right, Morgan, you're supposed to be the expert on these beings. These Prometheans, as you call them. You said if anyone could help us with our situation, they could. So now what are we supposed to—''

And suddenly a soft humming began to sound from the weapon. Then it began to build in intensity, vibrations spreading from it in all directions, becoming fiercer with every passing moment. Shelby felt her teeth rattling, and she had no idea what was happening.

That was when the planet dissolved around her in a sparkle of color. The next thing she knew, she and the rest of the away team were standing on the transporter platform of the *Excalibur.*

At the controls was transporter chief Polly Watson. She breathed a sigh of relief and then said, ''Transporter room to bridge! I have them, Captain, all in one piece.''

Shelby nodded in appreciation at Watson's quick work as she and the rest of the away team descended quickly from the platform and headed up to the bridge as fast as they could.

Boyajian had taken over Soleta's science station while she was on the planet, and when he had called out, ''Captain, energy spike! Something's happening down there!'' Calhoun had not hesitated a nanosecond.

''Transporter room! Get them out of there, now! Boyajian, keep me apprised!''

''Still building, sir. The exact nature of it is hard to tell. I've never seen wave readings like this, but if I had to guess . . .''

''Yes?''

''Sir, I don't think it's going to explode. I don't think it's a destructive force. Best guess is that it's similar to our subspace transmission waves.''

''You mean it's sending out some sort of message?''

''Best guess, yes, sir.''

Calhoun frowned. ''But who are they calling?''

''Captain!''

Calhoun had a sense for danger. Always had. Almost a sort of sixth sense that tipped him off about dangerous situations moments before they occurred. This time, however, there was no chance at all, for even as he suddenly felt that buzz of alarm, it was too late.

Space was beginning to distort all around them, the stars seeming to stretch as if the ship were suddenly kicking into warp speed . . . except the *Excalibur* hadn't budged from its orbit. A massive corona of roaring power was surrounding them, kilometers off in all directions but completely enveloping them like a gargantuan container. It was every color in the visible spectrum, flaring all around them. It was as if someone had plunged them into an ocean of blue, orange, yellow, every color imaginable.

"McHenry, get us out of here!"

McHenry scanned the area, looking for a path, a course to set, but he shook his head in frustration. "There's nowhere *to* go, sir! It's all around us! It's like we're trapped in the middle of a warp bubble! But its readings are totally different; it's like an alternate version of hyperspace, something that's sideways of us, different physical properties altogether."

"Shields up! Red alert!" Even as the klaxon blared, Calhoun moved quickly to McHenry, leaning over the instrumentation as he said, "What if we pick a direction and simply try to ram our way through?"

"Wouldn't do it, sir. Beyond the fact that it's warping space, I'm not getting any sort of a read on it at all. It could tear us to bits the second we come in contact."

The turbolift opened behind him and the erstwhile away team quickly assumed their positions on the bridge. Shelby stepped in next to Calhoun, who said, "Good to have you back. Any thoughts?"

"We're in trouble," she said tightly.

"On the same wavelength as always, Commander. McHenry, I'm not going to have us sit here and wait for the trap to snap completely. Set course one-five-eight mark four, all ahead full. Shields on maximum."

And McHenry was about to do it when suddenly it all became moot.

"Captain!" called Soleta from her station. "Whatever it is . . . it's dropping out of warp!"

"Where?"

"*Every*where!"

She was right. A vessel unlike any that they had ever known was materializing all around them, shimmering into existence out of the inadvertently named "sideways" of space. It did not seem to have any solid sides, no interior or exterior as was understood by the human mind. The ship was huge beyond their ability even to measure it, much less describe it, with shimmering waves of unearthly power radiating in all directions. It was as if a Dyson sphere were materializing around them, but one made of pure force.

This, then, was a Promethean ship.

Its very existence threatened to blast the *Excalibur* out of existence.

Everywhere there were energy waves pounding on them from all directions. There was nowhere for the ship to go, no defense that it could mount. Calhoun had never been so frustrated in all his life. There was no enemy to shoot at, no target to train his phasers on. It was as if space itself had come alive and was attacking them. The *Excalibur* shuddered under the pressure of a universe gone mad.

Never before had anyone seen anything like it. Usually in battle, if a missile struck one of the shields, there was a brief flare of energy as the shield absorbed the impact. Not this time. No, the shields were completely lit up along the entire length and width of the ship, wave upon wave of energy rolling over them, giving off light of such intensity that it was almost blinding. The shields were never designed to deal with that sort of punishment, and the energy levels of the shields dropped faster than Lefler was able to call them out. Within seconds there would be no shields in place at all, and the *Excalibur* would be pulverized, ground into bits only moments thereafter.

And there was nothing, absolutely nothing that Calhoun could do about it.

Selar had lost track of time.

She felt as if she had been floating forever, somewhere in a state of infinite comfort and bliss. She was no longer aware of her surroundings. Instead she felt a warmth, a peace such as she had never truly experienced before and—she suspected—would never know again.

There was something just beyond her, something that seemed in touch with a universe that had once seemed unknowable, mysterious, and even just a little bit frightening. But she was reaching out to it now, as it—in its slowly developing intelligence and sophistication—was reaching out to her.

She was unaware of her own physical presence against the warp core, oblivious to the concern of Burgoyne and the others. All she knew was it, was the beautiful entity that she was seeking out . . .

And then she sensed alarm.

It was too overwhelming for her not to notice. The shouts, the alarms, the fear that radiated throughout the ship, the terror of not knowing what was going to happen, the belief that this was, somehow, *it:* All of it began to pour into her consciousness.

She touched the mind, the spirit, of the entity, reaching to it as it had called to her, and she needed to find a concept that it would understand. And she sought out one of the oldest, simplest, most primal urges that any living being had: the instinct of self-preservation.

''Protect yourself,'' she whispered as her mind reached out and repeated, *Protect yourself . . . you must . . . protect yourself. . . .*

And that was when Sparky fought back.

''Complete loss of shields,'' called Lefler, ''in three . . . two . . . one—''

At that precise moment the trembling stopped.

Calhoun looked around, confused, as did Shelby. ''Ops, did we lose shields or not?''

''Shields are gone, Captain, but there's—'' She turned and looked at Calhoun in total confusion. ''There's something else. Some sort of . . . of energy barrier that just came into existence around us.''

And then Calhoun saw it. Something was indeed surrounding the *Excalibur,* acting as a barricade against the assault that they had been receiving at the hands of the utterly alien Promethean vessel. For a moment, just the briefest of moments, it reminded Calhoun of the great flame bird that they had encountered during the destruction of Thallon, but this didn't seem to have any shape to it. It was simply a massive shield of fire-like power that had surrounded the ship and was staving off any further assault on the vessel.

''Captain,'' Soleta said. ''I'm getting wave readings off the energy force that has surrounded us. They are identical to the wave readings generated by the creature currently housed in the warp core.''

''You mean that . . . *thing* in Engineering is protecting us?'' asked Shelby.

''That is correct, yes, sir. And it appears to be holding . . . with very little problem, sir.''

''Bridge to Engineering,'' Calhoun called.

''Engineering, Burgoyne here.''

''Burgy! Did you find some way to harness the power of that thing you call Sparky? Because right now it's the only thing between us and annihilation.''

''No, sir, it's not me. It's Selar. And we could use Soleta down here, because she's the only one who's got a shot at—''

The rest of what Burgoyne was saying was abruptly overwhelmed by a massive rush of noise. It was almost deafening, staggering everyone on the bridge, like a roar of millions of voices all at once in perfect unison.

Although Calhoun sensed it, Morgan was the first to spot it. A wave of energy beginning to coalesce on the bridge itself, taking shape before their very eyes. It was so intense that it almost demanded that Morgan look away, but she did not. For she sensed what it was she was about to see.

For years—for well over a century—she had sought the Prometheans, for her own purposes. In her time, she had witnessed many strange things, encountered many amazing races. She had seen beings of almost god-like ability. She had encountered races of almost pure thought, races who were infinitely grotesque, races who were so beautiful that to look at them moved one to tears. And in all that time, she had tried to imagine what the Prometheans would look like. These most unknowable, most all-knowing of beings; how would they appear? Would they be great, satanic beings with huge, bat-like wings and evil visages? Monstrous, dark and black, spider-like creatures? Would they be angelic, beings of pure light, with expressions of endless peace and serenity on their faces? No matter how much she tried to envision them, she always suspected that whatever she pictured would be wrong. That the Prometheans would be nothing like what she anticipated.

And as the Prometheans materialized aboard the bridge of the *Excalibur,* as Morgan Primus's long quest finally came to its climax and conclusion, she couldn't help but think of just how right she had been. No matter what it was that she had been expecting . . .

It sure as hell hadn't been this.

16

Hi. How y'all doing. Glad to be here. Really am.''

The Promethean was nearly six feet and looked completely human, a man in his late thirties, early forties at most. He was dressed in a fairly tight suit of purest white, much like a southern sheriff from the 1930s. His stomach was taut and flat, his jaw was squared off, and he had a thick head of blond hair.

He took a step down from where he was standing, smiled at Lefler and touched her cheek. ''Hi, little darlin'. You doin' okay?'' To Calhoun he said, ''My pardon if my accent is a little off. I haven't been to Earth in several hundred years.''

''I'm . . . fine, thank you,'' a stunned Lefler said. For no reason that she could discern, she felt an almost primal urge to scream in ecstasy and faint.

The Promethean nodded in approval, then clapped his hands together and rubbed them briskly. ''So, who's the captain of this fine vessel?'' he asked.

Calhoun eyed the newcomer warily. ''I'm Captain Mackenzie Calhoun, in command of the *U.S.S. Excalibur.*''

''Fine ship you got here, Mac. Can I call you Mac?''

''Under the circumstances, I think I'd prefer 'Captain,' if you don't mind. Particularly considering that this . . . this vessel of yours''—and he indicated the gargantuan sphere of power that still encompassed them—''damn near destroyed this fine ship.''

''We wouldn't have let that happen,'' the Promethean said confidently. ''Just wanted to see how much your ship could take. And who's this?'' he asked, facing Shelby.

''Commander Shelby, my first officer.''

He took her hand and gently kissed the knuckles. ''Charmed, ma'am.''

''You're . . . the Prometheans?'' she asked.

He smiled dazzlingly. ''If that's what you want to call us, that's happily a name we'll answer to, ma'am. Yes. We're the Prometheans.''

''I appreciate that,'' Shelby said in mild confusion. ''It's a . . . a pleasure to meet you.''

''Thank you,'' he said suavely.

''You're a Promethean?'' Calhoun asked.

''That's us,'' he said, slapping his chest confidently. ''I am them, they are me. We have a sort of all-for-one thing going, know what I mean?''

''May I ask a question?'' inquired Shelby.

''Ask me anything you want, ma'am,'' the Promethean said, his hands spread wide.

''How could you, an advanced race, possibly have made your technology readily available to people who clearly weren't ready for it?''

''We're the Prometheans, darlin'. We are the bringers of knowledge.''

''Your bringing of knowledge destroyed an entire race!''

He raised a scolding finger. ''We bring gifts, that's all. What people do with 'em . . . that's their business.''

He sauntered through the bridge as he spoke, occasionally shaking hands with crewmembers, patting them on the back. It was as if he was working the room. ''We go to various worlds, pick likely subjects, and introduce certain knowledge to the world—whether they're ready for it or not. Sometimes it works out. Sometimes it don't. (Pleased to meet you.) Ultimately, it's up to the people and races we choose. And we lay down puzzles and rewards for some really lucky folks. (Hi, how you doin'?) That's how we wound up here, now. We scattered some of our connector disks throughout this sector of space. Kept waiting for someone to bring 'em together and find where they go. (You havin' a good time? That's nice.) Only took a few hundred years. You folks are improving. Y'really are. We're proud of you. Really proud.''

''But that's irresponsible!'' protested Calhoun. ''If you're truly an advanced race, you would know that! Going around, doing whatever you want, without regard for the rightness or wrongness of your actions in terms of how they impact on others. You need to understand boundaries, to be aware of the result of the things that you do. You can't just interfere whenever you want. You can't . . .''

''Do what *you* do?'' asked the Promethean.

Calhoun hesitated, looking to Shelby. She shrugged. Clearly the same thing had been going through her mind. Calhoun turned back to the Promethean and said tersely, ''It's not the same thing.''

''It never is, Cap'n,'' said the Promethean. ''It never is.''

He had nearly completed his circuit of the bridge, and then he stopped as he got to Morgan. He stared at her for a long moment, scratching his sideburns thoughtfully. ''Do I know you, ma'am?''

She said nothing. Merely regarded him with amusement, her arms folded.

He snapped his fingers as if in recollection. ''Alabama. Nineteen thirty-four. Am I right?''

''Maybe,'' said Morgan, ''but unlike you, I've moved on since then.''

He pointed to Morgan but addressed Calhoun as he said, ''This is a very special lady. She's been looking for us for a long time now. You take good care of her now, hear?''

And suddenly the *Excalibur* was jolted. Then it began to shudder ever so slightly, and it seemed as if they could almost hear the sound of metal being strained.

The Promethean turned to face Calhoun, and he had a wide smile on his face. His teeth were remarkably white. ''So let's see if I understand you a'right, Cap'n. You're saying that we should not interfere. That we shouldn't help others with our advanced abilities. Well, you got a creature down there that could bust your ship here to pieces, and is about to, because he's in the process of getting hisself born. Now I could remove him from your ship, no sweat. Just another example of the Prometheans taking care of business. Or maybe I should just let him burst out, smash your engines to pieces, blow up your whole ship. Kill everyone on board. All in the interest of non-interference, y'understand. Is that what you're saying I should do?''

''No,'' Calhoun said tightly. ''That's not what I'm saying.''

''Then I want you to ask me for my help. No, better,'' and he grinned widely. There suddenly seemed something very dark and frightening hidden behind the ''aw-shucks'' attitude he displayed. ''Beg me . . . just like the captain of the *Grissom* begged you.''

There was dead silence on the bridge.

And then Calhoun said, ''Soleta, come with me.'' He pivoted on his heel and headed for the turbolift, Soleta obediently following behind, leaving the Promethean looking rather surprised at the rest of the bridge.

"Now don't that beat all," he said.

Burgoyne looked up as Calhoun and Soleta approached Selar, who was exactly the same way that she had been earlier. "Captain," s/he said formally, "Energy readings are building to an uncontrollable level. I think it may be time to abandon ship."

"Not yet. Soleta, do you think you can get through to her?"

Soleta studied Selar as if she were looking over a statue. "I believe so, yes."

"Is she in communication with the creature?"

"That would be my best guess, yes."

"Put me in communication with it," Calhoun said.

Soleta looked back at Calhoun and there was no hiding the clear surprise on her face. "Captain?" She was obviously not certain she had understood him properly.

"The two of you, working together . . . let me talk to it."

"We've never done anything like that, sir," Soleta said worriedly.

"Well, we're going to do it now."

Soleta looked from Calhoun back to Selar, clearly trying to figure out exactly how to proceed. Then, with grim determination, she said, "All right. Here, then." She pulled Calhoun over to her. "Clear your mind," she told him.

Calhoun did so. He washed away any thoughts of the imminent danger, any concern over what was about to happen. He allowed himself to descend into a place of calm and serenity, where nothing and no one could hurt him.

Soleta was somewhat impressed by Calhoun's powers of concentration and his mental control. *This might just work after all,* she thought to herself as she placed her fingers against his forehead. As she did this, she put her other hand against Selar's forehead. She let go of herself, of her consciousness and identity, and she whispered, "Our minds are merging."

And Calhoun suddenly felt as if he were falling, floating, and flying, all at the same time.

All of space laid itself bare for him, and he felt peace such as he'd never known, such as he'd never thought possible in his lifetime . . .

There was light and warmth all around him, and at first his impulse was to push away, to protect himself, but he surrendered that impulse, surrendered himself to that which was carrying him down, down and along to whatever it was that was beckoning to him. He was drawn to that very light, and part of his mind cried out a warning of what can happen when the unwary come too close to the light, but he did not care, he knew it was there, he knew that was where he had to go.

He felt alien whisperings in his mind, he felt cold and logic and emotion all wrapped up and bubbling within him, and there was Selar and there was Soleta, and there seemed to be a sort of chatter, the details of which he could not discern, but it didn't matter because he felt Selar guiding him then, pushing him in the direction he wanted to go, felt something pure and perfect and frightened brushing up against him . . .

And he saw it: It was void and without shape, but it *was* nevertheless. It was having a full sense of itself, and it was afraid, so very afraid. For all its power, for all its energy, it recoiled as Calhoun drew nearer.

No time, a voice called to him, and he didn't know if it was Selar's or Soleta's, or Burgoyne's own warning filtering through from some still tenuous link to the real world. All was blackness around him except for the light that the being gave off. *No time, hurry.*

You have to leave, he told it. ***You have to leave. You'll destroy us otherwise.***

It couldn't communicate in words. It didn't have the knowledge or understanding yet. It was a premature birth, a confused and disoriented being.

Instead every emotion it was feeling washed over Calhoun, and he drew in the sense of it and the comprehension of it . . . and he realized that the creature wasn't simply trying to be born, it was resisting its own birth throes, clinging scared and uncertain to the *Excalibur,* seeing her as the last link to its "mother," the great energy being that had deposited it there, almost by accident.

It did not know itself. It did not know its mother. It only knew fear. When it lashed out earlier, it was the actions of a terrified infant.

Feel this, know this . . . and Calhoun fed into the creature images of its parent. The massive flaming bird, glorious and powerful, enveloping all, spanning star systems, hurtling off into the void, truly one of the most amazing things that Calhoun had ever seen.

And it felt pride. Pride and eagerness, and joy at comprehending its own origins. Selar had not been able to project her own visions of the gigantic creature, for her mind had been fairly overwhelmed by the desires and needs of the being within the warp core, but three minds combined as one were able to handle it, to punch through the overwhelming need and give it what it truly did need.

You can leave here, he told it. *You can leave here without hurting us. Your continued presence will destroy us. Leave us now. Leave us in peace and go in search of your mother. Leave us.*

And the creature, emboldened, newly confident, gathered itself. Inspired by the images that it had seen, it drew itself up, up and out . . .

Selar gasped, taken aback, her hands slipping off the warp core. She staggered, her legs giving way, and Burgoyne caught her before she fell. Moments later, Soleta and Calhoun came out of their meld as well, Calhoun leaning against the core to brace himself, trying to pull himself back to the real world like a waking man trying to toss off the last vestiges of a powerful dream.

The creature coalesced all around the *Excalibur,* all of its being coming together at last, and then it tore loose of the starship, whirling above it, and it screeched in a voice that was heard in the voices of everyone in the ship. It had no wings yet, it had no complete sense of itself beyond the fact that it existed, but that was more than enough. It stretched out its essence, feeling the joy of deep space, feeling the full truth breadth of life.

Then, with a howl and an outraged scream of confusion . . . it vanished.

As did the Promethean ship.

Burgoyne's scans only confirmed what s/he already knew. "It's gone, Captain. Sparky's gone. Away from the engines, away from the ship."

Calhoun had sagged into a chair, still endeavoring to pull himself together. Nearby Selar was breathing deeply as Soleta stood over her, steadying her. "Our shield status?" he asked.

"Shields are gone, sir. At least three solar hours to effect repairs and bring them back up to full power."

"But we're still here," Calhoun said slowly, hauling himself to his feet. "Guess they found out how much our little ship could take."

Suddenly there was, once more, a burst of choral voices and a flash of light. A moment later the Promethean was standing there, looking cool and confident. "Thank you, Captain."

"Thank you for what?" asked Calhoun.

"Why, for our latest acquisition, Cap'n. That creature you had growing in there. Let itself go, let itself get born. And now part of our gestalt being."

"Let it go," Calhoun said angrily. "It's a free being, and deserves its freedom."

"Freedom?" laughed the Promethean. "Cap'n, you just don't get it. It's ours now."

Calhoun felt a deep, burning rage building in him. He'd felt the creature's fear laid bare, felt that—to some degree—it had even trusted him. "I said let it go."

"You got the stones to make me?" challenged the Promethean.

He was still laughing when Calhoun flattened him. His feet went out from under him and the Promethean hit the floor, never having even seen the fist that smashed into his chin. He lay there for a moment, clearly stunned and surprised. "Son, that was not a real bright move," he said slowly, rubbing his chin.

"Let it go," Calhoun said again.

The Promethean did not bother to get up. Instead he sat on the floor, looking up at Calhoun, shaking his head in wonderment. "You got a fire in your belly, son. I like that. I do. The fact that I like it is the only reason you're still breathing. But a fire can burn pretty bad. You took a major chance with me, just for the sake of something, until real recently, you were concerned would destroy you all?"

"It deserves protection. All beings do. Especially those that are alone in the universe."

"Well that all is a real nice sentiment, son. Just bring a tear to m'eye, but now you tell me this and tell me true: Let's say we let it go. Wave our hands and, *poof,* it's gone. And if I told you that, once we release it, it will seek out the nearest heavily populated planet and devour the inhabitants? Make a mighty big snack of 'em. What would you say then? 'Cause I'll tell you right now, that's what it's gonna do. Is that what you want? You get to choose, son. The creature . . . or a planetful of living beings? Decide."

All eyes were on Calhoun and, slowly, the captain realized that he had absolutely no choice in the matter. "All right," he sighed. "Keep it with you. But do it no harm."

"Cap'n! We are an advanced race, son. We don't hurt nobody 'less we have to." He rose, dusted himself off and, in a very offhand manner, added, "Oh, and Cap'n, just so you know. The nearest heavily populated planet is called Tulaan IV. Bunch of fairly nasty folks who call themselves the Redeemers live there. Had you continued to insist I release the creature I would have done it, and it would have blown 'em away for you. As it is, they are going to be coming after you in force before very much longer with the intention of turning you into space dust. Funny how there are no easy answers, huh?''

''Yeah. Funny,'' Calhoun said with absolutely no trace of amusement.

And with that, the Promethean tossed off a salute . . . and vanished.

''Soleta . . . Selar . . . you okay?'' asked Calhoun. He received nods from both of them, although Selar looked a bit more haggard than usual. Then he tapped his commbadge and said, ''Calhoun to bridge. Stand down from red alert. All stations at normal status. It would appear that the danger is past.''

17

There was no wind blowing on the surface of Ahmista. It was almost as if the entire world was waiting for something to happen.

Morgan stood there, contemplating the weapon. Nearby was Robin, and standing close were Kebron and Calhoun. Calhoun had been determined to see this superweapon for himself, and he shook his head in wonderment at something relatively compact, which, nonetheless, had nearly demolished his ship.

Morgan crouched down in front of the barrel, stroking the surface.

''Go ahead, Mother. Do what you have to do,'' Robin said softly.

Morgan looked up at her, her expression unreadable. ''What do you mean?''

''I'm not stupid,'' Robin told her. ''I figured it out. The reason you were seeking out the Prometheans. You wanted a weapon that could put an end to you. That would enable you to die, for certain. And now you've found it. You found what you've been searching for all this time. This has more than just fire power. You heard Tarella. It'll do whatever you want it to do. If you want to die, it'll do it for you. So, go ahead. Bond with it or whatever you have to do, and put an end to it. You know it's what you want.''

Her gaze flickered to Calhoun. He nodded. ''Robin told me what you are . . . what you want. Who am I to interfere in a quest of this magnitude? If this is your wish we'll honor it.''

She looked at the gun then . . . *really* looked at it. Then she looked to her daughter, who was—with effort—keeping her face neutral and determined. Her jaw was proudly set, her dark eyes free of tears.

An eternity of time passed. An eternity almost as long as Morgan's life.

She turned to Kebron and said, "May I borrow your rifle for a moment?"

Kebron looked questioningly at Calhoun, who nodded. He unstrapped his phaser rifle and handed it over to her. She cradled it, feeling its weight, and then with an impressive display of strength she braced it against her shoulder, took aim, and fired.

It took more than a dozen shots, but eventually Morgan succeeded in blasting the weapon into free-floating atoms.

Robin gaped at her, not quite believing what she had seen. And as Morgan handed the rifle back to Kebron she said, "When Tarella looked like she was going to shoot me, you got in the way. Even though there was no point to it, your instinct was still to try and save me. You were willing to die for me. The least I can do is be willing to live for you."

And Robin trembled, trying to suppress her sobs, but she was only partly successful as she half walked, half ran into her mother's embrace.

"What is with them?" muttered Kebron.

"That's what I like about you, Kebron," Calhoun said. "Your sentimental side."

Shelby let the warmth of the shower flow over her. As she did so, she mused about how things had turned out. They had come upon a tragic situation and made the best of it, but there were no easy or clean answers to this one. Sometimes there just couldn't be any.

At least the one upside to it all was that Mac had had thrown into his face a being who was the incarnation of Mac's philosophies, taken to their logical extremes. The Prometheans followed a sort of anti–Prime Directive, moving capriciously as they saw fit, an entire race governed by what felt right at the moment. And she had a feeling that Mac had seen something of himself in that. Perhaps he had come to some hard realizations about himself. Perhaps, thought Shelby, just perhaps, he was growing up a bit.

A few hours later, in the corridor, Zak Kebron approached her, looking puzzled.

"What's on your mind?" she asked him.

"Commander," he began, "the Promethean mentioned the *Grissom,* and you could have heard a pin drop on the bridge."

"Spit it out," Shelby said, although she had a good idea where the large security chief was going.

"So I was wondering, what happened on the *Grissom?* To the captain, I mean."

"I'm not at liberty to say," Shelby replied.

"And I take it you advise against asking the captain directly?"

"That's not a story the captain is ready to tell."

"And if I asked him about it. . . ."

"You might find yourself guarding the interior of waste extraction for the next six months."

"Thank you, Commander."

"You're welcome. That's what I'm here for."

In sickbay, Mark McHenry was having some of the bruises he'd sustained attended to by Selar. "You are becoming something of a regular customer here, Mr. McHenry," observed Selar.

"Wasn't my intention. Things just keep happening to me. Speaking of things happening . . . congratulations are in order, I hear."

"Thank you, Mr. McHenry. And I . . ." She cleared her throat. "I must thank you, I believe . . . for your ability to handle with such equanimity the rather odd relationship that has developed between myself and Burgoyne. I am, frankly, not sure if we are together or not together. It is very confusing, and—"

"Doctor," McHenry said confidently, "don't worry about it. Whatever happens, happens, and I'll be fine with it no matter what. There's very little that—"

At that point, Burgoyne entered and seeing McHenry and Selar together, headed over to them. "Burgy," said McHenry, "I was just telling the good doctor here that whatever ends up happening with you two s'fine by me. There's nothing that I can't take in stride."

"Well, that's good to hear, considering I've got some interesting news. Affects both of you, in a way."

"Oh, really? What?" asks McHenry.

"Well, Selar, it appears that your child is going to have a sister or brother."

"What?" She shook her head, not comprehending. "I do not understand, Burgoyne. I am not having twins. And if you are under the impression that we will be making a second child at some point in the future—"

"No, no. Actually, I guess I should have said half-brother or half-sister. You see . . ." Burgoyne cleared hir throat. "I'm a little surprised about this, I'm the first one to admit it. But, well . . . it appears that I'm pregnant. Congratulations, Mark. You're going to be a father.''

And Mark McHenry passed out. Slumped right back onto the med table unconscious.

''Well, well. Guess that proves there's some things he can't take in stride,'' observed Burgoyne.

Selar shook her head scoldingly as she reached for a spray hypo to bring McHenry out of it. ''That was not funny, Burgoyne,'' she said as she prepped the hypo. ''Making up something like that just to prove you could get a reaction out of him.'' Then she stopped, the hypo poised in midair as she said warily, ''Burgoyne, you . . . you *were* making that up, were you not?''

Burgoyne smiled cryptically.